"A gripping thriller that mov
tense run-up to war. Charin's resourceful ....
path between British socialites and Third Reich officers in a nan
biting plot set against the dramatic, real-life effort to help Jews
escape from Nazi Germany."

– Jane Thynne

*

'A sweeping novel set in Berlin and London during the last full year
before the Second World War. 1938 is often ignored in the context of
Nazi Germany but it provides a wealth of material for a novelist and
Geoffrey Charin's well-researched book expertly mines this period.
A cast of highly credible characters along with a clever plot involving
the escape of Jews from Germany and Nazi sympathisers in Britain
ensures *Without Let or Hindrance* is a highly readable book.'

– Alex Gerlis

*

"A powerful debut from a writer of great promise. Geoffrey Charin
takes us back to the time when too much of the British establishment
was ready to side with Hitler. A sharp eye for evocative period detail,
complex, well-rounded characters, an engaging protagonist and an
enthralling storyline make *Without Let or Hindrance* a must read for
fans of historical thrillers."

– Adam Lebor

*

I felt safe in Geoffrey Charin's hands knowing that this book was
expertly researched. It is wonderfully evocative.

– Clare Pooley

WITHOUT LET OR HINDRANCE

GEOFFREY CHARIN

The Book Guild Ltd

First published in Great Britain in 2021 by
The Book Guild Ltd
9 Priory Business Park
Wistow Road, Kibworth
Leicestershire, LE8 0RX
Freephone: 0800 999 2982
www.bookguild.co.uk
Email: info@bookguild.co.uk
Twitter: @bookguild

Typeset in 12pt Adobe Jenson Pro

Printed and bound in the UK by TJ Books LTD, Padstow, Cornwall

ISBN 978 1913913 397

British Library Cataloguing in Publication Data.
A catalogue record for this book is available from the British Library.

*To Miriam, who last saw her father when he gave
her sandwiches for her train journey to safety, and to
my grandparents, Geoffrey and Lily Charin,
for giving her a home.*

"...but the laments of these democratic countries have not led them to even now substitute their hypocritical questioning of our activities for any helpful action; on the contrary, these countries with icy coldness assured us that obviously there was no place for the Jews in their territory... So no help is given, but morality is saved."

ADOLF HITLER, SEPTEMBER 12TH 1938

ONE

29 SEPTEMBER 1938

AUGUSTSTRASSE, BERLIN

INSPECTOR STIEGLITZ LOOKED AT THE TWO WOMEN on the bed. Naked, they were lying on their sides face to face. The right leg of the blonde woman was draped over the left leg of the dark-haired one and, in between, they were loosely holding hands. The smell of gas lay heavy in the air masking the musky smell of death that the inspector normally associated with such scenes. The bedroom was small, claustrophobic even, situated towards the back of the apartment, originally the servants' quarters.

Elsewhere the gas had permeated further and his colleague, Sergeant Kuppers, stumbled into the room, handkerchief already clasped firmly to his mouth.

'My God,' mumbled Kuppers, seeing the bodies. The inspector noticed that Kuppers' face had now taken on a grey tinge and he gave an inward sigh.

He'll be throwing up soon, thought Stieglitz, sizing him up. Kuppers was from the countryside to the north of Berlin, below average height but strong and fit from many hours in the fields.

He'd doubtless slaughtered many an animal too but, when it came down to it, these youngsters who'd not seen war knew nothing. Stieglitz turned back to the bodies and concentrated on the women's faces. The blonde's eyes were closed but her face looked anything but peaceful, her teeth bared as if either in pain or in fear. The eyes of the older black-haired woman were open, as if she had been staring at the other.

'Maybe yes. Maybe no,' Stieglitz murmured to himself. His eyes scanned their bodies. The women were young but could have been anywhere between twenty and thirty years old in his estimation. Kuppers suddenly ran out of the room and Stieglitz heard him retching into the toilet.

Stieglitz walked round the bed to where the blonde lay and lifted her head from the pillow; it was heavy and he grabbed a handful of her hair to stop the head from dropping, long enough to take a good look. He grunted and put it carefully back down. Across the corridor he heard Kuppers pull the chain and moments later, looking embarrassed, Kuppers re-entered the bedroom.

'I'm sorry, sir. I thought I would be fine but suddenly… I've never seen a dead body before.'

'Of course. You wouldn't have,' Stieglitz replied. 'You got to be sergeant by beating people up, not killing them. Well, don't worry. If it's any comfort to you, I have a feeling you're going to be seeing many more from now on.' There was silence between them, as both wondered whether even a comment like that could be construed as criticism of the regime.

Kuppers moved round to the other side of the bed trying to look, Stieglitz realised, as if he was being professional and continuing to make observations.

'See here, Inspector.'

Kuppers had picked up a book from the bedside table and was flicking through the pages with his big farmer's hands. He handed it across and Stieglitz opened it to the frontplate. The two words at the top of the page in large black print were in what Stieglitz assumed to be Hebrew lettering and underneath in German was written 'Israelite Prayers in Hebrew and German'.

'Can't say I blame them, can you, sir?' said Kuppers as he watched Stieglitz put the book down on the matching side table.

'How do you mean, Sergeant?'

'Well, sir, not only are these two deviant, they're Jews too. Life must have been unpleasant for them and it's only going to get worse. Maybe they made a sensible choice.'

'Right,' replied Stieglitz, pausing for a moment. 'So really nothing to investigate then, is there? Who cares after all about a couple of dead Jews – straight or queer – doesn't matter. It's not as if we're going to prosecute anyone for this, are we?'

Kuppers grinned and nodded vigorously. Stieglitz groaned softly to himself and shook his head. The fact was, Kuppers was right, nobody would investigate this very thoroughly even though it was as clear as day to Stieglitz that this was no suicide pact of despair but a carelessly arranged murder. Yet something else wasn't right here. Why go to the bother of trying to stage a suicide if a murder wouldn't be investigated properly anyway?

'All right, Kuppers, let's pretend that this is a normal investigation and that we care. Take a look around, familiarise yourself with the scene. You know the routine.'

Kuppers could see that the inspector was testing him and he took another look at the women. He walked around the bed examining the scene from different angles.

'Take your time,' called Stieglitz, returning to the more spacious living room, down the corridor and past the front door which was hanging precariously off one hinge, courtesy of the Berlin fire brigade responding to a telephone call reporting the smell of gas.

In the living room, he took in the Wilhelmene-era two-seater couch and single leather easy chair arranged around a low table, on which were scattered a few books. He picked up one of them. *The Magic Mountain* by Thomas Mann. He grunted and returned it to its place giving the other titles only a cursory glance. The fact that Jews continued to read banned literature was hardly surprising. A sturdy oak sideboard stood against the longer wall opposite the door and dominated the room. On it sat the neat and compact VE301, or *Volksempfanger* wireless set. Whatever their reading tastes there was no chance these people had been listening to anything subversive: the VE301 had been deliberately designed to be unable to pick up any broadcasts from outside of Germany.

'Oh dear, oh dear,' tutted Kuppers, joining him. 'As if these Jews aren't in enough trouble already, they're in possession of a Party wireless set.'

Even Stieglitz had to smile at that one. Kuppers switched it on hoping to hear some folk music; it was always going to be either that, opera or classical. Beethoven's *Pathétique*, came through the loudspeaker – a relief to Stieglitz who was getting a bit tired of Wagner.

Noticing Kuppers' grimace and that he was about to turn it off again, Stieglitz said, 'Leave it on. I like it. It will help me think.' Stieglitz moved over to examine the diamond-shaped clock standing on the marble mantelpiece below a large fan-shaped wall mirror. Looking into it he watched Kuppers moving around the room being careful not to touch anything but looking at everything closely. Good man. He noticed that the wallpaper repeated the theme of the mirror itself patterned with multiple light green fan shapes – or were they sea shells? Stieglitz preferred plain white wallpaper himself. This crowded design, he felt, made this room, too, seem small.

'Inspector,' said Kuppers, clearing his throat. 'I have concluded that—'

'Not so fast, boy,' said Stieglitz. 'Take a look around the other rooms. The whole apartment is a crime scene after all. Try not to breathe in too much of the fumes as you go.'

An irregular swishing noise was coming from the direction of the window. The curtains were still partly drawn, adding to the gloom, though they billowed a little now in the breeze. The firemen had pushed the windows wide open to let in as much air as possible. Stieglitz now parted the heavy velvet drapes then wrestled with the inner curtains of white tulle behind. Strips of tape were hanging off the edges of the window frames and flapping noisily. Stieglitz slowly nodded to himself. It would be the same in all the rooms. Taping the windows was the first step to take when one decided to turn on the gas. He glanced down into the courtyard below, seeing that the three uniformed men of the *Orpo* in their smart blue double-breasted greatcoats had descended from their patrol vehicle, the chinstraps of their black shakos firmly fastened, as they lit up.

'And Kuppers,' he shouted, 'don't you dare light up in here. Smoking only in the courtyard, d'you hear?'

'Yes, sir, of course,' came the shouted reply.

Stieglitz returned his gaze to the courtyard below, so typical of the turn-of-the-century tenement blocks in this area of the city. His glance took in all the many windows, nobody gawping though he thought he saw some curtains twitching. It didn't pay to be too curious nowadays when the police were around. His thoughts returned to the dead women. He had noticed over the years that some suicide attempts were less serious than others. Sometimes it was as if people wanted to be caught before it was too late. On those occasions they probably wouldn't think about taping up the cracks between the windows. He hadn't come across many of these though, since Hitler had become Chancellor. Over the past few years he'd found that, once people got to that point, they gave it a really good go.

Pulling the drapes fully open, he let the net curtains fall back into place and turned as Kuppers came out of the little kitchen, his handkerchief again held to his mouth and nose and gasping a little.

'Kuppers, you look like my men at Ypres. The ones who didn't get their masks on in time. Come here and stick your head out of the window. Get some fresh air.' Stieglitz took off his own coat and wide-brimmed black hat and slung them onto the threadbare couch and loosened his tie.

Beethoven had now been succeeded, almost inevitably, by Wagner's *Ride of the Valkyries*. Stieglitz quickly moved across to turn it off before the violins gave way to the cacophony of trumpets and horns, and turned to Kuppers who was now breathing normally again and standing respectfully, ready to report his findings.

'Go on then,' said Stieglitz, 'what have you got for me?'

'Sir, I believe it was a suicide pact. They turned on the gas in the kitchen.' He paused, waiting to see the inspector's response, but Stieglitz said nothing. 'There's more, sir,' continued Kuppers, a little more nervously now. 'One of the women's clothing has been folded carefully and put on a chair in the corner of the room. But the other's clothes have been thrown just anywhere.'

Stieglitz nodded. 'And what do you infer from this?'

'The messed-up clothes belong to the blonde — there are strands of her hair on the woollen cardigan. Her blouse is still caught up in its sleeves.' He looked again to the inspector for approval and was pleased to see that he was still nodding approvingly. 'So, I think, the dark-haired one was waiting for the other one who came a bit later. And when the blonde arrived, she was so excited to see her. She didn't have time to fold her clothes.'

'No!' Stieglitz shouted. Kuppers stuttered to a halt, a lump of disappointment in his throat. The inspector made an effort to calm down before speaking again. 'No, Sergeant. This is not the time for your sexual fantasies. For God's sake, lad, you couldn't even hold your food down just now. That was what your stomach was telling you. Maybe listen to that rather than to other parts of your body.' He gestured vaguely to below Kuppers' waist. 'Use your brain, boy. Do you really think that if this was a suicide pact, either one of them would have been excited to fall into bed with the other? This is death. They'd have been sombre. You can guarantee that.' He paused, counted to three. 'But yes, I do agree that the blonde woman probably arrived a little later than the other one. However, there's another problem with that little scene in there.' He walked back into the bedroom, gesturing for Kuppers to follow. 'If you were going to kill yourself by turning on the gas in the oven, and you've gone to the trouble of taping the windows, would you really then go into the bedroom which is some distance away? Wouldn't you both sit around that little table in the kitchen, tape the door closed, and go as quickly as you could?'

Kuppers tried to say something but was so afraid of saying the wrong thing. He couldn't get any words out. Stieglitz watched the man's jaw working for a few seconds.

'Come on, Kuppers. I'm calm now. I won't bite. Speak freely – but sensibly.'

'Well, sir. All I was going to say is that, well, I don't know, sir. I mean the gas would get there eventually, wouldn't it? Maybe they wanted to die in bed.'

'Except that the smell of gas was at its strongest in the kitchen – there is far less smell in the bedroom. Go on, sniff the bedcovers – I have already done so. You see the expression on the blonde's face? She's not calm like the other one. Did you see the scratches on her thighs?'

'Yes, sir, but that could be when—'

Stieglitz interrupted impatiently. 'Lift her head up from the pillow.'

Kuppers moved around towards the blonde but hesitated. 'Go on, boy,' encouraged Stieglitz, 'just so you can see the other side of her face.' As he pulled the head up Kuppers could see where her left eye had been bloodied. He jumped back in horror and the head slapped back against the pillow.

'I think,' Stieglitz said, 'that killers were in this apartment waiting when Blondie here arrived and they were going to make sure both were dead before they left. This means that they would only have taped the windows and turned on the gas at the very end and for our benefit. But probably, because of the kitchen's proximity to the front door, the neighbour across the hallway alerted the fire department before the gas got as far as the bedroom. Make sure you bring the team in to dust the strips of window tape for fingerprints. I am going over there to No. 5. They must have heard something.'

'Surely, sir,' said Kuppers, 'if you're right, the murderers wouldn't have left their prints anywhere. Wouldn't they have worn gloves?'

'Exactly,' said Stieglitz. 'Well done. If there are no prints then I am right. If even one of the women's prints is on any of the strips, then I am wrong.'

TWO

23 JULY 1938

MAYFAIR, LONDON

VERONICA STEPPED CONFIDENTLY INTO THE DUKE of Wellington's entrance hall and surveyed the dozens of guests resplendent in their evening dress. She estimated there to be perhaps sixty or seventy couples. The air was rapidly filling up with laughter and the smell of cigar smoke which suffused everything in a warm filter, somehow making the women even more glamorous and the men more suave. The clatter of the many high-heeled shoes on the wooden flooring vied with the sounds of conversation. The women themselves seemed to be glittering, their eyes, and the jewellery on their gowns, reflecting the many lit candles scattered around the room, some set in trays on the top of the grand piano in the corner. Veronica's own gown was understated but in this company she felt that her youth shone brighter than the diamonds with which the women were all encumbered, either hanging from their necks, fastened to their evening gowns or encircling their fingers and wrists.

She felt herself relax. These were her types of people after all. This was where she was in her element. Her enjoyment was only enhanced by her companion Billy's palpable unease as he nervously tightened his grip on her arm.

A waiter materialised by her side. She took two glasses of chilled champagne from his tray and handed one to Billy, careful not to spill any onto her white satin above-the-elbow gloves. Billy's large neck was bulging over his close-fitting wing collar but at least, she noticed, the black bow tie was still in place. Billy's head, shaved bald, had a damp sheen to it and was reflecting the many lights of the giant chandelier descending ten feet from high above their heads.

The hall, with its high ceilings and paintings on every wall, was not as large as some of the stately homes she had visited as a child, but few could compete with its heroic associations. On the wall at the far end hung a massive portrait of the first Duke, swathed in a dark military cloak astride his famous horse, Copenhagen, and turning, one arm raised, to exhort his troops to advance. The first ranks of hundreds of men were dimly visible in the gloom behind him. The painting consisted mainly of dark colours but the Duke's face had been painted as if lit by a shaft of sunlight coming through the clouds and conferring on him a god-like status. The portrait itself was flanked on either side by a captured French standard; each hung at 45 degrees to the picture frame so that the eagles surmounting these standards seemed to be bowing in homage towards their conqueror. With that man as your great-grandfather, she thought, you don't need a giant hallway to impress.

Billy gulped his champagne down in one go.

'What the bloody hell am I doing here, Veronica?' His voice was taut. 'I think I'm the only Party member here. Do you see anyone you know?'

Veronica calmly sipped her champagne and wondered whether to make some withering rejoinder. She searched the faces of those close by, some of whom were also taking refreshment from the other waiters circulating with canapés. Most of the couples were old enough to be her parents. The men held themselves with the easy confidence that came from being raised as aristocrats born to rule. Only by convention did they defer to the women around them, who laughed easily at the witticisms of their men. She didn't recognise any of them but certainly she couldn't detect anyone or anything she should be afraid of. Everything seemed perfectly normal.

A sharp click of heels made them turn around. A man Veronica estimated to be in his late fifties was bowing slightly towards them in greeting. He wore a black and white sash which crossed over a white waistcoat, disappearing from sight under his tail coat. The light glinted off his round, horn-rimmed spectacles making his expression hard to read.

'Please allow me to introduce myself. I am von Dirksen. Heil Hitler.'

'Von Dirksen, of course!' Veronica replied, clapping her hands in evident delight. 'Billy, this is the German Ambassador.' Veronica felt a rush of adrenalin. Von Dirksen had been a noted pro-Nazi even before the Nazis had come to power.

'Heil Hitler.' answered Billy, a little uncertainly, shaking his hand. To Veronica it sounded as if this was the first time Billy had used the strange greeting. He'd no doubt get better at it with practice, she thought wryly.

'It is really wonderful,' said the ambassador, glancing around, 'to see so many people coming here to support the Anglo-German Friendship Club and so good of the Duke to lend his home for this event, don't you think?'

Veronica nodded and replied in German, knowing it would annoy Billy, 'Ambassador, we should do everything we can to ensure our countries never go to war again.'

Von Dirksen's face lit up in delight and he bent almost reverently to kiss the back of her gloved hand before turning away.

'What did you say to him, you bloody show-off?' Billy's flushed face stared into hers. 'You just stay close, you hear me? Don't start getting ideas about swanning off on your own talking German. Your place is by my side looking lovely. It's important for my status. And, my girl,' he added, 'the last thing we need is for you to say something stupid in any language.'

He glanced at her, hoping for a reaction. He did not get one. That Billy thought Veronica stupid suited her very well. During the months they had been together, she had made sure that he knew about her just what she needed him to know. He knew, for example, that she was excited by the dangerous circles he moved in and that when she was excited she could show him a very good time. He didn't know that that excitement didn't translate into any actual emotional connection to Billy Watson, the rising star in the Party.

'You'll have to give me a little bit of freedom,' Veronica said, 'if only to allow me to introduce you to any people I know. You're the outsider here, not me.'

Despite her brave words, Veronica did not expect to know many people here tonight: her refusal to indulge her parents and mix in high society for the past few years meant that she had had to rely on Daphne Peters for tonight's invitation. She sighed. Anything for the cause.

As if on cue, the announcement 'Tom Mitford' followed shortly by 'Lord and Lady Standish', interrupted her reverie. And suddenly there was Daphne, rushing towards her.

'Veronica!' she gushed. 'I was so glad to get your letter. It's been *far* too long.' Giving Billy only a perfunctory glance, she embraced Veronica, planting a quick kiss on her bare shoulder and murmuring in her ear, 'I knew you couldn't resist me forever. I love your evening gown by the way.' She pulled back and winked at her. Daphne still looked the same. Tall like Veronica, and with similarly fair complexion and long blonde hair. But where Veronica was thin with chiselled cheekbones, Daphne's face was plumper and her nose shorter, at least when viewed from the front. As Veronica returned her smile, she wondered whether the nose only appeared long because her mouth was so small. Daphne's lips were bow-shaped, just like Veronica imagined the lips of a cherub.

Daphne pulled at her arm. 'Darling V, I must introduce you to my husband Reggie.' Lord Standish was, Veronica thought, probably about forty years old, a good ten to fifteen years older than Daphne, which didn't surprise her in the least. In fact she wouldn't have been surprised if he had been twice that age, knowing Daphne's feelings towards men. Presumably Lord Standish needed an heir and she'd agreed to provide him with one. Veronica held out her hand and as Reggie bent forward, his lips hovering just above her glove, he glanced up at her and she saw in his defeated eyes the look she had seen in men before when they had thrown themselves at Daphne. 'You poor man,' she thought, but Daphne was already pulling her away, Billy following in their wake.

'Tom!' said Daphne, laying her hand on the young man who had arrived just ahead of her. 'Tom Mitford, meet Veronica Beaumont, who was also at St Margaret's with Unity.' She turned to Veronica. 'We were all such close friends, weren't we, Ronnie?' Veronica smiled but said nothing. Daphne may have been friendly with Unity but she'd have had to move fast. Unity hadn't been there for long and 'Ronnie' had kept well clear of her.

'Is Unity coming this evening?' Daphne was asking now.

'Afraid not,' answered Tom, 'she's in Germany again, though one of my other sisters is coming of course,' he said with a wink. 'In fact,' he said, looking around, 'I'd rather hoped Diana would already be here.'

'Oh Billy will be pleased,' Veronica said, bringing him into the conversation. 'Tom Mitford, please may I introduce you to William Watson.' She beamed at them. 'Billy,' she announced proudly, 'is a Fascist. A fully paid-up and, I must add, a high-ranking member of the BUF.'

Billy nodded uncertainly and shook hands. Tom was not taller than Billy but he appeared to be because he was so much thinner. He inclined his head of fair hair and smiled. 'High-ranking eh? My sister is with a fella in the British Union. D'you know him?'

'I doubt it, sir. We have thousands of members now,' Billy replied with confidence but Veronica noticed his horror on seeing Mitford turn and share a smile with Daphne. Veronica knew how Billy hated to be mocked. Daphne took a sip from her glass, coolly appraising Billy. Veronica thought perhaps the glass was concealing a smile of contempt but she could not be sure. Finally Tom said, 'Mr Watson, Diana's been spending much of the past five years in Sir Oswald Mosley's company.'

Blood rushing to his face, Billy bowed his head.

'Of course,' he said lamely, 'I know Sir Oswald quite well in fact. Forgive me, I didn't know Mrs Guinness was your sister.'

'Well, if you know him well,' grinned Tom, ' I daresay you've talked with him more than I have and certainly more than our parents ever have. We didn't choose him you know, that was all Diana – though Bryan, her poor husband, took it damned well I must say.' He laughed. 'Chin up, Watson! Don't give it another thought.'

Veronica saw Billy's humiliation at being spoken to in this way by a man who was maybe ten years younger than he was. Yet she felt no sympathy for Billy. Earlier that evening, as they had been dressing, she had tried to prepare him for whomever he might meet, and if he had listened he would have been saved the embarrassment. But when she had told him, 'Lord Redesdale and his son Tom Mitford may be there, which I think will be good for us, darling,' his answer had been, 'And who the fucking hell are they?' whilst crushing yet another cigarette into the plate on the kitchen table.

'Sir Oswald Mosley and Mrs Diana Guinness,' announced the footman at the door and there was an immediate buzz of excitement from the assembled guests. Perhaps the last time this room had witnessed such adulation had been when the Iron Duke himself had held court. Even Veronica, determined to stay calm and aloof, gasped as the couple walked into the hall. Sir Oswald, so well known from the many newsreels and speeches, was tall and thin with devilish good looks and an easy, confident smile. His black hair glistened with brilliantine and was combed back from his forehead whilst his thin pencil line moustache gave him a dangerous look. Or did she think that because of his reputation? She glanced at Billy but his eyes were fixed very much on Diana Guinness as she moved amongst the guests, smiling and shaking hands. Veronica well understood Billy's fascination. Diana was ravishingly good looking. Tall with blonde hair down to her bared shoulders, she had prominent cheekbones under carefully sculpted arched eyebrows and possessed the most incredible blue eyes which seemed to bore through you. She walked with such effortless grace that she appeared to be gliding across the room, her feet invisible beneath the long hem of her wonderfully stylish pale green evening dress. Veronica, herself a great follower of the latest fashions, recognised it as one of Madeleine Vionnet's new Paris collection. She wondered whether Mrs Guinness had had to pay for it or whether Vionnet had paid her to be a walking advertisement for her work.

Veronica knew, because Billy had proudly told her so, that some thought she and Diana to be lookalikes. Seeing her up close, Veronica now thought that comparison to be ludicrous. Veronica's model was Hedy Lamarr. She spent hours each week curling the ends of her hair to achieve the Hedy look in the new movie *Algiers*, though she would never admit it. That had been just as well: once, someone in a bar had commented that Veronica looked like Hedy Lamarr's fair-haired sister and Billy had knocked him out cold. They'd had to run for a cab with Billy unrepentant, cursing the man for daring to insinuate that his girl looked like a Jewess.

Suddenly, Diana's eyes were staring into hers and she realised she was holding out her hand in greeting. 'Miss Beaumont, is it?' she said. Veronica nodded nervously and shook the proffered hand as Daphne reappeared at her side. 'Yes, hello, Diana,' gushed Daphne, 'we were at school with Unity.'

Perhaps because of Daphne's rather inappropriate familiarity, Diana ignored her. She continued to look into Veronica's eyes so that Veronica began to worry that her mind was being read and that she would be powerless to prevent it. Diana had not yet released Veronica's hand. 'If you were in my sister's year you're what, twenty-four?'

Veronica nodded wordlessly. She wanted to turn away but her hand was still being held. Then Diana's stare softened. 'You're very pretty so keep away from my man, won't you?'

She laughed, let go of Veronica's hand and turned toward Sir Oswald, who at that very moment had just shaken Billy's hand.

'This your chap?' Oswald Mosley asked. Veronica looked at Diana, afraid that she had already committed some unforgivable sin, but Diana had caught sight of her brother and was already moving away.

'Yes, he is, Sir Oswald,' Veronica replied, 'I do hope he is behaving himself.'

Mosley laughed, 'Well, I don't know about that. There have been some recent rallies where he most certainly has not behaved himself, I can vouch for that.' He laughed again. 'This chap is just the one to have around when the damned Jews attack us. A violent riff-raff.'

'The Jews? Violent?' Veronica asked. 'I can't imagine it somehow.'

'Oh yes. The East End of London is a very dangerous place nowadays and we need to be prepared. But know this: whatever they seek to dish out, we will give it back to them with interest. The Jews have declared war on the British Union but we are up to the task.' He paused. 'I'm sorry, my dear, I am talking as if at a rally.'

Veronica shook her head. 'Not at all, Sir Oswald. You have a way of making things seem so simple and easy to understand. I'd like very much to hear more about it.' She looked around nervously but Diana was not in sight.

'Well, if you plan on sticking around for dinner, I've been asked to say a few words. Ah, they are calling us through to the dining room right now. Are you coming?'

For a moment Veronica thought that he had been about to offer to escort her through. Billy would probably have seen it as some sort of *droit de seigneur*, but Veronica was more nervous of how Mrs Guinness might act. It was with some relief that she saw Sir Oswald turn away, making a beeline for Diana.

Shortly after 2am that night, Veronica tested the temperature of the water filling up the bath and returned to sit at the dressing table. She stubbed out her cigarette and stared into the mirror. She allowed herself a smile, looked at her green eyes and winked. Her relationship with Billy had paid off tonight and it had been in the end thanks to Diana Guinness of all people. Veronica had been talking about her year in Berlin and, during the dinner, Mrs Guinness had invited her out to the terrace for a smoke just after her husband had sat down to a standing ovation.

'I'm off to Berlin in three days,' she had said. 'Shan't tell you why except that I'm going alone and could do with some intelligent company, and when I'm free you can show me places in Berlin that I perhaps don't know.'

Diana had been smoking from a long cigarette holder as she'd been speaking and Veronica had wanted to laugh, partly at how theatrical she seemed but mostly because it fitted in so well with her own plan to return to the city just a week later. This offer could solve a lot of problems. Containing her excitement she had asked, 'Why me, Mrs Guinness? Earlier you warned me to keep away.' But Diana had dismissively waved her cigarette holder in the air.

'That's why it is so perfect, Miss Beaumont. If you're in Berlin with me, Sir Oswald won't be able to pursue you. Oh don't look so shocked, darling, he collects pretty things.'

Diana hadn't seemed at all annoyed by this. In fact she'd smiled and given Veronica a light peck on the cheek.

'Do say you'll come. It will be such fun.'

Of course Veronica had agreed. She glanced now at Billy in

the mirror as she removed her makeup. As usual after their lovemaking he was fast asleep, and now he was lying on his back in all his naked sweaty glory, the crumpled sheet covering one of his legs but failing to cover any of his large belly. Everything about Billy, she thought, was large. He had a large head which he kept completely shaved – 'to inspire fear in the enemy' as he often liked to say. He had large fists most often employed against socialists, communists and Jews but 'never against a woman' as Billy also liked to say. This, however, was only true in the literal sense. Veronica had a couple of times felt the force of his open palm and had learnt never to question him in public, especially when he had been drinking. Still he always took care not to mark her face.

Tonight the talk had all been about the new pressure group that many gathered at Apsley House were hoping to form, tentatively to be called 'The Right Club'. She could think of a few people who would want to know of its aim of 'freeing the Conservative Party of Jewish control.' On balance it may even have been worth her renewing the acquaintance of the detestable Daphne, who would probably now start following her around again.

Walking up to Billy she bent forward and lightly slapped his face. He gasped, spluttered, turned onto his side and, for the moment at least, stopped snoring. Veronica glanced at the clock on the mantelpiece. He wasn't going to wake up any time soon and she could bathe in peace. She straightened, unclipped and peeled off the black stockings that Billy liked so much. Heading into the bathroom, she locked the door behind her. Two weeks earlier she had returned home to find Billy looking through her bedside cabinet. 'If you're going to see other men then I want to know about it.' She shouldn't have been surprised given the even more explicit request that he had made of her a couple of weeks before that. She hadn't decided whether he was a pervert or an ambitious schemer devoid of all morals, but her priority at that point had been to tighten security.

She took out the Patentex box from the cupboard, holding it upright so that the tube didn't fall out the open end. Inevitably, Billy never wanted to wear protection but there were many ways to ensure he was satisfied that didn't risk pregnancy and she used Patentex spermicidal jelly as a backup. She was careful now to leave the applicator screwed onto the tube and enough gel leaking messily from the end and oozing out of the red cardboard outer box to keep him from looking too closely. She kept the part of the tube that sat inside the box spotlessly clean. Billy found the whole thing repellent but the leaking applicator ensured it could never be mistaken for toothpaste. A clean, closed box might also have pricked his curiosity and could be opened from either end.

She removed the tube of gel, reached into the box and carefully extracted the tightly rolled-up message.

THREE

3 DECEMBER 1937

EIGHT MONTHS EARLIER, SAFFRON WALDEN

VERONICA LAY UNDER THE COVERS IN HER FOUR-poster bed reading Kurt's letter which her maid, Alice, had slipped under her door the previous morning, put aside until now. Veronica had been in no rush to read it but its proximity to her bed had been decisive. Like so many things in the Beaumont home, her bed had been in the family for a very long time. As a young girl Veronica had often tried to imagine what crane might have been used to guide the massive thing through the windows, and how they would have had to remove all the glass and wood from the window frames first. Later she realised that the house was even older and that the carpenters had constructed the bed inside the room. The fire in the hearth had gone out during the night and it would be a while before Alice would come by to set it going again. Alice always started with the fireplace in the morning room as Sir Ronald and Lady Beaumont were early risers and took their breakfast there. Veronica pulled the sheets up to the bridge of her nose so that just her eyes, the top of her head and the one hand holding up Kurt's letter were still exposed to the cold.

Kurt's writing was appalling and she would have struggled to read it even were it not in German. She probably had a magnifying glass somewhere but anyway, she could get the gist all right. Kurt would always have a place in her history, if not exactly in her heart. He had been her first, her only, discounting Daphne of course. Veronica hated her need to mentally add that caveat all the time. One silly mistake and it would now always be a statistic she had to dismiss. Well, Kurt had been her first man. He had been just 19, almost exactly two years younger than her, but he always seemed older and worldlier and she had been attracted to him in his German setting, though she would probably have ignored him had he been a 19-year-old Englishman. She had wanted to learn German from him. Never believing that she was beautiful, she assumed that he had been attracted to her because she owned a brand-new Opel Olympia Cabriolet. A young woman with her own motor vehicle would stand out in Berlin, especially a foreign one, which is why she had begged her father not to buy it for her. He hadn't listened of course. She could replay the discussion word for word, Father speaking, then Mother echoing whatever he said. Their dialogue always repeated that same ineluctable pattern. In her memories Veronica's own voice was rarely heard. When she did speak up she wasn't listened to anyway.

'I am not allowing my daughter to spend an entire year from home, in a foreign country no less, at the mercy of any man who happens to have a motor car and thinks he can thereby turn her head!'

Veronica had learnt to drive on the grounds of their estate when she was 15 and she had tried to teach Kurt the fundamentals as he had said early on that, when she left, he would like to have the Opel. Veronica smiled at how bad Kurt's driving had been. And of course his parents would never have been able to afford the vehicle, as Kurt had eventually accepted.

Kurt's letter was, she supposed, his way of saying goodbye. He wasn't so impolite as to say it directly but he had, he wrote, now joined the army and had met someone and they were very happy. 'I will always remember fondly our picnics together at Treptow.' You don't, thought Veronica, write that sentence unless you are saying goodbye. Poor Kurt. Had he not realised their relationship had ended the day she left Berlin? She had been happy to write to him but she had never seen their time together as anything more than ships passing.

She dropped the letter and pulled the covers over her head, *Sense and Sensibility* forgotten on top of the bedspread. She had very much enjoyed picnicking in Treptow Park. It had become a regular event on those weekends during the summer of '35 when she and Kurt, his childhood friend Michael and Michael's girl, Elke, had all squeezed into the Opel and they'd driven through Berlin with the top down. Her companions would sing marching songs they had learnt in school with her joining in as best she could: '*Millions, full of hope, look up at the swastika*'.

Veronica steeled herself to get up for breakfast. Just ten more minutes under the covers.

Downstairs, the morning routine was under way. Alice had ironed *The Times*, folded it into two and positioned it just to the left of Sir Roland's eggs and toast, ready to greet him when he joined his wife and daughter for breakfast. The eggs had to be soft boiled but not too soft and his tea cup warmed and ready.

Lady Cynthia Beaumont always made a point of looking at the newspaper before giving it to the maid so that her husband had the newspaper as crisp and uncreased as could be, but on this occasion, after the maid had gone to make the tea, she had carefully folded it to page eighteen so that Sir Roland wouldn't fail to see the photograph printed there of the Duke of Saxe-Coburg at the dinner arranged in his honour. She had waited at the other end of the long, heavy oak table for her husband's reaction, which, pleasingly, had come immediately.

'Aha!' Sir Roland exclaimed. 'The Grosvenor House event from last night. I was standing right there when the flashbulb went off. Couldn't see a damned thing for a few seconds after that. The scoundrel!'

'The photographer, or the Duke?'

Sir Roland smiled at his wife. He was a tall man with a still-dark moustache that contrasted with the thick silver head of hair he kept swept back.

'Very good, Cynthia, that was very good.'

She smiled and gave a brief wave of her hand in acknowledgement as Alice returned with the tea tray and carefully laid it down on the wonderfully carved Chinese elm sideboard that Sir Roland's father had brought back from Hong Kong at the turn of the century.

'Did you manage to talk to the Duke at all?' Lady Beaumont asked as she watched the maid carefully pouring their tea from the ornate Wedgewood teapot which was always used at breakfast. Alice served Sir Roland first, who added two lumps of sugar and stirred the tea before answering his wife.

'Not half. It turns out that he had met Mamma several times on her trips to Germany. I hadn't realised he knew her so well. He talked of her with great respect and affection.'

His wife nodded, unsurprised. Lady Eleanor's father had been half German and, long before the war, he had been prominent in German aristocratic circles. Sir Roland pushed the newspaper away, slowly and deliberately removed his glasses, rearranging the folds of his burgundy silk dressing gown over his knees.

'Delightful old chap,' he said, gesturing towards the photograph with his spoon. 'You know of course that he's a grandson of the old Queen? Originally born and bred here, so the perfect man to come over and promote closer relations between our two countries. And, because he grew up here, I can actually make out what he's saying, unlike some of those other buggers they send over.' He grinned apologetically at his wife who, he knew, didn't care for such words. 'I'll wager Veronica's German is better than some of their English, wouldn't you say?'

'I dare say,' smiled Cynthia, glancing towards Veronica's empty seat situated half way between them on the long side of the table. More often than not their daughter missed breakfast altogether, something they would not have tolerated when she was younger.

'Sending her there will, I think, prove to be a good investment,' he said. 'All the top people seem to be going there now and she will be well ahead of the game. She'll be in high demand.'

'Yes,' replied Cynthia, 'I am sure of it.' It had been two years since Veronica had returned home full of stories replete with German slang for which she had continually apologised. Of course Veronica had loved having to then translate for her dear old parents. 'She told me that it is all very well writing to the people she met but she really misses Berlin now. Apparently, two young men whom she knew well when she was there, and who had planned to become lawyers, have given that up and joined the army. I think she wants to see what all the fuss is about.'

'Of course we hope that they will never find out just how awful soldiering can be,' said Sir Roland. 'Which is why occasions like last night are so vital.'

'Speaking of letter writing,' said Lady Beaumont, waiting until the maid had left the room. 'I've had another letter from Sonia.'

Veronica made her way down the large central staircase. In recent months she tried to avoid joining her parents at breakfast. Years of being told that 'children should be seen, not heard', had ensured that she excused herself from that particular ritual just as soon as her parents agreed that she was old enough to make her own decisions. That had come a lot later than she would have wanted but it had been worth the wait. Often, she took breakfast in her room, and sometimes she ate with cook in the kitchen. Today, however, she had decided she would join her parents. It wasn't just the warm room that decided her. She didn't want them to think that she was avoiding them.

Striding along the corridor, she slowed down at the sound of her father's raised voice. What she heard him say stopped her completely, just outside the morning-room door.

'Your bloody sister will destroy everything. She can't come. Cynthia, you must see that.'

'Of course I see that,' replied Mother, whispering. 'Please keep your voice down.' Veronica suppressed her gasp. Sister! What sister? Until that moment, Veronica had been given to believe that Mother was an only child. Checking over her shoulder that the corridor was still empty, she crept forward the last few inches until her ear was almost touching the door, careful not to put any weight against it.

'It's just so unfair!' Mother sounded angry too now, though she was speaking in hushed, low tones. 'Roland, I hate being put in this position. She knows our stance on Germany. I wrote to her just last month about your role in the Anglo-German Friendship and I'd hoped that she would have got the message.'

'It is difficult for you, I know, my darling.' Father's tone was conciliatory now. Veronica could hear the delicate clink of cutlery on china and imagined her father buttering a bread roll. 'Whilst which religion you happen to have been born into, dear, makes not the slightest difference to me, hating Jews and supporting Germany seems to go hand in hand here. It distracts from the real issue, the Bolshevik threat. We all agree we need a strong Germany. This Jew thing is a damned shame.'

Veronica stood away from the door now, trying to control her breathing. She felt sure that her parents must hear her heart thumping. Why were they talking about the Jews? There seemed to be an implication there but that was surely not possible. She breathed in slowly, deeply and moved closer again to the door.

'And what does your sister have to say for herself?' Father was saying. 'Her coming back to England could be potentially embarrassing now. Especially if she makes a nuisance of herself at the German end.'

'Oh I'm not worried about Sonia. She's British after all. She's safe enough over there in Berlin. It's not as if she's in some far-out village at the mercy of some peasants. I agree, the last thing we want is for her to come over here bad-mouthing the German government—'

'Or worse,' interjected Father, 'bringing over her husband with his heavily accented English, frightening the horses. If only he didn't look so damnably Jewish. Forgive me, dear.' Veronica could hear the sound of a placatory kiss. 'No, I wasn't saying that you looked Jewish. Neither you nor Sonia do as a matter of fact. Perfectly lovely noses, the pair of you.' He laughed. She couldn't hear Mother laughing though. In fact she hadn't heard her mother in a while. Were those footsteps?

Veronica quickly moved across the hallway to the dining room. The room was only used when entertaining and all the furniture was beneath dust covers. It was a cold, gloomy place and always smelt musty. She absently patted the dust from one of the covered chairs and perched on the edge. The door to the morning room opened and quickly shut again. Her mother checking that neither she nor Alice were nearby.

So her mother was Jewish. How could they not have shared that with her? Veronica tried to imagine herself unknowingly passing this Sonia, her Aunt Sonia, in a Berlin street. She had never taken any interest in politics whilst she was out there. There must have been anti-Jewish demonstrations going on, but if she had seen anything it hadn't registered with her. Her German friends had never mentioned it. Or maybe they had. She felt a dull ache around her temples. The signs had been there if she had wanted to see them. She closed her eyes, not wanting to remember right now, shaking her head as if that would dispel any unpleasant thoughts. Why would they keep such an important thing from her? Perhaps it was the sensible thing to do with all that was going on in the world now. If she had been aware of Mother's religion, her experience in Germany would doubtless have been very different. She supposed it quite possible she wouldn't have been able to go there at all. Maybe, she reasoned, this was why her parents had kept all this from her. They'd been protecting her. This didn't comfort her. Instead she felt a growing unease, her world somehow under threat. Slowly and quietly she made her way back to the morning room.

'The things Sonia writes,' Mother was saying. 'Recently she has become quite frantic. Hysterical even.'

Father grunted. 'What sort of things?'

'Oh, it really doesn't matter. She over-dramatises everything.'

Almost too late, Veronica heard footsteps coming up from the kitchen and straightened up just in time. Alice stopped in surprise seeing Veronica standing there, but Veronica was already reaching for the door handle and about to go through to the morning room.

'I am frightfully late, I know. Alice, would you mind awfully bringing me some tea and a slice of toast?'

'Not at all, my lady,' said Alice, giving a little curtsey and going back towards the kitchen.

Veronica moved into the room and walked towards her mother. Lady Beaumont was staring at her husband trying to remember exactly what they had just been saying to each other and how much Veronica might have heard. Out the corner of her eye Veronica thought she saw her father gesturing to her mother.

Veronica quickly cut that off by bending in front of her mother and kissing her forehead. 'Good morning, Mother.' She walked over to her father and kissed him too. 'I must say you're both suddenly very quiet.'

There was an awkward silence before Sir Roland cleared his throat, stood up and folded his newspaper. 'Nothing to say, old thing. All quite boring,' he said, 'quite uninteresting.' As he walked past Veronica he gave her a quick kiss on the top of her head. 'I'm going up to get dressed.'

After he had closed the door, Veronica searched her mother's face for some clue as to what was in her mind. Perhaps now she would confide in her. Her mother was sitting ramrod straight, slowly stirring her tea, the relaxed action belied by the rigidity of her posture. Her face was still a little pale. Clearly she had nothing further to say on the matter. Veronica decided to give her every opportunity and sat down at the table.

'Mother, tell me. What is going on? I thought I heard arguing.'

'Darling, your father and I argue all the time! That doesn't mean that anything is going on,' said her mother, affecting a light tone but not quite succeeding, 'and you really don't want to know, or need to know, every little thing that we argue about after all these years.'

'Yes, I suppose so.' Veronica smiled, inwardly seething at the continued deceit. They looked at each other for perhaps a minute.

'You haven't eaten,' said her mother eventually. 'I'll ring downstairs and have them bring you some breakfast.'

'There's no need, Mother, Alice is already bringing me breakfast.'

'I'll leave you to it then, shall I?' Mother said and rose to leave. Veronica nodded absently, considering her options and only vaguely registering her mother's excuse that she needed to update cook about guests for dinner that evening. Veronica's mind was made up before Alice had come back with her breakfast.

Veronica wasn't often alone in the house. Even when her parents were both out Alice was cleaning and cook seemed to always have questions for her in her parents' absence. But now, whenever she could, Veronica searched for her mother's correspondence with her sister and, within a week, she had found it.

FOUR

7 JANUARY 1938

SAFFRON WALDEN

31 August 1936

Dear Cynthia,

We received your letter just before the Olympic Games opened and yes, the carnival atmosphere you asked about was really felt throughout Germany and especially here in Berlin. For a time it even looked as if your predictions might come true. Certainly all the foreign press thought so. Restrictions on the Jews were lifted – we could travel freely again, sit where we wanted in the parks. People who had frozen us out even began to carefully acknowledge us again – never has a slight inclination of a head made such a difference to my day! Well, the Games are over, the press corps has gone home – and all the restrictions are back. The large, intimidating notices are back up in our local park, 'Jews Forbidden'. I think that these rules against us are harder to bear coming as they do after a period when they had disappeared. Now we have seen how easily the hate can be switched on and off, and how easily the world can be reassured. But you, Cynthia? You must surely now know the truth. This nightmare continues here for me and for Manfred. You always assure us that everything will come right in the end, and I know this is meant to cheer us up, but sometimes I read your words and wonder if you really do understand what is happening here. I was talking about this with Manfred. He suggested that you and Roland should visit us here in Berlin. Would you come? See for yourself what has happened to the Germany I loved.

Please give our fondest wishes to Roland and to Veronica. It is hard to imagine that the tiny little girl I last saw all those years ago is now a woman. Your pride in her shines through your letters. If she should ever come to Germany, we would of course be happy to see her. Restrictions don't apply to Jews visiting on foreign passports and our apartment is a large one. Especially now the maid's room has been empty. I think I wrote to you last year about how she was no longer allowed to work for us, though we still exchange cards on birthdays.

All our love
Sonia

Lady Cynthia's Victorian walnut writing box had been concealed beneath a loose floorboard under the rug beside her bed. The house had always moved to its internal rhythms, bringing to Veronica's mind images of old sailing ships, creaking here, squeaking there. Over many years of playing hide-and-seek, Veronica had come to know where not to step if one didn't wish to be heard. She had also, on many an occasion, hidden under her parents' bed and had long known

about the particularly troublesome board under the rug. So
well in fact that, this time, when she had stepped on it whilst
searching her mother's wardrobe for her correspondence, she
had noticed the change in the sound from the one she had
remembered and she'd investigated. Sure enough, the once-
hollow space there had now been filled with a box. As she
brought it up onto the bed, she could see that it was a thing of
beauty with an intricate inlaid design along the edges. It had
a built-in lock, but whether because her mother had grown
lazy or she had never used the key, the clasp had opened
immediately. Opening the box, however, had not revealed
the stash of letters that Veronica had expected and at that
point, she had nearly given up. The box, at first glance, had
not seemed to have any storage space at all. Its insides were
designed to fold out once opened so that it was transformed
into a sloped writing surface covered in green baize. Veronica's
search had finally been successful only when she had realised
that the thickest part of the slope, towards what had been the
back of the box, concealed a compartment. Two bundles of
letters, each tightly tied by string. The larger bundle had been
the letters Cynthia had received from Aunt Sonia. The smaller
one comprised the drafts of letters written by Cynthia, the
final copies of which had presumably been posted to her sister
in Berlin. Both sets were typed or written on thin airmail
paper and covered the past two years.

Veronica looked again at the date at the top of the letter
in her hand, as if it might have changed since she had first
read the letter. August 1936. By then she had been back in
England almost nine months. She had spent an entire year in
Germany, much of it in Berlin, and yet her mother had never
mentioned this to her sister in Berlin.

She tried to remember whether, at that time, there had
been signs up in the public parks saying that Jews were

forbidden. She was certain there had not been because of one particular picnic in Treptow Park that she now wished she could forget. It had been towards the very end of the summer. She knew that because that was when Kurt and Michael had joined the Reich Labour Service for six months. She and Elke had had to endure a fashion parade as the boys showed off their brown uniforms and peaked forage caps. They thought the girls would be impressed with their pantaloons and shiny boots and Veronica had thought they looked smart enough, but when the boys had proudly said that they would be issued with spades the next day, she had been unable to contain her laughter. She'd refused to go to the park with them wearing their uniforms on such a hot day and fortunately Elke had agreed. In the end a compromise was reached. The boys would wear the dark shorts and running vest with the Labour Service badge on the chest. 'But you mustn't wear boots, mind!' Elke had said. 'No, that's right,' Veronica had replied, 'and you can't bring your spades either.' She shook her head at the memories, willing them to stop there. Remembering would do no good and she needed to concentrate on the letters in her hands.

She idly sifted through the pile of typed letters, taking care to ensure that they remained in date order. She noticed that, towards the end of the pile, Sonia had now started to handwrite her letters. Veronica picked up the first of these.

12 October 1937

To Cynthia, my dearest sister.
I cannot deny my sadness at your letter received today, but we must accept your decision. It is all very well to urge us to 'see it through' and 'don't let them break your spirit', but in fact our spirit IS broken. How could

it not be? Manfred's in particular of course. If we came to England we would lose almost all our possessions. Yet we have still asked you if you will vouch for us. Does not that alone tell you how serious things are? Writing that we should calm down and that things will pass, would be funny if you were not at the same time condemning us to suffering without end. I feel sure that you could only take such a stance because you don't know and cannot imagine what is going on here. Do you remember how sympathetic we were to Mrs Pankhurst's women and their fight for the vote? And I still have your letter describing your joy when you first voted. As you know, I too voted for the first time here in Germany.

Neither I nor Manfred are allowed to vote anymore. Will you not now fight for OUR right to vote? Sir Roland makes wonderful speeches in Parliament – and please pass on our congratulations of course, we try to read all his speeches! – but we can't help but notice that he never mentions the Jews even though he knows more than most, through you of course, the truth of the matter. I write this with pen and ink. You know how, as a left-hander, I have always disliked to do so. As you can see, I have not completely avoided smudging! Cynthia, I can hardly bear to write this: the police came round the other evening. Manfred opened the door and we stood there, struck dumb with terror as two big men walked into our home. They weren't rough with us, they were almost apologetic even, but they read out some regulation or other (there are so many!) and took away our typewriter. He said that Jews are not allowed such machines. We don't know if this is true or whether his family had need of a quality typewriter. Do you see now why we must leave? Please help us. It's all very well to say that I am British and can come. *But I gave up that right in 1914. And even if I hadn't, you know I would not leave Manfred and I am sure that isn't what you were suggesting.*

Please write back soon.

Your sister who loves you and who misses you,
Sonia.

It had taken Veronica nearly two weeks of stolen trips to her mother's bedroom before she had finally read through both bundles of letters. Two weeks which revealed the other side of the Germany where she had spent such an idyllic year. Her Aunt Sonia's clinical description of her life in Berlin was all the more shocking for what she was describing – the slow torture of Germany's Jews by their own government. The day when she and her husband, Manfred, had discovered that they could no longer walk in public parks, go to restaurants or visit their local swimming pool.

Cynthia's replies had at first been guarded but sympathetic. Veronica wished that they had been warmer. She could not fail to notice that, as later letters from Sonia began to explore the possibility of Cynthia's help in getting her and Manfred to London, Cynthia's tone had become worse still. Veronica read of her mother's indifference to her own sister's plight and she feared it. Feared it because she wanted to be angry and she could not be until she had confronted her own behaviour.

Two years and three months ago, on that day in Treptow Park, it really had been the very best of summer, the temperatures not as punishingly high as they had been. Veronica had never really liked the heat.

The four friends had played ball games, raced in pairs, the girls on the shoulders of the boys. Tired and happy they had finally settled down to eat when the first ball had rolled between them and onto the picnic blanket. It was a light ball but still able to knock over the tankard of beer in its path. It would have done too, if Michael had not managed to lean over, Elke's head still on his lap, snatching up the tankard and saving almost all of the contents. Only a little bit had splashed onto him, reaching Elke's face just as she opened her eyes to see what all the fuss was about. Her loud scream rooted the poor perpetrator, a little boy, to the spot, blanching with terror.

'Hey, hey, little chap!' Kurt had said, smiling reassuringly at the boy. 'Nothing to worry about. Everything is all right – you see?' As he was speaking he had been wiping the little ball clean and he then had rolled it gently back to the boy, patted him on the head and given him an apple as a gift.

'Best go now, little chap,' Veronica now recalled Kurt saying, 'before your mother thinks she's lost you.' The boy had given a slight bow and began running back in the direction from which he had come, happy once more. 'Do come and visit again, won't you?' called out Kurt before turning to Veronica, a big grin on his face. He knelt down and then rested his head on her lap, much as he had seen Elke doing, only this time he was face down, pulling up her blouse and making loud raspberry noises on Veronica's tummy until she nearly passed out from laughter.

Veronica walked to the post office, her letter to Aunt Sonia in hand, in which she asked that Sonia respond to her, care of a friend's address nearby. This had to be the strangest letter she could remember writing.

'*Dear Aunt Sonia, I don't know you, though you may have met me when I was very young. Just a few weeks ago I was told of your existence and I have read the letters you've written to Mother…*' Veronica had gone on to request that Sonia not tell Mother that she and Veronica were corresponding but she couldn't be sure she'd keep to that. Veronica had never deceived her parents before. She had even told them about Kurt though not that they had slept together. But even that, she felt, had been understood. She hadn't lied. But now, entering the post office, the act of writing to her own aunt felt like a betrayal. A betrayal that had begun with her searching for the correspondence she was not supposed to have known about. That her mother had deceived Veronica first didn't lessen the guilt. As if in a dream she saw herself buying the stamp and dropping the letter into the pillar box outside.

With her mind free once more to wander, it inevitably wandered back to Treptow Park and this time she knew she would fight the memory no longer. She felt tightness in her chest and sat down on a public bench and put her head in her hands.

The second ball to disturb their picnic that day had been a full-size, heavy leather football, tightly laced. This ball hadn't rolled onto the picnic blanket. It had simply rolled out from the nearby trees and come to a stop some yards away. Veronica wouldn't even have noticed it but for Kurt jumping up with a whoop and running to beat Michael to the ball so that he could get a good kick of it back to its owners as soon as they emerged from the trees. She could see him now, her tall, strong man, his well-defined biceps, bare and glistening with a thin layer of perspiration from the hot sun. As he reached down for the ball its owners had burst into the open. They too with big smiles on their faces. Which vanished when they saw Kurt straightening up, their ball in his hands, their eyes drawn fearfully to the Labour Service badge on his and Michael's vests.

From where she was sitting Veronica could not see Kurt's face, nor Michael's, but she could see them tensing, like wild animals ready to pounce, eager for a fight. What made it so bloody exciting was that the newcomers were clearly older than them by a few years and taller and stronger. Veronica found herself staring at the thickness of their thighs. And yet their powerful bodies slumped in submission to whatever it was that Kurt was saying to them. He was talking in short, rapid and low tones. To her astonishment, the men suddenly turned and ran back towards the trees, leaving Kurt holding their ball.

'Halt!' Kurt was yelling after them. Immediately they stopped and turned towards him. 'Haven't you forgotten something?' He waited until they had begun to move back towards them, eyeing the football, but still some distance away. 'I told you to leave the park as soon as possible, didn't I?' Kurt screamed. He then pointed away from the trees, over his shoulder to the gate they themselves had come through. 'Isn't that the closest exit?' And now Veronica could see his expression, transformed by anger, his teeth bared as if he was ready to attack. She clasped a hand to her open mouth, excited, wanting to see what would happen next.

'But sir, please, sir,' one of them had said, almost in a whimper. 'Our wives and belongings are through the trees. Can we not go and get them and then we will all leave, I promise.'

Kurt turned to Veronica and Elke. 'What do you think, ladies?'

Elke was laughing and said nothing. And Veronica — what had she felt at that moment? What had she truly felt? She didn't know what these men had done wrong. She only knew that somehow, Kurt had enormous power over them and that he was generously now handing some of it to her.

She felt dizzy. Elke tried to say something but was unable to get her words out and resumed rolling about on the grass, tears of laughter streaming down her cheeks. Veronica felt that somehow everyone else understood what was going on but her.

'Let them go, Kurt,' she said at last. 'If you think they've learned their lesson.' True power, she felt, was choosing to be magnanimous. Kurt seemed to understand this and he turned back to the men and beckoned them closer.

'Nearer,' he said, 'I need to tell you something.' They bent towards him. Before they could react, Kurt brought his hands up and slammed their heads together. They shouted in pain, reeling away, clutching their heads, one dropping to his knees. 'Now you've learned your lesson!' Kurt yelled. 'Go on then, run! Run, I said!' They started to make off but were disorientated and ran almost in circles at first, sending Elke into more gales of laughter. Veronica too could not suppress a smile, reminding her of a scene from a Charlie Chaplin film. As they ran back to the trees, Kurt shouted after them, 'If at the end of fifteen minutes all of you have not left this park, we're coming back for you.' He and Michael raised their hands in victory, punching the air gleefully.

'Jews,' Michael said as they sat back beside them, shaking his head.

'Jews,' Kurt had repeated as he flopped down beside Michael and slapped him on the back. 'We showed them, didn't we?!'

'They were so much bigger than you two,' Veronica had marvelled.

'Big apes. They gave way to their superiors. We are the Master Race after all.'

'To the victor, the spoils!' said Elke, sitting astride Michael.

Veronica watched them kissing for a moment, and then laughed as she saw Kurt looking hopefully at her. She took his face in her hands and kissed his forehead.

'My hero,' she whispered.

With a deep groan at the memory, Veronica tried to rise from the bench but her legs wouldn't immediately support her weight. Instead she sat back and tilted her head up to the sky. It had begun to rain and she welcomed the drops on her heated face. Kurt was evil; Michael and Elke had been no better.

'And me?' she asked aloud, looking up at the fast-moving grey clouds. Perhaps God would give her another chance.

Veronica made sure to visit her friend regularly. On the day she was informed that a letter had arrived for her from Germany, Veronica reacted as if it was the most normal thing in the world to receive a letter that could not be posted to her own address. Time passed slowly until, finally, she was able to get away and read it in private. It was cold outside and drizzling with rain but she didn't want to read it at home. Not this first time. She walked along the country lanes until finally she found a telephone box. Entering it, she took out the envelope and looked at the portrait of Hitler on the stamp. What a sharp nose he has, she thought. She ripped open the envelope, deliberately tearing the Führer's face in two.

29th December 1937

Dearest Veronica,

Where to start? Probably with a thank you. A thank you from the heart. Manfred and I read your warm words and we are not ashamed to say that tears were shed. Both of happiness that you had written but also sadness that it has had to be in secret. That of course confirmed our greatest fear – that your mother is not, shall we say, acting in a very sisterly fashion at present. We pray to God that that will change and with you there, we may hope that this will yet happen.

You asked so many questions and I am not sure I am able to answer you but will try to the best of my ability. In my day, the Jews tended to live in the East End of London, but also Hackney and Bethnal Green. Aldgate was another area as I recall. Perhaps a visit there might prove profitable. It is so wonderful that you wish to help. You asked about Jewish institutions and there too I really can't be sure now. Synagogues of course are focal points for Jews everywhere, so you might wander into one. No doubt they will be open on a Saturday morning. Actually there is one institution that I do remember reading about. It was set up, I think, by the League of Nations after the Versailles conference. Or perhaps a bit later than that, I am not sure. But it was called the 'Jewish Agency' and it has offices in London. I don't know where but I can try to find out. What else? We used to read a newspaper called the Jewish Chronicle. It was quite a good read, as far as I can remember.

A few weeks ago, Mr and Mrs Glickman were able to leave Berlin for England. They have a son in London who moved there for business about ten years ago. He is naturalised British and was able to vouch for them and pay for their passage. Mrs Glickman told me that they would be living in Hendon. Apparently that, and 'Golders Green' nearby, is where German Jews are settling now in London, but that is in the far north-west of the city in new estates that didn't even exist before the war. Certainly I have never been there but it occurs to me that if that is closer for you, you might go there to see if you can help at all.

Perhaps you will visit us here in Berlin. It is quite safe for foreign nationals. I do feel so isolated now. And to think you were here for a whole year. It is really too cruel. Please write back soon.

Love
Aunt Sonia and Uncle Manfred
(I have never signed like this before, how thrilling!).

Veronica kissed the letter before carefully refolding it and putting it back in her pocket. She wiped her eyes and blew her nose. She had been looking in England for something that would give her life some purpose when all the time it had been waiting for her in Germany. There she might also find atonement.

FIVE

21 JANUARY 1938

HENDON, LONDON

V ERONICA HAD NEVER BEEN TO EITHER THE EAST
End or to the north-west of London but was pleased
to take Sonia's advice. Hendon was a lot nearer than the
East End. She could hardly get a ride in the family motor
car, though, without questions being asked. She looked in
her purse for the coins she needed, picked up the telephone
receiver, dialled the operator and asked to be put through to
a taxi cab company.

The cabbie knew the route but nothing of its population
and he dropped her off, forty minutes later, outside Hendon
Central underground station. Veronica proceeded to wander
around looking for Jewish shops. She knew the Jews had to
eat kosher food, whatever that meant, and that they didn't eat
bacon, so she tried asking for a kosher butcher. To her delight,
everyone she passed seemed to know of one and she was rapidly
directed across the Watford Way until she arrived at shops on
a smart road called Vivian Avenue. She saw a kosher butcher
with a 'Closed' sign on the door, and a fishmonger with a large

notice saying 'Kosher'. Its shutters were down. She passed by one shop front that she had at first thought was a hairdressers until she realised that it was a shop selling women's wigs. She stopped for a few moments, fascinated by the variety on display. It was clear from the notices in the window that this was catering for Jewish women and she made a mental note to find out more about that. She forced herself to turn away, remembering that her aim in coming to Hendon, and its Jewish shops, was to find a Jewish newspaper, an idea she had got whilst reading Sonia's letter. Looking about her she saw a newsagents and was relieved to see that it at least was open. She walked up to the shop but paused with her hand raised to push the door, unaccountably nervous about going in to ask if they sold any Jewish newspapers. Would they see her as some sort of imposter? Would they laugh at the very idea of her asking for such a thing? Yet, when she finally pushed the door open, the loud ringing bell elicited no stares. Slowly she moved to the counter and in a low voice asked her question. She need not have worried.

'Of course! Which one are you after?' came the reply and then, seeing her confusion, the man added, 'English? Yiddish? What's your fancy?'

She walked out with a copy of the *Jewish Chronicle* and sat down on a bench to see what she might discover. The first two pages were filled with announcements of births, engagements and deaths within the Jewish community in Britain. She flicked through pages reading stories here and there when one paragraph caught her eye. It was headed '*Elimination of German-Jewish Business – The Economic Stranglehold*'. She rapidly scanned the words, sentences jumping out at her, verifying beyond any doubt everything her aunt had been writing to her sister. '*All the Jewish shops would be taken over by Germans.*'

'*As from January 1938, Berlin newspapers are forbidden to accept business advertisements from Jews.*'

The article went on to describe how three thousand Jewish doctors were to be deprived of their insurance cover and below that another article headed '*Caught in a Trap*': '*The first concrete indication of the Nazi Government's new decision not to let German Jews leave Germany came from the French and Swiss frontier stations this week.*'

Veronica shook her head in despair. What would she do if she were faced with such a situation? She turned back to the beginning of the newspaper and then, on page three, she noticed amongst the Personal Advertisements, cries for help, each more piteous than the next, from the terrified Jews of Germany, all giving mailbox numbers at the offices of the *Jewish Chronicle* itself and arranged in alphabetical order of the advertisements' first word:

> **Gentleman**, 62, former director of a bank in Leipzig. Nearly forty years' experience. Speaks fluent English. Requires permit. Eternal gratitude.

> **Hospitality** for 3 months would be greatly appreciated by a young man, German (26), well educated but must perfect his English before being accepted into America. Willing to help in any capacity.

Veronica's eyes had filled with tears at the desperation that must have been behind those placing such notices in a newspaper many hundreds of miles away, willing to leave everything behind to escape the growing persecution. Her mother's own sister was among them. Would she ever be able to speak to her mother again? She had forced herself to read on.

Is there anybody who will give a young Berlin lady, now in England, the opportunity to free her parents, or at least her endangered father, by giving a guarantee or a position?

Surely there would be some address in this paper of somewhere she could offer her services? If not, she had felt that she would go back into the newsagents and start screaming until someone told her what to do, how she might free herself from the suffocation she was now feeling.

Urgent. Will any sympathetic person act as guarantor for young Frankfurt man? Has finances to last for two months. Please hurry.

Would kind person release German Jew (45) from a concentration camp by becoming guarantor for entry into England until arrangements can be made for emigration abroad?

Tears were streaming down Veronica's cheeks. She hated her parents. She hated herself for having no real means of her own that would enable her to stand as guarantor for anyone. She had to get a job and she realised she would never go home again except to pack up her things and leave. She would do it when her parents weren't at home. Minutes passed as she sat reading these terrible messages on page three. Finally she'd begun to turn the pages again, remembering why she had bought the paper in the first place. She passed larger advertisements on subsequent pages, '*Fine Fruits of Palestine*', '*Daimler Car Hire*', interspersed with other articles about the worsening situation for the Jews of Europe. Everywhere antisemitism seemed to be on the rise, in Hungary, Austria and especially Rumania. How could she have been so unaware of what was going on? Finally, at the bottom of page twenty-two, she found what she had been hoping for. An interview on the worsening refugee situation conducted with a Mr Berl Locker, the head of the Jewish Agency offices in London. An advert towards the back of the newspaper for a part-time typist had provided the address and she had stood up to walk back to the underground station. If she hurried, maybe she'd even be able to meet Mr Locker before the rush hour started. Just then the man who had sold her the newspaper had come out of his shop and, to her surprise, the notice in the door window had been turned to 'Closed' and he was locking up. The time: half past two.

'Excuse me.'

Startled, the man had turned round. Then he recognised her and he lifted his trilby hat to her.

'Excuse me for asking, but why are all the shops around here closing in the middle of the afternoon?'

'It's Friday!' he said, as if that explained everything. Then, seeing her blank look, he added, 'It will be dark in another couple of hours. It will be *shabbes*.' Veronica must have still looked blank, because he gestured at the *Jewish Chronicle* he had sold to her. 'My apologies, Miss, I assumed that if you buy the *Jewish Chronicle*, then you must be Jewish. Tonight is the start of the Jewish Sabbath. We have to be home to prepare. All Jewish places will be closed now. I was one of the last to close today and I am running a bit late.'

She thanked him, wished him a good afternoon and walked back towards Hendon Central, aware that many men seemed to be walking there too. She wondered why so many would be heading into the city at that time of the day. Except that every one of them had turned away up Wykeham Road just yards after the station. They had all been wearing suits and ties under their coats and either bowler hats or trilbies, but none of them had been carrying a briefcase or even an umbrella. Veronica had stopped to look at them as they had walked past, an incongruous figure by comparison with her bag and rolled-up newspaper. Gradually it had dawned on her that these were all Jewish men and that they must be going to a synagogue. How many, she wondered, were refugees from Germany? She'd thought of trying to speak German with them but had realised how ridiculous that would be. She didn't notice that one of the men was wearing a suit and a coat that was not quite as sharp as the others, his shoes not quite as shiny.

But Harry Wolf, in his cheap suit and unpolished shoes, had noticed her standing on the corner, and briefly wondered why a young woman was standing there, just before the start of the Sabbath, holding a *Jewish Chronicle* but clearly in no hurry to get home. Was she not going to light candles and eat with her family? Before he had been sent down, he and his wife had been one of the more hospitable members of the community and they would have invited her to eat with them. But now nobody wanted anything to do with him, his wife had fallen ill with cancer and they ate alone. So, head down, he had passed her by and continued up Wykeham Road to the synagogue in Raleigh Close where once his artistic skills had been much in demand for invitations, certificates and birthday cards. Even here in the synagogue there was evidence of his work. One only had to look up, as Harry did now on entering the main prayer hall, to see the large marble stone fixed prominently high on the right-hand wall near the front, close to the Holy Ark containing the Torah, the sacred Scrolls of the Law. His eyes flitted over the words he had engraved there though he, and everyone else present, knew them off by heart, recited as they were every week during the Sabbath service.

He who giveth salvation unto kings and dominion unto princes, whose kingdom is an everlasting kingdom, may he bless:

> *Our Sovereign Lord, King George,*
> *Our gracious Queen Elizabeth*
> *Mary the Queen Mother*
> *The Princess Elizabeth*
> *and all the Royal Family*

Two years earlier he had been working on different wording but then, at very short notice, he had had to change it. If King Edward could have only delayed his abdication by just one more month, Harry would have already been paid for that work and he could then have expected to receive another commission for a wording for King George, though he couldn't think what would have come in place of '*Queen Elizabeth*'. Surely not '*Our Gracious Queen Wallis*'? He always smiled when he thought of that, even now. At the time though, he had not been sure against whom he should more direct his annoyance, Mrs Simpson for bewitching the King, or Dr Glass, the Synagogue's Honorary Officer who had paid him for his work.

Shortly after that, acting on an anonymous tip-off, the police had caught him with a forged painting in his house. Disputing the size of a commission for his engraving quickly assumed a very low priority. Fortunately the police, having found only two incidents where he had sold for profit, had been unable to prove that he was running a fully commercial enterprise, which is why he had only been given a few months' prison as a warning. His art studio, with its many works in progress, remained hidden but he didn't dare resume his work.

On his release, he had continued to attend services even though his old friends at the Synagogue had not stood by him. The Honorary Officers no longer invited him to participate even when attendance was low and they were pressed to find others willing to come up and take part. After a while he had got the message and moved towards the back of the hall where he could not feel the eyes drilling into the back of his head nor hear, or imagine that he heard, the whispering about him and what he had done. Harry seethed at this treatment. After all, who had he killed? Where were the victims? He tried to survive in a difficult world like everyone else. His wife was now an invalid for God's sake. Sometimes he wondered why he still attended as he certainly didn't pray but he went through the motions so that he could retain some regular structure to his week. He found the routine and the reading of prayers in Hebrew, which he could follow but didn't understand, oddly comforting.

Dr Glass, Harry noticed, was there tonight, wearing his black pin-striped suit and top hat, displaying the authority that Harry now despised. If the doctor had been a tall man, the top hat might have made him look imposing but as it was it seemed only to accentuate just how short Dr Glass actually was. The service ended and everywhere men shook hands with each other, saying *a guten shabbes*, the traditional Yiddish wish that they should all enjoy a good Sabbath. Harry was the exception of course. The most he got was a slight nod of the head from a few old friends but most of these tilted their heads so that their eyes were shielded from his under the rims of their bowler hats. As he turned to go he noticed Dr Glass, who seemed to be making his way towards him, and he began to move in his direction but at that point Raymond, the local school teacher, approached Dr Glass, said, '*A guten shabbes*,' shook his hand and began to ask him how his wife and two young daughters were faring. The doctor answered distractedly and tried by signalling with his eyes to Harry to stop him from leaving. *He does want to speak to me!* Harry found this both surprising and amusing. He decided to wait.

'I'm so sorry,' he heard the doctor say to Raymond, 'I need to speak with Harry Wolf before he leaves.'

Raymond looked at him curiously, unaware that Harry was now just behind him. 'You're talking to Harry again?'

Dr Glass paused. 'Ah well, I wouldn't put it quite like that. But excuse me and my regards to your wife, *a guten shabbes, a guten shabbes*.'

Harry was in the cloakroom getting his coat when Dr Glass finally caught up with him.

'Harry! Have you got a moment please?'

'*A guten shabbes*, Dr Glass,' he said pointedly and put out his hand. Dr Glass shook hands.

'Yes of course, *a guten shabbes*. May I have a moment of your time?'

Harry theatrically turned his head as if to see if Dr Glass could perhaps have been addressing someone standing behind him. There was nobody there. He turned back and pointed at his own chest.

'Me? You was wishing to talk to me, to Harry Wolf?'

Inwardly Dr Glass sighed. He had expected no less. Of course not. Glancing around nervously in case he was being observed, he leant in close to the man and said, 'Harry. I do need to talk to you urgently.'

'Urgently?' repeated Harry. 'Now it's urgent? Whatever could you and me need to talk about, eh?'

'Not here. Not now. Can I come to you tomorrow afternoon?'

'Dr Glass, come now, sir, let's be honest with each other,' said Harry. 'In the nine months since my court case, you've barely said a word to me. I come to synagogue every *shabbes*, but not once, not once have you allowed me to be called to the Torah or otherwise participate in the service. Me and Naomi. We're not invited to lunch with no-one no more. And ain't I right in saying that you have something to do with this? You can understand my surprise, I think.'

'Yes, yes, of course. But Harry, you were convicted of a crime. Surely we cannot have a convicted criminal say blessings over the Torah! That is an honour and the Rabbi is, understandably, reluctant—'

'But what about forgiveness? Rehabilitation?'

'*Have* you been rehabilitated, Harry?'

Harry grinned, revealing discoloured, uneven teeth. There were no gaps though a gold tooth showed on the edge of his grin. 'I was inside for four months. That's rehabilitation enough, ain't it?'

'Harry, you want honesty? We both know that your forging activities were not limited to being caught with a couple of paintings. So really, you haven't paid for your crimes. Also, one of the forgeries you are known to have sold, you sold to the Rabbi who paid you believing it to be genuine! You haven't offered to make good his loss, have you?'

'How can I? They put me inside. How can I make a living if I'm inside? Do they think of that?'

'In my opinion someone like you brings our entire community into disrepute. And with fascism all over the East End, you are a danger to all of us.'

Harry turned to walk away. It was now dark outside and beginning to rain. He turned his collar up. Dr Glass followed him outside and put out a restraining hand on Harry's arm.

'But Harry, this should only impress upon you the urgency if I nevertheless need to speak to you. Are you home tomorrow or not?'

'Well, I may be off to see Spurs,' replied Harry provocatively, knowing that Dr Glass frowned on people going to matches on the Sabbath. 'In fact, now, I am almost certainly going to go. And I'll tell you for why. Because, if you want to speak to me, then next *shabbes*, I want to be called up to the Torah to say my blessings. Once the congregation sees that, then I'll hear what you have to say.'

'Don't ask me that!' exclaimed Dr Glass. 'That's not just up to me. That is also a religious issue. The Rabbi wouldn't allow it. I couldn't help you there, even if I wanted to.'

'Your lovely pin-stripe suit is getting wet, doctor,' replied Harry. 'And I'm not sure it's good for your silk hat.' He contemplated the doctor for a few more seconds as Dr Glass grimly stood his ground. 'I tell you what then. Do something for me what you *can* do. I want you to invite me and my good Naomi to lunch. Next *shabbes* immediately after the service. Can you do that?' He saw the doctor's hesitation. 'What, you can't even do that?'

'No, it's not that. I can – I will. But I was hoping not to have to wait a whole week.'

'Well, nobody said life is fair, did they? Oh and that's not all. You must also invite another family to that lunch. I don't mind which one but another family from this community. I don't want you pretending that the invitation never happened. My Naomi and me, we need the community to know that you have invited us to lunch. We want it to be talked about and not hidden. Then we will receive other invitations and be accepted once again at least socially if not in the service itself. All right, Dr Glass?'

Dr Glass had indeed hoped he'd be able to meet with Harry without undue publicity. He nodded irritably. 'Very well. My Greta will discuss the details with Naomi.' He turned to get back into the Synagogue and out of the rain but Harry called after him.

'What? What, Harry?'

'*A guten shabbes*, Dr Glass. That's all.'

'*A guten shabbes*, Harry.'

SIX

21 JANUARY 1938

BLOOMSBURY, LONDON

V ERONICA HAD WALKED BACK FROM VIVIAN AVENUE to Hendon Central station because it was on a busy road and she hoped to be able to hail another taxi. However, whenever she had been taken to London as a child, she had always been driven by a chauffeur in Father's car and now, standing at the station, her curiosity to get on a train overwhelmed her. Almost before she knew it, she had bought a one-way ticket from the ticket office. Half an hour later, a convert to underground travel and the modernist simplicity of the underground railway map, she had arrived at Tottenham Court Road station. From there she had made her way to 77 Great Russell Street.

There were two people in the small office just across from where Veronica was sitting quietly in the narrow corridor waiting to be called. If they were being observed rather than doing the observing, it might have been thought that they made an incongruous pair. The man, Berl Locker, wearing a crumpled black suit, was a short, pale man with thick swept-back black hair but with a lined face that showed him to be in his early fifties. The woman was perhaps a quarter of a century younger, tall and gangly with a dark complexion that made her bright green eyes startling by contrast. To Berl's vague unease, she wore flat shoes to work. Worse, she had a mass of loose black hair that hung down to her shoulders and which didn't seem to have been brushed let alone been set or pinned. That, combined with her habit of ignoring the chairs in his office, made her seem to Berl like some dark giant spider perched on his desk. He again resisted the temptation to tell her to get her hair done, buy a decent skirt and sit with her ankles crossed, preferably on a chair. If she was a member of his staff he would have said it the day she arrived. Instead he looked through the blinds of his office towards the woman in the corridor. She, by contrast, blonde, pale and poised, looked as if she might well manage the girls in the typing pool downstairs.

'Another good Samaritan no doubt wanting to help us,' said Berl with a sigh. 'It is yet more proof that our situation is dire. These English adventurers are all very laudable but they can't in practice do anything – other than waste our time.'

'Just as well then, Berl,' smiled his colleague, 'that so few do come here offering to help. We politely turn them away just as their government politely turns us away.' She shrugged.

Berl looked at the woman whom he had known for barely two weeks but about whom he had received the telegrammed orders from Jerusalem that Sarah Levtov was being sent over to him and that she be provided with 'every facility'. She spoke to him with a seemingly unaffected lack of formality that still jarred though he knew that she was typical of the new Jewish woman that was being created in Palestine. If he was ever going to live there himself, as he intended, he had better get used to it.

'I'll leave her to you then,' said Sarah. 'I would love to stay but your office barely has room for two people and we don't want to overwhelm her.'

Of the three languages they shared in common, they had settled into speaking German when alone and English when with colleagues, with the odd Hebrew thrown in if the need for confidentiality outweighed the desire to be considerate. Berl watched Sarah walk down the narrow stairway to the right to where, if she chose, she could listen in via the tube as she sometimes liked to do. He stepped out into the corridor and signalled to Miss Veronica Beaumont that she should come through, and showed her into his cramped office.

Veronica shook Mr Locker's hand as he showed her in. She noticed that he was slightly shorter than she was, and estimated him to be about 50 years old. His hair seemed to bother him and he kept pushing it back from his forehead. He had a short toothbrush moustache which was beginning to turn grey. From the deep creases around his eyes and cheeks, she got the impression that he was a man who liked to smile a lot. He was all business now, however, as he gestured to the wooden chair in front of his desk and returned to his own seat.

'Please excuse the paperwork,' he said, gesturing at the piles of papers taking up much of the floor space around them. 'We have been so busy recently…' He had an east European accent, she thought, though his English was good. 'My name is Berl Locker. Now what I can do for you?'

'Why are you open on a Friday evening, Mr Locker?'

Berl, startled, looked at her more closely. 'Normally we would not be working now, but there's a crisis. People's lives might be at stake. Is that what you've come for, to tell me I am not religious enough?'

Veronica laughed, embarrassed and aware that that had not been the best opening line that she could have begun with. 'Please forgive me, Mr Locker! That was not at all my intention, I was simply curious. No, I am here because I want to help the refugees.'

'So do I,' Berl said, confusing her for a moment before he continued, 'but there are very complex issues involved. And, unless you are going to donate a very large sum of money to us, I am not sure how you could help.'

'I speak rather good German,' said Veronica, watching his face for some reaction. There was none. 'So I wondered whether it might come in handy.'

'My dear young lady,' smiled Berl gently, 'do you have any idea how many German speakers – native German speakers – we have in London right now? All arrived in the past five years. I really don't see—'

'Maybe, Mr Locker, but they are Jews and they can't go back.' She stood up. 'I, on the other hand, am going to Berlin in a few days from now, and I thought, surely you might have something for me to do.'

'Like what?' said Berl, rapidly rising to his feet too. 'Perhaps you could bring someone back in your bag?' Veronica could see that Mr Locker regretted saying this as soon as the words had left his mouth. Perhaps her face had betrayed her upset at his response. 'I am sorry, Miss Beaumont. We have a lot of offers of assistance by good people who are appalled by the situation in Germany today but we need money and we need visas and I don't think you are offering us either.'

There was silence as Veronica tried to think of something to say, but her mind was blank. She was sure that if she could only think of the right words, he might yet listen.

'You may have heard of my father? Sir Roland Beaumont?'

'Yes, Miss Beaumont, I have heard of him. You are his daughter? Does he know you are here? He is no great friend of ours, I think.' Mr Locker was now opening the door in confirmation that the interview was at an end. Dejected, she walked through the door and thanked him for his time in a voice so small that she wasn't sure whether he would actually have heard her.

Mr Locker smiled; he was not an unkind man. 'I do thank you for your willingness to be of assistance. If everyone in Europe felt like you did, there wouldn't be any refugees. Now if you will excuse me, I may not be a religious man but I don't want to stay here too late on a Friday evening and there is still so much to do.'

Veronica came out of the building and turned blindly down the street, her eyes beginning to sting with the first tears of frustration. It was getting dark now and there was a hint of rain in the sky. She walked quickly, turning the next corner, looking in her handbag for a handkerchief and with no clear idea of where she was going nor what to do next. She felt silly that she had imagined that anyone would have any interest in her and her great plans to save the world. She was angry with herself and angry with Mr Locker. Surely that stupid man could have at least...

'Miss Beaumont! Wait!'

She turned to see a figure rapidly closing the distance between them, waving her arm. Veronica's first impression was that this woman was quite as tall as Veronica herself but with the build and easy gait of an athlete. The dark hair and dark, tanned skin made her think that she might be Italian or Greek perhaps. As the woman came closer Veronica noticed her large dark eyes beneath thick eyebrows and eyelashes. The woman came to a halt in front of her, took a drag on her cigarette and expelled a plume of smoke from her nose down towards the ground. To

Veronica it seemed almost as if she was being confronted by a raging bull. The woman ran her eyes over Veronica and it was apparent that she wasn't impressed with what she saw.

'How do you know my name?' asked Veronica, attempting to keep her face neutral whilst quickly looking around her. In the late afternoon, just past Kingsway, and surrounded by the hustle and bustle of central London, she didn't feel afraid but nevertheless she clasped her handbag tightly to her.

'I see I have startled you, Miss Beaumont. My name is Sarah Levtov. I work at the Jewish Agency office with Mr Locker and had hoped to catch you before you left the building.' She handed her a folded piece of paper. Veronica took it and opened it. It was a blank sheet of Jewish Agency stationery, its letterhead giving the address she had just come from. Sarah stuck out her hand.

Veronica shook it, noticing the rough calluses on her palms. She wondered what life she led to get them into such a state. Her English was perfect but she had an accent that Veronica had never heard before. Her words infused with guttural consonants, sounded harsh. Mainly because she'd never heard any Turks speak, Veronica now wondered if the woman might be Turkish.

The wind was blowing Sarah Levtov's unruly hair across her face and she absently tucked the strands behind her ears. Veronica found herself reaching a hand to her own hair, suddenly conscious of the half hour she had spent that morning releasing her waves from her curlers, combing her locks and securing her hat with hair pins. A number 33 tram slowed a little as it turned into Theobald's Road and a man jumped off, nearly landing on top of them before steadying himself, straightening his jacket and melting into the crowds.

'Come. Let's find somewhere quieter to talk,' Sarah said. She gestured back the way they had come. 'How about the little park back there? There are some benches and, at this time of the day, we may be lucky and find one empty.' She looked up at the sky. 'At least until it starts to rain.'

Veronica found herself irritated by this woman's abrupt way of speaking. 'Do you know why I came to the Jewish Agency today?' Veronica asked, standing her ground.

'Yes, I do. That is what I wanted to talk to you about. I think Mr Locker may have been too hasty in reaching his decision.'

A glimmer of hope. She allowed herself to think once more of her aunt and uncle in Berlin and forced a smile. 'In that case, Miss Levtov, do lead on. Let's go and find your bench.'

There was one unoccupied bench in Bloomsbury Square. Veronica sat quietly for a while watching the passersby, deliberately not turning to make eye contact with Miss Levtov, who sat at the other end with her legs splayed, like a man. Was her future course really to be determined by this brash woman? Surely not.

'Mr Locker told me in no uncertain terms that—' Veronica began.

'Mr Locker was the first interview,' interrupted Sarah with a smile, 'I am the second interview and if I decide, then you pass. The Jewish Agency,' she explained, 'works to support the British Government in carrying out its League of Nations Mandate to build a Jewish home in Palestine. Right now, however, the British have begun to severely limit the number of refugees allowed in. Mr Locker can hardly be expected, in the name of the Jewish Agency, to encourage British citizens to help circumvent government policy.' She looked at Veronica for a long moment and then continued. 'And how does he know that you aren't some sort of agent provocateur? There are many

in the British Colonial Office for example who would welcome
an excuse to discredit the Agency.'

'But I am no such thing!' Veronica retorted, realising as
she said the words, how silly they sounded. Sarah nodded
dismissively.

'I lied to you earlier, Miss Beaumont,' said Sarah, speaking
quickly as if she were trying to keep pace with her own
thoughts. 'I don't really work for the Jewish Agency. I take
my orders from a new organisation in Palestine. Its name
in Hebrew is "*Aliyah Dalet*", and its purpose is quite simple.
It is to bring into Palestine as many Jews as possible from
Germany and, very likely in the near future, from Austria.'

'And you are able to make the decision whether to use me
or not?'

Sarah noted the tone of disbelief and barked a laugh,
revealing, Veronica couldn't help but notice, a set of strong,
filling-free teeth.

'You mean, how can I, a mere woman, make decisions?'
Veronica nodded. 'I am from *Eretz Yisrael*, that's Palestine to
you,' she added, seeing Veronica's confused look, 'and there,
on our farms, and in the Labour movement, women take
many decisions alongside the men.' She laughed again. 'Poor
Mr Locker is still getting used to it!'

Veronica turned away from the woman's dark stare,
feeling a touch of sympathy for 'poor' Mr Locker. This Miss
Levtov was bursting with an energy quite unlike anything she
had seen before.

'And do you think I can be of use to you and your
organisation?' asked Veronica. She could feel a fluttering of
anticipation in her stomach.

'That you go to Berlin is useful,' Sarah replied. 'That you
are not Jewish and, please excuse me, look like Germany's
ideal of womanhood, is even better. That you are your father's

daughter is best of all. Can he help us perhaps?' She was unashamedly looking at Veronica's pale, unblemished skin and her nose and chin, her expression seemed to be saying *you're a weak Daddy's girl.*

Veronica blushed and shook her head. She should never have mentioned her father.

'Well, can you get us to speak to his friends, or can you convey messages perhaps?'

Again Veronica shook her head. Of course that would be useful to them and that would be the reason for their interest in her. 'I am so sorry. I love – or loved – my parents, but I do not share their views and in fact have become quite horrified by them. I simply cannot discuss any of this with them and in fact would have to conceal from them any contact I have with you. I am sorry to have wasted your time.' She stood up.

'Sit down,' Sarah snapped and Veronica's knees obeyed the sharp command. Sarah was silent for a moment weighing up options. The fact remained that, other than Jews, few German-speaking English people came to the Jewish Agency, even fewer looked like Veronica and only one could claim Sir Roland Beaumont as a father. That father and daughter might be estranged didn't change that. Sarah threw down the end of her cigarette and ground it under her foot.

'Why do you go to Berlin?'

'Well, I am telling my parents it is to meet old friends from my year there in 1935. That is where I learnt German. They think the more contacts we can make with the Germans the more likely there will never be a war between us.'

'That is good. But how often can you go? You'll need a better cover story if you are to be helping us whilst you are there. People will get suspicious over there very quickly.'

Veronica said nothing, biting her lip. She would indeed find it hard to explain the time and expense of continuous trips, just one reason why she had needed help and had come to Great Russell Street in the first place. She lifted her head and turned to Sarah defiantly.

'Well, that's what your organisation can do surely? You are the experts. You get me a cover story!'

Sarah snorted as if that response confirmed the low opinion Veronica was now sure she had of her.

'Well,' said Sarah. 'First we would have to be sure we could trust you. Especially with your background, you could be a lot of trouble if you wanted to hurt us. This initial trip can be a trial run but I am going to need to get to know you a lot better. We won't give you anything very difficult to do and we will be watching you. I can get you some money, and maybe put you in touch with someone from our organisation there when you are in Berlin. You need to remember all the time, Miss Beaumont, that this is not a game. It's a very serious business. Are you sure you want to do this?'

Veronica nodded hurriedly. 'Of course.' As she said the words she repeated them to herself, steadying her nerves. The desperate, pleading letters to her mother from her newly-discovered aunt in Germany had shaken her as had those personal advertisements in the newspaper and she wanted to trust this exotic woman. She *needed* to trust her but at the same time she would have to keep some secrets. She couldn't bring herself to talk about her aunt or of her mother's treachery. Not yet anyway.

Sarah looked carefully at Veronica, aware of the danger that she may have been pushing this British innocent into a little too quickly. She did not think the British were trying to plant this woman into *Aliyah Dalet*. For one, it would be too soon for them to have heard about its existence. The organisation had barely begun its activities. The fact that her father was known to be pro-German made her story somehow more believable. If she had been trying to infiltrate them surely she would have tried to conceal her parentage? She sighed. This Miss Beaumont had no skills and probably lacked the necessary courage or inner strength. But her looks and background would make up for that to some extent. Sarah keenly felt that, for the Jews of Germany, time was running out. This rich, privileged little English mouse would have to do.

SEVEN

29 JANUARY 1938

HENDON, LONDON

'THAT WOULD BE LOVELY, MRS GLASS, THANK YOU,' said Harry Wolf, holding out his pale green china coffee cup and saucer for a refill. He had earlier checked under the soup plate to confirm that it was Susie Cooper. In his business he had to be able to appreciate the finer things in life and it wasn't just their set of china. The room was long and narrow but with enough room to pass the dining table on either side. Unfortunately its features were hidden by the thick white tablecloth but Harry appreciated the scrolled toes design of the feet which matched those of the rococo-style walnut chairs they were sitting on. Just behind his chair was a fireplace in front of which stood a wide neoclassic-style firescreen. He never understood quite the point of a firescreen, especially when the fireplace was not in use. From the look of it this one had not been used for some time. A shame. Harry preferred a warm fire over central heating and, on his return from prison, one of his first tasks had been to sweep his chimney clean.

Dr Glass looked at him and then around the rest of the table. Naomi was looking at him from her wheelchair. She seemed to understand the discomfort he was feeling and was even perhaps showing some sympathy. Which only made things worse. Raymond the school teacher and Rochelle, his wife, made up the rest of the gathering. They seemed to have got over the rehabilitation of Harry Wolf rather too quickly, Dr Glass thought, and had been laughing with the man all through lunch although careful to keep the conversation away from art and Harry's own particular skills. Now that the meal was over, Dr Glass was dreading the moment when Raymond and Rochelle would say goodbye and he would ask Harry Wolf to step into his study to hear his proposal. Best get on with it. He cleared his throat.

'I think it's time to say Grace.' They never bothered with Grace after any other meals during the week but on *shabbes*, he felt he ought to, given his position in the Synagogue. But that took five minutes at most and the moment it ended, he knew the others would leave.

'*Gut Shabbes!*'

'Thank you for having us!'

'Lovely to have you back with us, Harry!'

'Harry,' said Dr Glass, 'would you care to step into my study please? Greta and Naomi, I am sure, still have lots to talk about when we are out of their way.' He took a few steps down the corridor and opened a door.

Harry looked around the small room, taking in the charts depicting almost life-size men, drawn with various sections cut away to show how the human body worked, the digestive system, the respiratory system. Harry hated seeing how messy and complicated things were just under the skin. He would much rather not know. There was a large, heavy oak desk that took up the entire width of the room and almost half its length. The top of the desk was inlaid with green leather, a narrow, central drawer beneath it with a lock and key. Harry looked longingly at the ashtray and silver cigarette case placed tidily next to the pen and inkwell set and modern-looking telephone with its handset sitting in a cradle on top of its squat black body. Harry thought that he and Naomi really ought to get one like that. The top of the desk rested on two thick pedestals each with three drawers. A couple of these drawers, he noticed, were not fully closed, showing that they were full to overflowing with letters and medical papers. Other than that the room was neat and tidy. The sun shone through the window, casting a brilliant white light over the desk and the leather swivel chair in front of it. By contrast, the rest of the room looked gloomy. Dr Glass sat on the swivel chair, turning it so that his back was to the desk and to the window but facing Harry. He gestured to Harry to sit on one of the two straight-backed plain wooden chairs with thin cushions on their seats.

Harry's gaze went back to the ashtray and he thought that this would be just the right time of day and location for a smoke but he didn't dare ask for a cigarette on the Sabbath. He thought for a moment of jokingly suggesting to the doctor that if they both lit up nobody would be the wiser but then he saw the doctor turn slightly, unlock the centre drawer and take out a small passport-sized red booklet.

'Here, Harry, look at this. This is what I wanted to talk to you about.'

Harry took it. At the top there were two words in gold lettering; one of the words looked to be Arabic and the other he recognised as Hebrew. Some more words were at the bottom. He tried to read them but they weren't ones that he was familiar with from the prayer book. He tried to piece each word together letter by letter.

'You're looking at the back,' said Glass. 'If you turn it over, it's in English and you won't have to guess.'

You smug bastard, thought Harry, but did as instructed. It was, in fact, a passport and a British one at that. The words 'British Passport' appeared in gold lettering above the Royal coat of arms. Beneath the coat of arms another word: 'Palestine'. Harry raised an eyebrow and quickly flicked through the pages. It belonged to a man called Eisenthal. Harry turned the passport horizontally to look at the black and white photograph. He didn't recognise him.

'Where did you find this?' he asked.

'I didn't find it,' replied Dr Glass, 'Mr Eisenthal gave it to me.'

'I see,' said Harry, though he didn't see at all. He waited for the inevitable explanation. Dr Glass had not invited him here in order to not tell Harry more.

Dr Glass sighed. 'You see, Harry, the Jews in Germany are having a bad time at the moment. You know that.' He stopped and waited for Harry to say something and when he didn't he continued. 'Thousands are trying to leave but it is expensive and it is hard to find a country that will take them in. Many are desperate and, once they've decided to leave, they will go anywhere that will take them in. From this year the British have even made it harder for them to get to the Jewish National Home in Palestine.'

'I'm sorry, Dr Glass, I'm still not sure what this has to do with your friend here.' He held up the passport.

'Mr Eisenthal, on a visit to London, has lost his passport. He reported it missing shortly after bringing it to me. It is highly inconvenient for him as he has to stay in England a lot longer than he originally planned until a replacement passport can be issued to him.'

'And?'

'And there is a young man in Berlin, let's say his name is Otto Lipschitz, of a similar age to Mr Eisenthal. Otto is a talented musician, who has handed over almost all of his savings to the Gestapo, the Nazi secret police, in return for permission to leave Germany, but who now has nowhere to go.' He reached back into the drawer and brought out two other passports. 'A couple of others have also "lost" their passports in the last few weeks. Fortunately, the administration of paperwork regarding Palestine is chaotic and it takes months to cross-check the details of lost passports against those entering using those same details more than once.'

Harry frowned and flicked back to the man's photograph, examining it carefully and holding it up to the light. 'So you want me to swap the photos and copy the stamp onto the corner of the new one, so this man, what's-'is-name, can use it to go to Palestine. Is that it?'

Dr Glass nodded.

'And what about those?' he asked, pointing to the open drawer.

'Those are really quite special,' said Dr Glass. 'They could be used for a husband and wife. And someone with your skill could also add the details of children. You could save an entire family. We are waiting for the right people to come to our attention.'

'We? Who's "we" exactly?'

Dr Glass looked away sheepishly.

'I can't tell you that.'

'I see,' said Harry. There was a long silence. To Dr Glass it seemed to stretch for as long as a minute. He knew what was coming now.

'You are breaking the law, Dr Glass.'

There it was. The moment Dr Glass had dreaded for weeks had arrived. His eyes snapped back to Harry, noticing how the man was savouring the power he, the petty criminal, now had over him, the Synagogue President.

'Harry, these people will be thrown into concentration camps if they are not able to get away.'

'But it's still illegal what you're doing, ain't it?'

'I am not making any money out of this, Harry. In fact I am losing quite a lot of my own money by working on this.'

Harry raised an eyebrow mockingly, but said nothing.

'Yes, I am breaking the law!' said the doctor finally. 'But this is nothing like what you did!'

'I disagree,' said Harry quietly. 'The judge who sentenced me said that there is never any excuse for breaking the law. We live in a just society here in England. If there is anything that is wrong that needs improving, then we lobby for changes to be made. We have a free press—'

'That's true,' said the doctor, 'but—'

'You are a hypocrite,' said Harry, surprised to feel real anger beginning to well up inside of him. 'After all what you did to me over the past year. The shaming, the ostracising. And now you tell me you've been doing the same thing. No actually, you're worse. I was working alone, for me. You, though, are part of what I think in America they call "organised crime". You are a gangster, Dr Glass!'

'That is a distortion!' hissed the doctor, trying to keep his voice from being heard by the women in the dining room. 'I am, even in this guise, trying to save lives. Like I do as a doctor. You preyed on the gullible. You took their money.' He grabbed one of the other passports from the drawer and waved it at Harry. 'Who are the victims here?'

The two men contemplated each other from their chairs, silent, their knees almost touching. Through the door they could hear their wives laughing, quite loudly. They were both surprised by this.

'What makes you think I won't turn you in and take revenge on you?' asked Harry.

Doctor Glass nodded slowly. 'I've thought about that possibility of course. And I can't be certain that you won't. However, I decided the risk was worth taking for a couple of reasons. Firstly, the Jewish community in Britain has been galvanised as never before into trying to help the suffering of the Jews in Germany. You may have read in the paper about all the fundraising and donations of clothes etcetera that are taking place. Everyone wants to do what they can to help. If you were to "turn me in" as you say, there wouldn't be a door that would be open to you. If you thought you were being ostracised before, that would be nothing to what you would experience at the hands of the country-wide community.' Dr Glass looked at Harry carefully, glad that he had not been challenged on this. It sounded plausible but in truth, he had no idea what the country-wide community thought about anything, especially law-breaking of any kind in Britain. He didn't even know if there was such a thing as a country-wide community. There was the Board of Deputies of British Jews but they certainly wouldn't support him publicly even if they agreed privately with his actions. Ostracising could anyway only happen at a religious level and he was pretty sure it would have to be for some religious offence. But none of this had occurred to Harry so Dr Glass was able to proceed more confidently. 'Secondly, I am hoping you will want to help because you, like so many of us, have relatives left behind in Europe, for whose safety we worry every day. Everywhere now, it seems, Jewish communities are suffering growing attacks. In Poland and Rumania in particular. Your family is in Rumania, isn't it?'

More silence followed. Then Harry stood up and tossed back the passport he was holding to Dr Glass. 'Where is the photograph of this geezer?'

'I don't know who it is. Someone will bring it to me once they've identified a suitable person and once I tell them I have someone who can do the work.'

Harry nodded, turned, and put his hand on the doorknob.

'Will you help?' asked Dr Glass, also rising to his feet.

'Of course I'll help,' said Harry.

EIGHT

31 JANUARY 1938

SOHO, LONDON

VERONICA MOVED QUICKLY THROUGH THE vestibule of the Regent Palace Hotel and pushed through the swing doors at the far end and into the restaurant. The central court was bathed in bright natural light, the sun shining through the glass-domed roof, and Veronica had to shield her eyes as she scanned the room. She spotted Sarah in the far corner, head down and face covered by her loose mass of untidy hair. Veronica made her way to her, noticing that under Sarah's table her foot was tapping restlessly.

'You're late,' she snapped, looking up as Veronica pulled out a chair.

'I apologise,' Veronica said, attempting to keep her voice neutral, but she could already feel her hackles rising. 'My chauffeur was delayed in picking me up.'

Sarah snorted and muttered something that ended with the words 'public transport'.

She said nothing more and to fill the silence, Veronica called out to a passing waiter and ordered a pot of tea.

'Will you join me?' she asked Sarah, receiving only a grunt in return.

Finally, Veronica asked with a brightness she didn't really feel, 'Have you got something for me then?'

'I'm really not sure, Miss Beaumont,' replied Sarah, 'I'm really not sure.'

'What's that supposed to mean?' replied Veronica, uncomfortable at the way Sarah was looking at her. 'You asked me to come here.'

'I'm not sure we can use you after all.' Sarah stood up. 'I think it was a mistake.'

'You've brought me here for no reason?' Veronica realised that, whilst she was angry now, she was also afraid. She had to stop Sarah walking away. 'Tell me, why are you so rude?' she said. 'I'm offering to help. I don't expect much in return. Perhaps no more even than a word of thanks but I really wasn't—'

'Rude?' Sarah whispered, her mouth pursed into a tight line, her eyes glinting with a barely concealed fury. 'Rude? Why? Because I expected you to turn up on time for our meeting? Or do you mean rude because I refuse to treat you as if I'm one of your maids? Am I rude because I refuse to curtsey and tell you how special you are?'

Sarah looked towards the exit and began to walk away. Veronica's mouth opened and closed uselessly. She could think of nothing more to say. But, as she watched, Sarah retraced her steps, pulled out her chair and sat down again.

'It doesn't make you brave, you know, going to Berlin with papers. All it means is that you were born into that ruling class that allows you to do what you like. Your skin and your money and your bloodline mean you can hop from country to country, carrying whatever you want and never worrying too much about the consequences. If you make a mistake, Daddy will no doubt sort it all out for you anyway. In the case of many others going to Berlin, they would be putting their lives on the line simply by looking at someone the wrong way. But you? You, who were driven here by your chauffeur, you, even in Berlin, will have doors opened for you.'

Veronica listened to this flow of words, her emotions moving from astonishment to upset to anger before settling on a calmness she didn't know she possessed.

'And that's why you need me, Sarah,' she said quietly. 'That's why you have come back and sat down, isn't it?'

Sarah's hand suddenly launched forward and grabbed Veronica's wrist. She turned her hand over until their palms were touching. Veronica let out a yelp of surprise.

'You feel that?' Sarah said, rubbing her rough, calloused skin against Veronica's straining hand. 'That is what happens to a woman's hands when she has to work for everything she has. This,' releasing her grip, she gestured to her shoulders and arms, 'is the body of a woman who toils every day in the harsh sun, working the land. On my kibbutz, we never say "thank you" or beg each other to help. We just help. We just do. We sacrifice for the greater good, building our little community, building somewhere safe for our children. Safe from persecution.' Veronica watched as Sarah tossed back her thick hair and gave out a bitter laugh. 'Persecution,' she repeated. 'That is what takes me away from my home to this cold grey country, to meet the likes of you. So, no, you won't hear me thank you.'

Veronica felt Sarah's anger and she could see her pain. Yet all she now felt was exhilaration. The cause, as Sarah had clearly articulated, was a worthwhile one, she had not attempted to refute what Veronica had said and, more immediately important, Sarah was no longer walking away.

The tea arrived and Veronica smiled her thanks to the waiter. She stood to pour the tea. Now she could look down at Sarah and feel less intimidated.

'Sarah,' she said, calmly. 'How many of "the likes of me" do you actually meet? Most people are not like me. Most people don't give two hoots about how those beastly Nazis treat their own people.'

'You're right. It's unusual,' Sarah replied, watching as Veronica put the tea cup down in front of her. 'Which makes me wonder. Why did you really volunteer? From the goodness of your heart? Or because you need to compensate for past failings in your own life?'

Veronica, smiled, impressed at how close Sarah had come to the truth. 'Drink your tea,' she said as she poured a second cup for herself.

Sarah looked at her for a moment, then at her tea cup and then back at Veronica again as the latter sat down. Sarah smiled.

'Maybe you're not such a mouse after all.' She leaned forward, gesturing. 'How's the wrist?'

Veronica made a conscious effort not to rub it.

'I'll live,' she said.

'Listen to me, Miss Beaumont. What I said before, about Daddy being able to get you out of trouble – well, that may not be true in this case. The Nazis are not your normal European government. They are vicious and are led by a madman. It will be very dangerous. You've never been in danger before, have you? Not really.'

'No,' agreed Veronica, 'but I will prove to you that I am ready to face it.'

NINE

12 FEBRUARY 1938

SAFFRON WALDEN DANCE HALL, ENGLAND

VERONICA LOOKED AT THE SEVERAL DOZEN PEOPLE gathered outside the hall in the cold evening air, blowing into their gloved hands and shuffling from one foot to the other.

'It's fuckin' freezing, mate,' shouted one. 'Can't you open early and let us in?'

'Why don't you shut it,' answered another. 'You old woman.'

The first man swung around, searching for the person who had said that, clearly ready for a fight. He had looked ordinary from behind but was a fearsome prospect when he turned, with barrel chest, jutting jaw and a scar from his forehead to his cheekbone across one eyelid. Nobody spoke and quickly looked away as he searched their faces. Eventually, he turned back, hunched his shoulders against the cold, muttering.

Suddenly one of the two large men guarding the door lunged into the throng and pulled out a thin, middle-aged man wearing wire-frame glasses. 'You commie bastard!' exclaimed the first guard. 'I recognise you.'

The man was protesting his innocence, though this was quickly drowned out by the jeering around him and, as he was pulled towards the entrance doors, a few managed to land some kicks on him, laughing as he yelped in pain. The second guard had his fist ready for when his companion threw the man towards him, and struck him full on the face, sending his glasses flying. Veronica heard the man's nose break and she let out a small scream.

Would they spot her next? she wondered. She was trembling now, hoping people around her would think it was the cold. Though there were other women in the throng, she was sure she stood out, if only because she was alone. This had been a terrible idea and she wanted to leave. She looked around. The crowd had grown to perhaps seventy, spread out along the front of the building. Her dilemma was that she didn't feel it was dense enough to cover her escape. She would only draw attention to herself running away now. At that moment the doors opened and suddenly everyone converged on the single entrance, eager to get inside. As she was propelled towards the doors she felt her sharp heel stepping on the hand of the beaten man. She looked down in horror and for a fleeting moment she saw his bloody face but he seemed to be beyond feeling.

Once inside the hall the crush ended and people began to fill up the rows closest to the entrance at the back of the hall. She made her way to the front. After all, she was here to try to meet party officials. She spotted an empty row and sat down. She checked her heel for signs of the poor man, half expecting to see a skewered hand, but there was not even any blood. A middle-aged man, dressed in a pin-stripe suit, sat down one seat away from her. They exchanged brief smiles. Some of his teeth were missing, she noticed, and the cuffs and elbows of his jacket were worn. Hoping not to invite conversation with this man, she kept her eyes to the front, looking fixedly at the three empty seats behind the wooden table on a small dais constructed of wooden blocks. She felt a hand on her shoulder and stiffened. A woman's voice spoke into her ear.

'Are you expecting company?'

Veronica turned. The woman was about her own age, dark-haired fringe showing beneath a flowered scarf tied below her chin. She shook her head. The woman smiled warmly and gestured to her companions, two men and another woman. They smiled too.

'Well, if you're feeling lonely, you can always come back and sit with us you know. I'm Janice.'

Veronica, nodded and thanked her, glad to know that the people behind her were not hostile. The noise of scraping chairs on the wooden floor subsided and there was an expectant hush. From behind her came the men they were all here to see. Janice and her friends turned, their conversation forgotten.

There were three of them, dressed in brown tweed suits on top of black roll-neck jumpers, making their way to the dais to general applause. Veronica knew that following the rioting in Cable Street it was now illegal to wear military uniform in public. It seemed that in an effort to get around this restriction, the British Union had placed along the back of the dais enlarged photographs of each of the three men taken at rallies two years earlier. There they stood, with their peaked hats at an angle, black jodhpurs tucked into shiny boots and of course their black shirts buttoned tightly at the neck. Above their left elbows were the armbands on which was sewn the BU's emblem of a single lightning flash in a circle.

The man in her row leant across to Veronica and said, slowly and clearly, 'Perish Judah.' Veronica started, pretending not to hear. She could feel a tightness at the roots of her hair as beads of sweat quickly formed. Had he smelt her out as a Jewess? Maybe her own self-knowledge had changed her appearance in some way and she now stood out. If so, she was doomed.

'Come on,' he said then, a little more loudly now, 'Perish Judah!'

The cry was taken up around them: 'Perish Judah! Perish Judah!' She glanced around the room. Everyone was standing and Veronica quickly stood too. Nobody was looking at her. Hesitantly she began to chant it too. The man in her row smiled at her in acknowledgement before looking back at the three men and shouting even louder.

Billy Watson looked out at the crowd from the dais and signalled that they should all sit down again. He turned to look at the photographs on the wall behind him and his two companions. At a meeting in London he'd seen some newsreels and a screening of a Nazi rally. The experience had inspired him to splash out a small fortune on these photographs and he'd even brought in an artist to carefully paint in the red of their armbands and the blue background of the central emblem. He thought the splash of colour offset the black and white images brilliantly.

The hall was normally used as a dance club which meant a large floor space, now filled with over three hundred wooden folding-chairs though he could see that barely a third of these were occupied. Billy was irritated by the poor turnout. Although people were still coming in, the meeting was supposed to have started ten minutes earlier and there wouldn't be a significant influx now. The three men sat down. Billy glanced at Paul, a former policeman who sat to his right, and then at Nick, a schoolteacher, to his left. They were both steady men, reliable in a scrap, but both he and Paul knew that it was Nick's stupidity that had led to this situation tonight. Out of the corner of his eye, Billy knew that Nick was looking at him. It would be with that look of admiration that, most of the time, made him feel good. If he was to be a leader then he'd need much more of that. Right now though, Billy was irritated by it and pretended not to notice. It was Nick who had persuaded him that it would be a good idea to hold a political meeting some 40 miles north of London and maybe 45 miles from the East End.

'If we want to go national then we need to start testing the waters outside of the cities too,' had been Nick's argument. The result, thought Billy, could be seen in the empty seats and he knew the reason too. North of London there were no immigrants, no foreigners and not even any Jews. So there was no threat to the local white population, no fears to play on. The only thing they had going for them was that they were anti-war and that was striking a chord. Except that the government was also anti-war which, whilst positive in itself, was making life more difficult for the British Union right now.

Billy sat back in his chair and straightened his shoulders. He had just noticed one of the most beautiful creatures he could ever have imagined, sitting just two rows from the front. She was tall and slim, though not too slim; he could definitely see some curves there, and she had long blonde hair. As he was staring, she looked up and met and held his look, smiled slightly and then looked slowly around the hall. He resolved then and there that he was going to have this woman. If she got up and walked away now he would follow her even if it meant abandoning the meeting.

But Veronica had stayed and her presence had inspired Billy into giving one of the best and most fluent speeches of his life. He denounced the Jewish cancer in their midst, driving the country towards a war which would see the Jewish capitalists make huge profits and out of which the Jewish communists somehow would also profit. He even pounded the table as he'd seen Hitler do in those newsreels, and, a couple of times, he tilted his shaven head and stared down imperiously, his hands on his hips like Mussolini. He noticed that, whilst the woman listened raptly to every word, she didn't seem as enthusiastic as some of the others and he found himself trying harder to impress her. By the end he was almost talking only to her and he knew that she would be feeling a special rapport too.

Veronica listened to this stream of hatred, concentrating on keeping all thought and feeling from her face. Not too long before, she would have listened to such politics with the same sense of boredom that she would have listened to any ranting from any politician whatever his views. But that was before she had found Sonia's letters, before she had awoken to what was happening in Germany. It was the views she was hearing tonight, she now knew, that were responsible for those personal advertisements in the newspaper she had bought in Hendon.

She looked at the three men on the stage wondering with whom, if she had to speak to one of them, she could manage to hold a conversation. The one on the right, she felt, looked slightly less brutal than the other two but the enormity of what she was planning to do hit her hard at that moment. This had been a stupid idea. She decided to leave and had just got to her feet when the audience began to clap once more, signalling the end of the meeting. Everyone else rose too and began wrapping themselves up warmly for the walk home. At that moment, the fat, frightening one of the three leaders, the one who had been making the speech, came almost to attention before her.

'Good evening, Miss,' he said awkwardly. 'I hope you liked my speech tonight?'

She nodded slowly, searching for the words she had rehearsed to herself should it come to this point. She looked him in the eye. 'It certainly gave me much to think about.'

'Good,' he said and put out his hand. 'I'm Billy. Billy Watson.'

She shook his hand. 'Veronica.' He waited expectantly. 'Beaumont. Veronica Beaumont.'

'The lads like to go down the pub after meetings like this. I would be honoured if you would come with me. Just a quick drink?'

Veronica did not want to go. Was this the man she was now destined to become friends with? The reality of what she was getting into made her dizzy. A part of her had been sure her plan would come to nothing and she could at least say she'd tried. She quickly put both her hands on the back of the chair in front of her, grasping it tightly until she was sure she wasn't going to faint.

'Yes. Just the one drink perhaps. Thank you.'

TEN

20 FEBRUARY 1938

LONDON

S ARAH WAS ANGRY.

'Will you sit down?' Veronica said, trying to keep her tone light and friendly. 'People are beginning to stare.'

Veronica had picked their meeting place this time. She had chosen a more casual restaurant, but realised that in whatever place Sarah found herself she would stand out like a sore thumb.

'Let them stare,' Sarah snapped. 'I'll sit when I'm ready.'

Veronica looked down and attempted to focus on the menu. That proved impossible so she decided to watch the performance and try to keep control of her own temper. Sarah had clipped her hair back from her face today but stray curls still fluffed out around her temples. Veronica found herself able still to admire the other woman's cheekbones and strong jawline. There was definitely a good structure there, if only she would take better care of her looks. Perhaps, Veronica thought, she should recommend a good hair stylist. After all, Sarah was new to London; maybe that was why she looked so slapdash. Veronica was opening her mouth to suggest this when Sarah scraped back a chair and sat down.

'Ready to talk?' Veronica said with a smile, ignoring the withering stare. 'You could look at the menu, if you like. They do a wonderful afternoon tea here.'

Sarah said nothing, waving her hand dismissively in the air.

'You're going to have to talk to me,' Veronica continued, 'otherwise there's little point in our sitting here.' She gestured to the waiter. 'Could we please have the pastries and scones assortment with two Earl Greys? Thank you.'

'You don't need to worry, I am more than happy to talk,' said Sarah, leaning forward in that way she had, both elbows firmly on the table. 'I'm just trying to put in order everything I want to say to you. Let's start with the fact that you are now sleeping with one of Mosley's fascist henchmen. Do you think that is a good thing to be doing when we had talked of you going to Berlin?' Sarah saw that Veronica was about to speak but raised her hand to stop her. 'And do you think that the Jewish Agency wants to bring itself to the attention of British fascists when we have enough trouble with the German ones?' She again held up her hand and finished with an urgent angry whisper. 'And how is what you are doing going to get a single additional Jew out of there?' Sarah sat back with a look of furious exasperation.

Veronica looked at her trying to gauge how best to respond.

'These are questions I have naturally asked myself too,' she said, 'and I think that having a fascist as my companion makes me above suspicion.'

'You are the daughter of a pro-Nazi toff,' interrupted Sarah. 'That is more than adequate cover, I should have thought.'

'True, but then we need to also think about the future of politics in this country. It isn't impossible that Mosley will at some point play a part in the government of this country. Look at what is happening all over Europe – fascism is on the up and up. If I get inside the BU now, by the time they are either brought into government or have seized power, I will be trusted and at the centre of it all. And by the way I haven't been sleeping with him.'

Sarah snorted. 'You don't need to act innocent with me. That's going to happen and you know it.'

Veronica remained silent.

'And you think this Billy has good promotion prospects?'

Veronica shrugged.

'He might have. After all look at the non-entities surrounding Hitler? And they didn't have me at their side.' She smiled but Sarah didn't smile back. 'Anyway,' Veronica pressed on, 'I will be known and trusted within the Party. I will have the right credentials.'

'Fine, Veronica, if you want to do that, that's up to you, but you can't possibly work for us at the same time. It is just too risky.'

'Here you are, ladies,' the waiter announced, placing an elaborate tiered cake-stand, piled high with dainty cakes and scones, in front of them. Seeing Sarah's look of horror, Veronica couldn't help but laugh.

'I can hardly see you!' Sarah said, aghast, gesturing at the ostentatious gold handle of the cake-stand which towered between them. 'I see I still have much to learn about English polite society.'

She watched what Veronica was doing and followed her example, taking a scone and layering on some cream and jam.

'*Two* condiments,' Sarah muttered to herself and Veronica choked back another chuckle.

Sarah paused for a moment and tilted her head at Veronica, absently running a hand through her hair and dislodging a tangle of curls from her hair clip.

'Veronica, you're an unusual woman. Not someone I would spend any time with. But if I needed someone to teach me about the ways of the British, you would be my first choice.'

There was a moment's silence which Veronica wanted to think of as amiable, before Sarah destroyed that illusion.

'As I was saying, I am, of course, going to have to find myself another business partner. You simply can't have it both ways.'

'And if I tell Billy I am no longer interested, you would still want me?' Veronica made sure her voice was calm and betrayed none of the anguish she felt that Sarah might no longer be interested in her help. She felt that Sarah was showing her some respect now and her instinct was to buy herself some time to think because she did now truly feel that, more than before, she could help thwart the fascists by becoming a member of the BU.

'Possibly,' Sarah was saying, 'but you'd need to mean it, and do you think he'll take your rejection without making things unpleasant for you?'

Veronica said nothing, watching as Sarah enjoyed her tea and scones, thinking about how she too might have her cake and eat it.

ELEVEN

28 FEBRUARY 1938

THE HOUSE OF COMMONS, LONDON

A S HE SAT DOWN, HILARY LOOKED AROUND, ONLY now realising that his speech had had the impact he'd hoped for. Most of the House was in uproar, contrasting strongly with the utterly silent government front bench: every one of them sitting stony-faced, apparently oblivious to the mayhem around them. He glanced round at the sea of members waving their papers wildly in the air. He would remember later that Anthony Eden had managed to catch his eye for a brief second and smile at him. This gladdened his heart the most. Leo Amery turned round and shook him by the hand. From behind him he heard one say, 'At last we have another champion like Winston, but without Winston's tiresome baggage.' From the opposition benches he even heard a brief chant of 'Hilary! Hilary!' before the Speaker of the House finally succeeded in calling the chamber to order. Now perhaps, thought Hilary, when the Prime Minister listens to me, it will be because he truly appreciates my influence here, and not just because of our family ties.

At a meeting that took place later in the day at the Foreign Secretary's Office, Richard Austen Butler, known to everyone as 'Rab', was worried.

'I was too young to fight, but Hilary? He was out in France for God's sake and fought at bloody Passchendaele. Has he managed to forget what it was like? We cannot put the country through another war.'

Lord Halifax, the new Foreign Secretary, looked at his Under Secretary and nodded. 'I hear from everyone present that Hilary gave a masterly speech today. It will make Neville's work harder, certainly.'

And ours too, thought Rab, nodding.

'The Prime Minister has some sympathy with the Sudeten Germans' desire to be reunited with Germany—'

'Well, exactly!' began Rab, but stopped immediately when Halifax raised his right hand in silent admonishment. Rab focused instead on Halifax's false and motionless left hand, covered, as always, in a tight leather glove. Looking at it always put Rab in mind of the ex-Kaiser, the only other person he knew to have been born with a withered arm, though at least in the German's case the arm had included a hand at the end of it, however useless it had been to him. Rab realised his thoughts were drifting and concentrated again on the Foreign Secretary's words.

'...And if there's even some truth in the stories in the German press about the Czech atrocities on these defenceless people—'

'Well, they can't all be made up, can they?'

'Quite.' Halifax unwound his tall lanky form from his seat and walked around his desk. He perched on the front of it, closer to Rab who thought, and not for the first time, that Halifax looked more like a vicar than a senior member of His Majesty's Government and wouldn't have been surprised to see him swap his tie for a dog collar.

'We need to find a way to limit his influence with Neville,' Halifax said. 'You need to work both on how Masterson perceives himself and how Masterson is perceived.'

'You mean discredit him?'

Halifax frowned. He was indeed a God-fearing man and he didn't like to get into the dirty business of politics. This was quite apart from the fact that peers of the realm ought to be above all that.

'Well, you could first try to change his mind. But I'll leave it to you. Whatever you think best to get the job done.'

'Understood,' replied Rab. 'If it were anyone else we wouldn't need to worry. The PM would mark him down as one of Churchill's boys and that would be the end of it, but he refuses to view anything Hilary Masterson does as a personal attack on him. Quite the contrary, he has on occasion, following conversation with Masterson, asked us to check if *we* have erred somewhere in our own briefing papers. Masterson is a backbencher! This is not how policy should be made.'

'Don't you worry about Neville,' said Halifax. 'I'm going over to square things with him. On this matter we see eye to eye. You do your part, Rab, and I'll do mine.'

But, as Lord Halifax made his way over to the Prime Minister's room in the Commons, he found himself face to face with the PM coming the other way. To Halifax's disappointment, accompanying the Prime Minister was Hilary Masterson himself. Halifax's face must have failed to conceal his concern and frustration because, as the three men drew close, Hilary looked at him, grinning broadly.

'Ah, Edward,' the Prime Minister, Neville Chamberlain, greeted Halifax warmly, 'Hilary here is going to walk with me to Number 10. Care to join us?'

Halifax shook his head. He wanted to talk to the PM

about Masterson, not endure a walk during which they'd all be forced to chat about inanities.

'Forgive me, Prime Minister,' he said, thin-lipped, 'I'm going over to the Lords, but perhaps we could catch up later?' The three smiled at each other, raising their fingers to the brims of their hats.

Hilary watched Halifax go.

'He doesn't like me, you know.'

'I'm not surprised,' Chamberlain grunted. 'You know how vital he regards our appeasement policy. Lord Halifax is a dear friend as well as a member of my cabinet. I feel closer to him in fact than to any other colleague.' Chamberlain rarely smiled warmly at people but he did so now as he turned to Hilary. 'But you, dear boy, are Birmingham born and bred, and more family than colleague. So in regard to Edward at least, you are making things difficult, as I am sure you know.'

'And yet you are not annoyed with me. Does this mean you can yet be persuaded?'

Chamberlain let out a slightly high-pitched whine which was, Hilary knew, his restrained, strangled way of showing amusement. 'Unlikely,' Chamberlain replied. 'You surely cannot hope for such an outcome. And persuaded of what, pray? That Nazi Germany is not a nice place? I know this already.'

Hilary, however, remonstrated. 'I know I've not been long in the Commons and junior MPs should not presume, but can I talk to you on the basis of the friendship between our two families?'

Chamberlain nodded. 'Of course.'

'Will you not consider that trying to appease someone like Hitler is futile? Surely, it will only encourage him to take a harder stand. We let him take back the Rhineland without a fight. He will soon doubtless take over Austria despite that government's best endeavours. This is 1914 all over again. The German military machine is gearing up once more and if we let it, it could mean a worse war than the last one.'

Followed at a discreet distance by a detective from Scotland Yard, the two men had by now exited the Palace of Westminster, and were crossing over Bridge Street towards Whitehall, each striding purposefully with a long furled umbrella which they rapped smartly on the pavement. Every so often the Prime Minister nodded or put two fingers to his homburg to acknowledge the respectful greetings of police officers, civil servants, MPs and other passersby.

'That is not the whole story though, Hilary,' Chamberlain continued from where they had left off, but his voice lower now that they were on a public road frequented by many journalists. 'We went to war not just because the Kaiser had a big army he wanted to play with, but also because our own alliances seemed to threaten Germany with encirclement. This put the Kaiser under great pressure and especially from his generals. Maybe Herr Hitler simply wants his people not to be hemmed in. We must learn from our mistakes.'

'Prime Minister!' shouted a cabbie as he slowed down on the other side of Whitehall. 'God bless you, sir, for keeping us all safe!' Chamberlain raised his hat in acknowledgement. He turned back to Hilary.

'Hilary, I am not upset about your speeches because I know they are your opinions, honestly held. And I have no doubt that you, whom I have known since you were bouncing on your father's knee, are and always will be unswervingly loyal.' Hilary nodded earnestly as Chamberlain continued, 'I don't need proof, but if any were needed, your personal loyalty is obvious by your not having any truck with Winston, despite approaches that have been made to you.'

Hilary should not perhaps have been surprised that the

Prime Minister had known about those approaches. He had an effective Chief Whip who, clearly, must be doing a good job. God knows David Margesson had been in that role long enough. Hilary, however, had nothing to hide and the PM's analysis of Hilary's motives was correct, so he again just nodded in agreement.

'But on this matter,' Chamberlain continued, 'you are gravely mistaken.' He glanced around without slowing his stride. The street was empty. He put his hand on Hilary's shoulder and spoke close to his ear. 'Our economy is weak. We simply cannot afford a war now. And much of the country wouldn't support us in such a venture let alone our colonies and dominions. The Empire's very cohesion is at stake.'

They were fast approaching Downing Street which was now in view. Chamberlain paused, looking at the small turning. 'Hilary,' he said, speaking again at his normal pitch, 'as a backbencher with your finger on the pulse of the party, let me have your opinion on another matter which is bubbling up.'

'Of course, Prime Minister, but why isn't the Chief Whip giving you that insight?' He smiled, inviting the older man to share a confidence. But Chamberlain shook his head.

'I have every confidence in David. He does a fine job whipping all our MPs, but you can give me the raw view before the promises and the threats distort real opinion. And I know you'll always tell me the truth. The problem is the Quakers.' Noticing Hilary's raised eyebrow he hurriedly continued. 'Well, maybe not the Quakers themselves but the Jews.'

'Ah,' said Hilary.

'The Quakers are agitating, you see. They'd like us to take in a good number of refugees from Germany. The Quakers like to keep in the background but they are well connected. What do you think?'

Hilary didn't need to think. 'I'd be very much against that, Prime Minister. The trouble with bloody do-gooders is that they don't stop to think of the consequences. There are a lot of Jews in Germany. Once we say we'll take some, they'll be coming over in their hordes.'

Chamberlain frowned. 'I don't like to see what is going on there. It's uncivilised.'

'Of course it's uncivilised! That's what I've been saying all along. Those National Socialists are a disaster for us all. But we shouldn't have to pick up their bill.' He paused. 'Well, not here in England. But why not Palestine? It seems the obvious place, I mean we've been spending the last twenty years building up their bloody national home. I never much cared for it but it seems fortuitous now. The Royal Commission has recommended partition over there. So let's do that. Give the Jews their little state and then give them the problem of absorbing all those German refugees. And,' he smiled, 'once we have momentum, maybe they can absorb all our East End Jews as well.'

'The Arabs don't want partition,' said the Prime Minister, whispering once more. 'That's why we have a rebellion over there.'

Hilary too lowered his voice, speaking urgently. 'Yes but once partition's happened, they'll have to concentrate on governing their own piece of it and if the Jews can't take in enough refugees, well, that's their lookout and we're off the hook.'

'Yes, that's true,' said the Prime Minister thoughtfully, 'and if these were normal circumstances that might be a way to proceed.' He looked around and then lowered his voice still further so that Hilary had to lean in to hear. 'But there could be a European war and we don't want to have resources tied down in Palestine and possibly in the rest of the Arab world too. Mussolini and Hitler would be only too happy to cause trouble and we don't want the entire Middle East to turn into another Spain.'

'Then, please, I beseech you, Prime Minister. Stand up to that man. Make him back down and there will be no war in Europe.'

Chamberlain shook his head. 'No. You are wrong. If we can satisfy Herr Hitler's needs and we get an understanding with him, *that* will avoid war in Europe. It will mean peace for generations. He's a rational man we can do business with. Halifax has met him.'

He turned to look down towards No. 10, straightened and sighed. 'Well, Hilary, "Home sweet home" and all that. I have work to do. You are welcome though to come in and say hello to Annie, she is always most pleased to see you.'

'No, I had best not. If I were to be seen walking into No. 10 alongside you, you will have to spend all day tomorrow strongly denying that you have been persuaded to join the anti-appeasers. You don't want to have to deny it and I wouldn't want to hear the denial.'

Chamberlain inclined his head towards him in grateful agreement and, followed by his detective, turned into the street, deserted except for the solitary policeman standing vigil at the front door. Hilary, with a slight nod of his own, turned back towards Parliament. It was beginning to rain now and he unfurled his umbrella, humming *It's a Long Way to Tipperary* as he increased his pace.

TWELVE

2 MARCH 1938

LONDON

AS THE WEEKS HAD GONE BY, VERONICA COULD NO longer deny that Billy had a certain rough charm and, as long as he wasn't talking politics, he could be engaging and, sometimes, even funny. He worked as a welder at Strachans in North Acton, where he was on the team building the bodies of the Austin Taxi cabs which Strachans supplied to Mann & Overtons in Battersea. She didn't know much about the motor car industry but the fact that he was working on the production of London's taxicabs apparently commanded respect. At least this is what she had understood from Nick. Certainly Nick and his friend Paul always deferred to Billy and clearly, for them too, Billy possessed a charisma to which they were, unconsciously, responding, always making sure to laugh at his every joke.

Veronica did the same, and sometimes he was genuinely funny, but she was always on her guard, never drinking more than she could easily handle and always with an excuse to be somewhere else before it got too late at night. To his friends, there seemed to be no question but that she was 'Billy's girl', just as Stephi was 'Nick's girl'. Neither of them had any say in the matter, though Veronica could see that Stephi was more than happy to be with Nick. She reminded Veronica of Elke. That need of a strong man to tell her what to do and what to think. Just so long as she could belong. The choice Veronica did have, of course, was to leave and never look back, but once she had not taken that choice, she knew that sooner or later a man like Billy would make demands on her and that she would have to comply. She was going to have to sleep with Billy.

They had been greyhound racing and on a few trips to the cinema, and it was at the end of one of those evenings that Billy had said, 'When we next meet, Veronica, I expect you to be showing me a little more gratitude for our time together so far.'

By now she was adept at hiding her feelings. 'Gratitude?' she had laughed. 'Is that what you truly meant to say? Or were you simply saying that we should perhaps make our friendship more formal?'

Billy had quickly agreed that that was indeed what he had meant. He had then taken hold of her and kissed her. This had not been the first time he had tried his luck with her, but it was the first time she had let him. To her secret delight, she found that kissing Billy did not set her heart pounding and that here too, she would be able to remain detached. Billy was a brute but she could see an animal attraction there, so different from either Daphne or Kurt, the only other experiences she had to draw upon. Until this moment, she had worried that her emotions might let her down. Now, though, she was sure: she might sacrifice her body but as before, here too she would remain in control. She stepped back and looked at him. Billy seemed more sure of himself now that she had allowed him to stake his claim on her mouth. She supposed he saw her now as a sure thing. Perhaps, but she needed him to work for it.

There could be no suspicion that this was something she had planned.

'Veronica, I want us right now to—'

'No, Billy, I can't. I'm just not ready. And certainly not "right now". "Right now", I have to go visit my mother. She is ill.'

'When then?' He didn't bother asking after her mother and she wondered whether this was because he was an uncaring bastard or because he knew that she was lying and saw that as an inevitable part of the chase.

'Monday.'

'Monday? You're 'avin' me on. It's only Thursday now!'

Veronica put a finger to his lips. 'Shhh. On Monday I'll come to your rooms in London. Make sure you've not got your men with you else I won't come in. Is that all right?'

Mollified by the details she was giving him, he nodded and stepped back.

'Come at 7pm then. I'll be waiting.'

He moved to kiss her again but at the last moment she couldn't help herself and turned away so that he kissed her cheek. She quickly smiled at him. 'Good night, Billy, I'll be looking forward to it.'

He turned and within seconds was swallowed by the gloom beyond the streetlamps. Veronica watched him go, a worried frown on her face. She had bought herself a few more days to get used to the inevitable, but nothing more. She would have so liked to talk it over with someone but there was nobody. Certainly not her parents. The very idea was laughable. And Sarah, who was the only person who knew about it, had already given her views.

'Very well then, I'll do this alone,' she said aloud, watching the steam of her breath merge into the surrounding fog. She pulled up the collar of her coat against the cold and began to walk.

THIRTEEN

8 MARCH 1938

SAFFRON WALDEN, ENGLAND

R AB WAS STANDING IN THE SMALL CORRIDOR OF HIS constituency office having just relieved Billy Watson of his coat and hung it on a clothes-hook attached to the wall. The offices were normally closed at this hour and the usual helpers and hangers-on had now gone home for the evening. Rab had not wanted anyone to see him entertaining a member of the British Union.

'I understand you are planning to stand against me at the next General Election?' Rab asked, opening the door to the small room where he conducted his surgeries and gesturing for Billy to enter. He offered Billy a cigarette. Billy accepted it but then declined to sit, causing Rab, who had just sat down at his desk, to get up again. He wanted to avoid having to look up at this large man.

'You must see,' Rab began, 'that you stand no earthly chance in Saffron Walden – the last time the Conservatives fought and lost this seat was nearly 30 years ago and I personally have won the last three elections here. What can you possibly hope to achieve?'

Billy smiled back at him. 'The times are changing though, don't you think, Mr Butler? The people want strong leadership in difficult times and the BU can provide that. The people don't want another European war – every vote for us makes war less certain.' He waved his cigarette at Butler expectantly and Rab fumbled in his desk drawer for a lighter and found himself apologising for his omission. Not a good start.

'Look now,' said Rab, returning to the matter at hand and concentrating on keeping his expression friendly, despite his revulsion for the fat oaf in front of him, 'the Conservatives are the party delivering the appeasement policies that are working so well. There are things in motion now that will have reached fruition by the time of the 1940 election, and we will then be seen by all as the party of peace. We are going to win by a landslide.'

'But you're nonetheless scared of us.'

How insufferable these people were, Butler thought, deciding to sit down after all. Fascism might play well with the Italians and Germans but here in Great Britain, people treasured their democracy and the sense of fair play. With an effort he uncrossed his arms and placed his hands slowly palms down onto the table in front of him. But then he thought that might look too confrontational and the time for that hadn't yet come. He clasped his hands together and felt that this was the correct pose for now.

'Why would you think that, Mr Watson?'

'Why else would you ask me to come and visit you in your constituency office? You are going to ask me to give you a free run in this constituency, aren't you? You're going to warn me about splitting the vote and letting the socialists in. Well, Mr Butler, you can save your breath.'

Rab shook his head. 'I can assure you, sir, I don't care one way or the other whether you stand. Either way I win. I think that, if you did stand, as you have correctly stated, you'd probably split the Labour vote not ours, and help me increase our majority.'

'A bit of a gamble on your part, I think. But let's say for the sake of argument that you are right. Then what? Why are we talking?'

'I have a proposal to put to you, Mr Watson. Please, take a seat here by the window. I am not going to bite. Relax a little, my dear fellow.' Billy sat down. 'That's better. After all, I think that you want a lot of the same things as I do: good relations with Germany, and at least an indifference to the plight of the Jews there. Is that blunt enough for you?'

Butler noticed that though Watson was probably wearing his best suit for the occasion, it was distinctly shabby compared to the fitted suit that Butler was wearing which had been cut exactly to Butler's measurements. And that was what Watson really wanted in the end, Rab thought, as he lit his own cigarette and put it to his lips. Billy Watson wanted the money and success that would allow him to walk into Savile Row and order his own made-to-measure suit. Rab watched him, expressionless, through the clouds of smoke.

Finally Watson nodded. 'Yes, that's a good start.' He took a couple of long puffs and then began his well-practised ritual of flicking ash into the ashtray. 'Yes, please do continue, Mr Butler, tell me what you'd like the British Union to help you with.'

'Let's say that I have a friend. A dear friend. He likes a lot of things that I like, despises a lot of people I despise. That sort of thing. But there is just one issue, an important one. An obstacle really. This friend can cause a lot of damage that will upset a lot of important interests.'

'You're talking in riddles and,' Watson got to his feet, 'I don't have time for your game.' He had left home this morning after having finally bedded Veronica. He'd kept at her most of the night and she had been sleeping, exhausted, when he left. He was tired now but, more than that, he suddenly realised that he still wanted her to be there when he got back home and was anxious that she might not be. He was unaccustomed to such a feeling and that in turn made him even more anxious. He turned to leave.

'Wait,' said Butler and took a deep breath. 'Hilary Masterson.'

Watson reluctantly sat down again.

'Hilary Masterson? The MP? Are you actually and in all seriousness asking the British Union to nobble one of your own MPs?'

'No!' cried Butler. 'Not nobble him, whatever you mean by that. And not the British Union of Fascists or British Union or whatever they're calling themselves nowadays. I am turning to you personally. Think about it. You want to get on in life, we all do of course, but you are, ah, shall we say, starting from further away from where you wish to be than others. And you must know that there are many amongst us, both in the Conservative Party and amongst the lords of the realm across all parties, who believe that the new Germany can only be good for our country. We wish to do business with them – and so do you.'

Watson laughed. 'Easy for you toffs to do business with them. What chance for the rest of us. Those that weren't born with silver spoons in their mouths, eh?'

'And that's my point. I can get you to where you deserve to be. If you can ensure that Hilary Masterson is not able to influence our national policies – if you can simply cause people to at least doubt him – then you will find all sorts of things begin to come your way.'

This was the sort of work Billy enjoyed. Of course this

stuck-up bastard needed him. He stood and took his jacket off. 'Let's say I am interested,' he said.

Rab noticed his huge hands, thick forearms and biceps stretching the now-revealed shirt and it made him shudder involuntarily. He wouldn't like to be pleading for mercy from this man. He nervously licked his lips and tried to concentrate on what Watson was now saying.

'I need to know enough about him that can get me close to him. What are his strengths and weaknesses, in politics of course but more importantly his personal life? What does he like to do and who does he like to do it with? What's his family life like and what are his movements?'

Rab pushed a lever-arch file across his desk to Billy.

'It's all here,' he said with a smile, 'this is our intelligence file on him. Where he lives with his family in the country, his flat in London and so on and so forth. He is happily married, loves his wife and children, but there are rumours – unsubstantiated, mind – that he is partial to blondes and that he likes them young. He's said to have had a few affairs and his wife either doesn't know or doesn't care. He is very discreet. What we have is all in there,' he said, pushing the file a bit closer to Billy until Billy finally took it onto his lap and started going through it quickly. 'One thing you might well use to your advantage. He really doesn't like Jews much.'

'Who does?' said Billy.

FOURTEEN

23 MARCH 1938

LONDON, W9

VERONICA WAS LYING, FULLY DRESSED, ON THEIR bed reading *The Secret Agent*, by Joseph Conrad. It amused her to be reading a book with such a title in front of Billy though, disappointingly, the plot wasn't really a description of the sort of work she was engaged in. There were too many anarchists and she was hardly that. Neither were bombs in her repertoire. She had just got to the part in the book where the agent's wife stabs him to death, when Billy came into the room from the toilet, still buttoning up his trousers. After two weeks together she knew that he wasn't going to wash his hands. 'No need, is there, after a piss?' had been his reply the only time she had raised the issue.

'You want to go to the flicks?' Billy asked.

Veronica made a mental note of the page number, put down her book and stretched. Billy's eyes tracked her movement, lingering on her breasts. He wasn't even aware he was doing it.

'What's showing?' she asked.

'*The Prisoner of Zenda?*' said Billy with a grin.

Veronica groaned. 'Not again, Billy, we've already seen it twice!'

'Well, there's nothing else on that I want to see. We can go to the pub instead, I don't mind that, though you don't ever want to go there either.'

Veronica nodded in agreement. If she was to be able to bear his presence at all she had to keep him away from the heavy drinking that always turned him violent. She got off the bed and stood in front of the mirror to check her hair was still tidy and the clip in place at the back.

'Why don't we plan to do something interesting for a change?'

'Like what?' He didn't like it when she put forward ideas. It didn't seem the natural order of things to him.

'We could go to Germany.' She heard him laugh at the idea and quickly added, 'Not tonight of course. But let's tonight plan it at least and maybe we could go next week?'

'Why would we want to go to bloody Germany?' Billy asked. 'You're barmy you are sometimes.'

'Think about it. It would be good for your progress in the Party. How many Blackshirts can actually say that they have seen the Nazis in action? And what with their marching into Austria now, Hitler really is the man of the moment. You can tell them that you want to see what is happening there first hand and how their methods might work if they could be introduced into England.'

Billy thought about this. She could see that he liked the idea.

'Weren't you saying the other week that you know someone from there whom you met in London when he had been visiting his Welsh aunt? He was taking the opportunity to make contact with BU members as some sort of investment for the future. So you'd be doing the same thing.'

He grunted. She decided to push him a little further along. 'Perhaps he could show us around over there?'

He laughed at the very idea of that. 'I'm not sure you'd want to meet my friends,' he said cryptically.

'That's all right, Billy,' she answered quickly. 'We don't have to be together all the time. I can go sightseeing, do a bit of shopping maybe, see how Berlin fashions differ from London ones.'

'You've decided on Berlin then? Why not Munich? That's a really good place to see the Nazis, I think.'

Veronica paused. It had to be Berlin. 'Well, I've always wanted to see the Reichstag.' She could have kicked herself. Of all the places in Berlin why choose that one? Maybe he wouldn't spot it. Fat chance.

'Well, you're too late to see that, aren't you? The commies burnt that down years ago.'

'Yes, I know, but that just makes it more interesting,' she said weakly. 'I think Munich might be an awful bore though. Is that it then, if we go it has to be to Munich?'

He grinned. 'Nah. Berlin's the place to be. That's where the power is now.' He enjoyed seeing her confusion and answered her unspoken question. 'But it's my decision, where we go, not yours, darling. Though of course the Party won't pay so it's just a dream.'

She shrugged. She had money enough for both of them from her allowance. How to get him to accept it though? Easy enough, she thought, if one realised one was talking to someone who was a mixture of child and wild caveman. Without looking at him she put a foot up on the chair in front of the wide, three-mirror dressing table and angled one of the mirrors towards her. She hitched her dress up high and began to adjust one of her suspenders, concentrating on that task.

'Well, you can't expect me to pay for you out of my money, Billy. I'm not a charity.'

He swung round to face her and caught sight of her silk tap pants in the mirror. His anger was immediately tinged with lust and he grabbed her by the waist and threw her onto the bed, unbuttoning his trousers again.

'I'm not good enough, is that it? You don't think you should spend your money on the likes of me?'

'No! Of course you are Billy!' she shouted, rolling quickly onto her back. 'I'll do it! I'll pay for us both. Just don't hurt me.'

He was on her in a flash, reaching roughly under her dress.

'Good, you little bitch. That's all settled then. Now take this.'

Veronica gasped, her hands gripping his shoulders tightly. Putting her head back, she looked at the ceiling and thought of England. Well, not England, she corrected herself with a smile. Berlin.

The next morning, Veronica wrote to Aunt Sonia suggesting a date they could meet. Veronica thought it might take a week to get there and that she might get a reply a week later with Sonia's suggestion of a possible venue. It would take another week for Sonia to receive Veronica's confirmation. This meant that she could not possibly leave London for another three weeks at least.

7 APRIL 1938

Always eager to learn English idioms, Sarah worked hard at her English and indeed it was near perfect. Unfortunately she just couldn't lose the accent so was resigned to always being looked down on by the British whether in Palestine or here, in London. In Palestine, 'beggars can't be choosers' was a common phrase, uttered as it so often was, by patronising British officials telling both Jew and Arab what they would have to put up with next.

It was this phrase that had kept popping into Sarah's head when meeting with Veronica in Hendon Park. Spring had come late this year but the trees were now in blossom and a park bench was as private a place as any. Veronica's excited phone call informing her that she and Billy were now going to Berlin had come at a desperate time for Sarah and for *Aliyah Dalet*. The secret network had built up a nice stash of life-saving documents but had no reliable way of getting these to the intended recipients: Jews, some of whom were being harried by the German police and, in many cases, who would shortly be incarcerated in the feared KZs. These concentration camps seemed to be everywhere now. Worst of all, 200,000 Austrian Jews had now come under Nazi control. The clamour for forged documents would grow and though Sarah worried that Veronica was a risk, the time had come to take that risk.

'Some of my colleagues don't trust you,' Sarah said as soon as Veronica joined her on the bench, her thick hair hidden by a scarf and her eyes concealed by sunglasses.

Veronica began to say something but Sarah gestured to her to remain silent. 'They ask, why run the risk when the truth is that, we could, if we had time, very probably find someone else, better qualified, better trained, and less likely to compromise what we are trying to do?'

Veronica was shocked. 'Sarah, do you think I would do that?'

Sarah shrugged. 'Perhaps. Not deliberately. I only know this. We don't have any more time. Your value to us is in your ability to bring in documents and deliver them. Something that I am unable to do with the scrutiny I come under as a Jewess from Palestine. If they caught me breaking the law they really would throw away the key. As it is, I can't be sure how much my status as a subject of the British Empire would protect me should it be put to the test, especially with my own parents being from Germany. Other German Jews face the same issues. But you, you speak German, know Berlin and are going to be there soon with your fascist boyfriend.'

'I won't let you down, Sarah. I will act just as I acted when I lived there, full of fun and innocence.' Veronica frowned. 'I know the role of an English woman in love with Germany, in love with Germans.'

Sarah grunted. 'If we're going to do this, we will need to talk about your cover story and some basic tips for your own security and ours.'

Veronica nodded and from her bag removed a little notepad bound with some string, to which she had clipped a pen. Sarah rolled her eyes.

'You can't write any of this down!'

Veronica froze, her cheeks burning.

'I'm sorry,' said Sarah, giving her an encouraging smile, 'but there is so much you have to learn. You will have to remember everything. We can go through things over and over until you do, but all of it,' she pointed her finger at Veronica's forehead, 'has to rest in there. Do you understand?' Veronica nodded, and put her notepad back into her handbag. Sarah smiled.

Well, at least I amuse her, thought Veronica.

'Good then,' Sarah continued, 'let's start. I hope you hadn't any other plans for today?'

It was a couple of hours before Sarah felt that enough progress had been made to allow an end to the day's proceedings. A light rain had begun to fall and they moved over the road to a cramped café on Queen's Road just around the corner from the underground station. Veronica could see across the other side of the large roundabout the entrance to the road of shops she had gone down just three months earlier and where her journey of discovery had begun. How fitting, she thought, it was also that same day that she had first met Sarah. Perhaps it was a good omen. She sat herself down on one of the rickety chairs and squeezed herself in beside Sarah. Now that they were not talking directly about the mission, Veronica was expecting Sarah to broach the subject of Billy again, but this time she remained silent. Sarah, of course, would realise that having to turn to Veronica again vindicated her decision to join the BU. Nevertheless Veronica felt that the knowledge of what she was now doing with Billy Watson lay heavily over their conversation.

Drinking their tea from the chipped cups on cracked saucers, Veronica wondered if the café's entire crockery had been in a crate that had fallen off the counter. Smiling at the thought she related it to Sarah but was met with the serious answer that on the kibbutz they made do with far worse. Veronica's ill-considered comment that 'your kibbutz doesn't sound all that much fun' met with a hostile rebuke and an uncomfortable silence, finally broken by Sarah.

'I think I may have given you a distorted picture about my kibbutz and about my homeland. Yes, it is a life of hardship and deprivation that I am sure you would not be able to imagine, but there is also a beauty, a closeness to nature and a happiness that comes from building our national home after nearly two thousand years of exile.' Sarah paused, smiled apologetically. 'That was a little unfair too – the kibbutz life is not for everyone. And we do tend to see ourselves as the hardest, the strongest of our people. But there are many who are better suited to town life and they too are doing their bit. Just thirty years ago we lay the foundations for the very first new Jewish city since before Jesus. Today, Tel Aviv has more than 150,000 people and whole streets are built in the latest Bauhaus style, to the extent that this gleaming city on the Mediterranean is now being referred to as "the White City".'

Veronica, despite her earlier doubts, found herself being drawn in by Sarah's evident pride and excitement in what had been achieved and wished she could at least see it though she knew it wasn't really for her. She told herself that she was in no hurry to build Jerusalem in England's green and pleasant land, nor anywhere else.

There had been just one other customer in the café and he had now left, the bell over the door announcing his exit as it had their entrance. The café owner had gone back into her office and closed the door. As if this was a signal that Sarah had been waiting for, she stopped talking about architecture and pushed her cup away.

'Well, enough of that for now,' she said, sitting bolt upright in her chair. Unconsciously, Veronica did the same. 'I need to explain to you about what you will actually be doing and why.'

'Of course, yes,' said Veronica earnestly.

'There are two ways,' Sarah explained, 'through which people from Germany can get into Palestine: the legal way and the illegal way. The legal way is to join the queue for British entry visas to Palestine. Currently this is limited to just 12,000 a year. If people can get those visas then of course that is wonderful. But there are hundreds of thousands in Germany – and now Austria too – trying to get out this way. The second way is to supplement these numbers by getting people in illegally.'

'Do you mean by forging the entry visas?' asked Veronica, eagerly.

'Well yes, we do that when we have to but it is expensive.

There is also the problem that when we get them into Palestine some British official makes a note of the numbers of people coming in on their visas and simply counts them off against the quota. This means that all we have done is taken the place of some other refugee who would otherwise have got in legitimately.'

'So, why would you ever do that?'

'Sometimes it becomes necessary if, for example, someone is being particularly persecuted in Germany and might be sent to a concentration camp. Then that person might need to get out as a priority. In that case, if we get enough notice to prepare things – and often we don't until it is too late – we can help.' Sarah paused.

'Go on,' urged Veronica. She felt like she had when Nanny had been reading her a bedtime story and suddenly threatened to stop and turn out the light. Please. Don't. 'Please go on, Sarah,' Veronica said again.

Sarah smiled. Veronica smiled back expectantly.

'We can also forge or amend British-issued Palestine passports but the numbers involved are tiny and only used when the opportunity arises. It is also the most expensive way per person. But there is another way in. It is still quite limited in number but is far less costly and seems to be outside the quota system and so doesn't take anyone else's place.' Sarah drew a piece of paper from her pocket and showed it to Veronica. On it was a list of ten names.

'Who are these people?' Veronica asked.

'These are people around the age of twenty – some a couple of years older and others who may be nearly thirty. People who were studying in Berlin before their studies were terminated by the Nazis. They would like to move to the university in Jerusalem to continue their studies.'

Veronica was confused. 'There is a university in

Jerusalem? Surely you can't already have a university in such an undeveloped place?'

Sarah nodded. 'A lot of people say that.' She reached into her jacket pocket and brought out a small wallet from which she drew a few photos, each about an inch square. 'These are some photographs I took a few months ago at the Hebrew University of Jerusalem. It actually opened in 1925 and both the British and the Jews are really proud of it. The High Commissioner for Palestine was at the ceremony and even Lord Balfour himself was there and he was a former Prime Minister and Foreign Secretary of Great Britain.'

Veronica looked closely at the small images. She could see men and women standing around and in the background some modern buildings. On their own the photographs didn't really reveal much, she thought. She handed them back to Sarah who returned them, almost reverently, thought Veronica, to her wallet.

'These pictures are of students on Mount Scopus, one of several hills surrounding Jerusalem. It's the location of our university site. Young men and women fulfilling their dream. One day I will tell you just how unprecedented this project really is, but what you need to know right now is that the British Mandatory Government in Palestine agreed many years ago that a certain number of students applying to move from universities abroad to the Hebrew University could come over and not be included in any quota.'

'That's good. So where do you come in? I mean, if it is all working as intended, why get involved?'

Sarah took a hold of Veronica's hand in both of hers. She was very serious now and Veronica gazed into her eyes, seeing her intensity.

'Three years ago,' Sarah was saying, 'the British Government gave the university 945 certificates to hand out to students from abroad for that year's entry. Last year, they cut availability to just 291 certificates, and even then they held back 89 certificates with no explanation given. They are closing the gates just as our need is greatest. I, and the organisation that I work for, cannot sit back and let this happen. If only 200 students can get to the university legally, then we can at least get in another 200 illegally.'

'That will come as a surprise to the lecturers then. Their classes will be unexpectedly large!' Veronica smiled gently to show Sarah that she was not mocking her or what she had to say.

Sarah smiled thinly back, releasing Veronica's hand. 'The ones on forged papers won't ever attend the university. The university authorities know nothing about what we are doing and would stop it if they could. I can't go into too much detail of course but suffice it to say that, when these "students" arrive at Haifa and their documents are checked by British officials, their names will appear on the list of eligible students held by those officials. We've already managed to get three people into Palestine that way. The good thing about this method is that they use their own passports and it is a lot easier to forge these certificates, which are really not much more than a letter, than a passport.'

Sarah leaned forward. 'This is where you come in. There are ten names here of young people in Berlin desperately waiting for these certificates. They already have visas which we have provided for them. But the visas will only be valid if they are presented alongside these Immigration Certificates and they also need to be able to show a Certificate of Admission from the Hebrew University itself. I have arranged for these to be prepared here in London. I am going to collect them now. But we need someone to bring the certificates to each of the ten young men and women, two certificates each. Someone to act as a postman if you like. We need someone who is above suspicion as far as both the British and the German authorities are concerned.'

'Can't you just send them in the post?'

'Hardly!' said Sarah. Veronica looked at her, waiting for an explanation.

Sarah sighed and then gave her a smile of encouragement. 'Forgive me. You are an innocent in times that are far from innocent. Firstly, we can't risk the post getting lost. Secondly, the Germans open suspicious post, and bulky letters from England to Jews in Germany will certainly be opened. Even if they then let them be delivered, they will cause trouble if they can. Thirdly, the British themselves sometimes check the post going to Germany and we can't risk them finding even one of these documents.' She leaned back on her chair so that the front legs came off the ground. 'The documents are ready to be collected now. Here in Hendon. I need you to wait here whilst I go and get them for you. You understand? You can't come with me, I'm afraid. I shan't be long.'

With that, Sarah stood up, squeezed past and walked out, the bell jangling behind her. Veronica watched as she turned left into Queen's Road and disappeared from sight. She thought for a moment and then, acting really on impulse, she stood up, went over to the counter, called to the proprietor, paid for their teas and left the café. She looked up the hill and could just see Sarah, striding along, about one hundred yards up ahead. Veronica had no plan and she certainly had no chance of even narrowing the gap between them in her heels, however sensible they might be. She crossed over Wykeham Road, just where, not much more than two months earlier, she had stood and watched the men going to synagogue. It felt as if at least a year had passed.

The road curved away to the left but Sarah was now out of

sight. Veronica crossed to the other side of the road hoping that from there she might see Sarah for a little longer before she finally disappeared from view. A young couple, pushing a baby in a pram, were coming towards her and she craned her neck to see past them. There she was, in the distance. She was just passing a red pillar box, way up ahead, when she suddenly stopped. It was hard to be sure from where she was standing, but it seemed to Veronica that Sarah was checking around to see if anyone was observing her. She then turned quickly and went into the front garden of the nearest house. The front door must have opened because she was no longer visible. Veronica went no closer but stood, not sure what she was doing nor why. But it was a nice day and she had nothing else to do. It was nearly fifteen minutes before Sarah reappeared. Veronica quickly turned and went back down the hill, only crossing the road once she had rounded the curve. Suddenly worried that Sarah would realise she had followed her, she almost ran back the last fifty yards until, a little breathless, she got back to the café. Fortunately their table was still free and she sat herself down. A couple of minutes later, Sarah reappeared, carrying a large overnight travel bag covered in alligator skin – though it might have just been designed to look as if that's what it was. It had a hard leather shoulder strap long enough for it to be carried at hip height.

'I'm so sorry. It took a little longer than expected, but here you are.' She opened the bag and removed a large envelope.

Veronica took it from her and looked inside. She could see various certificates in a mixture of English and what she now recognised as Hebrew.

'Government of Palestine,' she read softly, 'Immigration Certificate.'

Sarah put a restraining hand on her arm when she saw her

beginning to take out one of the sheets of paper for a closer look.

'Don't do that here. Wait until you are indoors.'

She nodded. Sarah, though, retained hold of Veronica's arm for a moment and pulled her closer. Nervously, Veronica looked around her. There was nobody around and the woman behind the counter had her head down, ticking items off a list.

'Our man is very good at what he does,' Sarah whispered. 'These certificates are going to save ten men and women from the grip of the Nazis.' She pressed a small piece of paper into Veronica's hand, closing Veronica's fingers around it. 'This is the list of their addresses in Berlin, numbered from one to ten. On the backs of these certificates I have written the corresponding numbers. So there are two certificates with a one on the back, two with a two and so on. Do you follow me?'

Veronica nodded, squeezing Sarah's hand back before gently disengaging. 'Is that all you need me to do when I am there? It doesn't seem much.'

'It's dangerous work, Veronica. You will be going all around the Nazi capital calling on Jews who are relying on forged documentation to get out of the country. You will need to be careful and I will give you tips on how to make sure you aren't being followed.'

Veronica managed to keep her face impassive and not betray her elation at having succeeded in following Sarah just minutes earlier without her noticing. Admittedly she had been way behind her and lucky that she had been hidden by the couple walking their baby just at the right moment.

'This bag is for you to take with you,' Sarah was saying, now reaching for it. 'It has lots of room and apart from the certificates you'll be able to put into here almost anything else you would want for a day trip away from your hotel.'

Veronica shook her head. 'Thank you but I already have a set of valises which I am fond of so…' But Sarah waved her to be quiet. Veronica stopped speaking, mildly embarrassed by being halted in mid-sentence like that.

'This bag has a false bottom,' Sarah continued. 'I'll show you how to get it open when we are in a less public place but I can assure you it's very easy to manage. It means that you will be able to sail through all but the most thorough searches without fear of their finding anything compromising in your bag.'

Veronica remained silent, her mind trying to take in everything she was being given. She really was a secret agent!

'See this as a sort of test,' Sarah was saying. 'Do well with this task and, on a later trip, I'll be able to give you more to do. Trust me, Veronica.'

FIFTEEN

25 APRIL 1938

BERLIN

THEY HAD BARELY ARRIVED IN BERLIN AND CHECKED into their hotel before Billy was on his way out of the door saying that he had business to conduct and that he would be back in the late afternoon. She was barely able to contain her glee.

'But then we'll go out to dinner,' he said.

'Dinner?' she laughed. 'Billy, that would be wonderful!'

His exit left Veronica with nearly four hours of freedom. Adrenaline rushed through her, banishing all sense of fatigue after the long journey. She made some phone calls and was out of the hotel just thirty minutes after Billy had left.

The Königs lived in a modest apartment just off Barbarossastrasse in the Berlin district of Schöneberg. Culturally, it was still a Jewish area but in this part of town they were assimilated – or had been – and there were few Jewish shops, restaurants or places of worship.

Veronica took a taxi only as far as the main street, afraid to draw attention to her aunt, and now she walked slowly up the unfamiliar road glancing frequently at the little sketch she had made from a Berlin map that had been fixed to the wall in the hotel lobby. An elderly man walked slowly along the street looking at her carefully. Veronica assessed him to be harmless.

'Excuse me,' she said in German, crossing the small street towards him, 'I am a friend of the König family, Herr Manfred and Frau Sonia König. I wonder if you know them?' She was about to give their address when the man took off his hat and put out his hand.

'I am Manfred König,' he replied to her in careful English. 'You must be Veronica.'

'Oh my word!' Veronica exclaimed. 'I am so pleased to meet you! Have you been waiting for me in the street?' She was genuinely happy to see a man who, she reminded herself, was her mother's brother-in-law. She hoped that she had successfully concealed the shock she felt at his appearance. The man before her, she knew, had been twenty-two years old when he had married Sonia and that meant he was only forty-eight years old now, but he looked at least twenty years older than that. She thought him to be quite shy but it might have been his lack of English – though it was his choice not to speak German to her.

'I have often liked to take long walks around these streets,' he was saying to her now, 'so it has been no hardship for me. I find the fresh air envigorating. I knew you would be here eventually. May I help you with your bag please?'

Veronica politely refused. Of the two of them she felt herself to be the more able to cope with her bag albeit her hands were beginning to sweat with nervous excitement. Just a few minutes later, she and Sonia were face to face. The two women looked at each other in silence for what seemed to be a long while; it was hard to tell. Veronica thought that, unlike her husband, Sonia looked quite similar to how she had imagined. She was, perhaps, a little taller and darker than her sister Cynthia, but the eyes were the same and when she smiled, as she was finally smiling now, Veronica was reminded of the smiles she had always received as a child. Before she was really aware of it, Veronica was crying. Sonia reached for her.

'You poor child,' she said, hugging her tightly. 'You have nothing to cry about. Come in. Come in and sit down. I have some real English tea. I'll make up a pot. Or do you prefer coffee? We don't have English milk but we have good cream if that is something you could tolerate.'

'Tea, please. Two teaspoonfuls of sugar.'

Manfred, who had been standing awkwardly at this first exchange, now coughed politely.

'Come and sit down, Miss Beaumont.'

'Thank you. Please call me Veronica, Herr König,' and then she laughed through her tears. He laughed too but didn't invite a reciprocal familiarity and she felt that he would be uncomfortable calling her Veronica, at least for now. He handed her a silk handkerchief. She smiled gratefully and began to wipe her eyes.

'Here you are, Veronica,' said Sonia, placing the cup and saucer down on the small side table Manfred had placed by her chair.

'Forgive me,' she said, sitting down opposite her, 'I have to assume you look like your father's side of the family. I can't see any of Cynthia in you.'

'People have said I look like Father,' Veronica answered, 'but I have never been able to see it.' She took a sip of the tea, nodding her head. 'Thank you, this is wonderful.' Placing it carefully down again she looked at her aunt. 'I want to say, and I hope I won't cry again, though I fear I might, that I want to apologise for my parents' dreadful treatment of you both.'

Sonia, moved her hands as if to dismiss the very idea but Veronica had rehearsed what she would say for some weeks now and was not ready to give way.

'I have had the most loving wonderful relationship with my parents. I had an idyllic childhood and, as an only child, I have felt probably closer to my parents than others my age. To find that they could behave so treacherously,' she felt her bottom lip tremble and irritably brushed away another tear, 'has been a terrible revelation to me and something that I don't think I will ever forgive them for.'

'You mustn't say that,' said Sonia gently. 'Things are rarely black and white you know. I realise how difficult it would be for your mother to have me come back now. We are not allowed to take much with us, and Manfred,' she nodded to her husband, looking at him briefly, checking that he was listening and not about to stop her, 'well, Manfred would find it very hard to get work there after all he has been through. We would be dependent on your parents and we quite realise what a burden that would be. We expect nothing.'

'But Aunt Sonia,' she paused, ready to apologise for using what may be too affectionate a title so soon after meeting. Sonia nodded encouragingly. 'Remember that I have read your letters to Mother. You did have an expectation – an altogether reasonable one. You *did* expect her to be able to have got you both to England by now.'

Sonia was nodding. 'Yes, that is true – at the time of writing those letters that was certainly the case. I am glad she has kept them at least, so very glad. You know, as children we kept daily diaries and we wrote about what was happening in our lives. Often these would be our different interpretations of the same events at home. Then sometimes, even when we were supposed to have been asleep, we would put on our bedside lights, pick a date, it could be months or even years before, and read our entries to each other.' Now Sonia too was getting tearful at the happy memories. 'The best ones were when we had been arguing with each other. Reading our different views of long-forgotten arguments had us rolling around with laughter at the silliness of it all.' She paused, and bent forward to fiddle with the laces on her sensible shoes. 'I'd like to think that one day we will do just that about 1938.' She straightened, the awkward expression of that wish now behind her. 'I'm sorry, how did I get on to that? What were we saying?'

'That you think differently since you wrote those letters.'

'Ah yes. My point is that I was upset at the time but I have found that I can be quite useful here helping others. The crisis has brought our community together. I have joined the *Hilfsverein*. Until this year we were getting people out quite easily. Thousands even, if they had money and the right connections abroad.'

'*Hilfsverein?*' asked Veronica.

'I'm sorry. That's what we call the German Jewish Emigration Office. We're quite well organised. People who would never have talked to each other or even have known the other existed have become close friends and we even have some contacts with Christian groups abroad who wish to help.'

'That's good. I can see that. But I want you to know, Aunt Sonia, that I will work to make you and Mother look back together on 1938 very soon. That is one of the main reasons I am in Germany today.'

'That's very sweet of you, dear,' said Sonia, but Veronica didn't hear any excitement there or even belief that that day would come.

'I know that, if it became possible, you would still choose to come to England and I intend to help you.' She turned to Manfred. 'Both of you.' He gave her a small smile.

'I understand, dear, and I hope that it will happen. But those letters, those sad desperate letters, were written many months ago now, before Manfred was arrested, and anyway it is far clearer to us now that we would not be welcome in England – at least not together. And I will never come to where we are not, both of us, wanted.'

'You were arrested, Herr König?' asked Veronica, looking at Manfred. 'What had you done?'

He smiled at that but was slow to respond, struggling perhaps to find the right words. His wife answered for him.

'This is Nazi Germany, Veronica, you don't need to have done anything to get arrested. It is enough to be Jewish. It was just after the end of the Olympic Games here in Berlin. We will never know, but we think that perhaps the government wished to show people that, just because it had behaved so nicely during the Games when foreigners were visiting, the gloves were now off again and that we, the Jews, should realise that things were back to "normal". My husband was one of many Jews arrested in the week following the Closing Ceremony and they kept him for eight months at a place near Munich called Dachau. Eight months! Look at him now.'

Manfred was looking a little embarrassed by this but also strangely silent even though Sonia was now the one crying. He slowly got to his feet, reached into the top drawer of a heavy wooden chest and retrieved another handkerchief. He passed it to her and sat down again. Veronica wondered what he must have been through. He reminded her of some of the veterans she had come across who had suffered mental breakdown in the war.

'He survived the war unscathed,' said Sonia as if in answer to Veronica's thoughts. 'He was at Verdun, for God's sake, and survived. So many of his friends were not so fortunate and others were scarred for life. But Manfred? He came back a hero. The same wonderful, happy and vivacious man I had married.' She had placed some emphasis on the word 'vivacious', looking to her husband, so Veronica thought, as if willing him to return to that happy state. 'Some of the other Jewish men arrested that week, have still not come home. We think that it was his war record and Iron Cross that got him released, so I suppose we have that to be grateful for.' Sonia looked through the lounge door to the large grandfather clock which was standing in the hallway facing them. 'I am not so interested in uprooting and rushing to get to England right now. Of course, if we had papers, we would go, we would be crazy not to. But much of my energy is spent nursing Manfred and even more time is spent on helping others. With our men in a KZ like Dachau, we set up a group for the women. Some of them were completely unable to cope and I found that, in supporting and helping others, I was better able to manage with my own loss. I still am engaged in this work and I find it very fulfilling. I am a trained psychologist after all but am no longer allowed to treat non-Jewish patients.'

She looked over at her niece and held her gaze. 'I think in this at least, we are kindred souls, are we not? I think that you might like to help more than just your poor old aunt?'

'Yes,' said Veronica quietly, returning her aunt's gaze with what she hoped was the same intensity, 'there is nothing that I would want to do more.'

'Right then,' said Sonia, standing up, 'there is no better time than now. There are some very close friends of mine whom I would like you to meet. Let me just telephone them.'

'This very moment?' Veronica was alarmed. 'I only have a couple of hours and then I need to start travelling back to my hotel. We could do this another day perhaps.'

'Two hours is more than enough time. Don't fret. They don't live far.'

Schöneberg Jews tended to be middle class: lawyers, teachers and doctors who had, until recently, commuted to their offices in the city centre. Some of the entrances to the buildings they were now passing had plaques fixed at eye level announcing the qualifications of the people living in that building and most of them stated their opening hours too. It was clear that many of these men were now working from their homes. Probably, Veronica thought, it was safer as well as cheaper and most of their customers were anyway now likely to be Jews living nearby. As they walked, Veronica stole glances at her aunt trying to see her own mother in Sonia's profile. Over the four months of their correspondence, Veronica had unburdened her soul to the aunt she had never met. In her mother's hidden stash she had read how request after request to help had been politely refused. All that had been needed was a relative in England willing to provide shelter, to find employment, to cover the costs as Britain, still in the middle of a depression, would not contemplate providing any state aid. From her mother's writing box, Veronica had removed just one letter, a draft that Cynthia had written to her sister in Berlin and dated less than a year earlier.

'Please understand the very deep feelings that still exist in this country towards people of German blood and the terrible strains we would be under were we to take such drastic steps. We do feel, dear sister, that the situation in Germany as you describe it is ~~just too fantastic~~ exaggerated. Over here we read of the many great things happening in Germany now and we all watched with amazement the greatest of all Olympic Games last year. We remember your telling us about the unfortunate incident with Manfred but that is in the past now and nothing has happened to him since. Perhaps you need to see the bigger

picture? As my sister of course you do not need my help to come here. You are British, and always will be, whatever a piece of paper says. Naturally, we advise you not to leave your family but should you determine to do so then of course ~~we would see if we could do anything~~ you must stay with us. But understand that this offer could not be extended ~~to Manfred~~ at present to anyone else. In a year or two we truly believe you will thank us for strengthening your resolve to seeing through any present difficulties and by doing so retaining your beautiful Berlin home.'

That letter was back in London, but Veronica now knew it by heart including the crossings-out and the insights these provided. The cruelty and deceit that allowed her mother to use British dislike of the Germans as an excuse for inaction whilst, at the same time, being members of every pro-German club they could find, had changed her relationship with her parents for ever. If her mother could lie so brazenly then so would Veronica.

They turned into the entrance of one of the apartment buildings and walked up the steps to the first floor. Sonia knocked three times quickly and then a slower fourth time. Veronica heard footsteps approaching and the door opened revealing a tall, austere-looking woman wearing a dark, close-fitting dress that reached nearly to her ankles. She noticed that her shoes didn't have much of a heel so she really was very tall and her black hair being tied up in a tight bun made her look even more imposing. She wore glasses but probably only for reading as these hung from a chain around her neck.

'Hello, Sonia,' she said. Her voice was deep and rich. 'Why don't you and your niece come inside. The major is in the lounge.' She turned to Veronica, gave a small smile and shook her hand. 'You are very welcome in our house. I am Frau Gutmann. Come through please.'

Sonia smiled encouragingly at Veronica. 'Her name's Renate! Don't be put off by their formality, you know the Germans.'

The lounge was a large square room with bay windows that looked out onto the street and through which the setting sun cast a golden glow onto the white walls and onto the giant Persian rug which covered all of the floor apart from a margin of six inches where the highly polished wooden flooring could be seen.

Major Richard Gutmann was standing by the fireplace, a glass of white wine in his hand which he put down on the mantelpiece as they entered the room. He smiled and walked towards Veronica, his hand outstretched in greeting. Height-wise, he was about the same as his wife; a good match, thought Veronica. He had a full head of hair which was flecked with grey and a full moustache, curled up at the ends in the manner so favoured by the Prussian officer corps during the last war. His bearing was rigidly military but his smile was warm, revealing even, white teeth.

'I am afraid that I don't speak English much, but I hear that your German is good. That is quite a relief for me I must say!'

Veronica had to stop herself from bobbing a curtsy that would have been as much a surprise to her as it would have been to the others but there was something about Major Gutmann that commanded attention and respect.

'Won't you sit down please, Fräulein,' said the major, gesturing to the nearest of a pair of yellow chintz-covered armchairs. He then sat in the other one whilst his wife and Sonia sat on the sofa with its abundance of small cushions.

Major Gutmann looked at Sonia expectantly. Veronica

looked at his wife but she was looking at Sonia too. She saw that they were waiting for Sonia to speak but Sonia was trying to find the right way to begin. Finally she nodded to herself and turned to Veronica.

'Major,' Sonia began, 'is of course, a military title and is something that Major Gutmann is rightly proud of, but you should also know that before the war he had qualified as a medical doctor and although he joined the cavalry he was also on the medical staff.' She paused and turned to him. 'Over to you now, Major?'

'Yes. He can continue,' replied Frau Gutmann, leaning across to briefly stroke his cheek, a loving gesture that surprised Veronica, coming from such an austere woman, and was, she felt, all the more powerful for that.

SIXTEEN

25 APRIL 1938

SCHÖNEBERG, BERLIN

IT WASN'T THE STORY ITSELF THAT WAS MAKING HIM uncomfortable. He had told it to Renate and to Sonia before. Now, however, he was relating it for the benefit of this young woman who had come from England and who, Sonia had said, might somehow be able to help them. It was difficult to talk to someone so young – and all the more so because she was English. It was humiliating to ask for help at all and it had taken a lot of persuading for him to get to this point. If it were not for the two children, he would not be doing this. He decided to start his story with the war. That had itself once been a hard subject to talk about with anyone of whatever age. Yet in recent years, he found it was easier, therapeutic even, to take refuge in what was now the distant past and at least free of the uncertainties afflicting them today. He decided to speak in German so that he would not further embarrass himself. He could always translate any military terms should they prove to be beyond Miss Beaumont's vocabulary.

'There were two doctors assigned to the 2nd Guards Uhlan regiment on the Western Front in May 1917. Myself and George Spencker. This was, for us, a welcome reunion. George and I had studied together before the war at the Charité Hospital here in Berlin. Earlier in the war we had served at various field hospitals but never together. We had each seen some horrendous things, things that haunted us even then in our dreams. But things got considerably worse in 1918 following the failure of the *Michael* offensive, or *Kaiserschlacht* as we called the great advances of that spring. Then, as the army began to give ground that summer, our conditions, never good to start with, got worse and we came under almost constant shellfire.

'On one occasion there was a direct hit on our field hospital and I was buried under a pile of mud mixed with body parts. I wanted to scream but my mouth immediately filled with the stuff. I tried to kick my legs. I couldn't breathe.' He stopped for a few moments. His wife put a reassuring hand on his knee and he was able to continue. 'I knew I was going to die. But then, at the moment that hope left me, I felt hands grab my foot, and I was able to wiggle it around so they would know that this was part of a live body. Earth was shovelled away and suddenly air rushed in, my face was being wiped and I could see again – and there was George. He smiled at me.' He turned to Veronica, his eyes full of tears. 'Never had I ever been so glad to see him as at that moment when he grasped me by the armpits and pulled me out of hell.'

Veronica felt very small. Anything she could say would be inadequate or worse, trite. Finally she said, 'Do please continue.'

'After that we were closer than I had ever been. Inseparable. Until that terrible day, a few months later, when a shell came for George. It was an English shell.'

'I am so sorry,' said Veronica. She felt her cheeks redden. 'No, forgive me,' said the major. 'That was unnecessary. It isn't your fault. It wasn't even the fault of the men who fired the shell. They were trying to survive in the same way as we were. Anyway, I tried to save George as he had saved me. But all our equipment had been destroyed by the explosion. I had nothing.' He looked up at his wife as if, even now, pleading for her understanding. 'I carried him to the next casualty clearing station, trying not to slip in the mud and drop him. There was blood everywhere and only the pressure of his stomach on my shoulder was keeping him together.' He paused for a few moments more, seeing before him not the living room in Berlin but the remains of the field hospital in the aftermath of that shell. 'George was strong, mentally as well as physically. He survived for several more hours and during that time he told me how grateful he was that I had stayed with him. He told me where he had put letters for his wife and asked that I gather his personal effects and tell her that he had not suffered. Of course, he had suffered, but I obeyed his wishes.'

At that moment there was a sound of loud, incongruous, laughter. The door swung open, knocking against the back of the chair in which Veronica sat. She stood up quickly and so did Frau Gutmann, apologising for the rude interruption. Two children, a boy and a girl, had run into the room. The girl couldn't have been more than ten years old, dressed in a frilly white, long-sleeved blouse, buttoned to the neck, and a loose-fitting dark skirt that came down to just above her ankles. Her hair was light brown, arranged in two plaits. She had a light sprinkling of freckles over her nose and her green eyes were brimming, at that moment, with tears. The boy was a few years older, tall and gangly with short blond hair, wearing grey shorts with a matching jacket and long white socks.

'Peter's pinching me!' cried the girl, running to her mother and throwing her arms around her waist and burying her head in Frau Gutmann's neck.

'But Lise was annoying me again,' said Peter. 'I was trying to study and she kept pulling at my arm.'

'You promise to play with me but you never do!'

Peter, seeing that his mother was occupied with Lise, went to stand next to his father. He said nothing more but waited for his father to pass judgement. Veronica looked quickly at Major Gutmann to see how he would take to this sudden interruption to his narrative but, if he was upset, he did not show it. In fact he seemed to welcome the distraction, reaching out to Peter and putting a comforting hand on his shoulder.

'Peter does have to study, you know,' he said to Lise, but smiling to show her he was not at all angry with her. 'How about we all play a game together?'

'Will you?' exclaimed Lise, brightening immediately, raising her head from her mother's shoulder. She turned to Peter, her quarrel with him forgotten in a moment. 'Did you hear, Peter? Father is going to play with us. So you can stop studying now can't you?'

'Not just yet, Lise,' her father clarified. 'Peter must do some more studying and I have to conclude my conversation here. We have a visitor from England.'

Startled, both children turned to look at Veronica, noticing her for the first time. 'Hello, children. So you are Lise. I am so pleased to meet you.' Lise stared back at her. She made no reply but there was no hostility there. It was more that she was struggling for a frame of reference. Peter though, with an effort, recovered from his own surprise and took a step forwards, bringing his heels together and bowing slightly. 'Hello,' he said. 'I am Peter, Lise's brother. Are you a friend of ours?'

Veronica laughed. 'Hello, Peter. Sonia here is my aunt and yes, I hope very much to be your friend.'

'Are you English then, like Frau König?'

'Yes, I am. I have come here for a short holiday.'

Peter nodded at that, bowed his head and took a couple of steps backward. For a while there was complete silence as both children continued to stare at this foreign apparition.

'That's all for now, children,' said their mother, standing up and clapping her hands. 'You will have a chance to get to talk some more to Fräulein Beaumont later on.' She glanced at Veronica, who nodded her head enthusiastically. 'But right now, the grown-ups have to talk.'

'Is this about our horses?' asked Peter, moving reluctantly towards the doorway.

Veronica noticed that Frau Gutmann looked flustered at that and didn't reply. 'Come on, both of you. In one hour come back and get your father.' They left the room. 'And no listening at the door, is that clear?' Frau Gutmann waited until each had promised her and only then closed the door.

'Yes,' said Major Gutmann, 'in some ways, this is in fact about the horses. I will be coming to them shortly. First though, I was telling you about my last conversation with George.'

Veronica nodded solemnly. She was very aware that this was all for her benefit. She wanted to hear their story but at the same time, the more that they invested in the sharing of themselves with her, the greater would be their inevitable disappointment. For, surely she, a courier of university certificates, could not possibly help them. At least not this trip. Sarah might be able to help but she would then have to tell her about Sonia. She resolved to concentrate. It was hard enough following all the German without her mind wandering at the same time.

'On my very next trip to Berlin, I went to see George's wife. We had never met before but of course each of us already felt we knew the other. In fact, because over the years George had spent so much more time with me at the front, I probably knew so much more about her than she of me. But in any event, we quickly became friends and I believe that I was able to give her some peace in sharing with her George's last hours.

'Hildegard said that nobody could ever replace George and it is not as if there were anyway many men to choose from after the war and there were even fewer after the influenza epidemic. This meant she had never had children. Instead she threw herself into her work and developed the small stables that she and George had bought before the war. Soon she was housing the horses of the wealthy and teaching their children to ride. When our children were born, she in a way saw them as her surrogate family and of course she taught them everything they know about horses.'

He smiled at Veronica. 'Peter is quite the accomplished horseman,' he said proudly. 'As good as I ever was.'

Frau Gutmann now spoke. 'Nearly three years ago, we held a barmitzvah party for Peter. Do you know what that is?'

Veronica nodded. She didn't really know much more than that it was some sort of coming-of-age ceremony for Jewish boys at 13. She could ask Sarah for details of that too later.

'Hildegard was so much a part of our family that we gave her the place of honour at that party. It was September 1935 and I even remember the exact date of the party, because we had all been so relieved that it had taken place just days before the passing of the Nuremburg Laws which made such social interactions suddenly very risky for non-Jews, though technically not illegal.' Frau Gutmann looked over to her husband, signalling to him that she had said what she wanted to say.

The major took over the narrative. 'Even then,' he said, 'Hildegard continued teaching the children at some risk to herself. As a German woman, just under 45 years of age, she could no longer be employed by Jews in their households, but it was still unclear whether accepting their money for teaching them riding was forbidden given that they were leaving their household to be taught. It was a grey area. I think she was nervous though she tried very hard to conceal her fears from us. Then, a few months ago, I had been out riding with the children. Normally, Hildegard would come out to greet us on our return and make us something to drink. She always had some treats for the children and she liked to catch up on their news. But, that day she had instructed the stable boy to meet and take care of the horses and he told me that Frau Spencker wanted to see me in her office alone. I thought it was unusual but, naively, I still had no premonition that there was anything really wrong.'

Major Gutmann stopped talking for a while. It was too painful for him to carry on. The others waited patiently for a minute or two then his wife went and stood behind him and started rubbing his shoulders. He looked up at her, expressionless. 'I'm sorry, my darling. Perhaps in a few minutes?'

'Of course,' she said. 'We'll talk about other things and you tell us if and when you'd like to continue. I would rather you tell it than I, but of course I will if you wish it.' She kissed him and then went to sit next to Veronica and began to ask her more about herself. Major Gutmann sat perfectly still, alone with his pain, replaying in his head that last meeting with Hildegard, as he had already replayed it a hundred times before.

The wooden door with its large glass panel had been ajar and he had walked into Hildegard's spacious office-cum-living room. Hildegard had been reclining on a low, white chintz-covered sofa looking very much the part of a riding-school proprietor. She was short and lean, built like a jockey, and had been wearing her white high-necked blouse tucked into her cream jodhpurs, themselves tucked neatly into her shiny black riding boots. Clearly she had not yet ridden that day. She had greeted him with a solemn smile and gestured for him to sit. He'd chosen the chair in front of the fireplace below what was her favourite portrait of George.

It was an enlarged and slightly stylised photograph of him in his new uniform and officer's hat, a photograph just like so many other photographs taken of those fresh-faced, brave and happy men, eager for war. The portrait revealed that he had not yet won his Iron Cross and after he had won it there was so little time and no opportunity to sit for another portrait. Yet the medal was there all the same: hanging from the white and black-edged ribbon which was draped across the top right corner of the frame. It was he, Major Dr Richard Gutmann, who had brought it back from the front and given it to Hildegard.

Thinking back now, he realised that it must surely have made it harder for her to say to him what she had decided to say to him, with George looking down on her. For she must have known that George would never have approved.

There had been a tension in the room that Dr Gutmann had not felt before. He had even looked around the room carefully to see if perhaps someone else was standing or crouching in a corner. Perhaps the presence of a third party explained such an atmosphere?

Finally Hildegard had broken the silence. She had been unable to look either at him or at the picture of George. Instead she had looked fixedly at the fireplace. It had not been lit but afterward, when he looked back on this day, it seemed to him that she had been looking into the fires of hell.

'The problem for me, Herr Major,' she had said, 'is that I have always obeyed the law. I don't steal, I don't cheat my customers. Do you see?' He hadn't quite seen, but he had nodded anyway. She had taken a deep breath and continued. 'The government's job is to look after our country and to keep it healthy. If it cannot do this then we are all lost. Do you not agree? I think you once said yourself that when the Kaiser called on us to go to war, it was unthinkable for you not to go. Is that not so?'

'Yes, I did feel that, Hildegard,' he had replied, 'but forgive me, I don't know what you are trying to say.'

Hildegard, however, had pressed on. 'And when today the Führer says that he fights for Germany so that we can be strong again, he must equally be right.'

'Well, I don't know that I can agree with that—' he had begun.

'No? This is my point, Herr Major. My point exactly. Here is a man, from the most humble of origins who has come forward and made Germany great again. He has overcome the horrors visited on us by the Jews of Wall Street and made the economy strong again. He has stood up to the British and the French and reunited the Sudeten Germans with the Fatherland. And yet, some people still, after all he has done for us here, do not accept this.' She looked at him with a look he had never seen from her before. 'You, Herr Major, do not accept this. And even now, when I mentioned those Jews, I saw you start to object. Yet you cannot deny this.'

'Of course I deny it, Hildegard!' he had protested. 'How can you blame the Jews for the Wall Street crash? I want Germany to be great again. Of course I do. But Hitler wants to take us into another war and he will destroy all of us in the end—'

'No, Herr Major. I thought that once but I realise now that this is not and cannot be true. It suddenly came to me when I looked around at my friends. Good people. They have stopped coming to me because of you. Some have moved their horses elsewhere for stabling. Others send their children to other schools. I thought that they were all wrong and hated them for treating me in such a way. But then I realised, no, what is at stake here is something far greater. The Führer says, "The Jews are our misfortune," and I realise how right he is. You, Herr Major, are my own personal misfortune. I need to follow the Zeitgeist. It is I who have been out of step.'

'Hildegard! Have you taken leave of your senses? This is me, Richard, you are talking to. You say that I am your own misfortune. Have you been secretly reading Der Stürmer? Are not the Nazis our misfortune? How can you, after all these years, suddenly become one of them? If you were to say to me, "Dear friend, I care for you but I am not strong enough to stand against the tide so must hide our friendship," this I could accept. I would be terribly sad, of course, but only very few can be brave enough to defy the regime.' He had paused then, but had decided to continue. 'I had thought you were such a person.'

Hildegard looked at him but had not said anything at first and he had dared to hope that his words had had the desired effect. Eventually, she had leant forward, her hands on her knees.

'The Führer has said that you, the Jews, are not just our misfortune but our enemy. Dr Goebbels has warned that we may know Jews personally and believe them to be our friends, just like you, when really you are plotting the destruction of our nation. You wrongly assess the situation, Herr Major. I have been weak but now I am brave. I have been blind but now I really can see once more. I see that you are the enemy and I am brave enough to take the required action. You must not come back here again.'

He had gasped and staggered to his feet. 'You cannot be serious! And what about the children? They love you. Are they your enemies too? You cannot take this away from me, from them, from us. I beg of you to reconsider.'

Hildegard's bottom lip trembled but she held her nerve. 'It is a question of race. You are born impure. You cannot help what you are. But it is through purity that Germany is rising again. It is so clear. Perhaps you personally do not mean to contaminate but nevertheless, whilst you are here, contamination is taking place.'

Until this point he had been able to separate his hatred for the Nazis from his love for his country and wait for the 'real' Germany to emerge. But now, he had realised, there might not be any other Germany to emerge. Somehow, whilst he had been riding his horses and treating his patients, his country had slipped away, taken in by a man who told them that hating their neighbours was a good thing.

'What about the horses? I have nowhere to keep them. No other stable will receive them from us now. Have pity, Hildegard. If only for George's sake.' To his shame he had heard his voice shaking.

'It is true, you were George's friend and he died never knowing that his country was being betrayed. For the sake *of that bond, which never was itself contaminated, I will buy your horses from you at the full market price. That is more than generous.'*

He had walked quickly to the door, trying to maintain his dignity. 'I must gather the children then and say goodbye to the horses. Will you give us the time to do that at least?'

Hildegard had nodded. As he'd left the room, she had got up and closed the door behind him. What was really in her mind at that point? Did she feel like a monster or was she protected by that pamphlet written by Dr Goebbels and warning people about what to expect in such a situation? The Gauleiter of Berlin had written that such feelings of empathy to old friends would pass as long as one showed unflinching resolve. And maybe Hildegard was following a certain twisted logic. The Führer had been proved right in so many things, why shouldn't she owe him her unquestioning support?

He became aware that the other conversation in the room had ceased. He saw that they were looking at him, waiting.

'The children,' he sighed, 'think only of the horses. How their father will make everything as it was before. That nothing could be so bad that they could not be reunited with them.' He shook his head and looked directly at Veronica. 'Madam, it's not about the horses anymore, is it? There has always been antisemitism in Germany. It's been there, under the surface. But it was not talked about. One could live one's life and ignore it. But in these past years, things have changed. It has been gathering momentum since 1933. It may have started as the distasteful aspect of one political party, but when that party has taken power – then what? In just five years it has taken over the country and now even decent people, our friends, have fallen for it. Who knows where it will end? And so, we ask you, help us to get away from here. Whatever it takes, whilst we still have the means to make it happen. Please help us.'

SEVENTEEN

25 APRIL 1938

TIERGARTEN, BERLIN

'WHAT IS THAT TUNE YOU ARE WHISTLING?' ASKED Gunther.

'It's called *Tipperary*. We used to sing it during the war. Why, do you like it?'

'Not really, but it is in my head now. What is it about, Tommy?'

There were three of them walking down the Charlottenburger Chausee, the wide road that bisected the huge Tiergarten wooded park in the centre of the city: Gunther, his guest from England who spoke no German, and Gunther's friend Hans, who spoke no English. Gunther was beginning to find the need to translate quite tiring. For the past fifteen minutes he'd kept mainly to English and left Hans in the dark a bit. Hans didn't seem to mind.

'It tells of our homesickness for England. Gunther, you don't need to call me Tommy.'

'Ach so. Surely if you are remembering the war, I can call you Tommy – no? I recognise those places from my time in

London. But not the first place. Is that London also?' He looked at his friend, genuinely wanting to know. He had learnt his English from his Welsh step-mother, Angela, the only mother he had really had. They had lost contact after 1914, and only recently, on trips to England, had he managed to track her down again.

'No, Gunther, it is not in England. It was home though for many of us but now it's gone. The bloody Irish have taken it with them.'

'You know, you and I are much the same age, you're 39, right? Yes, I remember the Tommies in their trenches singing their strange songs.' He laughed. 'Did you ever listen to our songs, Tommy?'

'Tommy' laughed. 'If you're going to call me Tommy, then I am going to call you Fritz. How do you like that, Fritz?' He nodded towards Hans. 'And what about you, little Fritzy?'

'You waste your insults. He doesn't understand so is not offended. And also, he is only 36, so he missed the war altogether. He knows nothing of what we went through in the trenches in seas of mud. His first blood was killing Bolsheviks right here in Berlin.' He translated this last bit for Hans, who laughed, nodding his head vigorously. Gunther laughed with him, slapping him heartily on the back.

Gunther was the happiest he had been in a long time. He had a dutiful wife and a two-year-old son at home in a small but neat apartment in Fehrbelliner Strasse, just north of Horst-Wessel Platz station. Most of all, he was back in full-time paid employment and was once again proud enough to wear his brown shirt and breeches in public along with his shiny leather boots. His beloved SA, the Brownshirts, had had its membership cut by more than half by the purges but for Gunther this had meant rapid promotion. In just four years he had gone from being a lowly Truppführer, to an officer's rank. Obersturmführer no less.

To celebrate his new job, Gunther had taken Lotte to dinner at a classy little restaurant on Savignyplatz, leaving her mother to look after little Otto. The evening had been truly wonderful, but eventually, he had to bring this part of it to a close. He had been dreading the scene that inevitably would ensue when she realised they would not be spending the night together and had put off telling her for as long as possible. In fact he had realised that, even if she accepted the news quietly, he would now be late for the next part of his evening. But Lotte had not accepted the news well. She had clearly been expecting a more romantic finale.

'Gunther. Please don't do this to me,' she had pleaded with him, trying to hold back tears. 'I told my mother that we, *we*, would be back much later. What will it look like if I come back earlier and alone? Please, Gunther, I will be so humiliated.'

When Gunther had stood resolute, his long leather coat gathered now over one arm, ready to leave, Lotte had tried crying and then moved to blazing anger, following him as he had gone out onto the street. And now it was Gunther who felt humiliation. Here he was, in full SA uniform, being harangued outside on the pavement. Passersby would think he couldn't control his own wife. He could already feel their stares. Their romantic two hours now forgotten, he grabbed Lotte by her upper arm and half marched, half dragged her to the kerbside where he hailed a taxi and bundled her in, thrusting the fare to the driver through the partition. It could not be helped. Gunther was ready to start the second part of his celebration and that had no place for his wife. His friend from London was over and Gunther had promised him a special evening ahead. And special evenings always involved Hans, his best friend since school. Together they were unstoppable. Together they had joined the SA and when the purge had come, Hans too had emerged with enhanced responsibilities. Their invincibility was on show tonight and they would teach their English guest how to have some fun. Gunther looked at his watch and cursed. He was going to be really late.

In the old days it had been easier for the boys to have a fun night out. They and a few others would march into districts like Wedding or Friedrichshain and cause serious harm to any Bolshevik KPD supporters they met. But now that enemy had been so defeated he'd disappeared from the streets. The Reds had either fled the country, become good Nazis overnight, or joined the army. There was still fun to be had, however. You just needed to be patient, stay awake later and know where to go.

The three of them had eventually met up at Savignyplatz station and they had entered the woodland of the Tiergarten via Lichtensteinallee. But that part of the park had proved disappointing and so they had walked on. Gunther put a finger to his lips and their English friend finally stopped whistling his old song from the war. They left the road, moving into the woods and continued to walk, more slowly now, deeper into this enormous heart of darkness in the very centre of the city, whose undergrowth attracted all sorts of night life.

'Halt,' whispered Gunther, raising a warning hand and they stopped, scarcely daring to breathe. There it was; he heard it again, a woman's hushed giggle. As the three men crept closer they could hear heavy breathing and Gunther heard sounds that he thought were of people kissing. He hoped so.

There they were, in a small clearing illuminated by moonlight. They could see the woman up against a tree, one leg curled around the waist of a tall man whose hand was pushing up her skirt so that her stocking top was clearly visible. His face was partially buried in her neck and she had her head back against the tree, eyes tightly shut with pleasure.

'Good evening, my friends,' said Gunther cheerfully. 'It's a nice night for it, don't you think?'

The amorous couple pulled apart, the woman quickly adjusting her skirt so that once again it went down almost to her ankles. The man was gratifyingly thin, thought Gunther as he squared up to him.

'We are so sorry to disturb you but might I ask to see some identification?'

'Are you police?' asked the man.

'We're not, no. Not exactly,' answered Hans, opening his coat to show his brown SA uniform and breeches. 'But we are SA and we would like to know who you are and what brings you here?'

The couple exchanged frightened glances before the woman finally replied, 'We only left our houses very briefly. We live near here, if you wish we can go home and bring you our identification. We're not criminals.'

Gunther grinned. 'But you are not man and wife either, are you? You live in different homes and you meet at 2am in the Tiergarten for fun and games.' He shook his head. He turned to the woman. 'Are you a whore?'

'Certainly not!' she replied indignantly.

'Ach well, Fräulein, that was a bad answer to give me. Or should I say Frau.' He pointed to the ring on her left hand. 'You are adulterers. You are law breakers. The Party takes a very dim view of such immoral activity.' He turned back to the man. 'Are you a member of the Party?'

'Yes I am! I work on the S-bahn. We all have to be Party members.'

'I see,' said Hans, 'so you are a member of the Party by

necessity rather than by choice? What were you before that, a Bolshie?'

Gunther suddenly grabbed the woman to him, his hands squeezing her buttocks. As she instinctively opened her mouth to scream he pressed his lips hard against hers, muffling the scream, and then put one hand to her head to keep her there.

'Hey!' shouted her lover. It was the last thing he would say for many weeks until they removed the wiring from his jaw. Hans only needed to punch the man once in the face. He sank to his knees but before he could collapse fully to the ground, Hans managed to kick him into oblivion when his jack boot connected cleanly with his head. Hans removed the bloodied knuckle duster from his hand and put it back into his pocket, flexing his fingers.

Gunther meanwhile had thrown the woman to the ground and was unbuttoning his trousers. 'Your man doesn't seem able to perform tonight. And he had got you all hot and bothered too. Never mind, I think I can be of assistance.' He knelt down and thrust her skirt up. The woman's mouth had been opening and closing with no sound coming forth but Gunther could see she was about to finally emit what would be a very loud scream.

'Let me caution you, Frau whatever-your-name-is. We hold all the power here. The law is on our side. And most of all, if you scream, and you get lucky and someone comes to help you, what will you tell your husband?' He knew from her expression that he had correctly guessed the situation. 'If I were to give you honest, free advice, tailored to fit the unfortunate circumstances in which you are finding yourself, I would say that you should just keep your mouth shut, and lie back and enjoy.'

He shuffled forward, stuffing into her mouth a large handkerchief that he carried around with him for just such occasions. 'But I am celebrating tonight. So if you wanted to struggle and to try and get away from me that would be even better.'

He thrust into her. It felt so good, so empowering. There was a noise to his right and he turned his head to find that the big Englishman had finally emerged into the clearing and was watching closely.

'Tommy!' Gunther laughed in English. 'You want to go next? From the state of you I think if you watch too long, you'll be too late!'

But Billy Watson laughed self-consciously and shook his head. 'I think I'll pass this time. I can't help feeling the police may come at any moment.'

'Fuck the police,' panted Gunther. 'So what if they come? We're the law here now. This isn't London. Do here what you can't do at home!' At that point, Gunther had to turn his head away as he gasped out his pleasure. He waited another few seconds before slowly withdrawing. He looked down at the woman, her cheeks wet with tears but still with her mouth stuffed. She looked like she might be from a wealthy home. Maybe the *Kripo* might yet get involved. Oh well, too late to worry about that now. Just as well Billy was such a coward as they should probably put some distance between themselves and these two. They might know somebody important. But, just then, he felt a heavy hand on his shoulder moving him away from the woman.

'Okay, I'll have a turn now,' said Hans. 'Move aside, Gunther.'

Dinner earlier that evening had been most trying for Veronica too. Sitting with Billy as he talked about fascism and how, here in Berlin, there was so much to learn from the new Germany, was something she had become used to over the last few days.

She would smile and nod, nod and smile: the dumb blonde hanging on his every word, asking daft questions here and there. It confirmed to Billy just how little women understood politics. But to do this, right here, in this city, having just met the Gutmanns, was testing whatever acting skills she possessed. She just wasn't up to it. Fortunately though, it seemed that Billy too was not in the mood to lecture her. He was unusually quiet and constantly looking at his watch. He had already been cross with her for being ten minutes late.

'Bloody hell, Veronica,' he'd said in exasperation when she had finally arrived in a flurry of blonde windswept hair, 'I told you I have a business meeting immediately after this and I can't be late.' She had looked at him with that apologetic, quiescent way that she knew would distract him from his anger, though it also ran the risk of ramping up his libido. She calculated that this would not be an issue tonight given that he would be leaving her there and had already warned her that he would then not be back until early morning.

Now, however, dinner was over and he was unexpectedly hurrying her along Hindenburgstrasse, past the silent park and towards the Schmargendorf S-bahn train station. Veronica was finding the pace too fast in her heels.

'Stop, Billy! Please stop. You can go on and meet your friend. I don't need to go to Savignyplatz. I will just make my own way back to the hotel.'

'No! I told him we would be there. I just want him to meet you. It's polite. And from there, you can go back to the hotel.'

'So why are we taking a train? We could have ordered a taxi from the restaurant. It would be faster if you're in a hurry.'

Billy slowed for a moment. 'I wanted to. They didn't have a telephone.'

'Billy, they did have a telephone! I saw them using it. And you don't even speak German. I could have called a taxi. This is just silly and we'll never be able to hire a taxi on this road. All the ones that have passed us have been full. We should go back to the restaurant.'

'It's too far now, Veronica. We should just press on.'

Veronica reluctantly carried on walking for another few minutes before again speaking.

'Look, Billy, we are much nearer now to our hotel than to where you're trying to get to! It seems a lot of effort to meet someone on a train platform just to say hello and then you go off and have your business meeting, leaving me to make my own way home. This isn't reasonable, Billy. Why didn't you let me call a bloody taxi?!'

Billy looked at her, sitting now on a low wall and removing one of her shoes.

'Please, Ronnie,' he said finally, plaintively. 'The truth is, I'm not used to getting taxis to places. I'm not like you, going around everywhere in chauffeur-driven cars. It simply didn't occur to me that we could go anywhere other than by train or by tram. I have hardly ever used a taxi in my life.'

Veronica nodded, taking this in. It was a side to him he had not shown her before and she could see the irony of his helping to build taxis in London but never being able to afford to ride in one. Billy was sweating profusely; his large bulk had been struggling with this fast pace as well. She tried to imagine how it must have been for him growing up poor. On the other hand, he had just called her 'Ronnie'. She hated it when he called her Ronnie. He'd begun to call her that a few weeks ago and did so now when he was trying to be especially nice to her. She didn't like Billy when he was being nice to her.

'But why am I coming with you, Billy? What's the bloody point?'

'You're beautiful,' he said finally, looking down at her one stockinged leg crossed over the other as she massaged her tired foot.

'*What* did you say?' Veronica didn't know if that had been in answer to her question or a change of subject. Either way it was unwelcome, now more than ever.

'I'm proud that you're my girl and I want these Germans, who think they're on top of the bloody world right now, to see that I have something that they don't have. Is that so strange?'

Veronica regarded him silently as she put back her shoe. It was strange all right. But flattering somehow. And it was the game she had been playing. To meet people in Billy's world, to gain knowledge that may at some point be used against them.

She sighed and rose to her feet, slipping her arm through his. 'Go on then.'

The high vaulted underground ceilings of the station resting on their heavy curving columns were awe-inspiring. More grand and magnificent than anything she had seen on the London Underground. She would like to have had more time to explore and vowed to come back when it was less crowded. At this time of night the platforms were filled with late-night revellers enjoying the benefits of a revitalised and booming Berlin. Many of the men were in uniform, grey green for the army, brown for the SA and more than a few black for the SS. Men in civilian clothes looked curiously at them from under the peaks of their trilby hats. Posters on the subway walls appealed to patriotism for the Reich: the men to the Party and to the *Wehrmacht* or the *Kriegsmarine*, the young women to join the *Bund Deutscher Mädel*, the League of German Girls, known to all as the BDM. Others proclaimed the new virtues to which these girls should aspire once they had graduated to full womanhood. *Kinder, Küche, Kirche*, Children, Kitchen, Church.

One advantage of being with Billy was never not finding space on a crowded train. Billy simply pushed his way through and his bulk sheltered her from the pushing, and sometimes groping, endured by many other women travelling on the S-bahn. They got to Savignyplatz not more than two minutes after the appointed time and Billy found the kiosk where they were due to meet Gunther.

'Perhaps he was here on time and didn't want to wait once I was late,' said Billy, looking over the heads of the people swirling around them. This station wasn't as opulent as Schmargendorf and seemed to be even more crowded. After ten minutes, Veronica had had enough. She didn't voice her dismay though until fifteen minutes had gone. 'Five minutes more,' Billy had replied, highly agitated now.

Veronica waited five minutes exactly. 'I'm sorry, Billy. It's been a long day. I'm tired. I need to go and lie down. I am going to go now.'

But Billy held on to her hand. 'Wait five more minutes.' His tone was pleading but his grip was strong and unyielding. 'Then, if he is not here, you can go and I won't try to stop you.' She nodded and he released her hand.

'Goodbye, Billy,' Veronica said when five more minutes had passed. This time she held her hands tightly behind her back, but, to her surprise, he bent down and kissed her cheek.

'I understand,' he said. 'It seems that he isn't coming. I'll wait a while longer though.' But just then, as he turned away from her, he thought he caught a glimpse of Gunther coming down the steps. He lost him again and then he saw him embracing a man not fifteen yards away from where he was standing. 'Gunther!' Billy shouted, his accent making several people glance his way. 'Gunther!' he yelled again. Gunther finally noticed him, came over, shook his hand, slapped him on the arm and introduced him to his friend,

Hans. Billy saw Veronica half way up the steps on her way out. 'Veronica!' he bellowed. 'Veronica, come back, he's here!' Veronica continued up, not hearing above the din. Someone, standing somewhere between him and Veronica, but further over to the right, took up his call, imitating Billy's English in a very heavy German accent, *'He is here! He is here!'* Billy saw Veronica turn a little in the direction from which that shout had come, clearly recognising the English words but not their intended meaning. She smiled towards the source of that shouting, continued to ascend the stairs and was gone.

Hans was speaking to Gunther in rapid German.

'What's he saying?' asked Billy, both irritated by Veronica not having heard him, and envious of the two men in their brown uniforms and armbands. He could not wait until the BU would again be allowed to also strut around in their black uniforms and boots.

'He says, when waiting at the station earlier, he had wondered whether you were the friend but he hadn't expected you to have a woman with you so he didn't approach you.'

'Well, you've missed her now, Gunther,' Billy said, though turning to look at Hans, 'that was my girl. Did Hans see my girl?'

Gunther smiled and winked, and conveyed the question to his friend. Hans shrugged and said some words.

'He says he saw her but he was a little far away and she was turned towards you most of the time. But yes, Hans says from what he could see, she is very pretty!'

Billy studied Gunther's face for traces of mockery but decided there were none. He smiled. 'I had hoped to introduce you properly. Perhaps another time.'

'Of course,' said Gunther, 'but until then, let us begin our evening, yes?'

EIGHTEEN

26 APRIL 1938

MEINEKESTRASSE, BERLIN

BILLY DIDN'T COME BACK TO THE HOTEL THAT NIGHT and Veronica luxuriated in having the clean sheets and double bed all to herself. Every couple of hours she would wake, glance at the clock, reassure herself she was still alone and enjoy the bliss of snuggling back down and letting sleep overtake her once more. By the time the first rays of the sun were coming up, she had finally slipped into deep sleep which was uninterrupted for more than three hours.

In the strengthening dawn light, she didn't hear Billy finally enter the room, undressing as quietly as he could, making sure to avoid standing on the loose floorboard. If she had been awake Veronica would have recognised the look he had at that moment, the look he had when intently watching the curve of her breasts or her feet in heels or, as now, the curve of her bottom under the sheets.

Billy was cold, frustrated and very much in need of relief after what he had seen in the park. He was angry with himself too for not having participated with Gunther and Hans and humiliated by their good-natured taunts all the while they were quickly walking back to the streets to get as far away as possible from the Tiergarten before the police came. When he was naked, he stroked himself a few times to ensure maximum hardness, pulled back the sheets and moved on top of her.

Veronica woke to feel his urgency pressed up against her buttocks. 'No, Billy, please. Not now. Let me sleep a little longer.'

He moved her long hair to the side, kissing her shoulder and then up to her neck. He smelt of stale sweat and stale beer.

'I need you. Right now.' He lowered his hand and began rubbing her, gently at first and then, when he felt some damp, more quickly.

Veronica had never been able to dissuade Billy once his mind was decided and she willed herself to be accommodating so that he wouldn't hurt her too much. *I am not doing this willingly,* she told herself and tried to crawl away across to the other side of the bed. Effortlessly he dragged her back by her hips, forcing her up on to her knees, as she knew he would. Without really meaning to, she arched her back. She was ready for him now. 'Go on then, you bastard,' she said. 'Take what you need.'

Something had got him excited and he hadn't lasted long. Whatever it was, it clearly had nothing to do with her. He hadn't even seen her face. He had used her as a receptacle. *Well, who's using who, pal?* she thought. She bathed, dressed and went down to breakfast. Even as he had been thrusting into her, one hand slapping her and the other pushing her face down into the mattress, she had thought that this might actually work out very well. If he had been up all night he would probably have slept a good few hours anyway but now, having had her, he would likely need even more.

With luck, he might sleep through most of the day, this day when she had arranged to meet up with Sarah. She had been worried about what story she'd have to concoct and now she didn't need one at all. She couldn't avoid the occasional creak of the unfamiliar floorboards but she gently pulled the door open, only as wide as she needed to squeeze through, fearful that the squeak of the hinges might yet be loud enough to wake him. Closing it just as carefully, she was away, leaving a note on the door asking that the room not be cleaned.

She and Sarah had carefully co-ordinated to be in Berlin during the same week and they had chosen today to be when Sarah would look out for her at the Jewish Agency offices. At her insistence Veronica had memorised the address, 10 Meinekestrasse, just off the K-damm, and not more than fifteen minutes' walk from the giant KeDeWe department store, now under new ownership. Going shopping there was going to be her excuse to Billy had she needed one.

She turned into Meinekestrasse and started walking down the street, looking for No. 10. It would be further down on the right-hand side. It was now 9am and people were starting their working day. Ahead, there seemed to have been some sort of incident as she could see that a crowd of people had gathered. As she got closer she was struck by their complete silence. There was little movement and no apparent focus around which they were gathering. Nor were there any police. It was most strange. They were hugging the right-hand side of the street and on the other side, people were walking past minding their own business, paying no attention to the silent crowd that Veronica estimated to be maybe one hundred and fifty people. She realised that they were actually blocking her access to No. 10 and that she would have to try to go through them. The vast majority of the crowd were men but there were also a few women. She went up to one of them.

'Excuse me, madam, what is going on here?'

The woman looked at her, part curious but part afraid. 'Who are you?' she replied.

'I'm a tourist,' she said, 'from England. I wondered what is happening here, that's all.'

The woman laughed and nudged the man next to her who had been facing the other way. 'Heinrich,' she said in a stage whisper, 'there's a tourist here. Come to see the sights of Berlin. We're a sight, aren't we?!' And then she added in an even louder whisper, 'Says she's from England!'

The man turned around. 'England,' he said as if trying out the word for the first time. 'England,' he said again slowly, looking at Veronica for the first time. 'How can we get to England?'

She looked at them both, confused. Then there was Sarah, standing by her side. 'Come with me, Fräulein,' she said formally and Veronica stifled what would have been an inappropriate grin of recognition, made her excuses to the couple and allowed Sarah to lead her through the crowd which parted for them, staring at her curiously.

'Do you have something for me?' Sarah threw back over her shoulder.

'Yes. I've some letters from Mr Locker. But Sarah, who are all these people? What are they doing here?'

'They're queuing,' she replied simply. 'They start from maybe 5:30 in the morning and queue until the end of the day when they move away before the police come.'

They were now directly outside No. 10 and Veronica could see that the people were indeed in a queue, the head of which disappeared through the single glass door set to the side of the building's large ground-floor window. Through that window she could see the queue continuing inside the building. Above the window on the front of the offices, large letters proclaimed this to be the offices of 'Palestine & Orient Lloyd'.

'Wait,' she stopped and pulled on Sarah's arm to make her turn and face her. 'Are all these people waiting to see you?' She didn't know why but the thought frightened her.

'In a way,' said Sarah, edging them around the long reception desk where a lot of people seemed to be talking at once, and led her through to the back and up a narrow flight of stairs. 'This building houses the offices of the Jewish Agency, my official employer, and also some other Jewish offices.' She stopped in front of a door which opened into a small room but which was mainly empty apart from a couch and a couple of chairs. On the couch sat a thin young man of medium height with tight black curls and wearing round frameless glasses. Unshaven, he appeared to Veronica the way she had always imagined Bolsheviks to look and she shuddered despite herself.

'Stefan Gruenzweig,' said Sarah, 'please may I introduce you to Veronica Beaumont, a visitor from Britain who has come out here to help you and others like you.' Veronica didn't know whether this pomposity was said for the man's benefit or for hers but Stefan quickly stood up and shook Veronica's hand.

'It is an honour to meet with you, Fräulein Beaumont. Miss Levtov has been telling me about you just before you arrived.' He seemed uneasy, perhaps because he was unused to speaking in English. After a moment of deep thought, he chose to add awkwardly, 'You might want to be knowing that I have been a graduate from the University of Berlin.'

Veronica smiled as if this information was just what she'd hoped to hear.

'Please, Veronica, sit down.' Sarah pointed to the couch so that she sat at the opposite end from Stefan whilst Sarah herself took one of the chairs. 'The crowds down there, as you might have gathered, are trying to get themselves and their families to Palestine. They hope to get some of the visas still allowed under the latest British regulations, and travel there legally. The Jewish Agency is the go-between, representing these people to the Mandatory Government and trying, without success I might add, to squeeze more visas out of it.' Sarah noticed the look of concentration on Stefan's face as he tried to follow this. She went to look out of the window at the street below and didn't turn around although she continued to speak, but now in German and believing that Veronica's was up to it. 'Until these restrictions came into force, people who wanted them were getting their visas to Palestine fairly smoothly. The difficulty is mainly the obstacles put up by the regime here, which has levied tax after tax, intent on impoverishing whoever tries to get out, and causing months of delays as they fill out the mountain of papers legalising their theft. But now, people can sign away every last thing of value, their last painting, their business, their house, all to get them passage out and they might still not have anywhere to go to.'

'Those poor people,' muttered Veronica in German, thinking of her aunt and uncle who weren't even joining the queue, their plans and expectations having for so long focused on England and help from her parents.

'Yes,' agreed Sarah. She remained facing out but smiled at the confirmation this gave her about Veronica's German. 'Stefan here,' she continued, 'just a little more than a week ago, was one of this throng of people. He was as desperate as some of these though at least he was not encumbered by family. I plucked him out of the queue and asked if he was willing to take some risk to get to Palestine more quickly and with more certainty. He has agreed. That's why he is here with me and not down there with the others.'

'I don't understand,' said Veronica.

'In England, we have a passport from a Mr Eisenthal who, to his great regret, mislaid it whilst visiting the country from Palestine. His physical description matches that of Mr Gruenzweig here. We just need to change the photograph.'

She nodded to Stefan, who removed a small leather wallet from his pocket, removed three black and white photographs of himself and held them out to Sarah. Sarah took them and balanced them on the palm of her hand for Veronica to see.

'I could take these back with me to England but it is risky. As an emissary from the Jewish Agency, they search me and make my exit as unpleasant and as bureaucratic as they possibly can. I would like you to take them back with you and hand them to me in England. When the passport is ready, with one of these photographs in it and an entry stamp into Germany on one of the later pages, you can bring it back to Stefan on your next trip and voilà, he is Mr Eisenthal leaving for England having visited some of his relatives in Berlin.'

Veronica took the photographs into her hand. This is what she had come out for, to help people like this man. Her cheeks were hot with pride and excitement. 'Yes of course,' she said. 'I will be honoured.'

Stefan Gruenzweig said nothing. But he took her hand, bent and kissed it, too overcome to speak.

NINETEEN

30 APRIL 1938

PARK LANE, LONDON

BILLY DIDN'T KNOW ABOUT VERONICA'S PARENTS' flat next to the Dorchester Hotel. Neither had he ever visited the large well-apportioned place she was renting in Bayswater. It was important to Veronica to keep it that way, which meant always spending the night with him at his much more basic accommodation in Portnall Road, W9, one of three recently converted flats in what had been a middle-class home when it had been built at the turn of the century. Portnall Road ran long and straight with almost continuous and uniform terraced housing filling both sides of the street. Veronica found it hard to tell Billy's place from any of the other houses and relied on the fact that, approaching from the nearby Harrow Road, one of the front rooms of a property next door but one had a broken window which was now boarded up. Billy's flat was on the top floor. It was small and dark and access was up a very steep and narrow staircase. So narrow in fact that almost every significant item of furniture had had to be hauled up from the street and through the third-floor window. Not that Billy had all that much furniture. Whilst in Berlin, Veronica had let slip that her rental contract was coming to an end and Billy had immediately insisted she move in with him. She could hardly refuse. At least his place had two toilets, she reasoned, even if one was outside in a brick outhouse in the garden.

It meant though that she now had to be much more circumspect and her parents' flat suddenly became, as she had suspected it would, a key asset in her life as an agent. If her parents were out of town, then that was where she and Sarah could meet. She liked it when Sarah was here, as she was now, but she also liked being alone in the flat, a place where she could be herself, in comfort, and drop all pretences. Sarah seemed to be tracking her thoughts.

'You should not come back to Great Russell Street. Not now that you've been on a mission. You have to keep all connection to any Jewish institutions invisible.'

Sarah was sitting on the couch in the living room with Veronica lying down on it, clasping her knees, her feet pointing towards the person she might now consider to be her friend. The heavy curtains were drawn, and the only light came from the tall standing-lamp in the corner, its deep red lampshade giving off a warm glow. If she narrowed her eyes till they were nearly closed, Veronica could easily imagine that they were somewhere exotic and not in her parents' place in central London. She studied the shadow of Sarah's profile projected onto the wall opposite and wondered what she was thinking. Was she looking at Veronica, or at least at *her* shadow?

'Your value to us is as a non-Jew,' Sarah was saying now. 'The less you associate with Jews the better. Maybe you can be persuaded to patch things up with your parents?'

Veronica stifled a sigh. She had been trying to tell herself that meeting with her aunt in Berlin and being known there as her niece from England was no different from meeting all those other Jews to whom she had delivered documents, but she knew that this wasn't true. If it had been, she would have told Sarah about Sonia, Manfred, and the people she had met through them, Richard and Renate Gutmann and their children Peter and Lise. She had no hope of getting them out without Sarah's help but she knew so little about the extent of Sarah's work that she didn't know when the time would be right.

'I've done as much as I can do in that regard, Sarah,' she said now, making sure she told no lies she would have trouble explaining at a later time. 'I have not broken off all contact with them. They are unaware of my anger. As time goes by and they don't see or hear from me, they might begin to make contact but I've left written notes to them here so they know I've been using this place and leaving it tidy for them, and no, I have not told them that you stay here sometimes! I have been very careful to remove all trace of you.'

'Ah good,' she said, 'can I have my comb back then please? Last time I was here, before our Berlin trip, I left it in the bathroom. Possibly it dropped down behind the cupboard. Did you see it?'

Veronica rose and started quickly towards the bathroom, thinking of Sarah's long dark tresses and muttering to herself, 'Mother will have kittens,' before she realised Sarah was laughing at her. She swung round, hands on hips and glared at her before she too saw the funny side of it and sat back down again.

'You think you're very funny, don't you?' she said. 'But, joking aside, we need to talk about me and what I am doing for you and your organisation – one whose name by the way, I even struggle to pronounce. Maybe you need to give me some basic Hebrew lessons. What's it called again?'

Sarah smiled. 'It's a secret organisation. I don't want you saying it all over the place. Better that you can't say it, dear, don't you think?'

Veronica looked closely at her. 'You really mean that, don't you?'

Sarah nodded and shrugged apologetically.

'But I am serious,' Veronica continued. 'Two days ago I was in Berlin and suddenly I was asked lots of questions to which I realised that I don't have answers. I don't need to understand the politics. I'm talking about the practical aspects of this thing we're doing here. If I am to do this job well, I should have practical answers. Don't you agree?'

Sarah shrugged. 'That all depends on what it is you want to know. But where I can tell you, I will.'

'Oh there is nothing cloak and dagger about my questions I can assure you, just practical things such as, what are the work prospects of a German immigrant arriving in Palestine? What if he is a lawyer who only speaks German and wants to live in a city with an orchestra and not on a collective farm?' She was all business now, concentrating hard. 'I just want to know what happens to German refugees who get into Palestine.'

Sarah raised an eyebrow, smiled but said nothing. Veronica grunted with annoyance.

'I will get it all out of you in the end, you know!'

'Yes, I want to see you try,' said Sarah, always glad to see Veronica show some backbone. She managed to keep a serious expression on her face. 'I am a professional and I know how to withstand even the most intense interrogation.'

Veronica nodded as if seriously absorbing this new information. She looked at Sarah.

'How about you teach me something that isn't secret?' She paused for a moment. 'Wait. I have just the thing.' She went to the bookcase behind them and took down a book, opened it and pulled out a folded piece of paper. She held it up to her. 'Do you remember when we first met? You accosted me in the street and handed me this to prove that you really had come from the Jewish Agency.' She opened it up. 'There is an irony here of course because you then went on to tell me that you didn't in fact work for the Agency. But anyway, here it is, on the formal letterhead: "*The Jewish Agency for Palestine*". And above it – I presume it says the same in Hebrew, is that not so?'

'Yes, that's right,' Sarah nodded, 'but it doesn't actually say the word "Palestine", as in Hebrew we call it "The Land of Israel", just like it says in the Bible.'

'That's interesting.' Veronica nodded. 'I just assumed that everyone called it Palestine.'

Sarah shook her head. 'It's okay when speaking English I suppose, but for us, Palestine is the name the Roman occupiers gave to our country when they took it from us by force. It's just not a name we use amongst ourselves.'

'Well, there you are. I've learnt something new – you see? Now teach me to say this in Hebrew.'

Sarah laughed but Veronica continued to hold out the piece of paper to her. 'Read it to me,' she insisted.

'I don't need to read it. It says *Ha-sochnut Ha-yehudit le-Eretz Yisrael*.'

'Oh dear,' said Veronica. 'That sounds impossible. I'll never be able to say that!'

'Oh no, Ronnie, you can't back out now. It'll be easy enough, there's just one guttural you need to worry about and you can practise that. The rest you could just memorise.'

'Blimey,' said Veronica, 'you called me Ronnie. Appreciation at last!'

'Oh,' replied Sarah, frowning, 'you don't like it that I should call you that?'

'No, no. It's actually fine. I had thought I didn't like it, but somehow it sounds good in your accent.'

'Good.' Sarah nodded uncertainly, pausing to gather her thoughts. 'Then maybe another time I'll start you on the alphabet. It will be fun actually, now you've put this idea into my head. In half an hour I can have you saying these four words like a true *sabra*.'

'A *sabra*?'

'There's another word for you. It means cactus and is the name we give to the new Jews – the ones born in their biblical homeland. They're prickly on the outside but sweet on the inside as I am trying to be.' She smiled that bright smile of hers that always made Veronica smile back. 'Not like me of course…' Sarah added, 'I was born in Germany, but I'm trying.'

'Trying which? To be sweet or to be prickly?'

Sarah laughed. 'Now you, my darling, are the very opposite, aren't you? You're sweet on the outside, but I'm starting to see that you are quite tough on the inside.'

Veronica laughed, flushing with pride and hoping that the latter, at least, was true.

SCHÖNEBERG, BERLIN, 20 MAY

'When was the last time you handed in any homework?' demanded Peter. Lise shrugged.

'Race you to the colonnades!' she shouted and darted off towards the park which lay on the other side of the busy Potsdamer Strasse.

'No, Lise!' Peter shouted after her. 'We aren't allowed in parks anymore. You know that!'

Lise showed no sign of having heard him and Peter slowed to walking pace. He didn't want to chase his little sister into the busy road. Lise ran straight across, barely checking, it seemed to him, to see whether the road was clear or not. Peter, fuming, had to wait for the next gap in traffic and by the time he entered the park, his sister was well hidden. With a sigh he began to search, zig-zagging his way through the double row of columns of what was known as the King's Colonnades. Peter didn't know which King but assumed it was Frederick the Great. Having made a lot of noise until that point, Peter suddenly stopped moving and listened. Sure enough he could hear his sister's excited breathing from not too far away and was able to work out which pillar she was hiding behind. As he crept up behind her he was in two minds, but in the end his duties as an older brother won out and instead of grabbing her he silently got hold of her school bag and moved away again without her realising. Peter sat down and started going through her books.

'It's worse than I thought, Lise,' he finally said out loud, 'you've not been doing any work at all!'

He laughed at her squeal of surprise and then as she spotted him going through her books she actually stamped her foot in frustration.

'Peter, how did you do that?' She sat down grumpily beside him on the ground but smiling despite herself at how clever he was. 'Peter, there's no point anymore is there? The teachers either don't mark our books or if they do they will always give a low mark. And now Father has told us he's going to move us to a Jewish school…' She shrugged.

'Imagine if we all took your attitude,' Peter said. 'We have to keep studying and not let them win. They want us to fail our exams, so we should work harder to prove them wrong.'

'None of my old friends talk to me anymore. I have to be friends with Rebecca Gerhardt simply because we are in the same position, but we never liked each other before and I don't really want to be her friend.'

'Lise, what has that got to do with anything? Do you think I don't suffer the same things that you do?'

She looked at him with a very solemn expression for some moments and Peter thought she was going to say how sorry she was and that she understood the importance of what he was saying.

'Go on,' he prompted gently.

'Mother and Father have been writing to that Englishwoman who came round a few weeks ago.'

Peter groaned, exasperated. 'Lise! Stop changing the subject!'

'I'm not changing the subject, Peter. I think she is going to get us all to England and maybe we won't even need to go to another school here. In England I will work much harder than here, I promise.'

'Lise,' said Peter, with a grin, 'you are so silly.' He held up one finger. 'Firstly, Father would never agree to go to England. You know that. For one thing, he doesn't think his English is good enough. And you – what's your English like? If you find this homework hard, there it'll be a lot worse.'

Lise started to protest but Peter held up a second finger and ploughed on, ignoring her.

'Second, Fräulein Beaumont isn't even trying to get us to England. She said when she visited that her interest is in getting Jews to Palestine. You'll find studying and speaking the language even harder in that hot oven of a place. There have to be a million places other than England or Palestine we could go to. I'd quite like to live in Holland.'

'Mother said the other day that they were going to find out whether Fräulein Beaumont could help. I don't mind living in a hot place.'

'Maybe her organisation can help us,' said Peter thoughtfully, 'but I doubt that she can.'

'But I really liked her, Peter,' she said wistfully. 'She had a nice laugh and she seemed so kind.' Peter rolled his eyes. 'And I know you liked her too, Peter,' she laughed, jumping to her feet and starting to sing: 'Peter loves the Englishwoman, Peter loves the Englishwoman!'

Peter stood up angrily. 'Stop being such a silly little girl! I am going home now. You had better behave or I'll report you to Mother and Father.'

He stuffed her books back into her bag, dropped the bag at her feet and walked off fast. He left the park and moved along the street. After a while he heard Lise shouting to him. 'Slow down, Peter, I'm sorry! I didn't mean it. Please, Peter.'

Peter was cross though. Of course the Englishwoman with the exotic name was very pretty. He said her name under his breath, *Veronica*. But his sister could be so annoying. She really didn't understand anything about boys and girls.

'Peter!' she called out again more urgently this time. And then she screamed.

Peter spun round to see that a policeman had seemingly come from nowhere and seized hold of Lise's hair with one hand whilst his other was pulling her school bag from her grasp.

The policeman was shouting. 'What do you have in your bag today, Jewish piglet? What shit are you carrying for you to wallow in?'

For a second or two, Peter did nothing, too shocked to react. How could the policeman even know they were Jewish? He began to move. He knew the fathers of some of his classmates were in the *Orpo* so maybe one day when they'd come to collect their children, the Jews had been pointed out to them. He thought he might even know which classmate was responsible, but he'd deal with that later. Right now, Peter was running as fast as he could, back along the pavement to his sister and, bending low, he rammed his head into the belly of the policeman, in the process cutting his own eyebrow on the round buckle of the policeman's double-breasted greatcoat. The two of them tumbled to the ground, with Peter trying to grab the man by the throat so that he could lever himself up to a sitting position. The policeman's chinstrap came away and his shako rolled off his head into the gutter.

'Run, Lise! Run for your life! Go and get help!'

The policeman was recovering from his initial surprise. Peter was well-built for a fifteen-year-old but he was no match for the far larger man who was now pushing one gloved hand into Peter's bloodied face whilst with the other he was reaching for his truncheon. Peter could see that Lise was still standing there gasping and crying.

'Peter, who should I ask for help from?' She was frantic, wanting to help him but not knowing how. She had a point, thought Peter.

'Doesn't matter! Forget about me. I'll be all right. Just run!'

Lise took off without looking back as the policeman started laying about Peter with his truncheon.

'You'll be all right, will you, Jewboy? We'll see about that.'

GOLDERS GREEN, LONDON, 20 MAY

Veronica pushed the door of the wig shop on Golders Green Road, bracing herself for the inevitable ringing of the bell that signalled her entrance. This shop was much larger than the one she had spotted in Hendon when this idea had first come to her. From behind the stack of boxes on the glass counter in which were displayed a myriad of combs and brushes, a short elderly lady emerged. She was thin and bony but smartly dressed. She had a head of impossibly thick black hair which was clearly a wig and, Veronica thought, was hardly a good advertisement for the products she sold. It was far too young a headpiece for such an elderly lady.

'Can I help you?' Even her voice was frail. She had a strong European accent.

'Yes, I'm looking for a wig that will change me from a blonde to a brunette and which,' she said pointedly, 'will not look like a wig.'

The woman picked out two examples from boxes filling the many shelves covering the wall behind her and stood watching whilst Veronica tried them on. One of them was in the same style as Veronica's own hair and looked quite all right, she thought, looking in the small mirror standing on the counter, but it was clearly a wig.

'How can I make it less obvious?' she asked the old lady, hoping the woman wouldn't take it as criticism.

'We do get some women who think that way,' she said cryptically. 'They let some of their hair come forward at the front, and comb it over. That removes this hard line you have across the front here.' She pointed at her own head, clearly aware then that she had done nothing herself to conceal the telling edge. 'But it's not approved behaviour.'

'What isn't?' asked Veronica.

'Showing your own hair of course,' said the woman. 'But in any case, for you it's not an option. Your blonde hair can't be combed over the dark. Really you should consider having the same colour as your natural hair.'

Veronica looked again in the mirror, changing the angle to see what looked most natural. It wasn't as if she'd wear it for more than a few minutes. The woman seemed a little odd to her. Why go to the trouble of getting a wig if it was going to look just like what you had before? She realised she probably should have just dyed her hair, had a photograph taken and then washed it out again. She'd thought this way would be less trouble but now she was starting to think that she was mistaken. She hadn't even asked Sarah yet about whether she would let her have one of the passports that from time to time passed through her hands. She had a feeling she would say no, which would make this entire idea a waste of time.

'I think I'll take this one,' she said. 'How much is it?'

'Two pounds, seven shillings and ninepence,' the woman said.

'What? No, really,' said Veronica, 'I was thinking it couldn't be more than one pound at most?!'

The old lady cackled. 'Maybe in your mother's day. Feel it though. This is quality and made to last.'

'It's very expensive. I've seen places in London where I think these sell for a fraction of this price.'

'Yes, but those are not serious and not for an orthodox Jewish woman. These are made to last for years.'

The two women looked at each other in mutual incomprehension.

'Where is your ring?' asked the woman suddenly.

'I beg your pardon?' replied Veronica, amazed at her effrontery.

'Your ring. You aren't wearing a ring.'

'No. I'm not married.'

The little woman looked at her in confusion and sat down on a nearby chair.

'You're not married?! Then why?' She pointed at the wig and from the wig to Veronica.

'I'm really sorry,' Veronica said. 'I seem to have upset you. I wonder if we could come to an agreement. I really only want a wig for some photographs. I'm an actress, you see.'

'Ah,' said the woman as if that explained everything. 'You're not Jewish?'

'Not really,' said Veronica. 'It's a long story, but—'

'You see,' continued the woman, 'these are for married Jewish women. They're not really wigs like you mean, these are *sheitels*.'

Veronica nodded with what she hoped might be the required level of solemn understanding.

'Tell me,' she said, 'could I rent it for an hour or two? If I were to give you ten shillings. Would that be reasonable, I wonder?'

'Are you a film star?' asked the old lady, excited now. 'I love seeing those films that can carry you into a very different world. Is that what you do?'

Veronica laughed. 'Yes, I suppose that is a good description of what I do.'

'Well then. Ten shillings it is, young lady. But you have your photographs taken at that studio across the road with Mr Michaels. He is a good friend. We can make the arrangements and you leave the *sheitel* with him when you leave. Is that all right?'

Veronica laughed. 'Yes, it is.'

Half an hour had passed by the time little Lise had run home to her parents to tell them about the attack by the policeman. Every time she had seen uniforms of any kind she had hidden and waited until they'd gone. A further twenty minutes passed by the time Major and Frau Gutmann arrived at the street where the attack had taken place.

'Are you quite certain that this is the spot?' asked Frau Gutmann, tearfully clutching Lise tightly to her in the backseat of the car.

'Maybe they've arrested him,' said the major quietly.

'Oh please God no,' murmured his wife, stroking Lise's hair. The girl was trembling all over and Renate Gutmann thought that she was probably in shock. Major Gutmann parked the car, reached over for his black leather Gladstone bag in which he kept his essential medical equipment and got out. He leant his head back inside.

'I am going to go and see if I can find Peter. Please don't leave the car, and keep the canopy up. Don't wind down any windows either. I know it is going to be hot but we mustn't draw attention to ourselves.'

Renate reached over and kissed him lightly on his cheek.

'Please be careful, Richard. We cannot survive without you.'

The simple truth of what his wife had just said shook him. They had to get out of Berlin. Maybe there were now just three of them, but if so he wasn't going to let his remaining child have to suffer this for the rest of her life. It was intolerable. He began to walk, softly calling 'Peter' every few yards.

The tall columns of the Heinrich-von-Kleist Park were now visible in front of him but separated by the wide Potsdamer Strasse. And it was then in a lull in the traffic, as he prepared to cross, that he heard Peter's voice coming from his side of the road.

'Father! Father. I am here.'

Peter was sitting upright against a garden wall, invisible to anyone turning from the main road into what seemed to be a small carriage path leading to a mews behind one of the large houses on that part of the street. Unless people happened to be going down there, they wouldn't notice him. Peter's eyelids were so swollen his eyes were nearly shut and Peter was struggling to see. His lips were split and his nose looked to be broken. His father nearly didn't recognise him.

Major Gutmann sank to his knees and ever so lightly stroked Peter's cheek with the back of his hand.

'My poor, poor boy. What have they done to you?'

Any thought Major Gutmann had of walking Peter back to their car ended as he felt all around his son's body for further damage. Two ribs were broken, maybe three. Peter also had fractures to the tibia in both of his legs – and his left arm seemed to have a complete break to the humerus which was going to take a long time to heal, assuming he could even get a hospital to treat him. It occurred to Richard Gutmann, and not for the first time, that Jews could no longer afford to suffer injury or even fall ill in the Third Reich.

He gently rolled Peter over, shutting out the terrible sounds of pain coming from his son, sounds that Richard felt as keenly as if he himself was being punched. Apart from heavy bruising, he didn't think there was any damage to any internal organs. Looking at the bruised and battered face, Richard found a piece of unbloodied skin on Peter's forehead and kissed him gently there for a few seconds. He couldn't remember the last time he had kissed Peter and resolved that this would change from now on.

'Peter,' he said softly, his lips still pressed to his son's head, 'I have to say I am confused. You are maybe one hundred metres from where Lise says you were attacked. You have three broken limbs. How did you get to be here? Did someone carry you?'

Peter tried to answer but the strength seemed to have left him. His father bent in closer.

'Say that again, Peter, please.'

'I said, I used my fourth limb.'

His father sat back astonished. Peter had dragged himself one hundred metres on one arm. He felt tears pricking his eyes and fought them back. In the dark, awful world of the trenches he had seen such feats of almost superhuman strength and courage and he realised that here, in Berlin, his own son was now in a comparable hell. Peter was trying to say something more. He leant in again.

'The *Orpo* man. He went off. I was worried he'd come back with more of them, or with an arrest vehicle to take me somewhere. I had to get away. I had to hide.'

His father nodded and smiled his encouragement.

'Peter, you are a brave, wonderful boy. I can't carry you back to our own motor car without causing you a lot of pain. Do you understand what I am saying to you?'

Peter nodded, wincing with the effort.

'I am going to get the motor and your mother and I will lift you onto the backseat. Lise is with us too. Everything is going to be all right. I promise.'

TWENTY

10 JULY 1938

49 PARK LANE, LONDON

V ERONICA LAY IN BED STRETCHING AND WATCHING the rays of the rising sun picking out the trees at the edge of Hyde Park. She couldn't remember when she had ever been happier. Life was exciting and her heart rate seemed to permanently be beating at 100 miles per hour. The only cloud on her horizon of course was Billy and how soiled that made her feel. Not for the first time, she wondered if it had been worth it. What in the end had she gained from making herself available to him? He had provided her with good cover to go back to Germany and without him as a partner she probably wouldn't have had the courage to go to Apsley House, and she may not even have been welcome there on her own. And then she wouldn't have met Diana Guinness. She also loved the excitement of playing a role, being someone who was so different from her real self. As she had admitted one day to Sarah, she also liked the way it allowed her to be someone else in the bedroom. Billy saw women as not much more than slabs of meat to be pulled this way and that until he was satiated.

Sometimes, and as long as it didn't continue outside of the bedroom into real life, she found that she quite liked that too and, she conceded to herself, the very fact that she really did hate Billy might be what made it so good.

Sarah walked into the room, two steaming mugs of coffee on a tray.

Veronica smiled at her happily. She had forgotten that she'd asked Sarah to stay over in one of the two guest rooms. The night before, they had arranged to meet in the evening but Veronica hadn't been able to get away from Billy until it was far too late to talk.

'What are you so happy about?' asked Sarah with a smile.

'I was just thinking of the numbers of people I have now brought certificates to and how much more I can still help. On my first trip, you gave me the names of ten people. Last month I brought over twenty certificates. Next time, if you give me double that again, I will have made it possible for seventy people to get away from the Nazis and on to Palestine.'

Sarah carefully put the cups down on the side table. 'You did really well last month. I'm proud of you. I never thought you'd show such few nerves.'

Veronica beamed. 'Have I ever told you just how disgusting a creature Billy Watson is?' she asked Sarah.

'Many times. Many times.'

'Well, this time he's really taken the biscuit.'

'What's he done this time, painted lightning bolts onto letterboxes?'

'No. It's a little bit more than that. He wants to whore me out.'

Sarah put down the tray and sat on the bed looking at Veronica closely. She was about to say something but seemed to change her mind, instead reaching for one of the cups of coffee. She blew gently into the mug and took a tentative sip, looking over at Veronica sitting propped up against her pillows.

'Isn't that what I'm doing to you already?' she remarked finally.

That was unexpected. It took a few moments for Veronica to take it in.

'How dare you say that to me! Is that what you think? That I'm nothing but a prostitute?' She was angry and Sarah quickly reached to steady the other cup as Veronica threw back the covers.

'You misunderstand me, Veronica,' she said gently. 'I was not criticising you, but me. If it were not for me you would not be doing any of this. I have not only corrupted you but I have put you in danger.' Veronica got out of bed and put on a robe, tying a sash around her waist. She looked at Sarah for a while, her anger slowly receding.

'Listen to me, Sarah. You have not pushed me into anything, on the contrary you always said I was crazy to have sought out the British Union. It was my decision and it is something I have to live with. It is not always easy, but it will be much harder if I have to worry about your feelings of guilt. Nobody, except my parents, has ever told me what to do.' She moved to sit next to her on the edge of the bed, and seeing Sarah struggling to hold both hot cups, took her own cup from her. 'And the days when I listen to them have long gone,' she added darkly. The silence continued and she took it as a good sign that Sarah was not protesting the truth of her words. 'Anyway,' she said gaily, signalling that it was time to move on, 'I want to tell you about Billy's idea.'

Sarah noticed that Veronica's robe was gaping and she quickly looked away.

'Go on then,' she said.

'We were walking home last night after another pub round with his repulsive friends and he suddenly held me tight against him, kissed my neck and asked what I felt about having sex with others whilst he and I were still an item. Well, as you can imagine, all sorts of thoughts rushed into my head at that point. What people may have said to Billy about me and that he might have believed them. They are really a very nasty lot in the BU. I thought that I was about to get a beating, or worse. I pulled back a little to look at his expression. He was smiling. "You naughty thing!" he said. "I was sure you were going to yell and scream and say no!" I told him I was just too shocked to speak but he just laughed. He then said that I should look at it as an assignment in order to "help the Party".'

Veronica stopped suddenly, realising that perhaps this had, again, come uncomfortably close to what she was already doing for their own 'cause', but Sarah said nothing and she continued. 'I told him he was being ridiculous and that the Party didn't need me to do anything of the sort and that his suggestion was just another of his perverted fantasies.'

'Does he have anyone in particular in mind for this fantasy?'

'Yes. As a matter of fact, he does. A Member of Parliament, no less. Have you heard of Hilary Masterson?'

Sarah gave a start when she heard the name, putting her mug back down on the tray and standing.

'Yes, I have heard of him. Why does Billy want you to sleep with him?'

'According to Billy, this MP has been a thorn in the side of a number of people who want closer relations with Germany. He is also a personal family friend of the Chamberlains. Billy's idea is that I seduce this man, take him to my room in a hotel and then, at a pre-arranged signal, someone will burst in, take photos and ruin his career.'

Sarah nodded thoughtfully. 'What was your answer?'

Veronica laughed. 'What do you think I answered? I told him what he could do with his twisted little ideas and that I wasn't going to ever do such an awful thing. I mean to say, this MP, if he is with Churchill in standing up to Hitler, nothing would get me to harm him in any way. Of course Billy doesn't know that bit.' She laughed again and swung her legs over and lay back on the bed, propping her head up once more against the pillows. After a while, she turned to look at Sarah.

'You're very quiet. What are you thinking?'

'Shhh,' said Sarah and she went and stood by the window looking out for a few moments before turning back. Frowning.

'Do you remember I was telling you about the conference on refugees that President Roosevelt called last month, to see what could be done about helping the Jews?'

'Yes, of course. In Switzerland.' Veronica nodded. 'Yes, you said, "finally someone is going to help us," and how the United States' involvement would push for real action at last.'

'Exactly. Except that it hasn't turned out that way.'

It was Veronica's turn to frown. The newspapers had not given that much detail but from what she had read, the nations gathered at Evian had appealed to Germany to make it easier for Jews to leave, and committees had been set up to discuss how and where to settle the refugees.

'Roosevelt,' Sarah continued, 'had intended that Palestine be the main place where the refugees could be settled but, from the very start, Britain made it clear that Palestine would not be considered.'

'But what about the other countries taking part? Aren't they each going to take in some Jews?'

'Look, they are still discussing it but the United States has already made clear that it will not increase its already existing quotas, and if the United States doesn't budge then who else will?'

Veronica shook her head. 'I think you are too pessimistic. How many countries are at this conference, thirty? I refuse to believe that they have all travelled across the world to do nothing. That would be giving Hitler permission to persecute Germany's Jews. Nobody gains from that.'

'Well,' nodded Sarah, 'the Americans have made one small concession. Ever since they put quotas on immigration fifteen years ago, they put up so many obstacles that, in practice, these were never filled. Now they have promised to remove the bureaucracy and will expect to fill these quotas from now on.'

'Well, there you are, that's something, isn't it?'

'In Palestine,' Sarah continued doggedly, 'we have quite a good intelligence network, you know. We hear things and we have official observers at Evian who report back information that does not appear in the newspapers.' She picked up her mug, and took another sip. It was still a bit hot but drinkable now. 'In Parliament over here, the British Government is going to try to counter any softening in the US position by doing the exact opposite.'

Sarah paused, watching Veronica's look of disbelief. In some small way it validated her own fury at what was going on.

'It is incredible, isn't it? The British Government is worried that just the filling of already existing American quotas might lead to a surge of people passing through Britain who may, or may not, continue on as planned to New York. So it is going to set up a committee that will just happen to "independently" recommend tighter British restrictions on immigration.'

Veronica went to her wardrobe and began pulling out some clothes. 'Go on,' she said. 'What about this committee and why are we talking about it?'

'The government hopes that the committee will say that

there is no room to house large numbers of refugees and that there is a risk of violence should this happen. They will then use these findings to reduce official pressure on Germany to let people out. But it's not certain that the government will get its way. A lot of influential people are uncomfortable with putting obstacles in the way of already desperate people. In the end it really depends on who chairs that committee and how strong his views are in imposing his will.'

Veronica had chosen her dress and now let her robe drop to the ground. She was wearing only tap pants. Sarah paused, momentarily losing her train of thought. Veronica, oblivious, scooped up her dress, holding it in front of her, modesty restored.

'And?'

'We were hopeful that Francis Bendit would chair this given his previous experience with the Children's Inter-Aid Committee and his clear sympathy with people in need. He had already been listed to be on this new advisory committee. Unfortunately, however, he will only be deputy chair. The chairman of the committee is in fact going to be Hilary Masterson.'

'Oh, I see,' said Veronica, no longer smiling. Still holding the dress up with one hand, she reached for her brassière with the other. 'What are you trying to say then?'

Sarah shrugged. 'I am just giving you some facts about this man. You should know that what qualifies him to chair such a committee is his interest in this issue generally. Hilary Masterson was instrumental in stopping various Christian organisations in this country from getting anywhere with proposals to take in large numbers of Jews from Germany. He doesn't like the Nazis but nor does he want to help Jews.' She dragged her eyes away from Veronica and looked at her watch. 'Much as I hate to say it, I have to go now.'

'So you're just going to leave me with this information and then what?' She laughed bitterly. 'Now you really are whoring me out! You expect me to sleep with Hilary Masterson as well as with Billy Watson?! Well, I won't do it. Anyway, what difference will it make? You think I can change British government policy now?'

Sarah paused by the front door. 'I will never ask you to sleep with anyone. I do know that we are facing unprecedented dangers where there are no good outcomes.' She blew her a kiss and left.

HOUSE OF COMMONS, LONDON, 13 JULY 1938

She wondered if this is what silly young girls felt like in Hollywood, waiting anxiously outside the opening night of a film, hoping to see Clark Gable or Cary Grant and to perhaps exchange some words with them. She was glad to see that there were no young girls standing alongside her outside the members' entrance to the House of Commons. She was able to pretend that she just happened to be standing there, perhaps a secretary or the wife of an MP. The policeman on duty at least did not question her though she noticed him gawping at her when he thought she wasn't looking. Perhaps he thought she was a streetwalker.

At last he emerged, standing close by as he hailed a taxi. 'Mr Masterson!' she cried out. 'Might I have a quick word with you? I so admire your stand on Germany.'

She realised that the cabbies had been waiting for the end of the session in the House and were circling to take MPs. To her dismay, a taxi arrived immediately. Hilary smiled at her as he put his hand on the door of the taxi. 'Thank you. I would love to talk, especially to someone as pretty as you, but I'm afraid I really am a busy man.' He ducked into the taxi and was about to close the door, only to find, to his annoyance, that Veronica was now standing in the way.

'Madam, please,' he said, his voice hard with annoyance, 'stand aside, this instant.'

'I... I'm the daughter of Sir Roland Beaumont and I really must speak with you.'

Hilary paused, looked her up and down quickly and seemed to come to a decision. 'Hop in then.' He leant forward and shouted the address of his club to the cabbie.

Veronica got into the seat next to him and slammed the door closed behind her. The taxi pulled away. Hilary regarded her suspiciously. 'Are you really Sir Roland's daughter?'

Veronica stuck out her hand. 'I most certainly am. My name is Veronica Beaumont.'

He shook her hand. 'Better hurry up with whatever you have to say. They don't allow women at the club, you know, and I really am in a hurry. If you are his daughter then you will know that Sir Roland and I do not see eye to eye on many things and especially not on Germany. If he wants to talk to me, he can do so himself rather than throw his daughter at me.'

Veronica laughed, startling him in her freshness and her clear lack of deference to either his age or his position. 'I do not share my father's views and I certainly do not come here at his request. I really am an admirer of yours and I happened to be passing just now, having visited my father who is also in Parliament tonight, when I caught sight of you. It really is as simple as that.' Veronica was amazing herself at just how fluently the lies came out of her mouth.

'And are you willing to risk embarrassing your father by being seen with me?'

Veronica shrugged. 'I want to help you. I would want to help Mr Churchill too, except that he frightens me.'

It was Hilary's turn to laugh. 'Yes, I can imagine.' He looked at her appraisingly once more. 'I do hope I haven't taken you too far out of your way?'

'No, not at all. I had no plans and Pall Mall is hardly out of the way.'

The taxi was already stopping outside Hilary's club. Hilary opened the door to let Veronica out, got out himself and walked forward to pay the driver.

'I don't really have a meeting at the club,' he said. 'I just didn't want to be buttonholed on the pavement by a stranger.' He offered her his arm. 'Shall we walk a little? Sir Roland Beaumont's daughter's views on appeasing Germany? I'm intrigued.'

'But there was more, right?' Billy was sitting on the bed in his shirt and trousers, his braces stretched taut over his belly. He had kicked off his shoes and Veronica noticed he seemed to have bits of white fluff on his socks. Idly she wondered how they got there. She didn't think it could be from the carpet, nor from the inside of his shoes. Perhaps it was a man thing. She certainly never suffered from sock or stocking 'dandruff'.

'More?' asked Veronica disingenuously. 'Whatever do you mean?'

'Don't play jokes with me, girl. Is he interested? Did he try to grope you?'

'No! He was the perfect gentleman. He was interested in me and my views and I asked him if I could be of any use to him. He bought me dinner. He asked me if I would like to help type some of his correspondence. Apparently he gets sacks full of post supporting his anti-German views.'

'I bet he does. That might be useful. Noting the addresses of people who are against us.'

'Don't be stupid, Billy.' She allowed a note of exasperation to enter her voice. 'There are hundreds of such letters. From ordinary people. How could I possibly note down all their names and addresses? And what would you do with them? Surely the important ones to know will be the ones you already know.'

Billy grunted. 'Well, it's a start. You need to get him into a hotel room as soon as possible.' He looked at her, taking in her sensible skirt, flat shoes and thick stockings. 'No wonder he didn't get excited with you looking like that. You have to be sexy. Draw him in.'

'He's asking me to come to his constituency office during working hours. I can hardly go there in evening dress.'

'No, but you can wear higher heels and show a bit more ankle. Let your hair down a little. Like you usually wear it. In fact I've never seen you look so frumpy. The idea, remember, is to seduce him.'

'Darling, I know what you want me to do and I know exactly what needs to be done. But we don't want to move so quickly that he gets suspicious. You're going to have to leave it to my intuition.'

TWENTY-ONE

22 JULY 1938

HOUSES OF PARLIAMENT, LONDON

H ILARY LIKED TO WATCH VERONICA SITTING AT her desk typing up his letters. He loved how she wore her hair tied tightly back when she was typing but left ringlets of hair coming down over her temples falling to below her ears. He had always thought that women who wore glasses ruined their looks, but in Veronica's case, wearing her 'typing goggles' as she called them, only enhanced her beauty for him. Sometimes, she would pause, frown thoughtfully, and he'd watch spellbound as her eyes narrowed slightly.

Over the past ten days since she'd begun working for him, he calculated that he must have spent several hours staring at her, and many, many more thinking about her. Even whilst he was preparing speeches on the pace of German rearmament, he was thinking of ways to make her laugh or at least to tell her something interesting so that she would look in his direction. She seemed to be unaware of his turmoil, completely impervious to his efforts. She was polite, engaging, thoughtful and, when she did laugh, she lit up the room.

If she did fall for him, as so many other women had in the past, he promised to God he would treat her with respect. He thought that this would be so even if her father were not such an important figure in society.

For days he had promised himself that he would not be the first to break. But he had slowly come to the realisation that she wasn't playing any game. She didn't secretly find him attractive. He would have to move things along. He couldn't anyway remain silent any longer.

'What is it you want from me, Veronica? You clearly aren't interested in a dalliance.' He tried to sound sophisticated, a man of power and experience. Joking with her. To his own ears though, he thought he sounded old, pathetic, desperate even. He was sure that now, with one withering rejoinder, she would cut him down to size and walk out of his life forever. But better now he reasoned, than in a few weeks' time when he'd be completely besotted.

Veronica looked up at him from over the rim of her glasses. 'Hilary, you're old enough to be my father. What a thing to say! And anyway, what about Billy? Wouldn't he have something to say about it?' She smiled at him, not shocked, not disgusted, not even disappointed. Just her usual happy, unaffected self. Maybe it was all a game to her after all. Never had he been rejected so charmingly.

'Doesn't Billy already wonder where you are?' he persevered. 'Yet you still spend all this time with me.'

'Am I too dedicated, would you like me to spend less time here?'

'No. Don't do that, Veronica, whatever you do, do not stop coming to me.' Now, surely he was being pathetic. He didn't care. 'Is it just the politics for you then?' he asked plaintively.

She sat back in her chair and regarded him, holding a finger at the corner of her mouth as if thinking this through.

'Well, let me see. I do of course admire you for your politics and the way you see the Nazis for what they are. I admit, that at the beginning, coming here was partly to annoy my father, but not anymore. I enjoy your company. You are clever, charming.' She stood up with a warm smile. 'Can't we just be friends?'

'A lady who is so interested in politics is rare indeed,' laughed Hilary, taking her hand and shaking it. He was careful not to ruin the atmosphere by holding on to it for too long. 'I suppose it makes sense that you got this awareness from your father as he had no sons.' He went back to his own desk and made as if to sit down. 'I don't know that I've ever been close to a woman before who only wanted me for my conversation.' And then, at that moment, he couldn't help himself. 'I could easily fall in love with you, you know.'

'Really?'

'Yes really. But I'm not going to embarrass you, don't worry. At least not to your face. You want to talk politics? Then go ahead. I can't of course divulge confidential information but within reason I can answer you if there is anything you wish to discuss.'

He was panicking a little now, talking quickly to move the conversation away from his declaration of love, his declaration of vulnerability. Yet Veronica accepted his invitation to talk politics, and of course she would, he reasoned, if it meant steering him away from any awkwardness.

'What do you know about the Evian Conference?' she asked.

Hilary had expected questions about House of Commons protocol, perhaps the origins of Black Rod. Or she might have asked him about his constituency work. This surprised him.

'My goodness me, Veronica,' he smiled, 'you really do keep up with the very latest developments don't you?!' He paused, thinking of the best way to answer without making it too hard for her to follow. 'Well, Evian's all much ado about nothing, isn't it? Roosevelt felt that there was a need for some hand-wringing to be done over the plight of the Jews. So everyone dutifully wrung their hands at the conference. And now that it is over, we can all go back to the way we were before. No harm done and we all feel a bit better.'

'Do you feel better for it?'

'What do you mean? Why should I feel anything about it?'

'I mean you as a prominent British politician confronted with this terrible outbreak of antisemitism in Europe. Where should we stand morally on this issue? I was reading the newspapers a few weeks ago in the library and there was this quote from, I think, a speech that Adolf Hitler made before the conference had even started. I was struck by it so I wrote it down.' She pulled open the top drawer of her desk and pulled out a piece of paper with her handwriting on it. 'Let me read it to you:

> "*I can only hope and expect that the other world, which has such deep sympathy for these criminals, will at least be generous enough to convert this sympathy into practical aid. We, on our part, are ready to put all these criminals at the disposal of these countries, for all I care, even on luxury ships.*"

'What a horrible man to call them criminals,' said Hilary. 'We can expect nothing from that jumped-up little corporal.'

'But he is being proved right in a way, isn't he? I mean to say, if no countries do take practical steps to help the refugees, then aren't we giving him permission to do what he wants to them?'

Hilary shrugged. 'I don't think he cares whether he has our permission or not. I am not a heartless bastard, you know. I may not want an influx of Jews into merrie olde England, but I would help them. I'd let them into their national home in Palestine. But the Prime Minister won't have it.' He shrugged again. 'I even reminded him that we do have some sort of obligation there after all.'

'I'm confused. What obligation?'

'I tell you what, let's go and have some tea and I'll tell you a story.'

They went out of his tiny office, down the narrow carpeted corridors of the House of Commons and out onto the terrace where, unlike the bar, women were allowed if they were guests of MPs.

'You know of course that I, just like everybody else my age, fought in the war.'

Veronica nodded. 'Yes of course.'

'I was posted to the Western front in early 1915. By then the memories of fighting in open countryside had long faded. It was bitter trench warfare where we cowered in our dugouts as they shelled us, and then we shelled them. Shells are an expensive business of course and we would save up vast stocks of high explosive prior to the next "big push". We'd shell them for hours. Both sides protected their trenches with row upon row of barbed wire, dozens of yards deep. Cutting through it when facing concentrated machine-gun fire was suicide. So the idea was that our artillery barrages would not only pummel their trenches, but would blow bloody great holes in their wire. Big enough for our men to storm through and take their trenches.'

Hilary paused to sip his tea. 'I hope I am not boring you.'

'Not at all. I have no clue why we are talking about this but it is fascinating to have such a first-hand account. Father never talks about it at all. Do please go on.'

'Time after time, the big attacks on the German lines failed. When we got to the wire there were never enough gaps and those that were there were rarely wide enough. On those occasions when we got through to their trenches we found them to be largely unscathed. One theory we had was that the German dugouts were so much better built than ours that they stood up to our shellfire where ours would have collapsed. But after a while, the rumours began to take hold that the main problem was our shells – that they often failed to explode altogether, resulting in thousands of our men caught in the wire and left there to die.'

'But that was surely just a rumour,' said Veronica. 'Why should our shells be any worse than those of the Germans? And if they were worse, and it was as widespread as you seem to be saying, then we couldn't have won and beaten them back. We broke through their lines, they didn't break through ours.'

'That is exactly what I thought at the time. It was only once I had entered parliament that I was able to check and find out the real facts. We had been using more explosive than we could produce and so production lines had taken short-cuts in quality and quantity of explosive to be able to make enough shells to meet government targets. We were firing a high proportion of duds and weak shells. Then this scientist chap turns up, a Jew, Weizmann, and he works out a new way of making explosive. I forget the details exactly but suffice it to say that it turned things around for us and the government was extremely grateful. To this day, Lloyd George says that his decision to award the Jews their national home in Palestine was by way of gratitude and thanks to this Weizmann, who it turns out, was the head of the Zionist movement when he wasn't being a scientist.'

Veronica clapped her hands together. 'Hilary, that is an amazing story! It sounds like something Kipling would have written. Although then the hero would be an Englishman of course. Can it be true? Did Lloyd George feel he had an obligation towards the scientist?'

'I'm assured it is true. But of course there would be other factors. Lloyd George is a wily old bugger. (Excuse me for that.) He would have made his calculations on what was best for British interests. At the time a lot of people believed that the Bolsheviks in Russia were led by the Jews and that all Jews thought the same as each other and were all plotting together and that if you gave them their own place they'd be so grateful they'd keep Russia in the war fighting with us against the Kaiser.'

'And do all Jews plot together?' Veronica tried to ask the question seriously but grinned broadly at the end. Hilary took it in good part.

'Of course!' he laughed. 'Except for the fact that the Bolsheviks hate the Zionists and vice versa. The Bolsheviks want the working class to break down borders and have a united, drab grey world where nobody has anything of any value. The Zionists are socialists not communists. They want a workers' utopia as far as I can make out. But they want it in one place and that has to be to where God led them when they ran away from slavery in Egypt.' He laughed and shook his head. 'God-fearing socialists. Whatever next?'

'But you say the Prime Minister isn't convinced?'

Hilary shrugged again. 'Not the PM, not the Colonial Office and not the Foreign Office. They're worried that Mussolini will woo the Arabs and they'll rise up in revolt and kick us out of the entire region.' Hilary laughed. 'Bloody silly nonsense. The Arabs might not like foreigners but they know they're a damn sight better off with us than with fascist Italy. Everywhere Mussolini goes he commits murder and mayhem. The Arabs have no better friend than us British. The PM thinks that, as the Jews will always be on our side against the Nazis, we should put all of our efforts in the region into appeasing the Arabs. Appeasement is the doctrine by which the greatest Empire the world has ever seen demonstrates its loss of nerve.'

Veronica was silent for a moment or two, mulling it over and oblivious to Hilary, who was staring at her, looking at her every movement and flitting facial expression. It was, she thought, clearly complicated with a lot of factors, but in the end it seemed to serve only to mask the underlying immediate problem which was that there were real people in Germany who needed to get out of there fast. She sighed.

'So then what? Can't we just let those poor German and Austrian Jews into here?'

'Over my dead body! They'll fill the streets with beggary. We'll have dirty penniless Jews with their long beards and filthy clothes everywhere. People won't stand for it and Mosley's Blackshirts will have a field day.'

Veronica looked up, startled by this aggressive response, her cheeks burning.

'You're a fine one, aren't you, Hilary?' Veronica could hear the tightness in her voice. She couldn't help herself. 'One moment you want the Jews to have their home but the next you show such callousness. Yet you must know more than most what's going on over there in Germany and Austria.'

Hilary was taken aback by the turn the conversation had taken, but he had had years of parliamentary debate and he realised that he just needed to be patient with her. She would learn from him and respect him for his wisdom.

'Look, Veronica, it's all about British interests. It has to come down to that in the end. I want them to go to Palestine partly because it would be good for Palestine but mainly because it would mean there would be even less chance of those people coming here.'

Veronica stood up and got hold of her coat. 'It's late and I need to go home.'

Hilary stood up too. 'I am sorry. Have I worn you out, old thing?'

'Not at all. I just need to go home.'

'Have I upset you?'

It was Veronica's turn to shrug. She began to walk towards the door.

'Will you come here again tomorrow?'

She shrugged. 'Perhaps. If you'd like me to.'

'Yes. Yes. I would like you to. Always. I've never met anyone like you.'

Veronica laughed. 'You are just like all men. They find a woman fascinating and interesting – if the women are prepared to listen to what the man has to say!'

Hilary said nothing and Veronica suddenly saw how sad and bereft he was at her words. Without really planning to, she went over to him, put her hand lightly on his shoulder, stood on tip toe and kissed him lightly just to the side of his lips. She pulled away, keeping her hand on his shoulder, looking at his surprised, needy face.

'That's all there is, I'm afraid, Hilary,' she whispered with a smile and then added, 'at least until you learn how to be a nicer man.' She removed her hand and was out the door whilst he was still touching with his finger the spot where her lips had been.

TWENTY-TWO

23 JULY 1938

PORTNALL ROAD, LONDON

A SSURED THAT BILLY WAS STILL SNORING IN THE bedroom, Veronica removed the tube of Patentex gel, reached into the box and carefully extracted the tightly rolled-up note.

She had found it in her bag when she got home from Parliament earlier that day and had not known what to do with it. It was bad timing that her parents were using their Park Lane flat for the next few weeks.

Dear Veronica,

I feel like a schoolboy writing this note to you, too scared to give it to you in person and stuffing it into your bag as I will do if I can summon up even that much courage.

I am in an unfamiliar position. Usually women come chasing after me, but you seem immune to my charms. You laugh and joke and generally dazzle me but you never actually show much of an interest. And yet, I do sometimes detect affection, which gives me hope that I can petition you to consider me as a serious proposition.

If you haven't already torn this up then please read my analysis of our situation as I have thought about this over the weeks you have been working with me. I think the issue is that you are a deeply innocent young woman who would not look at a married man. I can only admire you for your moral standing.

'If you only knew the half of it, Hilary,' murmured Veronica. She thought of Billy snoring away in the bedroom and how simple it would now be to enact his plan, lure Hilary into a hotel and notify Billy to have his photographer at the ready. That would be the end of Hilary's career, the collapse of the anti-appeasement camp and the rise to fame of Billy Watson and his fascist gang. She continued to read.

It is true, I am married. I can hardly pretend otherwise. But she has tolerated my various misdemeanours over the years. There have been several, I admit. But, Veronica, you must know that what I feel for you is something so utterly different and new to me. I believe I have fallen in love with you. How else to explain my tongue-tied state whenever you say something witty. And so often you do!

Intelligent and engaging women are hard enough to find, and combined with your beauty?

I am not suggesting that you be my mistress. I would not insult you with such an offer. But if you will consider me, I will divorce my wife. You would not be ostracised by society, indeed you'd be the wife of an MP and who knows, one day soon, you'd be the wife of a cabinet minister. With you at my side I think the sky would be the limit.

If, when you next see me you say nothing to me, I will understand and feel foolish but happy that at least you know how much I adore you. But, if you can at least say you'll give all this some thought, well then you would make me the happiest man alive.

Hilary

'Well, I never,' said Veronica softly, carefully refolding the note and putting it back into the box and then sliding the Patentex tube back inside. Of course she wasn't going to use this to help Billy, but could she use it to help save lives? With Mrs Guinness' offer of companionship and a visit to Berlin and now this, she needed to talk to Sarah urgently.

'Veronica, do you know what this means?' Sarah practically shouted down the telephone line the next morning.

'Yes! I think I do. Perhaps H can be persuaded now to help us get people into Great Britain, or at least to drop his opposition.'

'I agree. But more immediately even than that you need to take Mrs Guinness up on her offer and bring forward our plans for the Berlin trip. Having her as your companion on such a trip presents a real opportunity. You must accept her invitation.'

'But that's in just a few days' time!'

'I have been getting together what you would need anyway, most of it is here and ready. I need to meet you. Are you telephoning from Masterson's office?'

Two hours later, they met in St James's Park next to the Guards Memorial on Horse Guards Road. They embraced quickly, looking around to see if they were being observed. Putting the large obelisk between them and the road, they hauled themselves up to sit on the stone base of the memorial.

'Will you now concede that I did the right thing joining the BU?' Veronica was smiling but she really wanted an answer. 'Without Billy, I'd not have known about Hilary.'

Sarah was silent for a moment. Slowly she nodded her head.

'Possibly. All right, yes. I did know about Masterson but would never have suggested such a course of action. If I'm being really honest, I don't think it would have occurred to me.'

Sarah shrugged. Veronica wasn't sure if that was a shrug of regret or that she was signalling to Veronica that sometimes you have to put morality first. She thought of asking her but doubted she'd get the truth.

Sarah handed Veronica a sheepskin pouch and began sorting through the documentation that she had brought with her, every so often handing Veronica batches of certificates to put into it.

'What made him write such a letter?' asked Sarah.

'I didn't go in one day to help with the typing. I already knew from you of course about his views concerning Jewish refugees but it was another thing to hear him say them to my face. I wasn't even that cross, but I just didn't feel like going in and helping him. So I took some time off – I think he must have worried I wasn't coming back.'

'And I assume that the contents are not the sort of thing that he'd want discovered?'

'God no! In a way I am flattered by the trust he puts in me. He has given me the power to destroy him.'

'I'd like to see the letter but it will have to wait until you get back from Berlin.' She handed Veronica another pair of certificates and leant back against the obelisk. 'I suppose that this would be the time that Billy's plan for the blackmail of Hilary Masterson MP would succeed. If you were the person Billy thinks you to be.'

'Yes, it would. Hilary is a fool though to be so easily led astray. It won't be long before he slips up and I won't be there to protect him.'

'Yes, I was thinking the same. We need to have him help us before he has to resign. He quickly needs to be persuaded to talk to his friend the Prime Minister to stop appeasing Herr Hitler and to open the gates of Palestine.'

She slipped the pouch with the last of the certificates into her bag, wondering why this time they were in a sealed pouch. 'And if I can achieve that, you'll be impressed, won't you, Sarah?'

Sarah laughed. 'Yes, Ronnie. If you can avert a war and give the refugees a home, I'll be impressed.' Her smile retreated to be replaced by determination. 'But on a more practical note, I want you to take this.'

From inside her document case she withdrew a large velvet drawstring bag. Loosening the string she showed her its contents: a small revolver with a pearl white handle. Veronica gasped and recoiled from it, shaking her head.

'Please, Veronica. If you were going on your own I could not see a way to get you this protection but, travelling with that pin-up Nazi, Diana Mitford or Mrs Guinness or whatever she calls herself, you're not going to be searched. You need this.'

'Sarah, I can't take it. I simply cannot.'

'But you've fired guns before. You've said so.'

'Yes, but that was clay pigeon shooting! It's not the same thing. I could never shoot at a human being.'

'That depends on your situation. If your life was in danger then you would. If they discover the documents you are carrying they would kill you anyway, so having a derringer pistol isn't going to make things any worse for you.'

Sarah laid the bag down gently but it still made a solid

clunking sound on the white stone and Veronica shuddered. Sarah put her hands on Veronica's shoulders and waited until Veronica's focus was once again on her.

'Please do this for me, Veronica. Last time I was there to keep an eye on you. Now you will be alone. You may never have to use it but at least you will have the choice. Can I show you how it works?'

Sarah let go of her shoulders and Veronica immediately looked away, saying nothing. Taking this as acquiescence, Sarah picked up the bag and held it open to Veronica so that she could see the pistol.

'This is the Remington 95 derringer. It has two barrels each holding a .41 cartridge. I will give you four such cartridges. Two spare and two to be loaded into the barrels.'

Veronica looked round at that.

'You want me to walk around with a loaded pistol?!'

'It has to be loaded because, if you ever needed to use it, you probably won't have time to load it. But don't worry, it won't be cocked. Now see here.' She put the bag into her hand. 'Feel the weight of it. Put your hand inside. Yes. Do you see this lever between the handle and the trigger? Pull the lever down – do it.' Sarah glanced into the bag, looking at Veronica's fingers. 'Yes, there – it releases the barrel part of the pistol to pivot away from the handle-grip allowing you to reload. You then just bring the barrels up and it snaps back into the handle grip.'

'But, Sarah, I have never fired anything like this.'

'It's really simple. You cock the hammer, point it and press lightly on the trigger. It's not hugely accurate so you'd need to be close to whoever it is you're shooting at. And remember that it doesn't fire both barrels at once. You press the trigger once, it fires one bullet. Press again and it fires the second. You get two chances.'

Taking the bag back from her, Sarah reached inside to load a cartridge into each barrel. Veronica looked into the bag again so that Sarah could show her the safety catch. Sarah then wrapped the small gun in a white cloth. 'I've wiped off the surplus oil so this cloth should soak up any remainder and prevent it getting onto the documents which of course are also protected by the sheepskin pouch I have given you. I wanted to put the pistol into a different pouch but it would make it too difficult to access in an emergency.' She tied the drawstring tightly, closing off the gun wrapped in the protective cloth, and handed it to her.

Veronica took a deep breath and reached for her bag. Carefully she took out her everyday contents and released the innocuous-looking clasp that opened up the false bottom. The wrapped documents and pistol fitted, just, creating a bulge at the bottom of the inside of the bag but still not noticeable if you didn't know it was there.

She shrugged. 'I'll take it but I can't conceive of any circumstances where I would use it. I'd have to be practically dead already.'

'Agreed.' Sarah smiled. 'In any other situation don't use it.'

TWENTY-THREE

24 JULY 1938

LONDON, ENGLAND

VERONICA WONDERED ABOUT MEN. SHE HAD practically thrown herself at Billy Watson and from the start he'd felt that he could push her around as if she was his property. She was distant with Hilary Masterson and this powerful man was now besotted with her. Thank goodness for Sarah, she thought, who at least seemed to value her for the person she actually was.

'You're being silly, Hilary,' she teased now. 'You don't love me. You may think you do, but you really don't.'

'I do, Veronica. Please don't talk to me as if I am a child. I knew there was something special about you from the moment I first let you share my taxi. And in the weeks and months that have passed since, I've...'

'You've...? What, Hilary?' Veronica laughed. 'Don't be shy!'

'My God, do you think this is funny?'

'Well, it is maybe a little incy wincy bit, don't you think? I am easily young enough to be your daughter.'

Now it was Hilary's turn to laugh though it came across as rather bitter.

'Well, first of all you aren't my daughter. And secondly, I've slept with women who have been even younger than you are.'

Veronica looked at him coolly. 'Am I supposed to be impressed by that? And what next? Will you tell me that your long-suffering wife doesn't understand you?'

'She doesn't.'

'I'm not surprised. I don't understand you either. You are a man with a great political future. People respect you. You are a personal friend of the Prime Minister. Yet you would risk scandal. What if one of your affairs became public? You would be ruined. You'd lose everything.'

'Be that as it may be, I would leave my wife for you,' Hilary muttered helplessly.

'And what about the fact that I am already with someone else?'

Hilary said nothing. She had from the very start let him know that she had 'her beau'. She pressed on.

'And what about your position alongside Mr Churchill? You stand for those of us who hate the way our country is cosying up to barbaric dictators. You are a man of principle. You would risk all that and leave appeasement the victor just because you want to sleep with me.'

Hilary was shocked to hear Veronica of all people speak in that way. He had heard prostitutes using vulgar language of course. But it was very different hearing Veronica saying it in her King's English. She affected him so strongly; every word she used seemed calculated to excite.

Veronica's anger, though, was real enough. His infatuation with her could scupper all her hopes and plans. She had to get him to focus on what was important. Until now, she had found it hard to bring up the subject of Jewish refugees when she was not supposed to know about the committee meetings he was chairing on the subject. Nor of his hostility to any schemes that would let large numbers of Jews into Britain. But things were only getting worse since the German takeover of Austria. Hitler was emboldened as never before and for the Jews of these two countries life was fast becoming unbearable. She had to take some risks.

'Come along,' she said, 'we've both had a very long day in this stuffy old place. Let's go for a walk up to Trafalgar Square and find somewhere we can have dinner.'

He looked up hopefully.

'No, Hilary. Not that sort of dinner. I want to talk to you about Nazis.'

In the end, they'd not found anywhere nice enough by Hilary's exacting standards and they'd walked through and out of the square and ended up walking along Piccadilly, drawn inexorably to the Ritz. Throughout their long leisurely stroll, Veronica had been careful to keep the conversation away from the too personal and her body a safe distance from his. She talked of her year in Germany as a young girl away from home for the first time. Hilary didn't seem to mind.

'What about you, Hilary,' she asked, 'have you ever been abroad?'

He shook his head. 'Apart from one short trip to America a few years back. I'm not a big one for travelling abroad. Of course I spent a lot of time in Belgium, three years in fact. Didn't enjoy it much. But then, Wipers between 1915 and 1917 was deadly for the Englishman abroad.'

Veronica nodded wisely, deciding to play along with the deadpan delivery. 'Yes, I can see that one bad holiday experience like that might make you think twice about your next holiday. So no plans to travel and see more of the world, or at least the Empire?'

'No. Unless you count Belfast as Empire. I have a cousin there so I might conceivably go there one day.' He looked at her and smiled. 'I *am* planning to go to the Isle of Wight. Lovely place and doesn't need a passport!'

Interesting. She made sure to laugh at that. He seemed to genuinely be enjoying her company. Which made her feel a little better disposed towards him. That, and the fact that she was feeling more like a successful agent than she had ever done until now. Sarah had said that one never knew how even the most innocent of conversations might yield useful intelligence. *Such a wise woman, Sarah,* she thought as they walked into the Ritz, a daring plan whizzing around her head.

The waiter showed them to their table, one of two which were demonstrating new chairs to see if they met with customer approval.

'What do you think of these?' asked Hilary with a smile as he pulled out a chair for her to sit on. Veronica remained standing though, gingerly pressing down on the back of the chair, expecting it to fall over.

'It's got no back legs. I'm not sitting on one of these! Can't we go to another table?'

'It's perfectly all right,' said Hilary. 'I've seen one of these before, somehow they're quite sturdy. It's one of those modern designs. Steel frame, you see.' To prove the point he sat down heavily on the chair and it didn't give way.

Quite astonishing, thought Veronica, finally persuaded.

It was a busy evening and the hotel's restaurant was full of couples laughing, drinking and smoking. There was a buzz of serious conversation all around, sometimes pierced by raucous laughter. Tastefully, in the background, the piano player, resplendent in his tuxedo, was playing Scott Joplin on the Steinway in the corner.

Hilary pulled out two cigars from his jacket pocket and offered one to Veronica. She shook her head and Hilary shrugged, returned one to his pocket 'for later', and began the ritual of puffing and lighting it. Veronica watched, fascinated. He winked at her before drawing his first puff and sitting back with satisfaction.

Keeping it chomped between his lips at the corner of his mouth, he said, 'It's a real Havana. One of the most beautiful and perfect cigars in the world.' He held it in his hand between his index and middle finger, his thumb supporting the bottom of it, flicking it with his nail. 'Winston gave these to me,' he said. 'I think he finds me fascinating.'

'Oh? And why is that?' Veronica asked with genuine interest.

'He doesn't seem able to get used to the idea that I am so close to the Prime Minister but at the same time I bitterly oppose Mr Chamberlain's politics.' Hilary slouched down in his seat, pushed his face forward and down so that his chin was nearly touching his chest, then took a long drag on his cigar. As he exhaled a large, dense cloud of smoke, he intoned in a very passable lisping imitation of Winston, 'My dear boy, you are Lord Stanley at the Battle of Bosworth. You command great forces, and you have the power to strike the decisive blow. But will you wield it for your King and the House of York, your master who has made you what you are? Or will you walk with destiny and support the younger outsider, the upstart, the man of the future, Henry Tudor?'

Veronica clapped her hand and laughed out loud. 'Hilary! That was perfect, you have him to a tee! How long have you been practising?!'

Still in character, he replied, 'I? Why, I seek only to serve, my darling. Only to serve.'

'You silly man.' Veronica laughed again. They sat in silence for a while, neither of them looking at the menu. The maître d' was too well trained and deferential to ever hurry them. He stood far away against one wall, effortlessly taking in the situation at every table: whose glass needed filling up, who was ready for the next course and who did not want to be disturbed at all. He knew that Hilary Masterson MP would definitely not wish to be disturbed.

'I meant what I wrote, you know,' he said now, in his own voice again, 'about leaving my wife for you.'

'Hilary,' she scolded, pleased that she could feel so very much in control. 'Why would you think that I would want to marry you? Oh, you can be very entertaining. But are you a good person?'

'Are you about to lecture me about my past affairs?'

Veronica waved her hand lazily in the air, dismissing the notion. 'I meant about refugees.'

'Now look here, Veronica, we've been through all this before. That's a load of tommy rot and you know it. It isn't I who brought about their terrible situation, it's that Hitler chappie.'

'But you and the rest of the government choose not to alleviate their suffering by letting them into Palestine.'

'Look here, Veronica, the Jews have waited what, nearly two thousand years for their homeland? They can wait a little longer. Is it any more urgent now than it has been before?'

Thanks to Sarah, Veronica knew that what was going on now in Europe might soon be comparable to the Chmielnicki massacres in the Ukraine three hundred years earlier when an incredible 100,000 Jews had been killed. But she wouldn't be expected to know any of this.

'And England. What about their coming to England?' she asked instead.

Hilary looked at her, a puzzled expression on his face.

'Why the Jews, Veronica? Why do you care so much about these pathetic nomads from central and eastern Europe? If we were to let them in here, Mosley would have a field day. I would be responsible for an increase in the number of fascists coming out of the woodwork. And besides,' he added, 'we could never be sure of their loyalty. These Jews are Germans after all, our sworn enemy just twenty years ago. Many of them will have fought for the Kaiser.'

'Hilary, my ancestors were Huguenots. They came here as refugees. Would you say that we don't have a right to be here?'

'No, of course not. They have been here for centuries and are British now through and through.'

'And what about you, Hilary? No foreigners ever in your family tree?'

'I genuinely don't think so. I'm sure my lot came over with the Normans!'

'And I am sure the Anglo-Saxons resented their coming over here and taking their jobs as well as their women and, I've no doubt, their lives.'

'That was an invasion. That's a very different thing.'

'I think, Hilary, that the point is that after a while, everyone becomes British and accepted. These Jews will too if you let them.'

'The problem is having to suffer their foreign ways until that happens. They won't be able to speak much, if any, English. Those who can will take jobs away from British people. Why should the people of Britain have to pay?'

She was suddenly minded just how much like the BU this Conservative MP was sounding. And he was supposed to be from the moderate wing of the party!

'Veronica, you are clearly highly intelligent for a woman. And as I wrote to you, I admire you for that, I really do. But do we have to talk about this anymore? I have to deal with this during the working day and it's now well into the evening. Can we instead talk about my letter to you?'

'What about their children then?' she persisted. 'If we take them in when they are young enough, then we can make little Englishmen of them from the very start, can't we? What was it the Jesuits always say? "Give me a child until he is seven and I will give you the man." Let's take in the young ones, the teenagers even, and educate them here. They can't take anyone's jobs and by the time they come onto the job market they'll be speaking good English.'

'That's what that damnable Refugee Council has been talking to me about.'

Veronica stood, went around to his side of the table. Masterson quickly got to his feet too. Veronica flung her arms around him, kissing him on the cheek.

'Hilary! So you are with the angels after all! You've been arguing with me this way and that and all the time you've been working on bringing over young Jewish children?' She kissed his other cheek and then held him tight against her. Hilary let her, though he was careful to do no more than put his hands lightly on her waist, almost as if they were dancing in a ballroom. As Veronica had hoped, her approach, both tactical and physical, put him on the defensive.

'Well, it's a wonderful idea, of course,' he replied, wanting her approval but at the same time not wishing to be later caught out in a lie, 'but what parents will send their children away unaccompanied to a foreign country, without any clear idea what will happen to them? That is simply unnatural. It won't happen. These things are complicated,' he grunted. Then he pulled his head back so he could look at her. 'That this is even being discussed is also highly confidential. You must not breathe a word of what I just said to anyone.'

Everyone who needs to know already knows, Hilary, she thought, but nodded dutifully. 'Of course,' she said. But as she said the words, she was still grappling with what to say. She was getting tired of all the lies and half-truths. She needed to tell Hilary who she was and then she would finally tell Sarah too. She needed to tell them both and see if either of them could help Sonia come home. She thought of Peter and Lise. The fact was, time was running out for all the Jews of Berlin; anyone who'd been there could see it plainly. Their livelihoods were taken from them and they were all living on dwindling savings. Things were going to get a lot worse before they ever got better.

'Hilary,' she said, 'I will keep your confidence, but you must ensure that those discussions bear fruit.' She took a deep breath. 'I also need to tell you something in confidence. Please sit down.'

Hilary sat down and signalled to the maître d'. The latter nodded and within seconds a waiter was standing to attention by their table. But Veronica shook her head.

'The last thing on my mind now is food.'

'My dear, we can't occupy a table at the Ritz and not eat anything at all. That's just not on, I'm afraid.' He smiled, ostentatiously playing with the myriad columns of cutlery set for his meal.

'Could we just have a pot of tea?'

Hilary smiled and left the cutlery alone. He looked up at the waiter apologetically. 'Just a pot of tea, this time, I'm afraid.'

The waiter gave a slight bow of his head. 'That will be right along, sir.' He turned to Veronica and nodded again. 'Madam,' he said and turned smartly on his heel as if he was on parade outside the Palace across the park. Hilary turned back to her.

'Hilary,' she said, fixing him with a stare. 'I told you that I am part Huguenot. That is true. I am also part-Jewish,' she said. Hilary frowned, trying to work out what game she was playing now. 'My mother is Jewish, you see. And that makes me Jewish. As I am told, it follows through the mother.'

There was a long silence. Then Hilary said, 'I don't think I have ever met your mother. I can't picture her.'

'I can assure you, Hilary, she doesn't comply with your vision of a typical Jewess.'

'That's not what I meant at all, Veronica.'

'Isn't it?' She shrugged. 'It doesn't matter. I am telling you this family secret for a reason. You need to know that I have family in Germany. I want your help in getting them out.'

Hilary looked around him as if frightened about who might be listening. He put a nervous finger inside of his collar to try to alleviate the heat that he was suddenly feeling.

'I can hardly expect my colleagues to take me seriously if I try to make exceptions for people I know personally. Policy is policy.'

'I know that, Hilary. I am not asking you to help just my family. I am asking you to help change the policy.'

He laughed. 'Veronica, you cannot know how politics works. Your father probably never saw the need to explain it to you and you've never had to worry your head about it. Take my word for it. Policy is never changed on the hoof as it were, and never by one person.'

Veronica suddenly realised she had had enough of his patronising attitude and was tired of the sparring, the denials. She stood up and, resting her hands on the table, leant towards him.

'Hilary. I know you see me as a woman just about capable of understanding your local constituency matters. Too stupid to understand the wider issues. Well, I know a lot more than you think. I know, for example, that you have been working to tighten the immigration rules following the conference at Evian. All you have to do is stop opposing the plans of others who are coming before the Refugee Council. Let their arguments prevail. Will you do that for me? That is all I ask.'

Hilary looked at her, standing there back straight, cheeks flushed, radiant in her anger. How could she possibly be so well-informed? Yet as a woman, she was too emotional. Unable to understand the wider issues.

'Will you, Hilary? For me, at least, if not for yourself?'

Wordlessly he nodded.

Veronica was embarrassed at her outburst and that she had revealed her identity when that had not been her original intention. She needed to get away. She took hold of her gloves and her handbag, just as the waiter arrived with the teapot.

'Not for me, I'm afraid, thank you. But I am sure my companion here will have two cups.'

She turned to Hilary.

'Thank you,' she said.

'Well, that was two days ago,' she told Sarah from the phone box outside Tottenham Court Road station, 'and H's undying love evaporated in an instant as if it had never been. I turned up the next day at his rooms, ready to work, and he hadn't come in. There was an unsealed envelope on his desk addressed to me. The note inside stated that he had been called away on urgent business, asked that I kindly leave the key to the office on his desk and added that I need not come back into work the next day or ever after that. He thanked

me for the hard work I put in and wished me luck for the
future.'

She paused and listened for Sarah's reply. There was a
lot of noise coming down the telephone line and she wasn't
certain for a moment that they still had a line.

'Are you still there?'

'Yes, V, I am here.'

'I'm afraid that I've rather messed things up, haven't I?'

'Look, it was always a long shot. It's your other news that
I am trying to absorb. You're telling me that you are a club
member?'

Sarah had got Veronica to memorise alternative words to
be used as a code if they ever needed to talk on the phone
which Veronica thought was silly and playing at spying. But
Sarah had been very certain that, as telephone operators
could listen in to any calls which they connected they most
certainly did, and you would never know on to whom they
passed the information. She thought it was probably mostly
to the British Police, but not if the receptionist happened
to sympathise with the fascists or with the communists. So
Veronica had agreed to swap 'Berlin' for any British city
beginning with a B, Hilary became Howard or 'H'. 'Club',
meanwhile, was the club to which Sarah and the people she
was trying to rescue belonged – the Jews.

'Yes. But it changes nothing,' Veronica answered her.
'Next month I go to Brighton again. I don't see that this
changes anything.'

'But what about Howard? You have told a person who
hates the club and all it stands for, and he has no obligations
towards you. This certainly wouldn't be good for you and
perhaps not for the rest of us either. I can't let you go there. If
those people in charge of Brighton found out? It doesn't bear
thinking about.'

Veronica couldn't help but giggle at the image of Brighton's local councillors mobilising to attack people like her because of the club they belonged to, but she then had the sobering thought that, just a few years ago, people would have scoffed at the idea that Berliners would suddenly turn on their Jews.

'I have thought about this,' she said. 'Howard can't tell people about me without revealing his infatuation and risking that I might publish his letter. He doesn't like the people from Brighton almost as much as he doesn't like the club. Who is he going to tell?'

TWENTY-FOUR

25 JULY 1938

HENDON, LONDON

VERONICA REPLACED THE RECEIVER AND PUSHED the button to retrieve her unused change, at the same time carefully looking through the glass panels of the phone box to see if she was being watched. She didn't really have any confidence that she would spot anyone looking at her. There were so many people crowding the pavement that she had to wait for a gap just to push open the door. She entered the station and stepped onto the escalator, taking the opportunity to retrieve and light a cigarette from the handbag on her arm and making sure to close the clasp tightly. The tube was even more crowded than the street but she had not wanted to leave this task to later in the day, when rush hour had ended. It would then have been too late for a house call and she would have had to postpone to the next day, which would have been too stressful with her flight to Berlin set for the very next day after that. Two men sitting next to each other immediately offered her their seats and she smiled and rather selfishly accepted the offer of the much larger man so that when she sat she wouldn't be squashed up against him. It was stiflingly hot in the gloomy, smoke-filled carriage and she closed her eyes and tried to sleep.

At Hendon again, her third trip there in the last four months, she once more walked up Queen's Road. She had never doubted that she would remember the house that Sarah had entered four months earlier but now that she had arrived, she was not so sure anymore.

To be more certain, she crossed the road at the same point she had done that day in March and checked her memory against the view that she now had of the houses further up the road. She remembered the pillar box, and was now easily able to identify the right house. She nodded to herself and continued up the road. It wasn't the steepest of hills but in the hot weather she was beginning to get breathless. When she was opposite the entrance she paused, tightened her bun under her hat, mopped her forehead and then her neck with her handkerchief and re-crossed the road. She walked up the front path and knocked sharply twice on the door.

'Coming,' said a voice from inside.

Veronica tried to imagine what the man would look like on the other side. All Sarah had said was that he was a shady character who was a skilled forger of documents. The only people Veronica knew who played fast and loose with the law were the ruffians from the BU, so she was expecting a Billy lookalike. When the door opened on its chain to reveal a timid, short, scraggy, balding man with a short white beard, Veronica rapidly readjusted her opinion and this harmless-looking man, kindly even, instantly replaced forever the imagined thug. Veronica realised that she had been tense all the way there worrying about what she was getting into. And suddenly the tension had disappeared. Billy would never, ever open his door with a chain. Relieved, she smiled at the thought and covered it by greeting the man looking nervously at his unexpected visitor.

'I am so sorry to disturb you,' she said, holding out her hand in greeting. 'I've been sent by the Jewish Agency.'

The man looked at her but said nothing. She hesitated, put her arm down and started again.

'You know Sarah Levtov. She said to tell you that she sent me. You remember Sarah?'

'I know her, yes, miss. But I am sure many people do. What is it exactly...' He trailed off, waiting for her to say more.

'Ah yes, may I come in?' She made a point of looking back and up and down the street nervously. It was a gesture made for effect. If she'd really been checking, she might have noticed Billy's BU mate Nick standing in the distance on the other side of the road just a few yards closer than where she had herself observed Sarah the last time she had been here. 'I don't particularly want my presence noticed,' she said, smiling reassuringly, 'and I don't think you would either.'

'Are you the Bill?' he asked suddenly, looking at her carefully.

'The Bill?' she asked, confused, worried he was talking about Billy. The man sighed.

'The Old Bill? Coppers. Bobbies!'

'Do you mean the police?'

He nodded, sighing again.

'No, of course not!' said Veronica. 'I am the person who took your Hebrew University certificates to Berlin,' she said. That, finally, did the trick.

'Oh are you now? Right, then you'd better get yourself indoors.' He closed the door for a moment, unhooked the chain and opened it again, wider this time. 'Come in. Come in then if you're coming in.'

Veronica walked into a dimly lit passage, along the length of which was a long wooden handrail that reached all the way back to the kitchen at the end. The wallpaper was old, a dark red flowered pattern that only contributed to the gloom.

'Go on through to the front room,' he said, pointing the way. He smiled, showing her his crooked teeth. Crooked with one, golden, exception. 'How long have you known Miss Levtov? What exactly is her special relationship with yourself?'

'I should imagine,' replied Veronica, annoyed with this man probing so shamelessly. 'That her relationship with "myself" is quite different from hers with you.' She couldn't resist imitating his bad grammar, at the same time berating herself for doing so.

'Ah,' said the man. He seemed somewhat deflated by that and Veronica felt even more ashamed. 'This is Naomi, my wife,' he continued as they entered into the room. Naomi was, Veronica realised, the reason for the long handrail in the passage. She watched as the elderly woman, stick in one hand, moved painfully and slowly towards the handrail that Veronica could now see was along the wall of the small front room too.

'I am sorry, I can't shake your hand, dear,' said Naomi. 'Can you?' She gestured to her husband, who was already pushing the wheelchair towards her and helping her into it. 'I'll be in the kitchen,' she said, wheeling herself out of the room. Her husband closed the door behind her.

'Please, miss, sit down, we don't charge for sitting.' Veronica sat down in one of the chintz-covered armchairs and the man sat in the other one. 'I'm sorry, what *is* your name? You can give me any name you like of course. I just don't want to be calling you "miss" the whole time.'

'Hilary, then,' she said with a smile. 'Let's go with Hilary.'

'Harry,' he replied, 'Harry Wolf.' Now he put out his hand and she shook it. 'No point in giving you a false name when you've come to me own front door!' His smile faded a little as he added, 'Everyone knows me around here, I'm a famous artist, I am.'

'I've come about this,' she said, removing the blue British passport from her handbag and putting it onto the round wooden table that stood between the two armchairs.

Harry took hold of it and flicked through the pages. He smiled at first. 'Ah yes. Hilary. Yes, I see.' But then his face became serious again and he stole a few sideways glances at her until he shut the passport and put it back onto the table. 'This is most unusual,' he said finally. 'Miss Levtov didn't send you to me, did she.' It wasn't a question.

'No,' she admitted, feeling her confidence beginning to drain away somewhat.

He pointed at the passport. 'I know of this man. I don't see him as someone who would willingly volunteer his passport to help foreigners get into this country. This could be very dangerous for me.'

'It's not for refugees,' Veronica admitted, 'it's for me. It's insurance for me in case I need it.'

'I see,' said Harry. He picked up the passport once more and looked again through the pages. 'You're tall for a woman,' he said, 'I noticed that as soon as I saw you. So I think that you'll get away with the height here. But it says you were born in 1896 and that you have brown hair. Normally we match people to the age on the passport. I'd have to doctor the letters here…' He trailed off, waiting for her reaction.

'I think I can solve one of the problems,' she said. 'Here is the passport photograph I think you could use of me.' She handed him one of those she had collected from Golders

Green a week earlier. 'Of course, if I ever needed to use this, I wouldn't actually wear a wig, that was just for the picture. If it came to it, I would dye my hair.'

'For me to change the date,' Harry Wolf continued, scratching his head. '…It can be done. The easiest date change I could make would be to 1906. That would make you 32 years old. You'd have to look older than you are, but for women this is easier than for men I think.' He nodded. 'Yes, you dye your hair, change your makeup. But it will take time and it will cost money.'

Veronica nodded. 'How much?'

'Fifty pounds.'

She exhaled softly. She had thought it would be something like that but it would make a real dent in her annual allowance and she was determined not to ask her father for any more.

'Yes, I can manage that,' she said.

'And half up front,' said Harry.

'All right,' agreed Veronica, 'I wouldn't want to carry that all in one go anyway.'

'Good. I'll need a few days to make the stamp for the photograph. It has to match exactly, you see, to the part of the stamp that will remain on the passport once his photograph has been removed. And then the change to the date of birth. We are going to have to hope this ink,' he tapped the date with his index finger, 'will respond to the chemicals I have.' He thought for a moment. 'I'll need a week. You can pick it up then.'

'Oh,' Veronica said. 'I was rather hoping I could leave it with you for an hour or two and take it back with me today.'

Harry stared at her, thinking she was pulling his leg. She was not. He reminded himself that she was just a courier, albeit apparently one with funds. He tutted and shook his head. 'Look, Miss, er, Hilary. This is skilled work. It has to be good enough to pass inspection. Work like that needs to be done properly. My own personal freedom depends on it even if you are willing to take risks with yours.'

Veronica looked at him. She hadn't given this enough thought, she realised. She was confident that Hilary wouldn't be needing his passport and he might not even notice it was missing for months until just before it was due to expire. It would not be particularly difficult to collect it after she got back from Berlin a couple of weeks from now. Whilst she was thinking this through, Harry Wolf got up and went over to a small cabinet next to the door. It had one drawer and beneath that a small lockable door with the key in the lock. He knelt down, turned the key, opened the door and reached inside. When he stood up again he was holding what seemed to be some sheets of greaseproof paper.

'If you need the passport today then I can only suggest the following. I will, whilst you wait, make a tracing of the stamps across the photograph. You had best leave that, at least, with me here today. With the tracing I will be able to prepare a partial stamp and put it onto your photograph so that all I will need to do is swap the photos around. I will also take a tracing of the date of birth. I can practise the size and handwriting for the date. Then all I'll need is a day. You then bring me the passport when you can. '

Veronica stood up. 'No. I'm so sorry. It was silly of me to think you could do this so quickly and I want you to have as much time as you need. I'll come back in two or three weeks. That should be enough time in view of what you just told me. I trust this is acceptable?'

Harry gave a quick jerk of his head to indicate that it was and tore off a corner of the greaseproof paper and wrote on it. 'Here is my phone number. Call ahead. Give me as much notice as you can.'

She nodded gratefully. Perhaps a little too gratefully for Harry, who had been watching her closely.

'And it will cost you another three guineas,' he said. 'And I would like that up front now as a deposit.'

'Why?' asked Veronica indignantly.

Harry shrugged. 'There is extra risk for me in having this evidence in my house for longer than necessary. And especially the added danger of working with a passport of a public personage. There could be greater police interest.'

Veronica hesitated. She felt he was exploiting her but she was in too deep now. She nodded. 'All right.' They shook hands.

'Let me show you out,' he said. As he reached to open the front door, he turned. 'I've always wanted to go to America. What was it like?'

'I've never been to America,' she replied, 'what a funny thing to say!'

'But you have been to America. It says so on your passport, *Hilary*.' He held the door open for her. As she stepped into the street, bewildered, he added, 'You'd better examine the stamps and work out a story. It's usually details like that what gets people caught.'

TWENTY-FIVE

28 JULY 1938

TEMPELHOF AERODROME, BERLIN

'M RS GUINNESS, YOU ARE OUTRAGEOUS!' EXCLAIMED
Veronica, laughing out loud as they descended the
steps from the aircraft. 'This is practically a guard of honour!'

Two shiny black open-topped Mercedes were drawn
up alongside them, the red, black and white Nazi pennants
fluttering above each front headlamp. Holding open the
passenger doors, and now standing to attention, were SS men
in their smart black uniforms wearing peaked caps.

Diana tried, but failed, to maintain a stern uncaring
expression. 'Yes, I know it is a bit over the top. I cabled the
Führer saying it really wasn't necessary but he is such a darling
and once his mind is set on something you really can't change
it.'

Veronica wanted not to be impressed by the obvious
name-dropping but in Diana's case it was so clearly not an
exaggeration. She could feel her mouth gaping, just the effect
that Diana had hoped for. Diana giggled with the excitement
of it all and took Veronica's hand as they got into the first car.

'It is all rather fun, I grant you. Now you can't go around calling me Mrs Guinness for the next few days. I insist you call me Diana.'

With her free hand she waved at the three men who had descended the steps behind them and who were now getting into the second car. Diana had introduced them to Veronica on the flight but she couldn't remember anything about them other than that one of them, called Freddie, was her lawyer and the others were business associates whose names she didn't catch at all.

'This is very much a business trip, I'm afraid, darling,' Diana had said to her as if in apology. 'It's all rather hush-hush so I'm afraid we shan't talk about it, but when I am not in meetings you and I will try to have some fun.'

Veronica had remained silent, thinking that this might, with luck, just be like the last trip with Billy when she was left very much to her own devices. Diana, mistaking her silence for consternation, gripped her hand tightly. 'Don't worry, V. I know some really important people. I'll make sure you get to meet some of them. But I must warn you, some of them use their powers to indulge in various perversions.' She winked as if expecting Veronica to understand, which somehow made what she was saying all the more alarming.

'I'm sorry, I'm not sure how to take that warning. Should I be afraid?'

'Oh no, not afraid, darling! They would never go too far with an English Lady – unless you wanted them to of course – but you should be cautious. Dr Goebbels, for example. He has a place on Bogensee, a lake about twenty-five miles north of here, to which he takes his latest conquests. His wife tolerates it of course.' She looked serious for a moment, adding darkly, 'That's a woman's lot in life, isn't it – whether wife or mistress – to put up with things?' She caught Veronica's expression, reflecting concern at her tone, and brightened again. 'Anyway, Dr Goebbels is having the place completely overhauled. It's going to be grand, as you would expect. So if he starts talking about the place, do *not* express any interest in building, architecture, design or development – none of that! He'll invite you to come with him to supervise the building work and then he'll just jump on top of you. The last lady who accepted wasn't seen in Berlin again for a week.' She laughed mirthlessly at the memory. 'She has never been quite the same since, come to that. But what did she expect? Men lust after women and men with power will always indulge themselves.'

Veronica smiled weakly, imagining what Billy would be like if he had that sort of power. But then her attention was drawn to the progress of their bags from the aeroplane's hold into the boot of their car. Her hands had suddenly become clammy. Fortunately Diana, who was still holding her hand, was wearing silk gloves; otherwise she would have been certain to notice. If her bags were emptied, the one with the false bottom would be noticed immediately if only due to its weight. At that moment she wished she hadn't been persuaded to take the bloody pistol. If that was found, these same smiling, deferential SS men would frogmarch her into one of their notorious camps. She thought of Manfred. Would she, like him, emerge from months in a camp prematurely aged and broken in spirit? She grasped Diana's hand back tightly and whispered, 'Thank you,' which seemed the most appropriate response to give. Diana smiled and gripped her back.

The cars swept out of the airfield's perimeter and through the raised barrier, the tyres sending out sprays of gravel from beneath the heavy mud-flaps. The helmeted guards at the gate had snapped to attention, an almost pavlovian response to the sight of the cars' fluttering pennants. Diana tried to return the stiff-armed Hitler salutes but her hand got stuck in one of the bags she had on her lap and by the time she'd freed herself it was too late – which had the two women giggling like schoolgirls, Veronica able to relax at last.

'Have you ever stayed at the Kaiserhof Hotel before?' asked Diana. 'It's the only place to stay when in Berlin.'

Veronica shook her head but her mind was already dwelling on the tasks she had set herself for the ten days of this trip to Berlin. If she succeeded, there would be thirty more 'students' admitted to Palestine, few, if any, of whom would actually turn up for the new university term in Jerusalem.

She checked her watch. There was still time to visit Peter Gutmann today. Aunt Sonia's letter had been guarded in tone, saying only that he had been badly hurt in a fight. Veronica had immediately sent a card to the Gutmann family and the reply received just a week ago said that he was still recovering in hospital and giving her the address and visiting hours. Veronica felt it was ominous that neither letter contained any detail. If they were too afraid to write what had happened then it must have been something to do with the regime.

'Here we are,' said Diana as they approached the huge hotel which occupied an entire block on the street, only five storeys high but reaching almost as far as the eye could see. Veronica squinted up at the imposing, almost baroque, façade. Diana followed her gaze. 'It is impressive. I absolutely love this place. All the best hotels here may have followed its lead in adding ensuite bathrooms, but not all of them have telephones in every room so this is still the one for me.' She laid her hand conspiratorially onto Veronica's arm. 'I've taken the liberty of booking your room next to mine. But I don't plan on having any gentlemen visiting me so don't you worry about any noise!'

Veronica felt herself blushing. 'Likewise, I'm sure,' she said.

'Right then,' continued Diana, suddenly all business. 'I have to meet immediately with Freddie Lawton after I've freshened up and from there I hope to be going to the Chancellery. Do you have any plans?'

Veronica shook her head. 'No, not really, I thought I would take a stroll down the Unter den Linden and take in some of the sights. Get a bite to eat in a restaurant somewhere.'

By this time, porters were taking their bags up to their rooms. Diana suggested they get a coffee in the lobby whilst their things were unpacked. Veronica spoke rapidly in German to the man taking her things, telling him just to leave everything inside the door of her room and not to unpack anything.

'That's very impressive German you have, dear,' said Diana, 'but I speak a little and understand even more. Why wouldn't you want your bags unpacked?'

Veronica shrugged. 'That's always been the way with me. Mother used to scold me over my refusal to let the servants tidy my room or touch my things. I can't explain it.'

'How interesting,' said Diana, using the stock euphemism of the upper classes for 'How very stupid you are'.

It was another hour before Veronica could get up to her room and check that everything was still in place and that nobody had opened any of her bags nor discovered the false compartment in the over-the-shoulder bag.

Veronica knew as she was leaving the hotel to attend to her business that Diana had not yet left to attend to hers, because one of the SS men was back in the lobby. Diana must have telephoned from her room. A Mercedes was waiting outside the front; a second SS man sat smoking in the driver's seat. She had assumed there would be taxis queuing up outside the hotel and was relieved that this was the case. Her nerves would have suffered further abuse if she had had to stand next to that car hailing a cab.

About to give the address of the Jewish Hospital in Iranischestrasse, at the last moment she asked the driver to take her to the Adlon Hotel instead. It was in the wrong direction and would double her journey time but she was beginning to act like Conrad's Secret Agent now, worried that the taxi driver might report back to some Nazi sitting in the Kaiserhof, checking to see where guests went to. She thought it was probably unlikely but Sarah had told her to act on her instincts as these would normally be correct.

At the Adlon she got out and walked around for a few minutes until she was sure that her taxi had left the area. A side benefit of this was that she could now truthfully say if Diana should ask, that she had walked along the Unter den Linden and could describe the street-life that day, at least in the vicinity of the hotel.

Hailing another taxi she closely watched the driver's face, but he didn't react when she asked to be taken to the Jewish Hospital other than to say, 'That's a bit of a long drive, Fräulein.'

Twenty-five minutes later they arrived at the *Jüdisches Krankenhaus* in the suburb of Wedding. The building was pleasant enough for a hospital and less austere than some of the London ones Veronica had visited. It was a large building, its long three-storey façade stretching down both sides of the street leading away from the corner on which she was standing. It looked to be a fairly modern building with the red-tiled sloping roof that Veronica had noticed seemed to be so popular in Germany. She entered the reception area and was about to approach the desk when she saw Major Gutmann with his wife – Renate – Veronica remembered.

The women embraced briefly whilst Major Gutmann explained that Peter was awake, that they had just visited him, but if she went up he would be very pleased to see her.

'Please don't go just yet,' asked Veronica, 'could you please come up with me to Peter? I think it would be less awkward for him and I do have some news that I would like to share with you and the sooner the better.'

The couple looked at each other wondering what that news might be but didn't ask and showed her the way.

'It's on the third floor so there are a few stairs,' explained Frau Gutmann, 'but we got him a corner room with a view so it is worth it we think. After all Peter isn't the one climbing the stairs.' She turned and whispered to Veronica, 'Richard knows one or two of the doctors here, one of whom studied under him. It is a good room and shared with only three others at the moment.'

Peter was sitting up in bed talking to a severe-looking dark-haired woman in her mid-thirties sitting beside him on the only available chair. Veronica had at first assumed her to be a head nurse. The woman quickly rose to her feet, offering the chair to Frau Gutmann, who insisted, however, that she stay seated, indicating the woman to be a friend. Veronica's focus though was on Peter. The smartly turned-out 15-year-old boy she had met in April looked different today. His face was broadly the same as she remembered but subtly different. His nose and cheekbones had been broken and although the bruising had gone down, his nose was slightly misaligned and his cheeks seemed more hollow now. Of course it didn't help that he had been confined to his bed for all these weeks whilst his broken limbs healed.

'Dear Fräulein Beaumont!' Peter greeted her with genuine enthusiasm. Once he had been well enough to answer her card, he had requested that they correspond so that he could practise his English. Now he was speaking to her in English too. 'You are looking at me this moment as if you are seeing a ghost, is this not so?'

'No, not at all Peter. It is just so good to see you again and sitting up as well!'

'You are shocked at what you are seeing of me, I think.'

She shook her head. She was definitely upset to see him in this way but she was not shocked, not anymore.

Major Gutmann went out to get some more chairs to put around the bed whilst Renate introduced Veronica to the severe woman, Klara Stein. Klara stood and shook Veronica's hand, bowing her head slightly as she did so. She was a full head shorter than Veronica, who was wearing heels, and quite thin, androgynous even. The smile she now bestowed upon Veronica was open and friendly and changed her aspect, Veronica re-evaluated, from 'severe' to 'correct'.

'I've heard a lot about you,' said Klara.

'Good things, I hope?' replied Veronica.

'Well,' replied Klara, pausing for a moment, 'I certainly think that you and I should talk.'

Veronica nodded, and turned to Renate, raising a questioning eyebrow.

'Klara,' explained Renate, 'is an old and dear friend. She has never held with Zionism. During the days of the Weimar Republic, she fought for social justice and was our local SPD representative, and,' she glanced at Klara, 'I hope you won't mind my saying so, was fairly senior. One of the good people running Berlin.'

But Klara was shaking her head. 'I wouldn't mind you saying so, Renate, if it were true. But I suppose I did as well as one could as a woman and as a Jew.' She saw Veronica's perplexed look. 'Oh yes, even then, being Jewish was an obstacle in the eyes of some. Of course, looking back, in comparison to today…' She shrugged and left the sentence unfinished.

Klara looked so desolate at that moment, no doubt thinking, along with everyone else whom Veronica was meeting in Berlin, of how over the past six years everything had become so much worse.

Major Gutmann returned, dragging in three wooden chairs, and at last they could all sit down. To break the silence, Veronica leaned to the side and rummaged in her bag.

'I have something for you, Peter,' she said, bringing out a small box with a ribbon tied around it.

Renate clapped her hands as she saw the smile brighten her son's face.

'For me, Fräulein Beaumont? You really shouldn't have.' He started to reach for the gift and gasped, his arm still not used to that kind of movement. Veronica stood and brought it close to him. Still he hesitated.

'May I, Father?'

'Of course, my boy. Open it.'

But Veronica kept her hand on the top over the ribbon.

'Not until you stop calling me Fräulein Beaumont,' she said with a smile. 'It makes me feel like an old maid.'

'An old maid?' asked Peter.

'Like someone who should have been married by now,' she explained.

Peter's face was reddening but it may have been more to do with her request than her explanation.

'I find your name hard to say properly,' said Peter. 'I can't say the "V" as is correct to say.'

'Well, all the more reason you should practise then!'

'Weronica,' said Peter and they all laughed.

'Go on. Open it,' said Veronica, taking her hand away.

The ribbon quickly disposed of, Peter lifted the lid of the box and drew out a model of two generals on horseback. As the figures revealed themselves, everyone in the room seemed to speak at once, extolling the model's beauty and how wonderful a gift it was. Peter gazed at it in wonder, unable to speak.

The figures were about three inches high made from cast metal and carefully painted. The horses and men were fixed to the same base, coloured brown and green to resemble muddy ground so that the figures were fixed in relation to one another, both raising their military hats in greeting. One of the men had white hair and was dressed all in black. The other, with brown hair, had white trousers, riding boots and a blue jacket.

'May I, Peter?' asked his father.

Taking the piece, Major Gutmann examined the piece closely.

'This is a really fantastic piece of work,' he said in German. 'And I think I know who these people are.'

'Really?' said Renate, turning to Veronica, who was smiling encouragingly at the major.

'Yes,' he said with a smile, pointing at the man in black. 'This, if I am not mistaken, is our Marshal Blücher?'

Veronica nodded, very pleased.

'And this other one must be your Wellington. This shows their famous meeting at the end of the Battle of Waterloo.'

'Yes! That's right!' said Veronica with a laugh.

'Oh well done, Major,' said Klara, 'how impressive!'

'Originally,' explained Veronica, 'I was going to get you just any soldier. They had Lord Nelson, for example, probably the greatest British hero of them all. But then I thought that you might get into trouble here, so when I saw this, I thought that it neatly solved the problem. A German hero and a

British hero.' Her smile grew even wider. 'It was just perfect too for another reason.' She put her hand into the box and drew out a folded piece of paper. 'I also got you this to keep with it in the box.'

Peter took the piece of paper and opened it. There was some handwriting on it.

'To Peter,' he read aloud, before shaking his head and handing it back. 'You read it please... Veronica. I can't read the handwriting.'

'To Peter,' she read. '*A brave boy who deserves this commemoration of brave men, signed, WELLINGTON.*'

Peter's eyes widened at that. His father whistled.

'But how?' gasped Peter.

'Oh it's not the original Duke of Wellington of course. But I do know his great-grandson slightly, the fifth Duke. I told him you had been in the wars, showed him what I'd bought for you and he graciously wrote this note.'

Veronica basked for a moment in the happiness and joy she had brought into the room and she certainly was not about to tell them that she only knew the miserable old codger because the fifth Duke was involved in the ongoing discussions about forming the Right Club of which he had become a key patron. As Veronica knew, this club was going to be different from those others driven primarily by a desire for peace with Germany. She'd heard one man at Apsley House saying that they needed to end Jewish control, 'with steel if necessary'. If the old Duke saw nothing wrong with that then she had no compunction in omitting to tell him that Peter was a Jewish boy in Berlin. When the Gutmanns were safely in England she resolved, she would remind the old man of the gift that he had 'autographed' and that it had been for a Jewish boy. Then she would never see nor speak with him again.

She turned to the major, who had given the model back to Peter but who was still looking at it with some fascination.

'Major Gutmann, I also wished to discuss some other matter with you...'

He waited for her to continue, watching her curiously as she flicked her eyes towards Klara.

'Ah. I see. Please speak freely. You can trust Klara about our affairs. She is almost family. In fact she and Renate have known each other since they were little children.'

Renate was nodding and Klara was looking fixedly at the model soldiers, suddenly very interested in the detail of horses' hooves.

'It's just that after I realised what had happened to Peter, I made more enquiries about what might be done for you through some contacts I have. I realised there must be some urgency as presumably the children can't go back to school now.'

Renate shook her head. 'We are thinking they might go to one of the new schools being set up by the Jewish community but as you can imagine there has been a sudden increase in demand. The facilities are poor, the classes are overcrowded and there is no prospect of getting any certificate of education at the end that would be of any use.'

'Even if there were,' added the major, 'they can't go to university here anyway.'

'I have been asking about getting a family of four into Britain as I know that would be your preference, but in the meantime I believe that I can get false documents to get you into Palestine. You would leave Germany on your German documents but once across the border I will provide you with what you need to make the journey to Palestine via ship from Italy.'

The parents looked at each other, saying nothing, and it was Klara who broke the silence.

'Look, you know me. I say what I think and have done since I was old enough to speak. So hear me out on this. I have always believed that German Jews should be fighting for social justice for all people here in Germany. I will not run away even though we are going through tough times. In the past I have, as you both know, had furious debates with the Zionists, condemning them for running away from the battle for acceptance and equality here to create some ridiculous socialist utopia in the middle of the desert. But that's me. I don't have a husband and I don't have children. It's an easy decision for me to make. And can I truly say any longer that going to live in a tent in the heat of the Levant, is a poor decision in light of what we now face here?'

Klara paused and looked at the people in the room. They were hanging on her every word, even the Englishwoman. Klara loved to debate and was used to being listened to. Never though had it seemed so important to her as this moment. She turned to Veronica.

'This is what I was going to say to you. You, whom I understand have never been to Palestine, come here, risking your life, to try to send people there. Is it Zionism or is it survival? I don't care anymore. I want to say that I admire you for doing something practical to help. You are resisting, and what do I do? I talk and sometimes I shout just like the rest of the Social Democrats. But when it came to it we were powerless and achieved nothing.'

'Klara,' said Renate, 'I've never heard you talk like this before. Are you saying we should leave Europe for the Levant?'

Klara stood up, went over to Renate and took a hand in each of hers.

'For God's sake, what are you waiting for? Didn't you tell me that you got a rejection from the Dutch Government?' Renate nodded.

'Well then.' Klara turned to Veronica. 'They gratefully accept your offer.'

For a few moments, nobody spoke. Peter looked from one adult to another, waiting to hear his fate.

'Yes,' Major Gutmann said finally. 'Of course, we accept. The main thing is staying together and anywhere will be better than this hell-hole.'

Veronica felt relief at their acceptance but no joy. She was very aware that in normal circumstances, none of them would have wanted to leave Germany.

'Peter will need to be fully recovered to be able to travel,' said Major Gutmann, sitting, his hands clasped between his knees, talking slowly, concentrating now. 'We will sell what we can, but the Gestapo will take most of it. They also require us to make a thorough inventory of everything we have so that they can steal what they want.' He looked up at Veronica. 'Your aunt is the local expert on the procedures we will need to go through. I understand it will be exhausting and humiliating.'

The major rested his forehead on his hand, deep in thought. Veronica kept silent watching him. From time to time he would talk aloud to himself as he went through his mental calculations, before finally looking up.

'We might be ready by the end of September,' he said. 'Will that be time enough for you to arrange things with the Jewish Agency?'

'Yes.' Veronica nodded. 'I return to Britain in a couple of weeks. It will take me a few more weeks to get things ready and then I will return with your documentation.'

TWENTY-SIX

4 AUGUST 1938

PORTNALL ROAD, LONDON

BILLY SAT IN AN ARMCHAIR IN THE FLAT HE SHARED with Veronica on Portnall Road and lit his pipe. His flat was tidy, and he had always kept it tidy even before Veronica had moved in. The large chair was upholstered in a deep red velvet. He liked to sit back in it, put his feet up on the wooden footstool and think that he was living the life of an Englishman in his castle. The chair was a heavy Edwardian piece of furniture, one of the few things left to him by his parents. The pipe, though, was new. A few days earlier he had realised that he was missing some accessories from the mental image he had of himself reclining in that chair as Lord of the Manor. For one, he needed to be nursing a drink and he had bought a slightly chipped crystal decanter and two glasses from a second-hand shop just around the corner. One was now filled with whiskey and stood on a little wooden trolley next to the armchair. The wheels squeaked horribly but if it was stationary nobody was the wiser. The decanter set a new tone for him, quite a change from the bottles of ale that had been stacking up in the kitchen waste bin, witness to the many trips to the local off-licence when he wasn't down the pub with his mates. Also, he was moving up the ranks now and a pipe no longer seemed as pretentious as he had thought it to be even a few months earlier. He calculated too, that once he had paid for the pipe, with its bag, tobacco pouch, tampers and cleaners, the running costs were lower than for cigarettes. Cigarettes were still good of course for public meetings and the pub – he remained too self-conscious to light a pipe in public, but now, in his armchair, it was perfect for him engaging in princely contemplation.

Though not the most sensitive of men, Billy knew that his relationship with Veronica had changed. At the beginning she had been so eager to please, had looked up to him, and he had felt that she was fascinated by his life in the new party of British politics. He knew that she had found him exciting too and he had seen her as the student and he the experienced teacher.

He didn't feel that way now and he wasn't sure exactly when things had begun to change. Perhaps it had been when they had gone to Berlin at the end of April. The more he'd seemed to praise what they had found there, the more she had seemed to withdraw from him. Was it possible, he thought, now that she had seen what fascist success looked like, that the British Union and its members looked pathetic by comparison? Maybe, he thought gloomily, she was one of those women who appreciated men by their success. Recently, they didn't seem to be seeing each other all that much and even when they were together they didn't have sex as often, or at least he was having to be more forceful with her than in the past. Until now he had blamed himself for that. He had been absent more, his time completely taken by BU work. With the Nazi takeover of Austria and the developing tensions between Germany and Czechoslovakia, the fear of war had seen a resurgence in support for Sir Oswald and his men after what had been a couple of bad years. They were the only ones taking a firm stand to keep Britain out of any European war, taking the line that British men shouldn't have to die fighting for the Jews. And that was the other thing Billy didn't understand. Veronica had secretly visited an old Jew in Hendon. Why would she do that? Nick had not found it hard to get information about the man. He was quite the local celebrity. A notorious art forger who had done time. It just didn't make sense. Billy knew it wasn't good. He just didn't know why.

The other factor of course was that Veronica was supposed to have been cultivating the relationship with Hilary Masterson and he'd accepted that this would mean nights away and other nights when she would have to keep herself rested. But she had first met Masterson six weeks ago and by now, surely, she should have been able to get the man into a hotel room.

He got up from the chair and laid the pipe down on the ashtray. It was the bloody situation with Masterson that was bothering him most, he realised. Maybe Veronica had fallen in love with the man. Butler's photographs had shown him to be a good-looking bastard after all, and powerful too. But Billy had expected it to be a quick operation. He'd get his hotel pictures and that high and mighty Tory minister would be in his debt. She should have given him this success by now. Thinking back on it, for the past couple of weeks or more, Veronica had been evasive whenever he had asked her to report on progress. He picked up the note she'd left him saying that she had 'suddenly' had to go to Berlin. What did that mean, why would she suddenly need to go back there without involving him? It made no sense.

Unless of course she'd not gone to Berlin at all and was with Hilary.

He went into the bedroom and, opening the wardrobe, he found himself burying his face in her clothing. Her scent was intoxicating. He was not used to being the jealous lover. Usually he took what he wanted and then lost interest. Part of the problem was that he had been with Veronica for six months which was a long time for him. No wonder things were going stale. He had earlier decided to tell her that if she hadn't managed to get Hilary Masterson into a hotel room a week from today, then she should abandon the operation and break off contact. But now he knew with a sickening certainty that that wasn't ever going to happen. She'd fallen for the man, he just knew it. Maybe his bare hands were no longer enough and he'd have to start taking a strap to her to bring her into line.

He moved to her underwear drawer and began to riffle through it. He began by lifting out some of the stockings and rubbing them against his face, but gradually, without even realising it, he was methodically searching through her clothing and then her jewellery box. It was as if his inner voice was telling him to do it. At first, he tried to put things back as they had been before but after a while he didn't bother. At some level, he was aware that he was acting compulsively. He was being driven partly by a fascination with her things rather than anything specific. He knew of course that she was from a different class to him but he was unprepared for seeing everything all at once and how all of it was of such good quality and taste. It made him angry how people like her bloody father had managed to feather their nests whilst he and others had risked their lives for their country only to come back after the war to the same grinding poverty they had left behind a few years earlier.

If she was sleeping with Hilary Masterson MP then there never would be a hotel room ambush. But was she? Acting on instinct now, he went into the bathroom and started opening the cupboards, looking at all the paraphernalia she had in there. Products for skin-care and makeup and hair. All the things that women used to make themselves desirable. Normally he never looked at this stuff. He liked to believe that a woman's beauty was natural and effortless and not an illusion created by products and by hours spent in front of a mirror, shaving here and plucking there. He'd always resented that moment when the girls he was out with would say, as they always did, that they needed to freshen up. It made him think of the female imperfections that needed hiding and of this big con trick girls were playing on him, mocking him for falling for their illusions.

He imagined Veronica telling Masterson all about his hotel plan as they made love in a hotel. Laughing at him. He started to empty the cupboard of her bottles and ointments, sweeping them into the basin; though some missed and broke on the tiled floor, others cracked open as they hit the basin. He hated being made a fool of. He cursed as he realised that, at some point, he had cut the back of his hand. The smell of perfume was overpowering. He paused. Enough. Angry at himself now and his lack of self-control he began to clean up the mess. If he was wrong, and Veronica returned to see the mess he'd made, he really would look stupid then. That mustn't happen.

He quickly ran the cold tap which spluttered and then suddenly gushed, bouncing off the bottles gathered in the basin and splashing heavily onto the floor where it mixed with the objects already lying there. Billy cursed again, dried his hands and bandaged the cut with a small veil of Veronica's that had been draped over the back of her chair. The cut and the cold water had taken the anger out of him as suddenly as it had arrived. He took a towel and began methodically to dry and clean the bottles which had not been broken, separating them from the spilled liquid of those that had been. One by one he placed them back in the cupboard until the basin had only broken items in it. In the end there had been only a couple of breakages. She'd never notice.

He turned his attention to the floor, covered in water and spilt perfume. Crouching down but careful to keep his knees clear, he began to separate the broken from the whole and picked up the tube of Patentex in its now soggy cardboard covering. As he did so, the box gave way, the tube fell out along with a piece of rolled-up paper. Billy nearly didn't notice it. He had thrown the torn box into the sink and was about to throw the paper in after it when he noticed it was handwritten and not printed instructions. He had only seen the ink at all because, damp, it was now showing through the paper. He picked it up, unfurled it and began to read.

TWENTY-SEVEN

5 AUGUST 1938

PORTNALL ROAD, LONDON

'VERONICA WAS LOOKING PUKKA IN THE PAPER yesterday,' said Nick. Billy had been unusually quiet today and he thought this might cheer him up a bit. After all, if he had a girl as beautiful as Veronica, he didn't think he would ever be unhappy.

'What do you mean, which paper?' replied Billy, fixing him with a look of such malevolence that Nick felt himself withdrawing into the back of the armchair he was sitting on.

'I said, which fucking paper?'

'Keep your hair on, Billy! It was the *Herald*. Why?'

'When? When did you see it?' Billy was still sitting but he had turned so that he was half out of his chair, fully facing Nick. Nick was uncomfortable. He didn't like to be frightened but Billy was frightening him now.

'Yesterday,' he said sullenly.

'What did the paper say, Nick?'

Nick frowned, trying to remember the exact words.

'Come on, man! What did it bloody say?'

'I... I can't remember exactly. It weren't really about her. It was a picture of Diana Guinness. You know, the woman who married into the brewers.'

'Yes, I know her,' Billy said, remembering back to the evening at Apsley House, and his humiliation. What the fucking hell was going on?

'Show me,' he said.

'Well, I don't have it with me, do I? Who fucking goes around with yesterday's paper?'

Billy could move quickly for a large man and before Nick could react, he had leapt out of his chair, grabbed Nick by his neck and yanked him to his feet. Billy pushed his face close to Nick with one hand on the back of his head drawing him closer still. As Billy spoke, bits of his saliva were hitting Nick's eyelids, causing him to blink rapidly.

'Well, you'd better go home and get it then, hadn't you?'

'Billy! Please. I live half an hour away. It would take me an hour, even if the buses are running all right.'

'You'd better hurry then,' said Billy, letting Nick go. 'I'll be waiting right here.'

It was an hour and a half later when Nick finally arrived, stammering an apology about the bus not arriving, then two coming at the same time and him having to find the paper in his dustbin which fortunately had missed the collection. Billy said nothing. He impatiently held out his hand.

'Show me,' he said again.

Nick turned to an inside page, folded it back and handed the paper to Billy.

The photographer had not been taking a picture of Veronica and she was only included because she happened to be in the background. But it was clearly her.

Britain's Valkyrie, read the caption. *Diana Mitford, formerly*

Mrs Bryan Guinness, was seen today leaving the Kaiserhof Hotel on her way to visit Chancellor Hitler.

Billy looked all over the page but there was no other reference. There was no by-line either. He stared at the picture a while longer before finally handing it back.

So Veronica really was in Berlin. Now he was confused. Did she also go to see Hitler? He had had no idea. Why hadn't she told him something so important?

But then there was the letter from Masterson. Suddenly he felt small, insignificant, a pawn in a game that was being played high over his head.

He turned to Nick.

'I'm sorry, Nick. I shouldn't have laid hands on you earlier.' He attempted a weak smile. 'Woman troubles. You know what that's like.'

Nick nodded uncertainly, and walked towards the door.

'No problem, Billy. I'd best be off then.'

Billy nodded absently, deep in thought.

'No, wait, Nick,' he said. 'I've just had an idea. Stay please. Take a seat, help yourself to some whiskey. I just need to think this through.'

Billy stared into space for a minute or two. He needed to talk to Gunther. Gunther would know what to do with Veronica. He'd also need Nick's help, and Paul's. There was nobody else he could trust.

Two days later, a paragraph appeared, this time in the *Evening Standard*. It reported on a robbery at the premises of a well-known Bethnal Green tailor, Morris Levy & Sons, situated just off the Commercial Road, established there, so the reader was told, since 1910. Three men had come in just as Morris Levy himself, 60 years old, was closing for the day. He was badly beaten, some of his display suits had been slashed and the robbers had made off with £48.10s in cash. Police were asking any witnesses to make themselves known to Bethnal Green police station. What the short paragraph did not report, because the police felt that, in these troubled times it would not be in the public interest to do so, was that 'Jews out!' had been daubed in white paint across the door leading to the office at the back.

What they also did not report, because they did not know, was that Billy Watson was now able to finance a flight to Berlin to sort out his Veronica problem.

TWENTY-EIGHT

15 AUGUST 1938

49 PARK LANE, LONDON

'YOU HAD THREE TELEPHONE CALLS WHILST YOU were away,' said Sarah. They were sitting next to each other on the living room floor, their backs against the sofa. 'Daphne Peters. I think she wants to get closer to you again, if you know what I mean.'

Veronica groaned. 'Don't say that! I knew that if I renewed contact with her she'd be all over me again like a rash. What did she say?'

'She asked me why I was answering the telephone and when she realised I wasn't staff, she asked me if I was your lover. I told her that if the two of you were such close friends then presumably she should already know the answer.'

Veronica sighed. 'I'll telephone her tomorrow. I had hoped that Daphne was happily married and would have other things to think about but it seems she's married *and* a free agent. She doesn't seem to care that there might be a scandal if she is seen cavorting around like she does. Society doesn't mind if it's kept a secret but she is so public about it. It's the brazenness of carrying on in full view that is so frowned upon.'

'So, a bit like Mrs Guinness and Mosley then?'

'It's interesting you should say that actually. Diana told me that she isn't really Mrs Guinness anymore.'

'Well, that's not news. Didn't Bryan Guinness remarry a few years ago?'

'Yes, but she's not even the ex-Mrs Guinness.'

'What do you mean?'

'She and I were together a lot in Berlin – when she wasn't dining with her beloved bloody Führer. And I'd see she often had her hand on her belly. You know, just resting it there.'

'You mean like those portraits of Napoleon?'

'I don't know about that but you know when a woman does that what it means.'

'That she likes to rest her hand on her tummy?'

Veronica lightly slapped her arm. 'Don't be silly.'

'Okay, okay. So she is pregnant.'

'Yes. Anyway, I asked her if there was anything she wished to tell me. A bit like you just now, she smiled at me and pretended to misunderstand. "You mean about my meetings with the Führer?" she said. "Well, you know I can't tell you about any of that." But then she said that whilst she couldn't talk about her business meetings, she didn't mind telling me about what they had talked about at dinner the evening before.'

Veronica put a hand on Sarah's upper arm to make sure she had her full attention.

'She said, "The Führer has decided to destroy Czechoslovakia as an independent country. He said that creating that country had been a terrible mistake and that he would rectify that mistake before the year was out."'

'My God!' said Sarah, freeing herself and getting to her knees to face her. 'What did you say?!'

She smiled. 'I said, "No, Diana, that's not what I was asking you about. I was thinking about your condition," and I pointed at her belly.'

Sarah stared at her for a moment and then laughed. 'My, you're a cool one. That is the perfect response for an agent. Go on.'

'Well, she admitted that she was already five months gone. She said, "It's fine to tell you as we're going to have to tell everyone soon anyway." But then she was anxious to reassure me that the baby was not as she said, "going to be born the wrong side of the blanket". She claims that she has actually been married to Sir Oswald Mosley for two years and that her former husband, Bryan Guinness, was okay with it. They apparently got married when they were both out in Berlin during 1936. So she's not Mrs Guinness, she's really Lady Mosley.'

'I'm so pleased for her,' said Sarah. 'But her condition is bad news for us, isn't it? She probably won't be making any more trips to Berlin for a while.'

'Actually, I may have gone one better than that.' Veronica tried not to look smug but failed. The thrill of impressing Sarah with her successes gave her a real rush. 'When I told her I'd be coming back again in the autumn, she said that I should tell her when and she would see if it was at a time that her sister Unity was visiting Berlin from Munich where she lives. I told her that I couldn't possibly want to put her or her sister to any trouble but she said she remembered meeting Billy at Apsley House.'

'I don't understand,' said Sarah, 'what's that got to do with it?'

'Well, Diana thinks that I could do a lot better than be with some ignorant working-class thug. Those were her exact words! She says Unity would certainly be able to introduce me to some good Aryan stock in Berlin. Maybe even from Hitler's own bodyguard. Apparently I am "absolutely their type". So I said that I would certainly be interested to meet Unity and could she tell me when Unity next planned to be in Berlin as I would try to arrange my visit to coincide.'

Veronica paused, expecting congratulations but saw that Sarah was looking very serious.

'I thought you would be pleased,' she pouted.

'I am not sure what being friends with that crazy bitch Unity Mitford will do to help you achieve what we want out there. Usually we try to look inconspicuous, not drawing attention to ourselves. Once again, you are going to be doing the exact opposite.'

'You have also always said that I should blend in. Their secret police will be less likely to search my rooms or listen in on my phone conversations. Who is going to suspect me with friends like the Mitford sisters?'

Her good mood was quite gone now and she was annoyed.

'But Veronica, you're not trying to infiltrate the Nazi leadership. You are trying to get Jews out and Unity Mitford is even less likely to help you than her sister – and that's saying something. Will you perhaps have an SS chauffeur ferrying you around from one Jewish house to another as you courier documents?'

'You know it isn't going to be like that. I will be seen with her. I will perhaps meet some of her Aryan friends but most of the time I will be independent as I have been on the other trips.'

'And the pistol – did your aunt take it for you?'

This was the first time Sarah had mentioned Sonia since she had told her she had family in Berlin. Sarah had not taken it well and she realised that Sarah was now trying to mollify her by showing that she had accepted the situation. Veronica appreciated the effort.

'I told you I wouldn't need it. Yes. I hated to ask her but she was very good about it. She said that if it helped us in any way given what we are doing for them all, that was enough for her. Only she won't tell Manfred as she doesn't think his nerves would be up to the stress. She has put it in a place where nobody would ever find it and she said that she'd have it ready for me when I next come. Everything went well.'

'Yes, but do make sure you pick it up again as soon as you get out there.'

Veronica didn't answer. She was still annoyed with her. Sarah took her hand and rested it on her lap, looking at her closely. Veronica could see her concern for her and sighed.

'Sarah, you're going to have to let me do things my way. I will take all precautions and yes, I will take the pistol back when I get there.'

'All right then. Thank you, Veronica.' Sarah nodded to her and continued to hold her hand.

Veronica gently took her hand away and rose to her feet.

'Well, there's no peace for the wicked. I'd better go back home to Billy. He wasn't around when I left for Berlin and it was so sudden I was only able to scrawl him a short note. It was a bit light on detail so he's probably wondering where I am.'

'Do you care?'

'In a funny sort of way I do,' she replied. 'If I'm acting as "his girl" then I ought to behave like it. I've just gone off for over ten days and with his paranoia who knows what he'll be like. He'll probably be demanding his rights when he sees me so I'm prepared for the worst.'

'We need to get you out of there, Ronnie,' she said, 'now that you have the Mitford contacts you don't need him anymore.'

'Maybe you're right.'

'But stay here a little longer, can't you? Tell me about Lise. Did she like the doll you got her?'

Veronica smiled.

'She is a lovely girl. She really liked it. She hugged me for quite a while. I always feel such a weight of responsibility when I meet them. I realise what I represent to them. For two thousand years the Jews have longed to return to Zion and suddenly this family, which was never interested in Palestine, is yearning for it as much as the most fervent Zionist. I'm really their Moses, going to lead them all to the Promised Land. It took a long time to be on first-name terms with Renate and have them call me Veronica. But even now, I daren't call the major "Richard". Well, you know how stuffy the Germans can be.'

'You mean just like you English?'

Veronica laughed and punched her lightly on the arm, their differences forgotten. 'You know what I mean – they have a certain type of rigid German formality that surely is more than we British, don't you think?'

'I do know what you mean, yes,' said Sarah. 'Though I don't think my own parents were ever like that. But there are a lot of recently arrived Germans in Tel Aviv and we call them "*Yekkes*" – which is a Yiddish pronunciation of the German word for "jackets". That's because, there they are every day, in scorching heat, sitting at restaurant tables wearing their homburg hats, ties and buttoned-up jackets, mopping their brows with their handkerchiefs, watching the *sabras* walking past in shorts and sandals.'

'Oh dear,' said Veronica. 'Is that the fate that awaits Major Gutmann?'

TWENTY-NINE

15 AUGUST 1938

PORTNALL ROAD, LONDON

KEEP VERONICA BEAUMONT UNDER
OBSERVATION STOP KAISERHOF HOTEL STOP
ARRIVE BERLIN TOMORROW STOP WILL
CONTACT YOU ON ARRIVAL STOP TOMMY

THE TELEGRAM SENT, BILLY RETURNED TO HIS FLAT
to complete his packing. He still had one more visit to
make before going to Croydon and it was right out of his way
so he'd need to be out early. It would give him time to reflect
on what he really wanted to do about Veronica's treachery.
First he needed to know whether she was important to the
Nazi Party. If she was, then however much her having an
affair with Masterson might hurt him personally, she was
untouchable in Germany. But even then he was thinking
some facial disfigurement courtesy of the SA – but delivered
anonymously – could not be traced back to him. Especially if
people thought he and Veronica were still together.

He was retrieving some of the stolen money from behind

his bed when he heard a noise outside his front door. He stepped into the corridor and could hear a key turning in the lock. Either he himself was about to be burgled now, or the only other person who had a key to his flat was about to make an unexpected appearance. Either prospect was undesirable at this moment. He needed to get back into the bedroom and restore the fistful of bank notes to their hiding place but he stood staring at the door, his feet rooted to the spot, his hair standing up on the back of his neck.

The door swung open and standing on the other side, small suitcase in hand, was Veronica.

About to step inside, on seeing him she too froze. And for a long minute neither of them moved a muscle, each rapidly sorting through in their own minds what their stories should be and what must not be said.

Finally, Veronica gave a cheery smile and walked confidently into the flat, shutting the door behind her.

'Hello, Billy! Is this the right way to greet me?'

'Veronica,' said Billy, 'I didn't know how long you would be away for. You didn't say.'

'Didn't my note tell you? I am so sorry. How silly of me. But don't worry, I'm back now.'

She walked up to him and gave him a peck on the cheek. She knew something was very wrong. Normally he would be hugging her to him and pawing at her. She moved back, smiled and went into the bedroom, prepared to let him recover his dignity in the only way he knew.

Billy waited outside for the reaction he was sure would come. He sat down as he heard her gasp. She went into the bathroom and started opening the cupboards. This made Billy smile.

Half a minute later, Veronica reappeared in the doorway to see him holding up Hilary's love letter.

'Looking for this, were you?'

'You searched through my belongings.'

'Was that very bad of me, Ronnie?' he said sarcastically. 'Should I have trusted you?'

Veronica thought about the pistol now with Aunt Sonia in Berlin. It turned out she needed it here in London. Oh God. She knew she mustn't show fear and looked towards the door, calculating how far she could get before he caught up with her.

'You'll never make it,' said Billy as if he had been reading her mind.

'Listen, Billy,' pleaded Veronica, 'it really isn't what it seems. I can assure—'

'Am I better than him, eh? Is that what you want to tell me?'

Veronica shook her head.

'Yes, I mean no. I – I don't know.'

'Yes? No?! Or you don't know? Make up your mind, you whore.'

'I meant "No, I didn't want to tell you that" and "I don't know", because, I really don't know. I've never slept with Hilary Masterson.'

Billy again held up the letter and waved it around.

'That proves that Hilary is infatuated with me, nothing more than that.'

'Well, if you are telling the truth,' said Billy, smiling now and getting to his feet, 'then you would have been carrying out our plan, wouldn't you of? I mean, this man is off his head about you and would be in a hotel room toot sweet if you just batted your eyes at him. So why didn't you? Why aren't we looking at some nice photographs of you and him?'

Veronica had to take a moment to think of an answer and said, 'I'm going to get some water from the tap, all right?' He let her go, watching her the whole time, like a cat, she thought – or a tiger – waiting to pounce. She took a glass from the cupboard and filled it from the tap. She took a sip, thinking. Then another. She turned to face him, glass in hand. 'I was going to talk to you about that, Billy. Really. I didn't want to have pictures of me without clothes on being shown around. I would lose too much.'

'Yeah but we discussed this, didn't we? I said we'd remove any pictures that showed your face. You are lying. Why not show me this letter instead of hiding it away? We were a team, weren't we?'

He took two steps towards her as she shrunk back against the sink and shut her eyes, waiting for the blows to come. Instead, she felt his breath on her face and his hand take the glass from her and put it down on the wooden surface. But then a pause and she opened her eyes again as he began to speak.

'I don't know what your game is, Veronica, but it's over between us. You understand me?'

He put his hand up and squeezed her cheeks so that her mouth was crushed into a distorted 'O'. She quickly nodded.

'Now I'm going away for a few days. When I come back all your rubbish is gone from my place. Understand?'

Veronica nodded again and he let go of her and stepped away. He took the letter from Hilary Masterson which had fallen to the floor and put it inside his jacket pocket. Then he went back into his room, retrieved his money and his suitcase and walked out, shutting the door behind him.

For perhaps two minutes, Veronica stayed leaning against the wall in the kitchenette where he'd left her, until she heard him exit the building and her trembling had lessened enough that she trusted herself to stand up unsupported. She thought she heard a taxi stop outside and walked to the window in time to see Billy get in and the taxi drive away.

She moved quickly to the bathroom and vomited into the toilet. Then again. Finally she was able to stand and wash her face over the basin. She was still trembling and lay down on the bed. She didn't understand how she had escaped serious injury. He had been almost understanding. It somehow felt worse that he was not acting as expected. And how was he suddenly able to afford a taxi? Exhausted, she fell into a fitful sleep where she dreamed that she was being chased into a tunnel on the Underground, the platform had disappeared but she kept running, stumbling over the rail lines. She knew she had to keep going just until the next station, but the station never came.

THIRTY

15 AUGUST 1938

HARMONDSWORTH, ENGLAND

BILLY WAS PLEASED BY THE WAY HE HAD HANDLED the unexpected encounter with Veronica. It was too late to cancel his trip to Berlin but he anyway still needed to tell Gunther what was going on so that they would be ready for the next opportunity. Gunther would of course know very quickly that Veronica had checked out of the Kaiserhof and right now he wouldn't even know why he had been asked to watch her.

The main thing, thought Billy, was that nobody should suspect him of having any ill feelings towards Veronica. He was proud that he had managed to restrain himself earlier. A worthwhile short-term sacrifice. He needed to be strategic now.

The taxi dropped him off at Nick's flat – a necessary additional detour in view of what had just taken place. Nick needed to be updated and take turns with Paul to start to follow her and see where she went and whom she mixed with. He no longer needed proof of her affair with Masterson but it would be interesting to know if she was meeting with Germans.

Nick assured him that he would be outside Billy's building within forty-five minutes. If Veronica had not left by then he would be able to track her. Billy was reasonably confident that, even if she decided not to stay on there for a few days more, she couldn't pack her things and leave that quickly. He checked his wristwatch. He was making good time still. He could get used to cab travel. The taxi dropped him off at Wembley Park station and he took the Metropolitan Line to Hillingdon.

Hilary Masterson's parliamentary seat was to the west of London and he held his constituency surgery there every second Monday, as Billy already knew. From Hillingdon he took another taxi and arrived at the scout hut on the edge of the Great West Aerodrome where Masterson met his constituents. Billy had only Butler's photographs of the MP to go on and when finally ushered in to the small office, he sized him up without even being conscious of doing so. Few men matched Billy for size and this was true in Hilary Masterson's case, but as the MP stood and came around the small table to shake his hand, Billy could tell that this was a man who could take care of himself in a fight even though he was, Billy estimated, ten years older than him.

'How can I help you, Mr Watson?' asked Hilary politely after returning to his seat and waiting until Billy had sat down opposite. The office of the scout hut was very small and Billy was reminded of Veronica's description of Masterson's room in the House of Commons. Maybe, when she had described that room as 'small' she had meant 'intimate', thought Billy now, the anger he had been suppressing since the day before flaring up once again.

He looked around at the walls covered with prints of scout leaders and their activities, and certificates of achievement.

Behind Masterson's head were the two ubiquitous framed black and white photographs which Billy assumed must grace every scout hut in the land: King George VI in his naval uniform, side on with his left hand resting on the pommel of his sword – and Robert Baden Powell wearing his trademark campaign hat, his arms crossed over his bemedalled scout shirt.

The walls of the office, Billy noticed, looked very flimsy, barely capable of supporting heavier pictures. He wondered, if he were to try to punch Masterson and miss, whether his fist would exit the other side, startling those constituents sitting patiently there. Would they intervene? he wondered.

'Mr Watson? How may I assist you?' asked Hilary a second time. 'No need to be shy,' he added encouragingly, 'there is no problem too small or too delicate that your local Conservative representative can't help you with.'

'I'm not sure that's true,' replied Billy, turning back the lapel of his brown tweed jacket and revealing his BU badge with its lightning bolt in a circle.

Masterson smiled again but this time there was caution behind the smile.

'That's not a problem, Mr Watson. If you live in my constituency you are entitled to my support even if you are a member of another party.'

'And do you support your local constituents by fucking their girlfriends?'

Billy had to give credit to Masterson, who managed to keep a smile fixed to his face, though he noticed that his right arm had dropped below the desk edge. He couldn't, thought Billy, have a revolver there surely, but maybe had some other sort of weapon in case of unruly constituents.

'Now look here,' replied Masterson, 'you need to understand that an MP is often the subject of all kinds of rumours and accusations. Young women can be prone to all sorts of dreams and fantasies. It doesn't mean that they're true. I can assure you, sir, that I have not been sleeping with your girlfriend. The idea is quite preposterous.'

'Oh but I have incriminating evidence,' said Billy, reaching inside his jacket.

'My dear fellow, I can assure you that your evidence is false. However, if you are thinking of attempting to blackmail me or threaten me in any way, I have my finger on a buzzer here. If I press it twice, someone outside from my local association will immediately put a call through to the local police station and they—'

'My girl is Veronica Beaumont.'

Masterson's whole demeanour changed at the mention of her name and he took his hand away from the buzzer.

'Really?' he said at last. 'You're her beau?' He looked at Billy, sizing him up for the first time. 'And my God, you're BU too. Incredible.'

'So you admit it,' said Billy. 'You have been sleeping with her. Tell me why I shouldn't break your fucking nose.' Billy stood up.

Hilary stayed seated and contemplated Billy for a moment, entirely unperturbed.

'Forgive me, Mr Watson, but I don't believe you can possibly be her beau. For one thing, you really don't seem her type. If you really know her at all, she... well, let's say, she mixes with fellows from public schools.' He put his hands out as if in apology for the British class system. 'She never mentioned you as being anything of that sort, I'm afraid.'

'Well, she wouldn't, would she? She's been mine for months now.'

Hilary smiled at that. 'A-hah. So why have you come all this way? Is it really to break my nose? I think you might have tried that by now. Or is it that you wish to blackmail me?

Well, it won't work, I'm afraid. I am not interested in your little game. You want to publish, then publish. I'll simply deny everything and say it's a forgery.' He stood up. 'Now, I believe that concludes our business. I have real constituents to attend to, so please excuse me.'

'Look, I won't bloody hit you,' said Billy almost plaintively. He had begun fiddling with his lapel badge, absent mindedly removing it from the back of his lapel to the front. 'I just want to know if you are sleeping with her or if you aren't. Can't you be man enough to admit it at least? If she has been doing the dirty, it's her I'll blame.'

Hilary Masterson looked at the BU badge and at Billy playing with it and began to laugh, softly at first and then full on and loud.

'What's so bloody funny?'

Hilary reached for the handkerchief neatly folded and protruding from the breast pocket of his pin-striped suit and wiped his eyes.

'Forgive me,' he said, 'but are you really a member of the BU?'

'Yes, I am. What of it?'

'And Veronica is your girl, and has been for some months, you say?'

'Yes. I fucking told you.'

'And I'm sure she told you then...' Hilary, paused for dramatic effect, watching Watson's face closely for his reaction. '...that she's Jewish?'

The look on Billy's face caused Hilary to guffaw with laughter. This was priceless: the sheer comedic value in having this overbearing fascist try to intimidate him and now ending up looking so completely crushed.

'Come now, Mr Watson, surely you couldn't have failed to see the close resemblance she has to that actress Hedy

Lamarr? I thought you fascists could smell a Jew a mile away?' Hilary brushed away the thought that he too had failed in that regard. 'I have a suggestion for you. You keep my letter private and I'll not let on that you've been completely bamboozled by a Jewess who has twisted you round her little finger.'

Billy thought of all the terrible things he needed to do to Masterson right now, but there were too many witnesses and he had a plane to catch. He let out a primeval snarling sound, turned and left the little office, slamming the door so hard that the walls shook and Hilary had to move quickly to save King George from jumping off the wall.

THIRTY-ONE

16 AUGUST 1938

FROM TOTTENHAM COURT ROAD
TO HENDON CENTRAL, LONDON

T AILING VERONICA WAS THE MOST PLEASANT TASK
Nick had yet been given since he'd joined the BUF three
years earlier. He had met her several times of course since Billy
had claimed her after she'd come to hear him speak.

'Another notch on me bleeding bedpost,' Billy would
most often say when she was not around and he had had a
few too many. He was right to brag about her, Nick thought.
She was a real looker. Paul and he had shared more than a few
beers discussing what they'd like to do with her. And now,
Billy wanted them to mount watch on his place, and report
back where she went and who she met.

'I want to know what she does now she realises she's been
rumbled,' Billy had said.

'Rumbled? How d'you mean? What's she gone and done?'
Nick was quite fond of Veronica. She seemed harmless
enough though he knew that there was sometimes tension
between her and Billy. Not enough though that he had ever

felt he might get a look in. He knew he wasn't in her league. Billy was the District Leader and he was certainly the more vicious. Nick was never going to get on the wrong side of Billy if he could help it.

So, even though Billy never answered his question, that first day Nick had dutifully followed Veronica, his hat down and newspaper up, as she walked round the corner to the Lyons Corner House where she'd ordered and nursed a cup of tea and eaten a sandwich for forty-five minutes whilst reading a paperback. She'd not met or talked to anyone. Paul took over from him and reported the same. Billy had said that they only needed to keep up this watch for two days. Any longer would have been an impossible strain for two men and he'd refused Nick's request that they bring in more men to share the long hours.

'No,' Billy had replied. 'Nobody else must know that we're fighting. I need to trust you on this, Nick.'

Of course Nick had agreed. He'd not had to wait long this morning though. By 7am she was already out of the building and marching quickly to the corner where she began to look for a passing taxi. Nick quickly sprinted to a parallel corner and aggressively flagged down a taxi within five minutes. He had the driver go around the block and was relieved to see that Veronica was still standing there. They waited until she got into a taxi and then Nick told his driver to follow her. This was an interesting development. The more so when they travelled all the way up the Edgware Road to Cricklewood before turning off towards Hendon. Until recently, Nick had known nothing about this part of London nor why anyone would want to come up this way, especially somebody as posh as Veronica. Yet here she was again, her taxi stopping nearly an hour later at that same address on Queen's Road. Nick asked the taxi to drive on a bit and stop.

'You're running up quite a tab, mate,' said the driver. 'I hope you can pay.'

'Yes, I can pay,' answered Nick and showed him a thick wad of notes whilst turning in his seat to watch Veronica go back into the house just beyond the pillar box where that Jewish art forger lived. She had asked her taxi to wait so Nick reckoned she wouldn't be long.

As he had thought, just fifteen minutes later she came out of the house, got back into her taxi and they went all the way back again to Billy's place on Portnall Road.

He needed to discuss with Paul what to do and waited impatiently for another hour and twenty minutes before Paul arrived for a change of shift. After a quick consultation, they decided that this would be more than enough of a development to keep Billy happy and that instead of wasting more idle hours in the street, Paul would contact his former colleagues in the police, patriots like them and sympathetic to fascism, to find out more about the art forger and why someone might want to hire a taxi to go all that way to visit him for just fifteen minutes.

This meant that nobody was watching the building when, the following day, Sarah turned up in a small lorry driven by a colleague from the Jewish Agency to help Veronica move all her possessions from Billy's place to 49 Park Lane, next to the Dorchester.

THIRTY-TWO

19 AUGUST 1938

GRUNEWALD FOREST OUTSIDE BERLIN

THE TWO MOUNTED RIDERS, MEN IN THEIR FIFTIES, wore civilian clothes but from their posture they were clearly military men. Neither Prussian nor aristocrats, they were both outsiders who had become generals. They had served with distinction in the last war and had thought Hitler a definite improvement on the decadence of the Weimar Republic. Now, however, it was their shared disillusionment with Hitler that had brought them together riding in the Grunewald.

'His mind is unalterable – as he often tells us,' said Beck, who was still Chief of the General Staff, but who had earlier that same day tendered his resignation. 'He wants a war against Czechoslovakia. It is of no interest to him that the army isn't ready for such a war. He simply doesn't care. But until yesterday, I thought I could continue to protest and that logic, sooner or later, would prevail. But now he demands that the army "up to and including the Chief of the General Staff" must give him total obedience and we are forbidden from interfering in whatever he decides are "political questions". What choice did I have but to resign?'

Oster, only a Generalmajor to Beck's rank of Generaloberst, decided not to answer him directly.

'Perhaps it is the time to update you on my progress so far?' he asked instead.

Beck, leaning forward and patting his horse's neck, nodded. 'Go on,' he said.

Afraid that even the trees might have ears, Oster waited until they were cantering in a vast clearing in the forest before continuing.

'All the pieces are now in place. General Witzleben's soldiers, on my command, are ready to move from Potsdam into Berlin to support a coup d'état. Von Helldorf, the Chief of the Berlin police, has come over to our side and guarantees that the police will not try to intervene.'

Beck looked over at Oster, clearly impressed, but said nothing.

'Munich will be ours too,' continued Oster. 'General Hoepner is ready to crush the SS garrison there and then come up to Berlin in support if needed.'

'That is all well and good,' said Beck, 'but the SS have secret barracks we know nothing about. If we can't get them all, there is the risk of a counter-coup and a swell of popular support for them. There'll be civil war.'

'Actually,' smiled Oster, 'we *do* now know the location of all of these secret barracks.'

Beck reined in his horse. 'How could you possibly know that?'

'It was easy. Von Helldorf knows them all. The police have to be informed about the establishment of every new brothel and no SS barracks is complete without one!'

Beck allowed himself a smile and a wry shake of the head,

watching their horses grazing, heads close together in the long grass.

'You've been busy, haven't you, Oster?' said Beck with real admiration. 'Perhaps I shouldn't have resigned so soon over Czechoslovakia. You could have done with me in a position to command some divisions in your support too.'

Oster nodded. He had been thinking exactly the same thing. If only Beck could not have been quite so principled and waited just a few weeks more.

'Well, maybe he won't accept your resignation?'

Beck shook his head. 'Oh, he'll accept it all right. He's been wanting me gone for a long time now.'

'It doesn't matter,' said Oster generously. 'Your support from the side will count for much with your prestige in the army. And we have enough to carry out our plan.'

'So what exactly is the plan?'

'When the time comes,' said Oster, 'we will simply surround the Chancellery. A group of officers will march inside and arrest Hitler.'

'You're crazy,' said Beck. 'There will be a bloodbath.'

'It won't be easy,' admitted Oster, 'his bodyguard will fight to the end but there are never more than forty of them. They will be overwhelmed.'

'And Hitler?'

'He'll die in the fighting,' said Oster.

'No!' I will not countenance such a thing. Nor, by the way, will your boss. I know that Canaris believes that Hitler needs to be put on trial so that everyone knows what crimes he has committed. If he is killed he will become a martyr and we'll never hear the end of it.'

'I think,' replied Oster, 'that if he is taken alive, we will also never hear the end of it. We will forever be at risk of a rescue attempt and more fighting, more deaths. We can still make his crimes known – but after he is dead.'

'The German Army does not kill its heads of state. It is a matter of honour,' insisted Beck, his eyes blazing.

Oster realised that there was no point in arguing further. He had already given instructions. Hitler would die in the Chancellery and Beck and Canaris could cry about it afterwards as much as they liked.

The men started to move their horses forward again.

'You said, "when the time comes", said Beck. 'When will that be exactly? Do you know?'

'Britain and France will never let Hitler take Czechoslovakia without a fight. Hitler will not change his mind. Therefore the moment Hitler gives the order to attack Czechoslovakia, we move in and take over.'

'How do you know that Britain and France will fight? They did nothing about Austria and nor, before that, the Rhineland and the Saar. What makes you think this time will be any different? Hitler is certain they are so traumatised by the last war that they'll appease him and appease him until it's too late.'

'I am highly confident,' said Oster. 'Neither Britain nor France want to see Germany take over a democracy with the most formidable defences and army on the continent, second only to France herself. I am also confident because I am letting the British know that they don't even have to fight: just the promise that they will do so will be enough. If Hitler backs down under their threats then his magic will have left him and he won't survive the humiliation. And if he doesn't back down – then we strike. Either way, he's finished and there is no war.'

'Have you and Canaris made contact with the British yet?'

Almost without being aware of it, Oster looked at the surrounding trees, perhaps looking for a glint of sunlight off binoculars. He rode a little closer to Beck and leaned in towards him.

'Yes, we have. Just yesterday our emissary went over to England. He is there now and will for certain be meeting with Winston Churchill and Robert Vansittart. Perhaps he may even meet their Prime Minister. The message will be clear: stand up to Hitler over Czechoslovakia and there will be no war, not now and not ever. But if you won't stand firm, then there will be war sooner or later.'

'All right. Let me know what the British say. I will do whatever I can to help. It's been nearly six long, dark years for Germany. We need to make sure the Nazis never get to rule for a seventh year, for all our sakes.'

THIRTY-THREE

22 AUGUST 1938

TEMPELHOF AERODROME, BERLIN

IF HE HAD VERONICA'S WEALTH HE WOULD STAY HERE for longer, thought Billy bitterly as he watched Gunther walk back through the Tempelhof exit and get into his car. Billy was no longer short of funds, but he still needed to work.

The revelation that Veronica was Jewish had changed everything. His first thought on the way over was that he needed to warn Mrs Guinness that her companion was not what she seemed. If she was taking Veronica to see Hitler there might even be a risk of assassination.

If Veronica was still in Germany, Billy would have done exactly that and let the Gestapo take care of matters. But she was in England and he was far from certain that Mrs Guinness would do anything more than have it out with Veronica and cut off all contact with her. From what he knew of Diana she was, unlike her sister Unity, a savvy political operator and would steer well clear of anything sordid. That did not suit Billy at all. He wanted revenge. Veronica had humiliated him and made him a laughing stock. She had slept with him and used him – he had slept with a Jewess. He felt physically sick. He realised he was also now a little scared of her. Who was she really? Clearly not the dumb woman who never stood up to him beyond the odd sulk that he expected from women from time to time.

Maybe Gunther would know how to find out the truth once he and his SA friends got hold of her. He had wanted to be present to witness that but Gunther had counselled against it. If this was to look like a German affair the presence of a giant Englishman would not go unnoticed and the trail would quickly lead back to Billy, which could also make life difficult for Gunther. The treatment of Jews in Germany did not extend to foreign Jews, though he was fairly sure that the death of one in Germany would not be investigated with any enthusiasm.

The only difficulty was knowing whether Veronica would even visit Germany again and, without knowing why she was coming in the first place, Gunther was doubtful. Billy, however, was certain that she would come again. At some point, she would come back to do whatever it was that kept her coming here and then Gunther would be waiting for her.

THIRTY-FOUR

7 SEPTEMBER 1938

REGENT STREET, LONDON

V ERONICA AND SARAH LIKED TO JOKE THAT THEY shared a birthday in that they had both been born on a Tuesday and both on the 15th day of the month. But Sarah was three years older and had been born in August and Veronica had been born in September. It was close enough though and proved, surely, they laughed, that their friendship had been predetermined.

For Sarah's birthday, Veronica, remembering Sarah's discomfort when they had eaten at the Dorchester once before and she had nothing suitable to wear, had bought her an evening dress. Although Sarah feigned horror at having to wear such a 'get-up', they immediately made plans for when Sarah could wear it. They would celebrate Veronica's twenty-fourth birthday one month later, just before her next visit to Germany, at the Café Royal in Regent Street followed by an outing to see the revue show *Frivolities de France* at the Prince of Wales Theatre.

Veronica had long accepted that Sarah was not the sort of

person to surprise her with a gift. She liked to plan ahead and leave nothing to chance. So it did come as a surprise when, with ten days to go, Sarah telephoned her to say that she had changed the restaurant reservation to that very evening and that they would eat somewhere else before the show on Veronica's birthday. Sarah refused to tell her why the change of plan but she could hear an edge to her voice. All she would say was that it was good news. In the remaining hours until she would meet her there, Veronica tried to think what might be so important. Perhaps Sarah was going to reveal the existence of a hidden lover and that she was pregnant. But that was absurd. Sarah was far too much the professional and if it did happen Sarah would not have seen it as 'good news'. It had to be something else, and it was with some anxiety that Veronica met her at the restaurant and they were shown to their seats. Sarah had chosen a small table at the very back where it was dark. Veronica immediately lit up, taking short and frequent drags of her cigarette. Sarah ordered wine to drink whilst they decided what to eat.

'Veronica,' Sarah said, 'that's your second cigarette. Are you nervous?'

'Why should I be nervous?' responded Veronica, taking another puff and blowing out a long stream of smoke towards the ceiling, something she knew fascinated Sarah as she was that rare beast, a non-smoker.

'Quite,' she said with a smile. 'It's not as if I am going to declare my undying love for you. I'm not Hilary.'

Veronica laughed and stubbed out her cigarette even though it was less than a quarter smoked.

'So what's the good news? Is it business?'

'Yes, in a way, I suppose it is,' Sarah replied. 'I have something to show you and it's good you put out that cigarette as I don't want you to get ash over it.'

It was at that moment that Veronica knew what Sarah was going to show her, and she looked at her with disbelief, excitement flushing through her. She glanced around to be sure nobody was observing them.

'You haven't, have you, Sarah?' she whispered, her eyes bright now. 'Oh Christ. You have. Show me, quickly please.'

Out from underneath her shawl, slowly, as if performing a conjuring trick, Sarah revealed, inch by inch, a British-Palestine passport and passed it across to Veronica. Comparing it in her mind to the ones she had seen before, this one was pristine, new, untouched.

'I got it back today. I knew you wouldn't want to wait.'

Veronica held it and stared at it for a long time, thinking about what this meant, how this simple little thing could bring such incredible joy and would bring even more when she handed it over in Berlin. She was already imagining the scene. Never before had she seen anything as beautiful as this.

'Aren't you going to open it?' Sarah asked, as if this was her own early birthday present to her friend, which of course, Veronica realised, it was. The best birthday gift in all the world.

Slowly, she reached out and traced the cover with just the lightest touch of her fingertips. She opened it gingerly to the first page. She took her time, savouring the moment, and read the fine italic script.

By His Majesty's High Commissioner for Palestine
These are to request and to require in the Name of His Majesty all those whom it may concern to allow the bearer to pass freely without let or hindrance and to afford _____

Here, in the blank space provided, someone had written in blue ink 'them'. Veronica gave a sharp intake of breath. It said 'them', not 'him' nor 'her'. She felt a solitary tear start from her eye and read on.

> *every assistance and protection of which* _____ and again
> the blue ink *'they' may stand in need.*
> *Given at Jerusalem the* _____

The date had been completed in the same blue ink followed by the clear handwritten signature of the High Commissioner, *H MacMichael.*

And there on the facing page, the name of the bearer, in the ubiquitous blue ink, *Dr Richard Gutmann.*

Veronica looked up at Sarah, both her cheeks wet now, and mouthed, *'Thank you.'*

She turned to pages three and four, her eye immediately drawn to the facing page and the two photographs of Richard and Renate Gutmann which Veronica had given to Sarah when she had got back from Berlin less than a month before. Silently she uttered thanks to Harry Wolf and his professional skills.

She was about to turn the passport to look at the photographs the right way up, when at the bottom of page three, she saw, in the section for the name, age and sex of children, laid out in neat copperplate handwriting, Peter's and Lise's details. She suddenly felt herself gasping for air and quickly handed Sarah the passport before huge sobs burst out of her mouth. She cried for a minute, maybe two, conscious of nothing but Sarah's hand gently covering hers. Vaguely she heard her telling the waiter, 'She's quite all right. Actually she'd just had some very good news. Could you bring us a jug of water, please, and some napkins?'

'Of course, madam, right away.'

Finally Veronica was able to calm herself enough so that

the sobbing was replaced by a little laughter. She was giddy with happiness.

'But how, Sarah? How did you manage this?' She saw the look on her face and quickly added, 'No. Please don't tease me. Not right now. Just tell me.'

Sarah inclined her head in acceptance of her demand.

'We have had this passport in our possession for a couple of months now waiting for a good opportunity. As you can imagine, some quite heated discussions have been going on. There was always agreement that a blank passport must be used for a family rather than for an individual, but the list of course is still very long. I had to call in a few favours.'

'You're a brick, Sarah, you really are. A saint.'

Sarah smiled happily at that and took a sip of water before continuing.

'One of our chaps who works near to the passport office in Jerusalem, over time had familiarised himself with who came in and out of the building – that was why he was working nearby after all. So he knew who worked there. One day, quite by chance, he's shopping in the Arab market in the Old City and catches sight of a face of one of those employees, an Englishman, talking animatedly to a young Arab boy. When the two of them leave the market he decides to follow them. They get into the man's car which has been parked by the Zion Gate of the Old City and they drive away. Our chap then informs his superiors and they have a car ready at the Gate to see if he comes back again. One day he does and this time, when he returns with the boy, his car is followed. They go to some open ground not far from the Jerusalem Railway Station.'

She shrugged as if to say that what happens next is best left to the imagination.

'And he took advantage of the boy?' Veronica asked, wanting to be sure she understood what she was implying.

'Yes, between a grove of olive trees. Money for sex. As you can imagine, when confronted, the man was willing to do anything to ensure that neither his wife nor the authorities discovered his dirty little secret. Apparently it had been going on for some time and he professed he loved the boy.'

'How old was the boy? You make it sound as if he was just a child.'

Sarah shrugged. 'I think he was around 15. Make of that what you will.'

'Your people told him to stop what he was doing, I hope.'

'I am almost certain we would have said nothing whatsoever! We told him that if he wants his secret kept, then he needed to help us.' She saw Veronica's look of disapproval. 'Oh come now, Veronica, we have enough on our plate without policing the behaviour between the English and the Arabs. That's not our fight! But there is an end to this story if you let me tell it.'

'Continue then.'

'Well, it turned out that he was a very good fish to catch. As you can see, passports have printed serial numbers on them. It's one thing to steal one but, if noticed, the police will be on the lookout for it and it would be dangerous to use. That's why we much prefer to be in control of who has "lost" their passports. Then we can delay the reporting of its loss until it has been successfully used or at least until it is too late for the British to update records in Palestine. In this case, we might have just a few weeks between the time the theft has been spotted and the passport's turning up at the border entry point at Haifa or wherever. But this fellow knew the process well enough to be able to amend the records to show that this passport was legitimately issued to the Gutmanns. It's as if they were officially issued a passport. It won't ever be reported missing and it doesn't come off the quota. It's the perfect crime.'

Veronica, nodded with excitement, her concern about the morals of the man forgotten for the moment. The possibilities were endless.

'How many of these can he provide for us?'

'Two,' said Sarah. 'This and one other that he got for us before this one.'

'What? Two?! Why so few?'

'Because he's dead. His mutilated body turned up in the village of El Azariyah just to the east of Jerusalem. We think the boy's family found out what was going on and took matters into their own hands.'

'And the boy. Is he at least safe?'

'I don't know. The British are reporting this as just one more atrocity justifying the harsh methods they are now employing to suppress the Arab revolt over there.'

'Are we ready to order?' asked Veronica, upset now, both out of concern for the boy and for the lost opportunity to save others that could at least have come out of the situation. She signalled to the waiter without waiting for Sarah's reply.

'Have you thought about how this is going to be financed from the Gutmann side?' asked Sarah. 'Even if they succeed in selling their home the Nazis are not going to make things easy.'

Veronica blushed and now she looked distinctly uneasy, refusing to meet Sarah's eye.

'What have you done this time, Veronica?'

'You won't like the answer and maybe you'll have to sack me as your agent. But I've allowed them to transfer much of the balance of their bank account into my British account where the Nazis can't touch it. Whenever they need to cover expenses I will give them cash.'

Sarah sat back violently in her seat. Veronica felt sure that if they were not in a public place Sarah might have shouted at her for the first time since she'd known her.

'You might as well stand at the Brandenburg Gate, stop the traffic and shout, "I am a secret agent. Please torture me and lock me up."'

'I know, Sarah, I know. But it's their money and I don't think the risks are all that high. Nobody is watching me, nobody cares about one Englishwoman. I felt perfectly safe there last time, for all your warnings.'

'But it's not just that, Veronica. When they strike, you won't see it coming. And the Gutmanns will then be unable to access their own money. Their lives are now completely in your hands.'

THIRTY-FIVE

18 SEPTEMBER 1938

SCHÖNEBERG, BERLIN

S ONIA AND MANFRED WERE BECOMING USED TO
their niece's visits to them. They never asked her for details
of what she was up to and certainly never looked inside the bag
that had been with them now for over a month. For a Jew in
Germany knowing things people didn't want you to know was
how to end up in a KZ. They had made a solemn pact on his
return from Dachau that Manfred would never go back and
that they would kill themselves rather than let that happen.

So they never questioned Veronica this morning when
she came in from England once more, asked for her bag and
slipped in some more envelopes and pouches. The bag once
again secured, Veronica sat them down and told them that she
had been working on their behalf – that Sonia and Manfred
would be allowed to come and live in England after all.

'The paperwork is being prepared and in a few weeks' time
I will come back again and personally escort you to London.'

Sonia and Manfred looked at her uncomprehendingly
though she and Manfred instinctively held hands.

'Is Cynthia agreeing to be our guarantor?' asked Sonia. 'She hasn't written at all this year,' she observed finally. Veronica had expected the question.

'Did you know, Aunt Sonia,' she asked now, 'that Mother and Father have a flat in central London?'

Sonia shrugged and looked at Manfred but, as often the case, she got no response.

'She may have mentioned something many years ago, I don't really recall.'

'Well, that's where you will be staying. For as long as you like. There may be some forms to fill in saying that you will have steady paid employment as the live-in maid, but that's British bureaucracy for you. You will in fact be living there independently as if it were your own home, until such time as an alternative can be found. You won't actually be working.'

'But Veronica, dear, I know about these schemes. I would need to have an employer agreeing to pay me a salary. Who is going to do that?'

'I will, Aunt Sonia! I will be paying you to clean your own flat! It is a perfect solution.'

Aunt Sonia was not reacting the way Veronica had hoped. She sat there silently for a few moments. Thinking.

'And you say that Cynthia is in agreement with this?'

Veronica forced a bright smile and a nod.

'Yes! She has finally seen how bad things are here and she is now completely supportive.'

'And supportive of Manfred too? Even though he is German?'

'Yes. They live miles away from London and they rarely visit, so if you're worried about any uncomfortable meetings, don't be.'

Sonia was silent once more. Then she looked Veronica squarely in the face.

'I don't believe you, Veronica,' she said.

Veronica stopped smiling and returned the serious look.

'I understand why you think this way, Aunt Sonia. But you are wrong. On my next visit I will have with me a letter from Mother that will set your mind at rest. But in any event, it doesn't really matter what we say. It will be the documents that speak. These will get you and Manfred out of this place of insanity and into England. If I am lying about that then you'll know because you won't be leaving here. Do you really think I would get your hopes up unnecessarily? What do you have to lose?'

Manfred cleared his throat. Immediately the two women stopped talking to give Manfred their full attention, Sonia trying to remember the last time Manfred had initiated conversation.

'My view on this is that we thank you, Veronica, for what you are doing. We are coming. We are dying slowly here and you are offering me a chance to live again as a man without fear. We are coming. Thank you, my dear, for my life. Thank you.'

He bowed his head to hide his tears but his heaving shoulders hid nothing. Sonia and Veronica got up and knelt either side of his chair. Each took one of his hands and said nothing, for there was nothing to say.

Veronica had returned home from Berlin on 15th August. How long would it be before she went back there again? Billy had been asking himself this day after day and was at the point where he couldn't think of anything else. What if she had gone there just a week later and stayed a week? Gunther would have missed her. And if she was there, could Gunther and his SA friends really scour every hotel in the hope of finding her?

Finally, when one month had passed he dared not wait any longer. When they had returned from Apsley House back in July, Veronica had been so excited to have made contact with Diana Guinness and thrilled that she had been given her phone number. It had been written on a pad by the telephone stand and it was still there. Apparently a number in Staffordshire. The thought of dialling someone as powerful as a Mitford filled him with trepidation and he had prevaricated for a further three days before realising that it would be much easier to telephone her now, on a Sunday, than to try to fit this in during his working hours. So now, he stood in the telephone box across the street making a trunk call and, with a tight voice, he asked the operator to connect him. Whilst he waited he cleared his throat several times.

'Connecting you, caller,' said the clipped voice of the operator and there was a click on the line and the sound of his coins dropping into the box.

'Hello, who is this please?' answered a male voice.

'Ah, my name is William Watson. I am telephoning to speak with Mrs Guinness please.'

'May I ask the purpose of your call, sir?'

'You could tell her that it is Right Club business and that we met at Apsley House at the introductory meeting there in July.'

'One moment, sir, I will see if she is available.'

'Hello?' A female voice this time.

'Yes, hello,' said Billy, making sure to pronounce the H. 'Is that Mrs Guinness?'

'Yes, this is she. And who did you say you were?'

'I am William Watson. I was accompanying Miss Beaumont at Apsley House when we met.'

There was a pause.

'Ah, you must be "BU Boy", am I right?'

'Er, yes, ma'am, I am in the British Union. But I'd rather you thought of me as a "Mosley Man" rather than as a "BU Boy".'

Diana had the good grace to laugh at that.

'Very droll, yes, very droll indeed. Well, what have you telephoned about?'

'Ma'am, I was wondering if you knew the whereabouts of Veronica – Miss Beaumont – I... er, I...'

'What? Are you trying to say that you have mislaid Veronica, is that it?'

Billy held the earpiece away from his head whilst he fed more coins into the phone, quickly pressing Button A before he got cut off. He knew that she would humiliate him. Toffs were all the same, fascist or not. *I'll be there when the tumbrels start to roll again*, he thought to himself.

'No, Mrs Guinness. It's just that I have something of hers that she would want back.'

'Well, I'm afraid you've missed her. She's gone to Berlin so you'll have to wait till she returns. But who knows when that will be? I believe she is expecting my sister to introduce her to some strapping, handsome, blonde-haired, blue-eyed Adonis.'

'I see,' said Billy. Not too long ago this would have made him sick with jealousy. Now he knew better and he could take these Mitfords' schemes with a pinch of salt. 'Do you know how I could contact her? I would like to at least send her a telegram so that she knows it's been found.'

'Yes, I am sure that would be fine,' replied Mrs Guinness. 'You can send it care of the Kaiserhof Hotel. It's a famous hotel so don't worry, the GPO will know its telegram number. Unity is staying there too, in the very next room in fact. Obviously I don't divulge room numbers but the hotel will deliver the telegram to her. Now I really must be going, but – I'm sorry, what did you say your name was?'

'William – but people call me Billy—'

'Well, William. I wouldn't keep your hopes up. I don't mean to be unkind, but I think she's moving on if you know what I mean. Good day.'

'You bloody bitch,' muttered Billy after slamming down the receiver and pressing 'B' repeatedly, in the hope that he would get some unused coins back – none came.

The next morning he sent a telegram – but not to the Kaiserhof. It read.

V NOW IN KAISERHOF STOP STAYING
WITH UNITY MITFORD STOP THE
NEXT ROOM STOP TOMMY

Now Gunther could make his plans.

THIRTY-SIX

19 SEPTEMBER 1938

KURFÜRSTENDAMM, BERLIN

It was on her second day in Berlin that Veronica began to sense that she was being followed. At first she dismissed the feeling. She had been too influenced by her last conversation with Sarah. No wonder she was paranoid.

But the feeling persisted. She was walking down the busy K-Damm, window-shopping, mostly watching people sitting outside restaurants having coffee in the still-warm afternoon. A tram had gone past and, turning to look, she thought she saw a sudden movement in the reflection of the glass on the windows as it trundled by. From that moment, every so often, she'd stop and turn suddenly and on some of those occasions she would see more sudden movement amongst the crowds.

She couldn't say why, but a couple of times she had had the impression it might be a woman following her. A hint of swirling skirt or cardigan, a bobbing hat.

Would the Gestapo use women to follow women? Of course they would, she reasoned. But surely, if the Gestapo wanted to follow her, they would make sure that she didn't notice them. Unless they wanted to be seen. To frighten her. Did they prefer to terrorise their victims before pouncing with an arrest warrant?

She had the pistol but could she use it and if she could what would be the point? There would be too many of them and she'd never get away. She had promised Sarah that as soon as she had visited her Aunt Sonia she would retrieve the false bottomed bag. She shifted it from one shoulder to the other, hardly reassured by the weight.

She was aware that for a while she had been walking very fast, elbowing people to try to put as many people between her and whoever it was out there on the street. She should have been hot but instead she was shivering and cold. She increased her pace and then, as she approached the junction with Fasanenstrasse, she quickly turned into that street and hid in a shop doorway. For maybe fifteen seconds, she noticed nothing unusual. Then a woman appeared at the junction, stopped with her back to Veronica, looking around, uncertain of what direction to take. As she turned, her profile came into view and Veronica stepped out from the doorway.

'Daphne?!'

Daphne Peters spun round to face her.

'Oh there you are! I thought you'd given me the slip.'

Veronica's relief that she was not being followed by the Gestapo was quickly replaced by annoyance at what Daphne had put her through for the last twenty minutes.

'Why have you been following me, Daphne? Why are you in Berlin?'

Daphne looked as though she was about to answer her but then smiled coyly and, nodding towards the Kempinski restaurant, said, 'Why don't I tell you over a cup of coffee and some strudel? I was here yesterday and the coffee is simply wonderful.'

Veronica agreed, needing anyway to sit down and drink some water. She let Daphne chat away about the interesting sights of Berlin until Daphne finally paused for breath.

'Now tell me why you are here, Daphne, and where is Reggie?'

'Reggie? Oh he would never come to Germany! Says he will only visit when the monarchy is restored.' Daphne looked at Veronica for a moment, and leant forward across the small table until Veronica thought she was going to kiss her. 'Bugger Reggie. You know why I am here. You are why I am here.'

'Oh, for God's sake, Daphne,' said Veronica, 'you came all this way, just to follow me around the streets of Berlin?'

Daphne pouted and then brightened.

'I saw your photograph with Diana in the *Standard* and made some enquiries. I thought, "Why should you two have all the fun?" You looked wonderful together.' Her smile faded. 'Have you two been sharing a room at the Kaiserhof?'

'Don't be ridiculous,' retorted Veronica angrily.

'I thought you might have been. I wanted to see for myself. But when I booked into the Kaiserhof it was Unity I found there and she told me that you and Diana had left and that you were now at the Adlon.'

'Thank you, Unity Mitford,' sighed Veronica. She had moved out of the Kaiserhof because, after just one day, she hadn't wanted to be anywhere near Unity. Unity had invited her to tea in her room and insisted on showing her the latest copy of the vile antisemitic *Der Stürmer* which Unity kept on dignifying with the term 'newspaper'. Apparently she knew the editor personally. Unity had pointed out one particular cartoon. It showed beautifully drawn German workers: men, women and children, kneeling and supporting on their backs a heavy table top around which were sitting capitalist bankers playing cards across that table, dollar bills falling out of the pockets of their jackets which were buttoned tightly around their fat stomachs. More bills, sterling this time, were stuffed in the bands around their top hats. The faces of the bankers were grotesquely drawn, with thick moist lips and huge hooked noses. Stars of David were drawn on their hats just in case, Veronica thought, the message would otherwise be too subtle for its ignorant readership.

'This is what is happening in England too,' explained Unity, 'but the greedy capitalist Jews are too cunning and hide so well behind the scenes. The day of reckoning is coming.'

'But Unity, in England as in Germany, surely it is the aristocracy that owns all the land and has all the money?'

'And quite right too!' Unity had replied without any sense of irony. Veronica had frowned at that. As she knew from the past few months, there was no reasoning with an antisemite. That wasn't the only reason she had had to move. The publicity around Unity was far worse than it had ever been with Diana. But, so as not to upset Unity, Veronica had told her that she was going to the Adlon because people had been telling her that until she had experienced the Adlon for herself she didn't really know the meaning of luxury. That had been the best she could come up with. She turned her attention back to Daphne.

'And what do you want from me, exactly?'

'Sex. Veronica. Wicked sex. Just like that night.'

'You are insane, Daphne,' hissed Veronica, looking around, worried that the words Daphne had uttered had been overheard. 'That was five years ago and I was drunk!'

'Maybe. But I wasn't. And then, when you contacted me again last year, I knew that our fates were written in the stars. What's your room number at the Adlon?'

'I shan't tell you that!'

'No matter,' said Daphne with a laugh. 'I moved into the Adlon last night.'

Veronica sat back and looked thoughtfully at Daphne. The woman was clearly unhinged and could seriously compromise Veronica if she let things spiral. Yet Veronica could hardly call the police and she didn't have many options, other than to go home to England of course. But she was not going to do that when there were people relying on the documents she still had in her possession.

'Daphne,' she said in a calm voice, smiling now. 'I am flattered of course but I do prefer men.' Daphne started to speak but Veronica held her hand up to stop her. 'What you want is something that I, until now at least, have thought was not for me but, perhaps we can try to be friends first? I need to feel comfortable with you. Talk about other things, and then, over time, who knows what can happen?'

Daphne grinned, her perfect teeth revealed.

'I can be patient. For a while, that is. Yes, I can do that! And is Diana coming out here again?'

Veronica shrugged, remembering that Diana would now be six months pregnant. 'I doubt it. Why?'

'Oh nothing really. It was when I saw the picture in the paper. I thought that if I could only join up with you two we would look the most desirable women on earth. I was imagining the headlines: "Three Blondes for Hitler!" or "Proof of our Aryan heritage, these girls show the way!" – or something like that.'

She noticed that Veronica remained silent. 'Of course, if you are not interested maybe you can help me be in a picture with Diana and Unity – that would work just as well. But it would be so much better if you were there.'

Daphne had this irritating way of gushing when she was

excited. Veronica realised that she had to meet her some of the way, show her a little enthusiasm.

'Maybe the four of us would work nicely together,' she conceded. 'How about "Four Fräuleins for Fascism"? Or better still, "Four Fascist Femmes Fatales"?'

'Yes!' shrieked Daphne, and this time heads definitely turned, somewhat disapprovingly, at the two tall blonde English women who had no sense of decorum.

'Shhh,' whispered Veronica. 'You must keep your voice down. Tell me, are you even a fascist? I remember that politics didn't interest you.'

Daphne rolled her eyes.

'Oh God, don't get me started. I just don't have the head for it. I can't remember the difference between a fascist and a communist.'

'So then why? Why are you talking as if you are a fascist?'

'Well, if fascism turns *you* on, darling, then that's good enough for me. And it's very much in fashion, don't you think?'

An hour later, Veronica knew not only about Daphne's non-existent politics but far more than she cared to about her marriage. If Daphne were to be believed, once she had performed her duty and given Reggie an heir, she had refused to sleep with him anymore, telling him at first that she was tired as a new mother and then, once a wet nurse had been hired, that she wasn't in the mood. In the end she had threatened to leave him, relishing the power she held over him once she realised that nothing frightened him more than a divorce.

If the taxi driver, who had driven them from the Kufürstendamm to the Adlon, had understood English he would have learnt about Daphne being free to take as many lovers as she wished as long as there was no scandal.

'So you see, Veronica, dear, how perfect it is here in Berlin. Nobody really knows us, we're not famous like Diana and Unity and we don't have men around to placate. We can stay in our room all day and nobody would be the wiser.'

They were now standing in the lobby of the hotel. Veronica was not going to collect her key until Daphne had collected hers. When Daphne protested, Veronica stood her ground.

'Do you give me your solemn word that you will stop following me?'

Daphne hesitated.

'If I find you have followed me then I will never speak to you again. But if you behave we can at least be friends. All right?'

Daphne did a little dance for joy.

'"*At least* be friends"? So more than that if I behave?!' Before Veronica could move away, Daphne had quickly kissed her, chastely enough thank goodness, on the cheek. 'I can't wait,' she said.

Veronica watched her get into the lift and the doors close.

'Over my dead body,' she muttered to herself.

Gunther wished that he hadn't sent the telegram to Billy quite so quickly. It was an admission of failure and one that would really upset his English friend. As he had walked out of the telegraph office, he realised he wasn't ready to give up so easily.

It had read:

UNITY AT KAISERHOF STOP BUT NOT YOUR FRIEND STOP PLEASE ADVISE STOP FRITZ

Unity Mitford put on her bathrobe and hurried to the door.

'Who is it?' she asked in German.

'Flower delivery, Fräulein,' came the response. She opened the door. A bell boy, with greying hair, was standing there in his ill-fitting jacket and silly forage cap on his head. Frankly he looked ridiculous, thought Unity, but she forgave him his appearance as he was holding a huge bouquet of beautiful flowers. Unity laughed with delight. The Führer must have heard that she had arrived and sent her one of his many gifts. Such an adorable, generous man.

'Come in then. Hurry.' She gestured to the small round table in the middle of the suite. 'You can put them there in that vase. Please fill it with water.'

As he went to the bathroom to fill up the jug, there was a shout of annoyance from Unity.

'Stop! Come here.' She paused a few seconds but could still hear the water running. She went to the bathroom and stood at the open doorway. 'I said stop. You won't be needing the jug. You are taking these flowers back down with you.'

The bell boy stood up slowly – perhaps insolently, thought Unity for a moment.

'This card,' she said loudly and slowly in her deliberate German, 'is not for me. It says here that these flowers are for Veronica Beaumont. Take them away, bell boy.' She emphasised the word boy, taking pleasure in saying this to a man who was clearly twice her own age.

'I don't understand,' said the bell boy. 'I was told that Fräulein Beaumont is staying in this room.'

'Well, you were given wrong information,' said Unity. 'She no longer has a room anywhere in the hotel. *Your* hotel, apparently,' she said, jabbing a finger against his chest for emphasis, 'isn't a patch on the Adlon and frankly I can see her point. Why don't you take them there, boy?' She laughed and closed the door.

Gunther turned away, delaying his own laugh until he

had walked up two floors to his own room to change back into his own clothes, on the way depositing the bouquet of flowers into the large ceramic vase that stood on the carpet opposite the bank of lift doors.

His second telegram was received by Billy just four hours after the previous one.

FRIEND HAS BEEN FOUND STOP ADLON HOTEL
STOP WILL EXECUTE PLAN STOP FRITZ

THIRTY-SEVEN

19 SEPTEMBER 1938

ABWEHR (MILITARY INTELLIGENCE) HQ, BENDLERSTRASSE, BERLIN

'IT WAS A WASTE OF TIME,' LT. COLONEL HANS OSTER reported, glumly. 'No better than the visit of our emissary last month. Our Chargé d'Affaires Erich Kordt, in London, again spoke to senior officials of the British Government and this time he even managed to get to speak with Lord Halifax himself. Halifax was polite and seemed to show some interest, promising to relay the message to the Prime Minister and even said we should expect a favourable statement in the next few days. Either he never did or the Prime Minister wasn't interested but we have had no response. A few weeks before that we had a lawyer visiting there who talked with Sir Robert Vansittart of the British Foreign Office. Nothing. They either don't believe us or they do and they don't care.'

He looked at the other two Military Intelligence officers but they refused to meet his eye. This, more than any words, conveyed to Oster the depth of their disappointment. Finally Rear-Admiral Canaris turned to his *Abwehr* subordinate, Major Helmuth Groscurth.

'Well – where do you think the problem lies, with the British Prime Minister or with his Foreign Secretary?'

'We think that Halifax would have reported back to Chamberlain,' replied Groscurth. The rear-admiral had asked them to drop their acknowledgement of his superior rank for the duration of these types of 'private conversations', as he called them. Oster felt it was the man's way of acknowledging that what they were doing was against the law and, if known, would result in their imprisonment or worse. 'Halifax is a faithful servant of the Prime Minister and talks with him frequently. It is inconceivable that he would not have reported our plans back to him.' Groscurth spoke calmly enough but he was feeling the heat and he had to keep pushing his round thin-framed glasses back to the bridge of his nose. Where his hair had been shaved close to his scalp in the Prussian military style, his skin was glistening. He would have liked to have loosened the top couple of buttons from the tight neck of his military tunic but knew that in that regard at least, the Rear-Admiral was fastidious. 'It is my view that the British just don't think we are powerful enough against the Nazi party and that the *Wehrmacht* will overwhelmingly remain loyal to its oath to the Führer. They think that we are few in number – and we are indeed but a handful of men.'

Canaris looked from the Lt. colonel to the major and back. He was a short man with a head of white hair and with bushy white eyebrows flecked with grey. He thought Groscurth was a good officer and hoped he would manage to hold his nerve. Catching Groscurth's eye he gave him a flicker of a smile to let him know he was still appreciated by his commander.

'We may be few,' said Canaris, 'if by "we" you mean those of us in the circles with access to Hitler, but we have the support of most of the army and police commanders and we know that the people don't want another war. If they think one is coming, they will support us in avoiding it. In my opinion, the British don't respond because (a) they are wedded to negotiations almost as a way of life and (b) because in the end they don't feel that they are threatened in any way. Most Englishmen wouldn't be able to point to Czechoslovakia on a map; it's too far away from them and if it were to disappear, it would be no skin off their noses.'

Canaris had said the last few words in English and smiled, enjoying the confusion on their faces. He was an accomplished linguist and had even been known to throw in a few Japanese words from time to time.

'We can go no further on this,' said Oster eventually. 'We've talked to so many British politicians now and they have decided they don't trust us. It doesn't matter how many officers and lawyers we send and how many diplomats we talk to, if we can't get to Chamberlain it means nothing.'

Major Groscurth cleared his throat. 'We also know that the British intelligence services have become more active in Berlin. This might be because they are trying to see for themselves whether there are the conditions for a coup. They seem to have descended on Lichterfelde like a flock of geese. Every one of us in that district seems to have a car outside his house, round the corner or a man at a nearby café.' He shrugged. 'We thought it was the Gestapo!'

'Well, it might as well be,' said Oster. 'What do they think they are playing at? They are inviting the Gestapo to take an interest in us.'

Canaris was deep in thought. 'I think this must be their reply to us. They are telling us that they believe we are coordinating all our approaches to them with the Gestapo. In their minds SS or Army makes no difference. They are daring the SS to arrest us and when they don't it will prove that we, Himmler and Goering are all in this together.'

'And when we *are* all arrested?' Oster was pacing up and down now. They all knew of 'perfidious Albion' but never could they have foreseen this.

'Well then,' replied Canaris with a wry smile, '*then* they will realise their mistake and shrug their shoulders. For us, however, it will all be over.'

'Assuming that those men watching us are all British Embassy employees, we can't arrest them,' said Groscurth gloomily, 'but can't we at least move them on and state that their activities are not what should be expected from an embassy?'

'No. Not without creating a fuss and drawing it to the attention of the Gestapo,' replied Canaris. 'However, this may yet be an opportunity. Can you find out whether their monitoring in Lichterfelde also includes the home of General von Strasser on Kadettenweg?'

'Jawohl,' answered Groscurth formally, without thinking. 'I can already confirm that this is the case. It is the most worrying of all for us given how close his house is to the SS barracks there at the top of the street.'

Canaris nodded. They all knew the area very well. Before the barracks had been handed over to the Berlin Police in the days of the Weimar Government, it had been the military academy and all three of them had graduated from there. For the past five years it had been the divisional home of the 'SS Leibstandarte Adolf Hitler'.

Canaris now turned to Oster. 'And do you think General Beck still has a copy of Case Green?'

'Yes, I am sure he has,' replied Oster. It was over Case Green that General Beck had resigned as Chief of the General Staff just a few weeks earlier though the news had not yet been made public. Beck too had tried to warn the British about it and he would definitely have kept a copy. 'But why is this important, Herr Admiral?' Oster knew he shouldn't question his superiors but Case Green was the name for the detailed plans of the invasion of Czechoslovakia. Oster recognised the signs that the wily admiral had something in mind.

'Good, we need to move fast,' said Canaris, ignoring the question. 'Get a copy today and bring it here. We have time for one last effort, I think.' Oster stood and clicked his heels. 'But Oster,' added Canaris with a twinkle in his eye, 'send someone else round to General Beck's house to get them. We don't want to get those Englanders excited.'

KAISERALLEE, BERLIN, 21 SEPTEMBER 1938

Veronica had never thought that her picture would be published in British newspapers. How naive she had been to think that, because the photographers had been interested only in Diana, her own identity would be safe. Now she was uneasy and regretted her decision to leave her bag at Sonia's. If only the Jewish Hospital wasn't so far out of the way. She had, she realised, developed a habit of putting her hand deep into that bag and taking momentary comfort from the feel of unyielding metal at the bottom. The hospital, however, as a Jewish institution, was regularly inspected. If her bag were to be searched, the pistol would mean certain incarceration in a camp for all of them. By the end of the month the Gutmanns would be out of Berlin on their way to Palestine. She was not going to risk that.

How quickly though, had she learnt to be afraid. The very city in which she had spent a carefree year, now felt overbearing and oppressive. And that was when the sun was shining. Right now it was getting dark and the electric streetlamps were starting to warm up. She hurried her steps along Guntzelstrasse and turned left into Kaiserstrasse towards the taxi rank outside the U-bahn station. She was tired and nervous but she had promised Peter she would visit him one last time there before he returned home. She knew how important she was to him, a tangible link to a free world. It was a sobering burden to carry but it made her proud too. Before she had left England she had undergone intensive sessions with Sarah, bringing her up to speed on all aspects of life in Tel Aviv for a new German arrival. Their absorption would be smoother than most as there was always a need for doctors.

For a moment her introspection had made her less alert, although it was doubtful she could have done anything had she seen the danger. One moment the street was empty, the next a huge Mercedes was alongside her and a very large man in a long dark coat and wearing a black, wide-brimmed trilby was standing right in front of her with one of his hands on its open back door. She thought for a moment about ducking under his outstretched arm and making a run for the station. Then she realised that he was grinning at her, watching her, reading her mind and waiting for her to make just such a move. This was like the confrontation with Billy again, only this time she knew it would be much worse. Her limbs felt suddenly heavy and, defeated, she bowed her head and got meekly into the backseat of the enormous beast.

Just a matter of minutes later they pulled up outside an imposing building on Tirpitzufer alongside the canal. There were not too many men inside the large vestibule, just a couple at a desk inside the entrance to whom she was asked to hand over her passport, the details of which were carefully noted into the logbook. Veronica was scared and wanted the toilet but was too afraid to ask. Dimly she noted that all the men around her were wearing German Army uniforms. This included the two huge men who had brought her here, now that they had removed their hats and coats. They then took her handbag. She tried not to react as if there was anything of any particular importance to her there, but she anyway let out a little scream when a soldier behind her suddenly ran his hand down her leg. He quickly moved to her other one and she realised he was checking to see if she had anything hidden on her body. He patted every inch of her, dispassionate and thorough in his work, and she found this somehow reassuring. The two men now escorted her down the wide stone steps, along a narrow corridor, down a shorter staircase, and then into a small cell lit by a single low-wattage light bulb. There was a cot bed with a thin mattress covered in a sheet, on top of which had been thrown a threadbare blanket, but no pillow. The only other items in the room were a metal bucket about one third filled with water, a roll of toilet paper, a bowl of water and a tin cup.

'Good night, Fräulein Beaumont,' said the first man, 'pleasant dreams.' He laughed as he walked away, leaving the door open. Seconds later the other man came in and he did close the door.

'Take off your skirt, Fräulein,' he said, taking off his jacket.

'No,' said Veronica, backing away. 'I'll scream.'

'Oh you'll scream all right. But it would be so much easier if you co-operated. It's nothing personal. It's just a perk of my job.'

He started to move towards her and she darted past him trying to get to the door though she had no idea what to do if she got out of the cell anyway. His open hand slapped into the side of her head with such force that her body was thrown against the wall and she slumped to the ground clutching her head with one hand and her shoulder with her other. He grabbed a fistful of her hair, pulled her up and then threw her onto the cot. He started to unbutton his trousers.

'Wait!' shouted Veronica, her mind desperately racing. 'You can't touch me, I'm a Jew. Your race laws forbid it!'

The man laughed. 'That's a new one, Fräulein, and so pleasingly foreign. No German woman would dare claim to be Jewish. But you're no more Jewish than I am.'

'No, you must believe me. You would be a criminal in the eyes of your own legal system and you would be severely punished.'

'Enough. Stop your mouth or I'll shut it for you.' He raised his fist menacingly.

'*Ha-sochnut Ha-yehudit!*' Veronica shouted. '*Ha-sochnut Ha-yehudit!*' She tried to remember the other words from the letterhead that Sarah had taught her but in her panic all she could remember were the first two. She continued screaming them over and over again.

The man looked at her with astonishment for a few moments. Then he turned, grabbed his jacket and left the cell, locking it behind him. Veronica fell to her knees on the stone floor, her hands and legs trembling. She crawled to the metal bucket and started retching.

THIRTY-EIGHT

21 SEPTEMBER 1938

LICHTERFELDE, BERLIN

ROGER TUCKER HUNCHED AS LOW AS HE COULD IN the old battered DKW saloon car. He'd been handed the car for this assignment and it was not one of the Embassy's motor transport pool. It was just as well. He felt conspicuous enough as it was. There were a few other motor vehicles parked on the narrow leafy street but not nearly enough for him to hide amongst and he'd had to park quite a way down from the house. This cloak and dagger stuff wasn't really his style but for this week they had been told it was 'all hands on deck'.

General von Strasser lived in a detached house with mustard and brown decorative brickwork. It was two storeys high but with a very wide front, two pairs of windows to the left of the front door and three pairs of windows to the right. Some generals, Tucker mused, were living very well under the Third Reich. Until just a few years ago this area had been home to a mix of military and industrialist families, many of the latter Jews. Now that the Jews were all gone, their homes had been given over to senior officers both from the *Wehrmacht* and the SS. He wondered if von Strasser had been a beneficiary of this state-organised theft. The trees in the General's small front garden were losing some of their leaves now but the branches themselves were very thick. Visibility was, to some extent, also restricted by some large pine trees which lined the pavement on this part of Kadettenweg, or Cadets' Way, named after the large military barracks at the end of the street which Tucker knew had been, back in the Kaiser's day, the German Army's Sandhurst.

A couple of SS soldiers with the rank of Obersturmführer walked past, laughing. He had really picked the short straw here. Although the general and his wife had gone out an hour ago and the house was deserted, with the SS barracks so close by he had to be alert at all times and he didn't dare get out and stretch his legs in case someone tried to speak to him. His excuse for being in the area was no better than being a lost tourist poring over a map. At least, of the many of his colleagues sitting in cars across Lichterfelde that night, he was one of the very few to know why they were doing this. He'd known his boss at Harrow when most of the other staff were either from Eton or Marlborough, so he'd been given some inside information – but warned it was to go no further.

Harold Davis had drawn him aside, theatrically looking down the corridors of the Embassy to check the coast was clear.

'Keep it to yourself, old boy, but the chaps at the top are hoping to find evidence of Italian-German collusion over the Czech negotiations. Mussolini is putting himself forward as an honest broker. My Aunt Fanny! If we find any Italians having contact with certain members of the General Staff, then we'll know that we are right not to trust the buggers.'

Right this moment though, Tucker was itching for a fag. Smoking on the street would draw attention but he wondered if he could get away with it in the car. He reluctantly decided that that would be nearly as stupid. Passersby might not notice him slumped low but a car filled with smoke would definitely draw attention.

Just then a light went on in the general's home. Someone was in the study of what was supposed to be an empty house.

Oh hell, now what, *now what?* thought Tucker. He tried to calm himself: there could be any number of innocent explanations for this. Maybe there was another person beside the general and his wife who had remained in the house when they had left. Except he had seen them lock the door. But maybe they had forgotten they had a guest. Yes, unlikely, but still...

The light went out in the room. Tucker waited for a minute, took a deep breath and decided to get out of the car. He needed to get closer to try to understand what was going on. He headed towards one of the large pine trees next to the low garden wall. He hoped the thick branches would be enough to cloak him in the dim light... He walked briskly but quietly in the near silence. Suddenly, ahead of him, he heard a noise. Someone was opening a ground-floor window.

With a jerk of panic that hurt his neck, Tucker backed away from the tree to return to the safety of his car, all the while keeping his eyes fearfully on the window. There was a man, barely visible, his dark clothes blending into the shadows. Tucker could make out only a flat cap and the outline of a briefcase. As the man turned to gently close the window behind him, Tucker took the opportunity to sprint back to his car. Just then, from further down Kadettenweg, from the direction of the SS barracks, an SS trooper was walking in his direction, whistling tunelessly. The lights of one of the houses reflected off his gleaming jackboots. Tucker hesitated. So far he hadn't been spotted, but if he got back into his car, the soldier might wonder why, by the time he drew abreast of him, he hadn't driven away. If, on the other hand, he drove off, he wouldn't be able to report on an event his superiors would want to know about. But if he just hung about in the street, he would look suspicious and the burglar might notice him too. All three of them were on course to meet right in front of the house. Tucker decided to keep away from his car and walk up the street as if he was a simple pedestrian. But just as he was about to turn left from Kadettenweg into Weddigenweg, the man with the briefcase started running, overtook him and turned right into that road.

The SS man coming from further down Kadettenweg shouted, 'Halt!' and began to run towards the junction. Tucker, wishing the earth would swallow him up, pressed himself as close as possible to the garden wall in Weddigenweg, not looking back. Behind him from the burglar's side of the junction, a car's headlamps were suddenly switched on, its engine roaring to life. Despite himself Tucker turned his head, just in time to see the burglar run up to the car, chuck the briefcase through the back window and jump into the front passenger seat whose door had already been swung open.

As the car drove towards the crossing with Kadettenweg the SS trooper arrived at the junction, waving and shouting. The car knocked him aside without any attempt to brake. The young man was flung into the air, twisting like a rag doll. He slammed back into the road and lay motionless as the car roared down Weddigenweg, passing a petrified Tucker. There were, Tucker noticed, three men in the car.

As the noise of the engine faded away, Tucker was left alone in the quiet street. Although there was some street lighting, it was not enough to penetrate the gloom of the junction. He edged towards the SS man. There was no sound, no groaning and as he got closer he could see the trooper's legs had been broken at the knees. From the way he was lying, his neck was broken too. Lights were coming on now in some of the houses. Tucker walked quickly back to his car, willing himself not to run, got in, let off the handbrake and reversed silently, turning the wheel hard until the back of the car rolled across to touch the opposite kerb. He opened the door and momentarily put one foot on the ground to get up some forward momentum. Door closed, he looked anxiously around him but all was still quiet. Turning the wheel again he held the clutch down and rolled slowly downhill away from the junction, his headlamps off. Only after he had gone another fifty yards did he finally turn on the engine, praying that the engine would catch at the first moment of asking. It did. His hands were trembling violently now and so were his knees. He was in no fit state to drive but he would not stop until he was safely back inside the Embassy.

ABWEHR HQ, TIRPITZUFER BERLIN,
22 SEPTEMBER 1938

'It's a lovely morning outside, Miss Beaumont,' someone said to her in English, on Veronica's second day of incarceration. She was escorted, blindfolded, into a room somewhere else in the large building, up several half-flights of stairs and along corridors that she couldn't picture other than that the floors were hard and uncarpeted. 'I fully expect that you will soon be able to see that for yourself,' the voice had continued. She had no faith in his assurances and Veronica was more afraid than she had ever been in her life. For two days she had been left more or less alone though food had been brought to her and her bucket was emptied regularly. Sarah had told her that being left alone with one's thoughts was a technique used to break down prisoners' mental defences and she was shocked to experience just how effective this could be. For two days her imagination had been running riot in her head, playing on her greatest fears. She fully expected that some of these would now be realised. Her legs were shaking so much on the walk to this room that the two men had practically had to hold her up in the air so that her feet barely touched the ground. Her escorts now lowered her onto a hard wooden chair. She was aware of someone standing just behind her, his breath tickling the back of her neck.

'I am sorry for the blindfold, Miss Beaumont, but it is important, for reasons I shall make clear, that you cannot identify me, nor even where we are in this building. I will sit behind you for our conversation. Do not try to look at my face. You may call me "Captain". To help you not to make a mistake, we will turn on a very powerful light situated behind me. There. It's a very blinding light so please don't try to turn around. Now, I hope you had a good breakfast?'

Veronica didn't reply. Her blindfold was removed. She was sitting in a small room lined with files and some books, just in front of a large walnut desk that took up most of the room. On the desk were some more files and on one she could see her name had been written in large bold gothic letters. Unable to look at the man seated behind her, she looked down and into herself.

During the past two nights, she had been too afraid to do other than sleep fully clothed and her skirt and blouse were terribly creased. The pain in her head had gone but her shoulder was still throbbing. Her hair was not brushed and what was left of her makeup felt like paste and her eyes full of grit. She had not been able to clean her teeth and this made her reluctant to open her mouth. The young captain sitting behind her doubtless had just come out of the shower and she could smell his cologne very clearly. Her own smell would be far more pungent but she would not apologise for that. She was glad if it offended him. He had created it after all.

'I do hope your stay has not been too intolerable,' he added politely.

'Do you mean not too intolerable given the insanitary conditions I have been forced to endure, or that I was assaulted by one of your guards as soon as I arrived? I don't think your humour is very amusing.'

'Forgive me, Miss Beaumont, I don't know what you mean,' said the captain. Veronica began to think of him as 'Captain X'.

'Of course you don't,' Veronica replied. She knew it was pointless but she had nothing to lose. 'Just spare me the polite talk. You, as well as your men, are responsible for what happens to me here. You therefore are a rapist too.'

'Miss Beaumont, this is the army, not the Gestapo. We are not criminals, you know.'

'Actually, I would say that you are criminals and that I am not. I am, however, a British citizen and I demand to be put in touch with my Embassy. You have no right to treat me in this way. I should be in my hotel, not having to go into a bucket.'

'You are also Jewish apparently.'

'Right,' she said, fighting to keep her voice steady. 'So you've been talking to the man who wanted to rape me. If you are the civilised man you say you are, you'll do something about him.'

The captain sighed. 'I have had his report. He says nothing other than that you started to speak in the Jewish tongue. He does not know why you did this but felt it was his duty to immediately report it. You yourself just now said that the guard had wanted to rape you. Your choice of words indicates that he did not. Is that correct?'

Veronica nodded.

'So you are asking me to punish a good man because of a rape that never happened?'

'It's about intent.'

'Not really, Miss Beaumont. It's about actions. If nothing happened then there really isn't anything to investigate. Now please can we move on? The quicker we can do so the quicker you can go home. Or are you really intending to spend another night here, Miss Beaumont?' She could hear him sitting back in his chair and she imagined him tilting the chair slightly as he talked to her. She determined not to show her dislike of his constant and unnecessary use of her name, knowing that it would only encourage him. It felt like being back in school again. She heard a movement from the captain behind her. She tensed, expecting him to touch her, but instead he leaned over her shoulder and flicked open a nickel-plated cigarette case.

'Would you like one?' said a voice close to her ear.

Eagerly Veronica took hold of the cigarette. The case, she noticed, was engraved with an eagle grasping a swastika in its talons. The captain stood, lit his own and then leant across to light hers before resuming his seat. Veronica normally smoked only on social occasions but she allowed herself to make an exception this morning.

She took a long drag on the cigarette, closed her eyes and put her head back, exhaling slowly, making the most of it. She could sense Captain X watching her. She remembered Sarah saying that if she ever found herself in this position, she should try and build some sort of rapport in the hope that it would encourage them to be more open to her in return and less likely to do anything really horrible to her.

'Your English is really very good,' she said. 'How is that?'

'I was a student at York University. I was in lodgings just off Micklegate. Do you know York, Miss Beaumont?' She nodded. She had been there a few times. In fact she too had stayed near Micklegate. This could be something they had in common and which she could leverage. 'Actually, I tell a lie,' he continued. 'It was at Bristol that I went to university. I rented a room in Clifton from a very strict landlady called Mrs Venison. Do you know Bristol at all?'

'Very funny, Captain. You like to play with your victims, I see. You know I spent time in York.' The momentary calm from the welcome cigarette had been replaced once more by her fear. She felt this man could turn off the charm very quickly.

'I am an Intelligence Officer. I ask you questions but you don't get to ask me any, I am afraid. I hope that I have made my point to you. After all, if I told you where I learnt my English in England, you might be able to have your MI6 friends work out who I am and that would never do. For all you know, I may not even be a captain. I could be a lowly corporal or I might be the very model of a modern major-general.' He laughed again, proud of his ability to reference British culture. 'Don't be angry with me, Miss Beaumont. I have just given you some very good news, don't you think?'

'Another one of your games, Captain?'

'Not at all. Just think about it, Miss Beaumont. It means you will be going home to England. If you were to be executed as a spy, I wouldn't care if you knew my real name, where I lived in England or indeed what I look like.'

'Well, I am not a spy, so what have you brought me here for and why have I been treated so badly? And when can I contact the British Embassy?'

'Questions and more questions! I do think you are a spy

though, Miss Beaumont. Oh, don't act so surprised. Let's see: you befriend Mrs Diana Guinness who believes you to be sympathetic to Germany. I wonder what she would say, should she know what you've been doing here. Then look at the company you keep when you are here. Does the wife of the head of the British Union of Fascists even know that her travelling companion is Jewish?'

'Actually it's not called that anymore, you're out of date. It's known simply as the British Union now.' It was a small point but it gave Veronica a tiny measure of satisfaction to be able to correct the arrogant all-knowing captain on a completely inconsequential fact.

'Oh! Is that right?' The captain contrived to answer her as if somehow she was wrong, and that he hadn't made any error. What an insufferable, evil man he was. She decided to imagine him to be a sweaty, revolting-looking man in an ill-fitting, dirty uniform, who had only showered because it was that time of year for him. She allowed herself a small smile.

Stubbing out the last of his cigarette into the ashtray, he leant over her, moving her blindfold back over her eyes, and then removed a sheet of paper from the file on the desk. She could feel that he was now facing her, very close, leaning back and resting against the desk.

'Here we are. You have met several times with various members of the Gutmann family. You are friendly with the former politician Klara Stein and you also know Gloria Braun a Zionist.'

'But so what?' exclaimed Veronica. 'This doesn't make me a spy. These are people who simply wish to leave Germany. Germany doesn't want Jews and these Jews want to leave or help others to leave. I really don't see—'

'But that's not the whole truth, is it?' She could hear him rustling papers. 'Klara Stein is a known homosexual communist and member of the KPD before she joined the SPD. Gloria Braun has contacts with the British colonial government in Palestine. There are colleagues of mine who would look at these visits and come to only one, very serious conclusion.' He paused to let this sink in and then took a deep and audible breath, conveying to Veronica that he was trying really hard to remain calm. 'The point is, that those people don't like my country, my government. If you were the innocent friend that Mrs Guinness or, indeed, Miss Mitford, takes you for, you would not be contacting any of these people. Yes, our policy here in Germany is to allow the Jews to leave. But am I not right in saying that the papers you have for the Gutmann family allowing them to enter Palestine are in fact false papers?' Veronica said nothing. The ghost of his cologne lingered even though he had pulled away.

'How ironic then that you ask me to put you in contact with the British Embassy when it is British law that you have flouted, not German law.'

'I'll take my chances with British justice then, shan't I?' retorted Veronica.

Her blindfold was removed for a second time.

'You may want to take your chances,' he said, 'but what about these poor Gutmanns who dream of starting a new life in Palestine?' Tears began to roll down Veronica's cheeks as his arm reached past her to lay out the Gutmanns' documents on the table in front of her, removed from her bag. 'These are very high quality forgeries, Miss Beaumont. How they must be relying on you. Your return to England without ever seeing them again would cause them much pain.'

Veronica was tired. She wanted to be brave but how to be brave when there is no longer any hope? She didn't know where she had made a mistake. Perhaps others had given her away. But she realised now what an amateur she was

and how childishly stupid she had been to think she could
have prevailed. His mentioning her return to England gave
her reason to believe that she, at least, might live. They knew
about some of her friends, it seemed, but not all and, crucially,
they had not mentioned Aunt Sonia and Manfred. Perhaps
they only knew about the Gutmanns because she had been
carrying their passport with her. Equally though, it might be
another one of the captain's games.

'What now then?' she said, without turning her head.
'You have everything. You know everything. What do you
want from me?'

'I have for you an easy task. So easy, that you may think
that it is a trap. I assure you it is not a trap. I want you to take
some papers back to England for me and hand them over to
someone who needs to see them very badly. I want you to take
them to him.'

'You want me to act as your go-between and help you
contact your spies in England? I would be betraying my
country!' She shuddered at the very thought of what leading
such a life might be like. How could she ever look Sarah in
the eye again? How could she live with herself knowing the
people she was abandoning in Berlin? There may be no hope
but she could meet her end with dignity. She shook her head.
'Captain, I think the punishment for treachery is much worse
than the punishment for obtaining false papers.'

'This man in England is not our spy. In fact he is no friend
of Germany's. He thinks that Hitler cannot be trusted, that
the Führer is spoiling for a war and that when Hitler says
he only wants the German-speaking parts of Czechoslovakia,
that is just a first step and that he won't stop until he has
marched into Paris.' He moved away and she heard him open
his desk drawer and extract a large envelope. 'The man who
thinks such thoughts is your lover, Hilary Masterson MP.

And the documents in this envelope,' he pulled them out, 'these prove that everything he suspects is true.'

Veronica gasped with surprise, trying to form words. Eventually she said, 'I'm sorry, but I don't understand. Why would you want to help Hilary if he is not one of your spies?'

'It is entirely understandable that you should not trust me. Let me reassure you in the best way possible. I believe your German is good enough, so I will not only let you read these documents, but I will help you to understand not just those military words you might not know but also why they are important. I am going to trust you with secrets, Miss Beaumont. We are giving Hilary Masterson what he needs to avoid a devastating war between Germany and Great Britain.'

Standing behind her, he reached over her shoulder and gathered up the package of documents destined for the Gutmanns.

'Going by the dates on these forged documents, I am afraid that by the time you get back to us from Germany – and we very much expect you to report back to us, Miss Beaumont – your friends will have, literally, missed the boat. Do I use the idiom correctly?' Veronica stayed quite still, overcoming her instinct to nod. Not that the captain waited for any response. He pressed right on. 'But they would certainly want these passports, don't you think?' Again Veronica said nothing. He already knew that the passports were vital. With them she could replace the other documents comparatively easily. 'That you are a Jew,' he continued, 'and you feel the need to help these wretched people doesn't interest me in the slightest. But we are going to keep all your Jewish friends here in Germany until you have carried out your mission.'

The package was removed from view and seconds later was replaced by an air ticket.

'Your plane leaves in just under three hours. A car will take you to your hotel where you can clean yourself up and it will then take you to Tempelhof. We notice that you are booked into the Adlon for another week. We have kept that booking, and what items you have in your room will remain there until the week is out. So hurry back to us, Miss Beaumont. You must be under no illusion about what will happen to these people if you should fail.'

'But if I fail, I won't come back to Germany so that your men can attack me and no doubt kill me. But you must know this. So my question is, what if I succeed and Hilary succeeds, and there is no war? Will you at least let me visit my Jewish friends and help them?'

'My dear Miss Beaumont, if Hilary Masterson succeeds, your friends won't even need your forged documents.'

'But will you let me see them?'

'Miss Beaumont,' Captain X replied without any obvious trace of irony, 'you have my word as a German Officer.'

LONDON, 23 SEPTEMBER 1938

'My God, Veronica, have you gone mad? I didn't expect to see you again. I thought I had made that clear. And even if we *were* friends, you will recall that I imposed few rules, but one hard and fast one has been to *never* engage with me when I am with my wife. Yet you practically ambushed us there in Green Park. Were you following us?'

Veronica nodded, sat down in the armchair, unlaced and kicked off her shoes. She was exhausted from the long flight followed by an equally long cab ride from Croydon aerodrome.

'Hilary, please sit down, I—'

'Dammit, Veronica, if you think I'm going to—'

'I said to bloody sit down and hear what I have to say!'

Veronica had never shouted at Hilary before and suddenly he saw steel that he'd not known was there. Something about her look made him obey her and without realising it, he was sitting on the couch opposite, his own anger entirely dissipated. Veronica reached into her bag and took out a folded copy of the *Daily Mail*. Unfolding it she then removed from its inner pages a sheaf of typewritten paper which she handed to him.

Hilary didn't read German but he recognised the eagle and swastika emblem at the bottom of the last sheet. He looked up at her, then back down at the papers, then back to her again.

'Jesus, Veronica, what have you got yourself mixed up in?'

Veronica pointed at the sheets of paper. 'These were stolen a few days ago from the home of a German general in Berlin. They demonstrate more clearly than anything you've ever seen until now, what Hitler plans to do if we give into him at Munich.'

'Look, Veronica, I don't know who gave these to you, but I should tell you that this is not the first time some Germans, disloyal to Hitler, have tried to persuade us that, once he gets the Sudetenland, he then plans to take over the rest of Czechoslovakia, and even that he will attack Poland. The Prime Minister is aware of all of this but frankly, we cannot know for sure whether any of it is true, and even if it is nobody cares. Those of us who do care are unable to show any evidence and there is little trust in the sources who are informing us that the army will overthrow him.'

Veronica started waving her hands around to interrupt, but Hilary was having none of it. 'God knows I've tried, but our British sense of fair play is such that it is impossible to get past the feelings of disgust held for men who would betray their country. And that's the reaction of those few of us who believe them. By far, the widest view held is that these Fritzes are in fact simply trying to tease us into starting a war for which we are hopelessly unprepared.'

'France,' finally interjected Veronica.

'What's that? What do you mean, "France"?'

'These papers are not about Czechoslovakia or Poland. These are plans to attack France.'

For a moment, Veronica thought that Hilary was going to collapse. He sat down hurriedly and reached for the whiskey bottle on the side table. He looked at it unseeing for a moment before reaching for a tumbler. With a shaking hand he poured himself a measure and finished it in one go.

'Show me,' he said.

'These plans are called "Case Brown",' said Veronica, crossing over to him and kneeling on the floor beside his chair. She put the file on the floor and started passing sheets up to him, indicating where she had made translations in the margins.

'The first paragraph talks about the situation in which such a plan would be put into effect. These lines here say, "Once Czechoslovakia has ceased to offer resistance, we will be able to turn West." And here, further down, it says, "Whilst Britain and France are led to believe that our interest is in Poland, the Soviet Union will be assured that this is not the case. A quick and massive bombing campaign will get that message across." On the next page here, Hilary,' Veronica passed him another sheet, 'it says that, "Those army formations capable of rapid deployment must, within the first two to three days force their way through the Maginot Line with speed and energy." Here in the middle paragraph it details a large-scale bombing attack on Paris. Here is the detailed list of numbers and make of aircraft expected to participate. There are nearly 200 planes altogether counting fighter escort.'

'My God,' said Hilary, struggling to keep up with the speed with which Veronica was reeling off these plans and how she seemed to have changed into something quite formidable and frightening even. 'If this is genuine, the Prime Minister will have no choice but to act.' He looked at the wall, unseeing for a moment, and then slowly turned to look at Veronica.

'But first, I need to understand a lot of things. You can start by telling me what you were doing in Berlin, who you are and who gave this to you and why I should think this is anything more than a trap.'

THIRTY-NINE

24 SEPTEMBER 1938

DOWNING STREET, LONDON

NEVILLE CHAMBERLAIN WAS NEARLY 70 YEARS OLD and he was exhausted. Apart from a couple of years in the 1920s when there had been a Labour government, he had held ministerial office since 1922. Having never flown abroad before in his life, this month he had now flown twice to Germany and back and needed somehow to hold some reserve of strength in case he needed to go again.

He imagined that some people may have thought that to fly to Munich, to Cologne, was something to be envied, what with all the pomp and ceremony and staying in the best places. But Adolf Hitler was not an easy man to deal with, keeping him waiting and then giving little ground when they did finally talk. Last night's talks had gone on till early this morning. Hitler had been frightfully aggressive, making one demand after another, and Chamberlain wondered how he would have been able to stand up to him if he were not Prime Minister of Great Britain, the most powerful nation in the world, ruler of a quarter of the world's lands and supreme ruler of the seas. No wonder the poor Czechs were being browbeaten by that man.

Although as Prime Minister he could never say this to anyone other than his wife, Adolf Hitler was, in Chamberlain's opinion, quite insane.

Usually on the weekends, Chamberlain tried to get away to Chequers and rest a little from the pressures of the capital but, though they had landed at midday on Saturday, he knew he would not get any rest this weekend and directed that from the aerodrome he be taken directly to Downing Street, where he planned to sleep until evening. Hitler's latest ultimatum would not go down well with the cabinet, let alone Parliament, and he needed Sunday to prepare for what would be yet another critical day in the House. Duff Cooper was proving to be more and more temperamental as First Lord of the Admiralty, constantly agitating to take a firm line against Hitler, something that would undoubtedly bring war closer and play into Winston's hands. Duff had sent a note requesting to speak to him urgently about the Navy. He wondered, and not for the first time, whether Duff was leaking the detail of cabinet discussions to Winston. Someone was certainly. There were so few people in politics that one could trust.

He had just got into his pyjamas when there was a knock on his door.

He was not expecting interruptions when he was in his private rooms upstairs, and certainly not on a Saturday. He glanced at Annie who had been reading quietly in an armchair opposite him. She lowered her book and was also looking peeved, but with a hint of concern. He put on his dressing gown.

'Enter,' he called.

Lord Dunglass, his parliamentary private secretary, appeared in the entrance.

'What is it, Alec? Aren't you supposed to be at home today?' asked Chamberlain.

'I am sorry to disturb you, Prime Minister,' Dunglass nodded, bowing slightly to Annie, 'and Mrs Chamberlain. I was just catching up on some work downstairs so I happened to be the one to see Hilary Masterson arrive. He is asking to see you. Normally of course I wouldn't let anyone come and disturb you on a Saturday, especially as you have only just arrived, but, um...' He hesitated a moment, not sure how best to allude to Masterson's personal relationship with the Prime Minister, a closeness that itself was starting to become a political issue. '...well, he wouldn't quite say whether he was wishing to see you on a private matter or a political one, sir.'

'I understand, Alec. It's quite all right.' Chamberlain looked over at his wife. 'We are always happy to speak to Hilary, even on a Saturday when we've had little sleep. Ask him to come up.' Annie nodded with a smile. She had been worried that they would be bothered with politics even today. But Hilary was different.

'Alec,' Chamberlain called after the retreating figure, 'no need to hang around. You should go home just as soon as you're finished down there.'

Hilary came into the room dressed in a suit as if it was a normal working day. Chamberlain and Annie stood to greet him, both smiling warmly.

'How lovely to see you, Hilary,' said Annie, 'will you take tea?'

'Dear Mrs Chamberlain, that is so kind of you, and I see that I have come at an awfully inconvenient time but I am afraid I come with some really urgent information that cannot wait.' He stopped and looked expectantly at the Prime Minister. It took Chamberlain a moment to fully take in the insolence of this young man who had used their personal connection to conduct parliamentary business just as he was trying to get to bed. He was weighing up the cost of showing anger and regretting it later. Hilary pressed on.

'Sir, I am fully aware that I have exploited our families' friendship to come in here today and I only ask that you indulge me and judge me afterwards if you feel that I have not acted as you would expect.' He paused and looked at Annie expectantly.

Chamberlain felt the muscles on his face tighten with anger. Was Hilary asking that Annie leave the room in her own house?

'I see,' he said stonily. 'You'd better sit down then. This is most irregular.'

Annie began to walk towards the door, her cheeks reddening, when Chamberlain stopped her. 'No, Annie. Please stay. Hilary would not expect you to leave the room,' he turned to face Hilary, 'not with the relationship we have. Isn't that so, Hilary?' he challenged.

Hilary knew better than to argue and to his credit answered without the slightest hesitation, 'No, of course not! Mrs Chamberlain, I hope you didn't for a moment think that this was my intention?'

Annie smiled. 'I was only going to arrange for a fresh pot of tea and perhaps some cake too. I won't be a moment.'

Hilary was already taking documents out of the envelope he had removed from his briefcase and was laying them out on the low coffee table. 'Prime Minister, I am afraid I have received from an entirely reliable source, the most astonishing evidence that indicates that if Czech defences are handed over to Germany, far from preserving the peace, it will in fact lead to an almost immediate attack on France.'

'But that is preposterous!' exclaimed Chamberlain. 'The

Chiefs of Staff have made it clear that the German army is not capable of fighting both France and Britain.'

'These documents, Prime Minister, are the German army's plans for France. I have had the key passages marked and translated but essentially they intend to rely on overwhelming air power to devastate Paris and France's communications networks. They refer to the experience they have gained in Spain and their certainty that, as soon as the Czech defences are in their hands and the Czech army powerless, they can defeat France before the RAF can come to its aid.'

Chamberlain walked over to the coffee table, paused and then turned away with a sigh. 'I had better get my reading glasses.'

LONDON, 26 SEPTEMBER 1938

They had agreed to meet in Queen Anne's Gate, tucked in between St James's Park underground station and Birdcage Walk. Rab's idea had been to find a bench in the park and have a quiet, unobserved discussion and then quickly return to work at the Foreign Office. When he caught sight of the tall, bulky figure of Billy Watson lumbering towards him though, he realised he'd need to revise that plan.

'Where is your hat?' he asked Billy in response to the latter's greeting.

Billy shrugged. 'I haven't got one.'

Rab looked at him for a moment, unsure whether this was the man's attempt at humour. 'Why not?' was, in the end, all that he could think of in reply.

Billy shrugged again.

Rab felt as if he was, in fact, being made a fool of. He didn't need to look around to know that no other person, man or woman, was hatless. Apart from anything else, didn't this fool realise that he would stick out when what was required was a low-profile meeting?

'I've got better things to spend my money on,' added Billy as an afterthought.

Rab fished in the pocket of his waistcoat and brought out a ten-shilling note, but then thought better of it and stuffed it back in. Tempting as it was, he wasn't going to rile the man just yet. He stood up.

'I can't be seen talking to you if your head's not covered. It's far too risky.' He pointed back towards the station. 'I'm going to walk up there. Wait five minutes and then follow. At Broadway, turn right and I'll meet you in the Adam and Eve pub on the corner.'

Rab had deliberately chosen 11am to meet, when most civil servants would be at their desks. The park had been a good place for hiding in plain sight, but this pub was at least not a known Foreign Office watering hole. He was reassured on his arrival there to see very few people sitting at the dozen or so tables in the pub and he was able to find one unoccupied in the corner. He passed a shilling across the bar, ordered two pints of mild ale and carried them back to the table. Billy walked in at that point and followed him. He took the pint Butler pushed towards him and drank half the glass before putting it down again, saying nothing.

'You asked to see me, Watson. What do you want to say?'

Billy shrugged again. 'I've done what you asked. My agent has been in place.' He paused, thinking of Veronica in Hilary's arms. 'Very firmly in place in fact.'

'Really?' snorted Rab. 'You have some photographs then?'

Billy shook his head. Rab snorted again. 'No. But I have something possibly even better.' He drew Hilary's letter from his pocket, unfolded it and laid it out carefully on the table, first checking the surface with his hand to be sure it was quite dry. 'This,' he paused for effect, 'is a love letter from your MP to my agent.' He sat back smiling, waiting for Butler's reaction.

Rab took the letter and quickly scanned it. He knew Masterson's handwriting and it made interesting reading. What an insufferable cad Masterson was. He tossed it carelessly onto the table and sat back.

'You're too late.'

'How do you mean?' asked Billy, scowling.

'You said you would be able to move fast. You've taken months to get me this. You've bloody failed.'

'What do you mean? I don't understand.'

'Hilary Masterson has been to see the PM over the weekend. I don't know what he has said to him, but Chamberlain has had a change of heart. Our policy is to be turned on its head.' He leaned forward so that only Billy could possibly hear and said slowly, breathing straight into his face, 'Tomorrow, we are going to send a statement to Germany stating that we will join with France to counter any German military aggression.' He sat back again. 'You are a fucking failure. I don't know why I ever bothered with you. You can expect nothing from us.' He stretched out his hand to take up the letter again. 'However, I'll be taking this.'

Billy for a moment had been contemplating lashing out and throttling this snotty-nosed superior Tory toff for daring to talk to him in such a way but his anger was tempered by the realisation that he had let nearly two weeks go by before he had decided how best to use this letter and now it appeared that he'd made a mistake. He was glad Masterson hadn't dated the letter. Instead he moved quickly to snatch it off the table ahead of Rab.

'I don't think so. I will keep hold of this,' he said. He folded it carefully along the old folds and put it inside his wallet which he returned to an inside pocket. His mind was working fast. 'I can sort this out. Don't you worry.'

Rab Butler laughed derisively. 'How? How can you possibly undo whatever Masterson has done? We're bloody going to go to war and it'll be your fault.' Butler stood up and Billy did too.

'You'll be amazed what I can do,' Billy said. 'And you'll come to me and ask for forgiveness.'

Butler turned and walked out of the pub.

'You mark my words,' Billy shouted to his retreating back.

FORTY

26 SEPTEMBER 1938

LONDON

BILLY HAD ALWAYS BEEN AFRAID OF HIS FATHER. IT seemed to Billy that his father would reach for his belt as often as he would drink and that was most nights once Billy had passed his tenth birthday. Most of his friends at that time were beaten by their fathers and if their fathers were dead or absconded, not a few of these were also beaten by their mothers. If anything, Billy told himself, he had been lucky because sometimes his mother showed him signs of affection. Looking back he realised she probably would have been kinder to him had she not been so afraid of his father, who seemed to get jealous of her showing affection to any other person, even to their own son. Many years later a girl he'd been seeing had told him she thought that his mother, by showing him such little love, had been trying to protect him. What a load of bollocks. What he did know was that, at the time, he had tried harder and harder to win a smile from her, a constant and exhausting struggle that only rarely paid off.

One of those occasions had been his eleventh birthday when she had bought him a present. Possibly the first since he had been five or six. It had been a book, *India's Story*, his first grown-up book. It was, it noted towards the front, just one of several in a series called *Our Empire Story*, the others being *Canada's Story*, *Australasia's Story* and *South Africa's Story*. Billy hoped that if he was a really good boy his mother would buy him the others in the series. When he thought of it he would try so hard, offering to help her hang up washing or sweep the floors. But she never did buy him any other book and he was left with just the stirring tales of the White Man's triumphs in India. *India's Story* contained far more words than pictures, though the three or four colour plates planted throughout the book stirred him: Great Britain, victorious at sea against the French and on land, breaking the siege of Lucknow. His favourite picture had been of his hero, Clive of India, displaying true leadership '*Clive fired one of the guns himself*,' stated the caption.

But there had been other stories in that book which had affected him far more deeply and which he had never acknowledged. One night he had read how, during the great Mutiny, one hundred and forty-six British men, and one woman, had been forced into a tiny room just eighteen foot square, by an Indian mob. That room became known as the Black Hole of Calcutta. Billy had not been able to sleep that night for fear that he would wake in that dark hole. The next morning, he had read, only twenty-three of them, including the one woman, had still been alive when the door to the room was finally opened.

Perhaps Billy would have been able to move on from there if it had not been for his father who, wanting to enforce his conjugal rights in a room which was divided from Billy's by only a paper-thin wall, had suddenly grabbed his son, flung him into the small cupboard under the stairs and locked him in for twelve hours. Billy had screamed and pleaded but nobody had come to him. In his fear he had thought he'd heard rats scurrying about just as they had no doubt experienced in the Black Hole and he wet himself spending the rest of the night trembling in his smelly sodden clothes.

The claustrophobia he had developed that day stretched to any situation where he felt trapped and, after the encounter with Rab Butler, Billy was certainly feeling it now. Butler had pushed him into a corner where he stood to lose everything. His heart was pounding not just with humiliation but with the surfacing once more of his childhood fears.

He had already done things that society would not approve of but not much more than that. He included in this category the favour he had asked of Gunther. After all, it was no more than Gunther and his mate Hans were already doing to Jews all over Germany.

But now, for the first time, he began to contemplate getting blood on his hands, his own hands, here in England.

Anything to escape the trap.

A daring plan began to come together in Billy's head and he was quite proud of his ability to think logically and plan every step and every death along the way which, at the end, would see Butler grovelling in apology and Billy famous throughout the British Union as the man who could achieve real results.

That same afternoon as Mrs Wolf, using her two sticks, struggled back from the short walk to the pillar box to post a letter, two men helped her up her front garden path. At first she was grateful although, she said, it was really not necessary, she needed to try to do this sort of thing herself. Seconds later, when their grip on her arms was painful, she was protesting fearfully and begging that they let her go or she would scream. But by then they had opened her front door with her key, pushed her inside and punched her unconscious.

'Harry?!' Nick shouted. 'Your wife is in a lot of pain. Please can you help us?'

From up the stairs they heard a thumping noise and then sounds of exertion. Nick looked at Paul, who nodded and sped up the stairs. Harry Wolf was half way through the toilet window leading onto the flat roof before Paul grabbed his legs and pulled him back into the house. Harry, his hands flailing wildy in the air, grabbed hold of the long chain hanging down from the toilet cistern, but if he had hoped to use it as a weapon it simply wasn't long enough and he only succeeded in flushing the toilet as Paul grabbed him and dragged him down the stairs. Harry stopped struggling when he saw Naomi lying unconscious on the floor. Paul let him go but stood over Harry as, with a wail, he threw himself down onto his wife, kissing her cheeks, and moaning, 'What have you done to her? What have you done?'

'Don't worry, Harry,' said Nick softly. 'She'll live. But for how long, depends on your co-operating with us.'

'What do you want?' sobbed Harry, cradling his wife's head in his arms.

'We have a car outside. We want you to come take a drive with us. We have a job for you that can't wait and we will pay you handsomely – by agreeing not to kill your wife.'

FORTY-ONE

27 SEPTEMBER 1938

BELGRAVIA, LONDON

'NICK, YOUR BIRD, IS SHE RELIABLE?'

Nick smirked. 'She does everything a man could ever wish for if that's what you mean, Billy!'

'Actually, no, Nick. I weren't meaning that. I mean, can we trust her politically to keep secrets? Or to put it another way, would she steal for us, would she break the law for the British Union?'

Nick thought about this carefully. 'It's interesting. If you was to ask, would Stephi break the law for you and I? Nah, I don't think she'd do that. She has a high respect for what's right. But for the BU, she would be loyal to the end, without a shadow of a doubt.'

'Good. It's a bit short notice but by this evening I am going to have what I need to carry out an urgent job. You, me and Paul, we've done some pretty hard stuff recently and we're going to need to do just a bit more. We'll need Stephi with us tonight…'

Nick nodded. 'I'm wiv yer. Things are moving our way,

aren't they? So we have to be brave and show daring. I'm up for anything and I am sure that Stephi feels the same way.'

'And you know how proud I am of you and how proud the Party is of you, Nick. It's going to be very straightforward as far as Stephi is concerned. And she doesn't even need to know everything, but I do need her to do exactly what she is told and not to breathe a word of it to anyone...'

PARK LANE, LONDON

There was no getting around it. She was too afraid to return to Germany.

It really was that simple. She didn't think she could take a night like the one she had spent in that military cell and it wasn't even a concentration camp. She thought of Manfred and the months of incarceration that he had suffered. Of course, not to go back would mean that Manfred would never get out of Germany. That made her cry. For Manfred and for Sonia, for the student Stefan, for Renate and Richard Gutmann, and for Peter and Lise. All these people to whom she had made promises. Sarah might have been persuaded to try to help them despite having her own priorities but Veronica hadn't dared contact her, afraid that the horror of her experience would come spilling out and she would lose her respect.

The fact was that these Jews were now different from other German Jews. Thanks to her, and her association with them, they were now marked for special treatment by the German army. If she didn't go back these Jews in particular would face new levels of persecution. On the other hand, if she went back it might make no difference and she would simply share in their helplessness and suffering.

She had been back in England five days. Four days since

she had revealed what she knew to Hilary and three days since he had gone to speak to the Prime Minister. She had tried to contact Hilary after that but he had not returned her telephone call. If she left it any longer the fate of those she had abandoned would be sealed.

In her heart she knew she would not return to Germany. She would try telephoning him at work and if he didn't speak to her, that would be it. She would stay in London and try to forget that those people over there, her people, had ever existed.

'Hello, Hilary Masterson speaking.'

'It's me,' she said, speaking rapidly, afraid he would cut the connection. 'I have to know how your meeting went. Lives depend upon it.'

There was a deep sigh from the other end of the line.

'My life may depend upon it, Hilary. I explained this to you.'

'I will not divulge my discussions. You know I cannot do that.'

'I understand. Just tell me if you think he was persuaded. You need not say anything else.'

There was a pause. She could almost hear the cogs turning in his mind, calculating how much he might divulge both to her and to anyone listening on the line.

'I can tell you,' he said finally, 'that the message definitely hit home. I owe you that much. I can even say that I believe that, whilst the lion may not quite be ready to roar, he is raising his head from slumber and shaking his mane.'

'Vigorously?' she asked.

'Oh yes, I would say vigorously.' He mumbled something that sounded like a convoluted and final 'goodbye' and the line went dead.

She stared at the phone for a minute after replacing the receiver. If she were to go to Berlin, she would at least have something positive to report to those men. But nothing concrete. And she would be relying on Hilary, a man she had jilted, his lion and the word of a Nazi officer. It would be madness to go back.

That evening, to her surprise, Sarah agreed with that assessment.

'It's too risky, Ronnie. The Nazis now know who you are. You could compromise our operations there and make it harder for us to get anyone else out.'

'But I've achieved almost nothing. If I go one more time I could take, what, twenty more certificates with me?'

'Veronica. No. Your days as a courier are certainly over. You must see that. Anyone you are seen delivering certificates to would now be in danger. If you're caught with certificates on you – and you will now almost certainly be searched – we might never be able to use that method again. You can't work for us anymore.'

Veronica heard what Sarah said and she knew she was right but that didn't lessen the pain.

'You have achieved a lot, Ronnie, you really have,' Sarah said gently. 'Eighty certificates. And not one stopped en route to Palestine. That's eighty people saved from their clutches. How many people can say the same?'

Veronica reached for a handkerchief and dabbed her eyes. 'I'd hoped for a hundred,' she whispered.

As the two women talked, just a few miles away Hilary had locked up for the night and was about to take a bath. Naked, he tested the water with his foot but it was far too hot. He hated it when he didn't get the temperature right. He ran some cold water and keeping his hand right beneath the cold water tap, he scooped the cooler water into ever-widening circles to try to quickly cool the water down. At that very moment though there was a knock on the door.

He frowned; it could really only be Alec, the PM's PPS, coming to confirm that the negotiations with the Germans were now about to end following Britain's new firm line. It was a bit early for such a reaction and doubtful they would think to inform him directly anyway. Yet it was hard to know who else would have got in through the downstairs lobby to even gain access to this floor, especially at such a late hour. He shut off the tap, put on his bathrobe, tied it tightly, added some slippers and went to the door.

'Who is it?' he called through the door.

'I'm Stephanie,' came a young strong, voice in reply. 'I'm the new neighbour from downstairs. I've locked myself out but nobody is answering. You're the first person who seems to be home tonight. I wondered if you could please let me come in and use the telephone so my parents can send someone round with the key?'

She sounds lovely, thought Hilary. Her accent was not quite upper class and he had a feeling she had been trying hard to maintain what there was of it. How wonderful, he thought, someone with an interesting background and probably beautiful too. He put the chain on the door. If she really was as wonderful as she sounded, he'd let her in. He pulled the door open. Stephanie was indeed a vision of loveliness in her low-cut tight-fitting red evening gown, her face slightly concealed by a charming veil pinned to her short blonde hair.

'You've been out on the town, have you, Stephanie?' asked Hilary with a smile.

Stephanie looked down demurely. 'Er, yes,' she stuttered. 'I – I was out with my man. He kissed me at the door but went away in case my parents were around. But we've only been to the theatre!'

Hilary grinned. How charming she was. Especially her need to reassure him that she wasn't a bad girl. A nice touch, he thought as he closed the door, released the chain and opened it again.

Nice touch, thought Nick too, admiringly as he watched Stephi's performance, his back flat against the wall on one side of the door, Billy on the other.

Stephi smiled at Hilary as the door opened – and that was the signal for Nick and Paul to barrel their way in through the door, knocking the startled Hilary onto his back in the process. They fell on top of him, Billy, following in their wake, closing his hand over the MP's mouth and stifling any call for help.

'Off you go, Stephi,' said Nick, 'we just need some answers from this man. Close the door behind us. We'll see you tomorrow. Not a word to anyone, all right?'

Stephi smiled, and shut the door.

Nick removed a sock and a silk tie from his pocket and forced the sock into Hilary's mouth whilst Paul held the MP's head and sat on him. Nick then kept the sock in place by winding the tie around Hilary's mouth and tying it tightly at the back of his head. Hilary's chest was heaving with fear. They dragged him into the nearby dining room.

'Right,' said Nick, rising to his feet. 'I'll check around the flat, see if there is anyone else here.'

'There now, Hilary,' said Billy, looking down at his victim. He put a foot down on Hilary's neck, with just enough pressure to ensure that he didn't try to get up or do anything silly. 'You ain't so cocky now, are you? Not like last time. Mocking me, weren't you? Having fun at my expense.' He leant his head down so that Hilary turned to focus on him.

'You might be wondering why I ain't breaking your nose, or kicking you in the stomach, or giving you a black eye?' He reached down, grabbed one of Hilary's hands and began to bend the struggling man's fingers back. Hilary let out a muffled scream. 'Or,' continued Billy, 'you might be wondering if I am going to break your fingers one by one.' He abruptly let go of Hilary's hand. 'But I ain't going to do any of them things. You want to know why?'

Hilary's eyes bulged and he was trying to say something. Nick returned.

'It's all clear,' he said. 'There's a full bath down the corridor.' He jerked his head to indicate to Billy where he'd found it. 'He must have just run it. It's steaming.'

Billy grinned. He looked down at Hilary.

'Now what was I saying? Oh yes. Why am I not hurting you? Well, truth is, I was planning to kill you. I was going to hang you from that large chandelier you have here and have it look like suicide. You stood on that fine oak table and simply walked off the edge, see? It would look mighty suspicious if someone had beaten you up first. And with broken fingers, you wouldn't even be able to hang yourself so the police would be immediately suspicious.' He saw Hilary's eyes bulging with fear and felt the thrill of complete power. He smiled down reassuringly at his victim. 'But I've had a change of heart,' he continued. 'I ain't going to hang you after all.'

Hilary moaned and lay his head back on the carpet, relief coursing through him.

'Tell you what, Hilary,' said Billy. 'There really is something I want to know from you. If you answer me truthfully, I might let you go. You know, change of heart like I said. But if you lie, I'll cut your ears off. Do you understand me?'

Hilary's face was red and sweating, his eyes wet with tears

of fear. His bathrobe had come loose and his pale naked body was lying there under Billy's weight making breathing even harder. He quickly nodded.

'Right then, Hilary, have you or have you not fucked my girl?'

Hilary shook his head emphatically no. Billy pondered this denial, trying to work out whether it was true or not. Surely Hilary Masterson would say anything at this point to not antagonise him. 'Not sure you're levelling with me Hilary,' he said menacingly. 'No sex of any kind? She to you or you to her?'

Hilary shook his head again, more vigorously.

'But you wanted to and tried to, didn't you?'

Hilary hesitated.

'The fucking truth now or I swear to God...' Billy raised his clenched fist in the air above Hilary's head, ready to come crushing down.

Hilary nodded fearfully, telling the truth even though he assumed it was the worst answer to give.

'But you didn't?'

Hilary shook his head.

'She wouldn't let you?'

Billy put his fist down, satisfied. She hadn't cheated on him. He wondered why it was so important to him. Veronica had got to him, he realised. The bitch. He glanced at Nick and Paul.

'Come on then, let's get him on his feet.'

They hauled him up and Billy led them down the corridor, away from the dining room and the well-fixed chandelier. Hilary looked at him, his sweaty face now creased with an agonised hope.

'Yes, I was going to hang you, me old fella,' said Billy, dragging it out and giving time for Hilary's tears of gratitude to start to flow. 'But, if you've got a hot bath waiting, we don't want all that hot water going to waste, do we?'

Hilary's face crumpled. 'That's right,' grinned Billy. 'Suicide in the bath works just as well. You probably found cutting open your wrists the least painful way to go. Am I not right?'

As they got into the steam-filled room, they took Hilary's robe off him and together Paul and Nick pushed him into the bath. Hilary started writhing wildly, water pouring over the sides and soaking the two men's trousers, making them curse.

'I think the water's still a little too hot by the looks of things,' said Nick thoughtfully, pressing hard on Hilary's shoulders to keep him in the bath. 'Don't worry, Hilary. You'll get used to it in a moment. Next time,' he laughed, 'maybe you'll run some cold at the same time.'

'You've been a naughty boy,' said Billy, having waited until Hilary got a little more used to the heat. 'You've been whispering things in the Prime Minister's ear. Suddenly, appeasement's out and we're about to go to war.' Hilary jerked his head back in fear as Billy leant in close. 'What have you been saying to him to change his mind, eh?'

Hilary closed his eyes. There was a resolution about the set of his jaw. Billy saw the change, stood up and laughed.

'You think you've worked it all out, huh? You think, "Ah Billy Watson wants to know my secret and I won't tell him." Maybe you think you can die a martyr's death, be a hero. Better than dying for nothing, right?' He leant in again. 'Or maybe you're thinking that, if you hold out, I can't kill you and maybe you'll be able to drag things out until someone comes looking for you. Well, think again, Hilary. You think you are so smart, rich and successful and all the pretty girls queue up to get into your bed.' Billy stood up and patted his own chest. 'Well, Billy here is not as stupid as he looks. You see, I don't actually need to know what you told old Neville. It don't matter.'

Billy took a folded piece of paper carefully out of his coat pocket, holding it high and well away from any splashes. Unfolding it he held it up to Hilary.

'Look, Hilary, is this your handwriting?'

Hilary squinted to get a look but couldn't quite read the words. He nodded.

'And you see your signature on the bottom?'

Hilary craned his neck forward and then nodded again – but then he did a double take, an expression of confusion on his face.

'You just noticed the date under your signature, am I right?' asked Billy.

Hilary nodded, still confused. He couldn't have written the letter dated with the current day's date. He had written no letters today. Billy kept his expression unchanged but he rejoiced at this confirmation of the quality of the Jewish forger's work. He pretended to read the letter carefully, looked up at Nick and winked.

'Hilary, here, has been a very busy man today. He's been writing to the Prime Minister no less.'

Nick looked down at the naked MP and whistled with admiration. 'Has he now? My oh my. You must be very important.' Nick looked to Billy. 'Read what it says, Billy.'

'Yes, all right. But first, let's take his gag out. I'd like to hear if he has any questions, and with the bathroom door shut I don't think he'll be heard anyway if he starts shouting.' Billy looked down at him. 'Though if you do... '

Leaving the threat hanging, Billy cleared his throat and began reading the words Harry Wolf had come up with two days earlier.

Dear Prime Minister,

I have known you since I was a child. Our families have been close. Loyalty has meant everything to me and I have been so proud to be at your side in these difficult times. Knowing that you could always rely on me gave me the confidence to be forthright in my views and, though this has made me enemies, it has also made me friends, some of whom you count amongst your closest colleagues.

Billy broke off from reading and gestured to Nick. 'Do it now, otherwise it will take too long, he'll still be able to ask any questions while he bleeds out.' Paul pressed down hard on Hilary's shoulders and his mouth and nose sunk beneath the water. Nick caught Hilary's flailing arms and with his knife cut deeply into Hilary's wrist. As he drew the knife up along the vein, blood began to stream out. Paul lessened the pressure and Hilary's head reared up, gasping for air.

'There,' said Billy. 'All done. Not bad, eh? You can just relax now whilst I read to you. A bedtime story if you like. One that will send you into a looong deeeep sleep.' He laughed and resumed reading from the letter.

The other day, I gave you information that I believed to be of vital importance to our nation and to your premiership. I was happy to see that you trusted in me so much that you changed your policy. Happy that you trusted me, yes. But also happy that we were now doing the right thing for Great Britain and for the Empire.

I have to tell you now that I today received the devastating news, from an unimpeachable source, that I was misled, and that I in turn misled you: I now realise how critical it is to reach agreement with Herr Hitler and how near I came to dragging this country into an unnecessary war.

I understand that this revelation will cause you much pain and I cannot bear to be the cause of this. To see your disappointment in me will be the worst of all, the eclipse of my career a trifle by comparison.

My fervent hope is that my death will absolve you from any responsibility for the actions you have taken at my behest and at the very least will distract your enemies so that you can continue to lead us along the path to peace, a role for which I truly believe you to have been chosen by God.

Signed, Hilary

Billy looked up at Hilary. 'Any questions?'

Hilary started to answer but decided there was no point. This letter would bring war and bombs on France and maybe even on England. He had done his best. He closed his eyes. The heat of the water was unbearable. He felt as though his skin was peeling off as if he'd been on the beach. He remembered he had been terribly sunburnt once as a child and his nanny had put soothing balm on him and scolded him for not keeping under the shade of their umbrella. He supposed, now he thought of it, that his nanny had been afraid of what his parents would say. After all, she was supposed to have been watching over him. He tried to remember what had happened to dear old nanny. Must have been before the war of course. The war. Yes, he could remember being wounded. He'd had a similar pain in his arms then. A feeling that he couldn't move his arms, that they had been too heavy. He tried to move his arms now − no, they weren't moving. Just like at Passchendaele. When he woke up this time, he wondered, would it be like back then? Would there be a pretty nurse by the bed with a pitcher of cold water? That would be lovely. He thought he was already asleep. He'd look forward to that cold drink when he woke.

FORTY-TWO

28 SEPTEMBER 1938

PARK LANE, LONDON, MORNING

If Veronica had not decided to jump on the 16 bus as it drew up briefly at the stop near to her on Park Lane, she may well have never gone back to Germany. She couldn't even remember the last time she had ever taken a bus. Perhaps not since she had been a child when she had come into London with her nanny. Today the bus had drawn up and stopped, as it was required to do, even though no one was waiting. Or was it, she thought, because she had happened to be walking towards the stop, that the driver had halted, assuming she wanted to take it? Veronica had felt almost obliged to get on. As she'd stepped onto the low platform, the driver had accelerated and, being a novice, she had been taken by surprise, losing her balance and falling heavily against the conductor.

'Steady on, miss,' he'd said, his tone implying that she could have avoided him if she had just tried a little harder. Flustered, she had quickly sat down on the first available seat, crumpling the newspaper the man on the other side of the seat had been reading. He grunted irritably and moved to give her a little space, folding his copy of *The Times* in half, holding it up as a barrier between them. The inside pages were full of news of Czechoslovakia, teaching its readers for the first time about a country few had even heard of.

The page facing Veronica discussed precautions that Britain was taking, the handing out of gas masks, trenches being dug in St James's Park and on Hampstead Heath, but nothing that seemed to indicate that Britain was hardening its stand. One headline she could see, '*If we have to fight*', seemed promising but the way the man had folded the paper made it hard to read the article itself. The man shifted in his seat and refolded the newspaper, and then she saw it, in the very next column but one, and she couldn't stifle her excitement. She must have exclaimed out loud because at that moment the newspaper was lowered to reveal the top of an elderly man's face. He had a thatch of yellowy nicotine-stained white hair and was wearing heavy-framed glasses. The lenses too were very thick and magnified his eyes until they seemed to fill the lenses. They were staring at her. She tried to smile but he was now speaking.

'Do you want to take over my newspaper completely, young lady? You practically took my seat so why not my newspaper as well?'

'I'm so sorry.' She hung her head as if in shame but her need to read what she had just seen made her so very determined. 'It's just that my husband is in the navy and I saw the headline.' She pointed at it. 'It says "*The Fleet to Mobilise*". Does it mean that he is about to go to sea? Please tell me, if you won't let me read it.'

The man lowered his newspaper completely at that. She now estimated him to be in his mid-sixties. He was probably a City financier, she thought, observing his business suit and tie, his briefcase on his lap and his bowler hat resting on top…

'Your husband is in the navy?' She nodded. 'Well, that's different. Now let me see.' He turned the paper round to see the article for himself. *I could have read it in half the time,* thought Veronica. Finally he lowered the newspaper again. 'Well,' he pronounced, as if he was the teacher and she the pupil needing tuition. 'Yes, the King is to issue a Royal Proclamation calling up the naval reservists. All men belonging to the Royal Fleet Reserve Class B are to proceed to their depots on Wednesday. It says that this is just a precautionary measure. Well, they have to say that, don't they?' He looked at her with some sympathy. 'My dear, it is for the best. This will certainly give Herr Hitler something to think about. The French have mobilised fourteen divisions too.'

'Really?' said Veronica, amazed. 'May I see?'

'It's not here,' said the man, 'I heard it on the wireless yesterday. I don't know what's finally woken them up but we're getting tough at last. Bloody Germans.'

Veronica suddenly stood up and rang the bell. The man looked up at her in surprise. 'I'm so sorry,' she said again, 'I simply have to get back to my husband then and say goodbye.' The bus stopped and Veronica got off. Immediately she hailed a taxi to take her back to 49 Park Lane. She felt light-headed. Had she, by her own actions, called up the navy's reserves? Naturally Chamberlain had shared her information with the French. She had brought those papers back, had translated them for Hilary and had thereby mobilised the forces of the world's great democracies. Surely, she thought, the *Abwehr* would be impressed. The scales had tipped in her favour and she felt it was time to gamble. She was going to go back to Berlin, she would get the Gutmanns' passport back from the *Abwehr* and get her aunt and uncle over to England.

FORTY-THREE

28 SEPTEMBER 1938

ADLON HOTEL, BERLIN, EARLY EVENING

'SO THERE YOU ARE,' CAME DAPHNE'S ACCUSING VOICE. Veronica had hoped that Daphne would have returned to England by now. 'I was so sure you'd done the dirty on me and fled back home.' Daphne tossed back her mane of hair, flirtatiously, thought Veronica, and with difficulty overcame the urge to slap her. 'But you're here now,' said Daphne, 'so perhaps I'm not so angry after all.'

Veronica looked at Daphne, unable to summon up any words. The past few hours had been among the worst of her life; she was on the verge of tears, her life was in danger, and she still had to fend off this lecherous lesbian. It was too much.

'You're staring at me, V!' said Daphne. 'No, that's not quite right. You're staring *through* me. You're making me nervous. Is everything all right? Where have you been these past few days? Your room had a "do not disturb" sign on it.'

How efficient of the Abwehr, thought Veronica, bitterly. When she had left her room a week ago, she had not expected to be away longer than a few hours and had not worried about the cleaning staff. But, when she had returned this afternoon, all was still exactly as she had left it, her document pouch fixed up high against the back of the curtain. She realised that Daphne was still speaking.

'Last night I insisted the manager check inside in case you were in there dead.'

Veronica snorted but Daphne wasn't even pausing for breath, her long slim fingers flipping open a gold-plated cigarette case as she talked. 'And he did, you know – search the room. But the stupid oaf insisted that he do it alone as I had no right to look into a privately paid room. I told him I was a Lady but he said, "Madam, the Adlon has entertained kings and princes. The rules are the same for all." You should have heard him. The pompous man. And what a ridiculous accent, speaking English the way he does and expecting to get respect.' She took a drag of her cigarette and Veronica watched as Daphne contorted her mouth to one side of her head to exhale the smoke whilst at the same time concentrating her eyes on Veronica.

'*You* don't speak German, *do* you, Daphne?' She regretted the barbed comment the moment she said it. She needed to end the conversation not encourage the bloody woman. She thought that right now there probably was no woman she hated more in the entire world.

'No, I jolly do not!' Daphne replied. 'Everyone speaks English. Or everyone who counts for anything at any rate.' She prattled on for a while until Veronica decided she could take no more. She wanted to throw herself onto her bed and cry her heart out. She also knew that she absolutely had to hear the news on the large wireless set she had insisted on having brought to her own room. She had to tune in and find out how much tougher Chamberlain was going to be with Hitler. She was looking forward to falling asleep listening to it.

'You've taken a lover, haven't you?' Daphne moved to block her path to the lift.

'Don't be silly, Daphne.'

'Yet you don't deny it.'

'Yes! I deny it! Are you happy now?'

Daphne laughed.

'More than happy! I'll come to your room tonight.'

'No. You. Will. Not.' Veronica put her face close up to Daphne. 'I need to be alone.'

Daphne saw something in Veronica's expression and she stepped back, slightly afraid.

'But you promised.'

'Oh, for God's sake, shut up, Daphne. I promised. Yes. But I didn't say when. All right? Good night.'

She got into the lift, waited until it had moved up a floor so that Daphne would not be able to hear her through the doors, and finally she could burst into tears. Was it just this afternoon that she had been shown into a room at the *Abwehr* HQ? Once again it had been set up so that she could not see Captain X. He had listened to everything she had done since they had last met and he had gone over and over her meeting with Masterson and what exactly Masterson had said until he had left to go and see the Prime Minister. Word for word too on her telephone conversation with Masterson just the day before...

'Fräulein Beaumont, one day the world will know how you played your part in saving us all from a terrible war and you will be famous.'

'Thank you, Captain,' she replied. 'Now you must keep your word to me.'

'Of course, Fräulein,' he agreed. 'The moment I get authorisation from my boss, you will be free to return to

England. Today you can go back to your hotel. I don't need you.'

'And my friends?'

'You mean your Jews?' He waited, letting her know he expected an answer.

'Yes, them,' she said finally.

'We will stop monitoring them. They will of course remain subject to the law, but will not be treated differently from other German Jews.'

'And the Gutmanns?' Veronica tried to keep her voice calm, just another question.

'The same applies to them,' replied the captain.

'I mean their passport. Can I take it back to the Adlon with me?'

'No, of course you can't,' he replied, and in that moment her world began to spin. The Gutmanns could not leave without the passport because they had nowhere else to go to. Yet they had sold their home.

'Please,' she said. 'I'll do any task you set me. Just please let them go.'

'Miss Beaumont,' he said, using her English title for the first time to make it clear to her there was no flexibility. 'You should be grateful that you have not been punished for bringing those forged documents into our country. We have been more than lenient with the Gutmanns. The former Major Gutmann encouraged you to commit this crime. People have been sent to concentration camps for far less than that. You cannot expect that the German army would connive with such an international criminal enterprise and give you the forged illegal passport back so that you and he could continue to commit criminal acts in our country.'

Veronica had hung her head and said nothing, tears rolling down her cheeks. Then she had begun to beg him. Screaming, wailing, anything just let her have their passport back. It was such a small thing for him after all. It wasn't even a German passport, what do they care about forged Palestine passports for God's sake? But he had laughed, saying that nobody should feel themselves above the law. Then, tiring of her noise, he had slapped her. Hard. She had passed out and when she had come to she was being carried out of the building's side door and bundled into a taxi, supposedly civilian, but in reality an *Abwehr* vehicle which had deposited her back at the hotel. The last thing she had remembered the captain saying to her was, 'You're very lucky that you brought us good news.'

On an upper floor in the same cavernous building at Tirpitzufer, but a world away from the bare floors and windowless walls of the interrogation rooms, a celebration was taking place. As Admiral Canaris entered the room, a dozen pairs of legs, the grey uniformed trousers with their burgundy stripe tucked into shining jackboots, leapt to their feet and, as one, clicked their heels. Nobody raised their arms in salute.

Major Groscurth raised his champagne glass from the table behind them.

'I propose a toast. To our great commander, in recognition of what must be the greatest intelligence deception plan in history – certainly the most successful. Prost!'

'Prost!' came the reply from everyone gathered around their diminutive admiral as they drank to him and to their moving a significant step closer to taking over the Reich.

'Lt. Colonel Oster,' smiled Canaris, acknowledging the other officers with a quick smile and a wave. 'It seems the hour of decision is near. How are we placed?'

'Herr Admiral, all is ready. The men have been on red alert for the past twenty-four hours. We even finally have the commander-in-chief with us now. As soon as Hitler returns to Berlin and gives the order to attack the Czechs, Brauchitsch will issue counter-orders and we storm the Chancellery.'

At that moment, a lieutenant entered the room and handed a note to Oster, who read it and frowned. He cleared his throat.

'Gentlemen, we've just been informed that Mussolini is coming to Munich to help with negotiations along with the British and the French.'

For a moment there was silence and then suddenly everyone was talking among themselves, trying to make sense of this unexpected development. Who had asked Mussolini to come? What did it mean?

EARLIER THAT DAY: DOWNING STREET,
LONDON, MORNING, 28 SEPTEMBER 1938

Annie had taken the news of Hilary's suicide as badly as the Prime Minister had expected and she had retired to bed crying. He had at one point thought he would shed tears too but it seemed that he had forgotten how. Politically, everything was still salvageable. But he needed to regain Hitler's trust. Damn Hilary Masterson. Now he would have to meet with that awful man one more time. Only a face-to-face meeting would give Germany's leader the reassurance he needed. But God, Munich was so damnably far. Next time he'd insist that Hitler come over to London.

'You see, Alec,' he said to his PPS who was sitting at the far end of the three-seater sofa, 'the last time we met with Hilary, both Annie and I were quite cross with the man. But he had felt the news he brought us too important to delay and he practically barged in on us. Of course, Alec, you remember, you were there. And, as you know, what he had to say was so awful we felt then that he'd been right to interrupt. We forgave him the impertinence.' He took another sip of sherry and then refilled his glass immediately. 'How ironic, is it not, that Hilary's interruption, it transpires, was completely unjustified after all.'

He looked at Alec with such sadness that the young man felt moved to reach out and comfort him in some way. But he didn't dare. 'The thing is,' Chamberlain continued, 'we would have forgiven him. I saw the material he had. It seemed authentic. Even now I find it hard to believe it was not what it seemed and I fail to understand the lengths someone has gone to, to drive us to a war that would cause such terrible deaths from the air.' He shook his head, exasperated at the deviousness of mankind. 'Of course, we would have forgiven Hilary his error. It was well intended.' He sat back, his head leaning against the back of the sofa, his eyes staring at the ceiling. 'Such a senseless waste of a life. I remember him as a child!'

The young Lord Dunglass was not at ease in role of comforter.

'Sir, how do you think he found out he had been hoodwinked?'

The Prime Minister shook his head wearily.

'I don't know which contacts gave him this information in the first place. The police are investigating but I wonder if we'll ever know. Clearly he subsequently unmasked some attempt to use him and his closeness to me to subvert our policy.' He sat up straight and cleared his throat. Back to work.

'I immediately sent a note to Herr Hitler once more telling him that he could get all he wanted without delay and without resorting to war.'

'That's jolly good going, sir,' said Alec, quickly adding, 'if you don't mind my saying so, sir.'

'Maybe so,' nodded Chamberlain. 'But we need more time to get organised. We have been going from peace to mobilisation and now we need Herr Hitler to hold back his troops from the Sudetenland just a little while longer whilst we redraft an agreement.'

The Prime Minister took off his half-lens spectacles and rubbed his tired eyes.

'Then, just in the past hour, an idea came to me: Signor Mussolini. For all his pantomime, he wants a peaceful Europe. Yet he is a dictator of the same ilk. If he were to join the discussions, Herr Hitler could hardly refuse him. And that gives us a few days at least to head off any attack on the Czechs, during which we can reassure the Germans of our peaceful intentions and of the need to avoid war at all costs'

'The First Lord of the Admiralty will be unhappy,' said Dunglass. 'He still thinks you're set on a clear military stand. With Hilary's information passed to the French, he has them ready to bring things to a head right now if need be.'

'Duff will probably resign,' conceded the Prime Minister. 'So be it. We of course need to let the French know that what we told them previously was incorrect. It will be embarrassing but we have to move forward. They will be relieved too not to have to fight. It will be peace for our time.'

'"Peace for our time"? I say sir, that sounds rather splendid.'

ADLON HOTEL, BERLIN, MORNING,
29 SEPTEMBER 1938

Veronica was woken from a deep sleep. It took her a second or two to realise that the noise was the telephone ringing beside her head. Irritably she picked it up, looking at her watch. She had been back in her room just fifteen minutes but it had felt much longer.

'Veronica? Oh thank goodness you are there, we were getting desperate!'

'I'm sorry,' said Veronica, still disorientated. 'Who is this?'

'Klara, silly! I've been phoning you since yesterday. I didn't dare leave any message with the hotel reception of course. We have an arrangement for this evening.'

'Do we?' Veronica said. She sat up and pushed her hair back, trying to remember.

'Oh dear!' laughed Klara. 'Stefan Gruenzweig – do you remember him?' She waited for a second and then laughed again, a little more strained this time. 'Have you been asleep? It's nearly eleven in the morning. Have you had a wild night? God, I remember those. You're so lucky to be a foreign national.'

She suspected that Klara, who was now reminiscing about the great times before 1933, was deliberately giving her some time to pull herself together. She was grateful. With her own hotel reservation ending the next morning she had her train ticket ready for a departure the next day. She had decided weeks ago that, with the German intelligence services now likely to be following her every move, she would leave by an unusual route. But, with all that had happened, she had completely forgotten that Stefan Gruenzweig was also going to be on that train. She had arranged documentation for him as she had for the Gutmanns and on the basis of that, he too had sold what belongings he had. Unlike with the Gutmanns' documents, Stefan's had been in the pouch in her hotel room when she had been arrested. But now, she realised, she had been so upset about the Gutmanns that she had nearly failed Stefan too. What sort of secret agent was she?

'Tomorrow, Veronica,' Klara was now saying, 'his departure is tomorrow on the same train as you! We didn't agree exactly when you would hand over his documents, but the poor man assumed that he would have met up with you by now. To be honest that was my assumption too. You do remember he is staying with me now – 10 Auguststrasse – you have been here once before, apartment 6. You have to come today, with all the documents.'

'Yes. Yes of course. I hadn't forgotten,' lied Veronica. 'And yes, of course I know where you live! I am so sorry I've not been in touch. I will explain when I see you.'

She looked at her watch. She had to sleep for an hour otherwise she would be no good to anyone. Then she needed to bathe. Then a taxi to Aunt Sonia. They would want, of course, an update from her on their November plans to join her in London. She had some good news to give them too. Her bond was posted, she had written her letter of guarantee and Sonia and Manfred would soon be receiving a letter directly from the British Home Office. It was wonderful to her that they would be coming over using real, legitimate documents. They were as good as out now.

'Shall we say 6pm tonight then, Klara?'

For more than a week the reception team at the Adlon had noticed the presence of one or two officers wearing the brown shirts and breeches of the SA sitting on the plush chairs in the lobby itself or, more often, seated in the bar laughing loudly and drinking large tankards of ale. The hotel didn't really approve of the SA but didn't dare approach them and ask what they were doing there. If it was only one or two of them then the hotel could pretend they weren't there. Also they were always dressed smartly: clean, pressed uniforms and shiny boots. Most of all, they didn't disturb other guests. What the reception desk wasn't aware of was just how friendly one of the two, Hans, had become with Helga Schmidt, one of the switchboard operators. She was a small, wispy, dark-haired young woman with disproportionately large breasts who had been alone since her last relationship had broken down nearly eight months earlier. Lonely but shy, she had been completely unable to resist the tall Nazi who had taken her out to a show and who subsequently continued to be so attentive to her. She knew what he really wanted of course. She was no great intellect but she knew men. Why else would he be interested in her? She hadn't, so far, let him more than squeeze her breasts and put his hand up her skirt. She thought it a good sign that he had nevertheless continued to pay her visits, and did not push her to give more than she felt comfortable giving. She was both surprised and grateful. None of the men in her past had shown such patience. She felt guilty and wondered how else she might please him, at least until she was ready to give herself to him fully.

Hans was terribly impressed with her fluency in English. He couldn't speak it at all and she had got used to translating the conversations of Miss Mitford for him. She would bring the transcripts to a room that he had booked. Helga believed Unity Mitford to be the most debauched woman she had ever come across. At first, she had been too shy to tell Hans what the woman got up to. It seemed Miss Mitford had a penchant for SS men. She could see that Hans was annoyed by that so she often left out SS references and just concentrated on the sex talk. There was so much of it! It was whilst reading this that Hans would put his hand up her skirt. Naturally they paused out of respect whenever Unity Mitford talked of her friendship with the Führer. Helga and Hans were both in awe of her close ties to him.

'The other Englishwoman is back too,' said Helga that evening, pulling out another slip of paper from her bag. 'She's only had one telephone conversation though and, compared to Miss Mitford, she has nothing interesting to say.'

'Translate it for me, clever thing,' said Hans, standing up and moving to the window so that she wouldn't see his interest.

'No need,' said Helga, 'she spoke in German. Here, see for yourself.'

Hans took the piece of paper and read it through quickly.

'Forgive me, dearest,' he said. 'I have to go.'

Helga watched him go, wondering what he might suddenly have remembered that could cause him to move so quickly. He'd clearly been flustered, she reasoned, because he'd taken the boring transcript with him. She shrugged; she only ever brought the carbon copy to Hans. She always left the top copies on file as those were the ones collected each week by the Gestapo.

FORTY-FOUR

29 SEPTEMBER 1938

PORTNALL ROAD, LONDON

B ILLY HAD THOUGHT HE WOULD BE ALL RIGHT BUT he wasn't. True, he had shown true leadership in front of his men. Nick and Paul had seen him ruthless and determined, revelling in doing what needed to be done. But now, in the dead of night, Billy was afraid. The sadistic glee he had experienced from looking into Masterson's terrified eyes had been replaced by the memory of just those eyes. He couldn't sleep, tossing and turning, his sheets a mess.

What if Scotland Yard suspected foul play and sent in detectives? If they determined that the letter was a forgery, how soon before they linked it to the Jewish forger in Hendon? The forger was himself a big worry now. They'd left him for dead but when a few hours later they'd gone to collect the body, he'd gone. Billy was sure the man would never talk to the police if only because, if he admitted to the forgery and with his criminal past, they would probably charge him with being an accessory to Masterson's murder. It had meant, though, they'd had to let his wife go too. The Jew wouldn't otherwise be able to explain her disappearance. That had been a near miss. If they'd already killed her, the whole plan would have unravelled and they'd be on the run now.

Billy would have loved to confront Butler and have him admit that Billy had indeed sorted things out. But Butler would anyway know that he was the one who had done it. It'd have to do. The important thing now was to maintain complete silence. He knew he himself would never talk, but could he be so sure about Nick and Paul – and what about Stephi? Would they boast to other BU members? The police might have infiltrated the movement. They would be keeping a close ear to the ground. He wished Paul hadn't painted those words inside the Jew tailor's house, though at the time they had all laughed.

On the other hand, the suicide letter might never be doubted. And even if it were to be, there would be many people who wished ill of a man such as Masterson. It would take them a while to piece it all together and maybe never. It was the not knowing he couldn't stand. That in three or maybe four days there might come a knock on the door and an invitation for him to accompany them to the police station. He wondered how Gunther was getting along with his own plans. Gunther had once told him that the first killing was always the hardest. After that it got easier.

'Just the same as it was in the trenches, Tommy!' he'd laughed.

But in the trenches, thought Billy, we at least had our country's permission to kill. He grunted. Gunther's position in Berlin was so much easier. Which is why Billy's plan couldn't be carried out in England.

As light dawned on the morning of 29th September, Billy gave up on sleep. He would, he decided, sleep next in Germany. He needed to feel the respect that was paid automatically to people like him over there. He packed his suitcase, took the rest of the money from its hiding place behind his bedroom wall and his passport and by 8am was already on his way to Heston aerodrome.

He would stay in Berlin until his money ran out which ought to be enough time for him to know if the Metropolitan Police were looking for him. He'd have to give up his job at Strachans. They wouldn't take kindly to his disappearing for so long without notice. He'd find work in another car manufacturer based on his experience. Or at least he hoped so. If not he'd turn to robbery. He seemed to have a talent for breaking and entering.

BERLIN, SCHÖNEBERG, 29 SEPTEMBER 1938

Veronica had visited Sonia, but she could not face the Gutmanns. She'd told her aunt only that she'd been picked up by Military Intelligence and then released, but had given no details of the deal she had made with Captain X, nor of the resulting short week in England. Sonia had been understanding. At her suggestion, Veronica had used the telephone in Sonia's kitchen to speak to Renate. Renate had cried. Veronica had promised she would find another way to get them out. In the meantime she would help them to rent a place. There were enough once-grand Jewish houses in the area where the woman of the house was alone, her man arrested, her children fled to relatives abroad.

'We'll try again,' Veronica had promised. 'I will get all of you to Palestine one by one if necessary. It is quicker and easier than waiting for family documents. I will not let you down.'

Veronica had not been able to control her voice at the end but Sonia had been on hand to quickly cut the connection.

'You must remain strong for the Gutmanns,' Sonia said now, filling the kettle with water. 'If only we weren't forced to sell, they could have stayed here.' She looked around her spacious apartment. 'Manfred and I have lived here for twenty-five years. It is hard to think that we will be leaving.'

She put the kettle on the gas ring on top of the cooker and turned to her niece, more hopeful than Veronica could remember seeing her until now. 'I would never have believed how good it would feel to be leaving this place.' She clapped her hands. 'To be able to live again! And in England, at last, with Manfred.' She took Veronica's hand, concentrating now, earnest. 'And once we're over there, we will get to work. I have it all planned. Through the *Hilfsverein* I have good connections in England. Some Quakers. Christian bishops even. Manfred's first-hand account of suffering will raise awareness. We will soon get Renate out and all of her family.'

She let go of Veronica's hand and turned to light the gas. 'Though I must tell you, Manfred and I had a long chat last night. We really think that the point will come soon when everyone will get sick of the Nazis. People will wake up to what is being done in their name and things will slowly become normal again. This can't go on much longer. This is a great and proud country. Things will go back to normal, I am sure of it.'

It was four in the afternoon when Veronica finally took her leave from them and hailed a taxi from the corner. As the Tiergarten came into sight, the sun broke through clouds and lit the trees, their leaves a thick, shimmering tapestry of brown, orange, red and purple. If she was being followed, the long straight road through the Tiergarten might be a good place to find out. Seemingly on a whim, Veronica asked the driver to turn and drive through the Tiergarten and, just beyond the huge traffic circle of the Grosser Stern on the northern edge of the park, she got out and paid the fare. As the taxi drove off she stood for a couple of minutes carefully looking at the drivers of each of the passing vehicles. None of them spared her so much as a glance. She looked at her watch. She had quite a bit of time left before she needed to be at Klara's and she could do with the walk. In her flat shoes she reckoned that she could walk along the south bank of the Spree, with the river on her left and the Tiergarten on her right until she got to the ruin of the Reichstag and from there it would be a short walk down to the Adlon.

Twenty minutes later, disaster struck. One moment she had been looking up at the *Siegessäule* Victory Column, towering ever higher above her as she got closer to it, and the next she had caught her foot in a small pothole and tripped. As she fell, she felt her shoe give and her ankle buckled under her weight. Veronica cried out, pushing her hands in front of her to break her fall enough so as not to hit her head. As far as she could see from where she was lying, there was nobody else nearby. Slowly she sat up and began to assess the damage. The most pain was in her wrist, but she thought her ankle might be worse. She reached to put her shoe back on only to find that the ankle strap had snapped. She removed the other shoe and put both into her bag. Breathing heavily she rested for a moment, aware now that time was moving on. Finally, using her good hand and leg, she levered herself up until she was standing. Her foot hurt but she hadn't broken anything. She looked around. She knew that the Victory Column was just in front of the Reichstag and that from just beyond there, she would be able to get a taxi.

But as she limped up the road towards the Königsplatz, she found the approach blocked by road barriers and temporary fencing. She rested once more, her good hand pressing against the rough wood for a few seconds to rest her aching feet. She peered through a gap in the fence and could see a large number of construction workers swarming over the base of the column, the blackened parliament building forming a dramatic backdrop to their labour. Its ghastly burnt-out hulk a fitting metaphor, she thought, for what had happened to Germany's democracy.

As someone who appeared to be a foreman walked close by, she called out to him through the fence and walked gingerly along, parallel to him, until they both arrived at what was a temporary gate. It was locked with a chain but there was a wide enough gap around its hinges to be able to hold a decent conversation.

'What's going on here?' asked Veronica.

The man gestured up in the sky, pointing to the golden Goddess of Victory statue high up above them.

'We're moving her,' he said.

'You're moving the statue?' Veronica could see now that the men were erecting scaffolding all around the column. 'Where to?'

'Not just the statue,' corrected the man, 'we're moving the entire column. But not far. The Tiergarten will still have its *Siegessäule*, only it will be at the Grosser Stern junction over there.' He pointed behind Veronica's head in the direction from which she had just come. She didn't turn to look.

'But will you let me through please? I really need to get to the other side. It's urgent.'

The foreman shook his head.

'I can't do that, Fräulein. Barriers have gone up all around here and there is a lot of equipment everywhere. We have instructions not to let anyone through whilst we're doing this job.'

'But that could be days!' she said. 'Look, I've broken my shoes. Please let me through.'

The man again shook his head. 'Days? Weeks more like, I would say. I am sorry, Fräulein, we have our orders.'

'But why?' asked Veronica, really more to give herself time to think. She looked at her watch and began to turn away, vaguely hearing him replying something about 'by order of the Führer'. Whether he was referring to the decision to move the column or to the refusal to let people through, she couldn't say. It was nearly 5pm. She was expected at Klara's in just over an hour although she presumed she could be a little late. After all Stefan Gruenzweig was going nowhere without the documents.

She started limping towards the bridge over the Spree, thinking that maybe from there she could get a taxi but even if she found one it was a much longer route over the river and she could see that the traffic on that side was moving slowly as the working day had ended and made worse by diversions caused by the newly closed roads. Then she saw a public phone box just before the bridge and had an idea.

'Heil Hitler. This is the Adlon Hotel, how may I help you?' came the voice of the hotel receptionist eventually.

Veronica couldn't bring herself to return the Hitler greeting as was expected but, to compensate, made no effort to hide her English accent. Everyone was still forgiving of ignorant foreigners.

'Please could you connect me to the room of Daphne Peters, who is staying at your hotel. Tell her it's Veronica.'

Veronica waited, listening to her heart beating, praying that Daphne would be in her room. Seconds later, her prayers were answered.

'Veronica, is that you?'

'Yes, Daphne. I need your help. It is quite urgent actually.'

'Sounds interesting. What do you need me to do, darling?'

Veronica had had a few minutes to work out how to do this and now asked her to take down the number of the telephone box. She then instructed her to get the key to her room from the lobby and where, once in her room, she would find the document pouch stitched into the top of the curtain.

'You really do have an exciting hidden life!' was Daphne's first response. 'But why will they give me your key?'

'This time you pretend to be me. It's a risk, but I hope that they view one tall English blonde as looking fairly like another and won't even notice. They care about Unity but not other Englishwomen.'

Veronica's ankle was really throbbing now. All she wanted to do was to sit down on a bench and there was one, taunting her, about fifty yards away. She couldn't move that far or she would miss Daphne's call back. She wondered whether it was normal for a woman to stand expectantly by a public telephone. Every so often she glanced rapidly around but nobody seemed to be interested in her. She told herself to stop: if she was being watched she'd never know anyway. It felt like an hour, but her watch told her that just over twenty minutes had passed before the telephone finally rang.

'I'm in your room,' came Daphne's voice, 'what are you up to, Veronica?' Daphne sounded much more on edge than before, but this too was something that Veronica had anticipated. 'This Stefan fellow,' Daphne said, 'his name sounds Jewish and his photograph doesn't reassure me.'

'He needs to leave the country, Daphne. It's not illegal for him to leave, you know.'

'But that's hardly the point,' she answered. 'We're fascists, aren't we? We don't help Jews! Come on, Veronica, you know that.'

'I think we've established, Daphne, that you're no fascist. The point is, I want to help this Jew, and I am asking that you help me to help him.'

In a few minutes she told Daphne about her fall and that she was now trapped at the north-eastern corner of the Tiergarten. All Daphne needed to do was take a taxi to 10 Auguststrasse Apartment 6, hand the documents over to Klara and return to the hotel.

'How important is it that I do this for you?' said Daphne.

'It's really important. This poor man is relying on us to see that he does not miss his train tomorrow.'

'This is one hell of a favour you're asking of me, Veronica,' said Daphne, 'yet you've not given me what I have been asking for and I've come all the way out here for you.'

Here we go, thought Veronica.

'I know. And I'm sorry. I've just been so busy. But if you do this for me now, I promise that I will do what you want.'

'Oh yes?' Daphne gave a short humourless laugh. 'You've promised before. I think that you're just—'

'Tonight, Daphne,' said Veronica, 'I'll sleep in your bed tonight. Leave a spare key at reception. When I come back to the hotel I will pick up your key and I will be waiting for you when you return.'

'Really?' Daphne's voice was excited once more. 'On your parents' lives?'

'Yes, I swear it on my parents' lives.' Not so long ago, thought Veronica, I would have refused to say that on principle.

'All right. I'll bloody do it! V, your life is *so* exciting. You're always busy doing important glamorous things. First fascism and now this! I really do love you, you know.'

'I know you do, Daphne, I do know that.'

FORTY-FIVE

29 SEPTEMBER 1938

10 AUGUSTSTRASSE, BERLIN, EVENING

STIEGLITZ KNOCKED ON THE DOOR OF No. 5. THERE was no answer, but he thought he heard a noise on the other side. He knocked again more sharply. 'Police!' he shouted. 'Open at once!'

'I am coming, please wait,' came the muffled reply from somewhere on the other side. Eventually he heard the key turn in the door and it opened a fraction to show a rather plump woman, he estimated to be in her early sixties. Her hair was tied up in a bun and she seemed to be wearing some kind of capacious house coat.

'I am sorry to disturb you,' said Stieglitz. He held up his disc. 'I am Inspector Stieglitz of the *Kriminalpolizei*. There was an incident at the apartment opposite earlier today. It's Frau Bernstein, isn't it? I understand you were the one who called the fire brigade. I just have a few questions. May I come in?'

Frau Bernstein gave a little shake to her head. 'I did the right thing, didn't I? Calling the fire brigade? It was the smell of gas, you see, when I went out into the corridor.'

Stieglitz nodded enthusiastically. 'You definitely did the right thing! I wonder though whether you heard anything before you smelt the gas? If I could just come in?'

'I don't think I can help you, Inspector. I didn't hear anything at all.'

'I understand,' Stieglitz said affably, not believing a word. 'I am sorry for having bothered you.' If, he thought, she had said that she'd heard men stomping up the stairs, knocking loudly on the door, followed possibly by some screaming but had been too scared to open the door, that would at least have been plausible. She moved to close the door only to find his foot firmly in the way. 'However,' he continued, 'I would like to come in all the same and just check that everything is okay.'

'It really is, sir. Everything is fine.'

'Let me in, Frau Bernstein, I insist. I won't ask again.'

She opened the door, her face a rictus of fear. It wasn't a large apartment and he walked into the living room to see a young man sitting there with a suitcase. He too looked scared and gawped at the policeman ashen-faced.

'And you are?'

'Stefan Gruenzweig.'

'How long have you known, Frau Bernstein? Are you a friend? A relative maybe?'

The man didn't answer. Stieglitz pointed to the small suitcase.

'Where have you come from? Or are you going somewhere?'

Again the man didn't answer. Stieglitz took two steps towards him and struck him hard across the face.

'I don't have time for this. What do you know about the murders next door?'

Stefan Gruenzweig clutched his burning cheek, tears starting from his eyes from pain. And then he started sobbing.

'Murders?' he gasped. 'They are dead?'

'You knew them?'

Stefan nodded.

'Good. Then why don't you tell me who they are? Frau Bernstein – why don't you make us both some coffee? I just need to go back over there and talk to my colleague. Do not close the door behind me.'

'Kuppers,' he said on re-entering the apartment. 'I am chatting with the woman over the corridor and taking her statement. Remain here to make sure nobody else comes in, whether police or curious neighbours, doesn't matter. Knock on the door if there's anything you don't think you can handle.'

Kuppers nodded and sat down on the sofa. Stieglitz was amused to see him pick up the book by Thomas Mann and decided not to tell him it was one that had been banned.

He came back to Frau Bernstein's living room just as she brought in three cups of coffee on a tray. Both of them were clearly terrified – he needed them to be relaxed if they were going to talk freely and quickly.

'Listen,' he said, taking a cup and sitting down on one of the chairs there. 'I am not *Gestapo*. I am *Kripo*. So just you co-operate with me and you will both be fine. You understand?' Stefan nodded; Frau Bernstein however, did not.

'Frau Bernstein. You earlier lied to me, which is obstructing a police officer in the performance of his duties. But to show you how you have nothing to fear, if you fully co-operate from now on, there will be no charges. Do you understand now?' This time Frau Bernstein nodded too.

'I've done nothing illegal, sir,' said Stefan. 'I am allowed to leave the country, I made my application and I paid everything that was demanded of me.'

'That is good,' said Stieglitz, not really sure of the relevance at this point. 'Why don't you start at the beginning then?'

Once Stefan began to talk, he hardly paused for breath and Stieglitz had to interrupt quite forcefully when he had a question to ask. Gradually he got a picture of the desperate plight of Berlin's Jews in a similar predicament to that of Stefan Gruenzweig. It was something that the inspector had known about already of course, but the Gestapo might be interested in such detail. He was not, however, minded to share it with them.

'So, you were waiting for this Englishwoman Veronica to come by with your rail and ship tickets to England and that is why you were sitting with Klara in apartment 6?'

Stefan nodded.

'You have described how you have known Klara, a former member of the Social Democrats, for several years. Had you met the Englishwoman before?' Stieglitz didn't want to say her name again if he could help it. He had heard how Stefan had pronounced it and wasn't sure he could pull it off.

'Describe her to me.'

Stefan's description of the young, blonde Englishwoman matched that of the second body in the room.

'Going back to Klara, for a moment. Was she "warm"?'

Stefan looked confused.

'Did she have girlfriends?'

Stefan looked horrified at the question.

'What do you mean?'

'It's a simple question. What type of person did she like? Could you describe that typical person? Did she ever have gentlemen callers?'

'How could I possibly know this?' cried Stefan. 'Why would you ask me such a thing? I have no idea anyway. We never talked of such things. Never!'

Stieglitz nodded, already thinking of the next question. 'Can you think of any reason why someone would have wanted to kill either of them?'

'I originally thought that they were after me,' said Stefan, tears in his eyes again. 'We saw two Brownshirts arrive in the courtyard and Klara told me to go and wait here with Frau Bernstein. But I now know that they were after Veronica, not me and not Klara.'

'How do you know this?'

'Because the men waited in that flat for nearly an hour after they arrived and they didn't leave until after I heard Veronica arrive. They must have been waiting for her.'

Stieglitz nodded. This tallied exactly with the evidence in the flat. 'You said that the Englishwoman was bringing you your travel documents. Is it possible that they were after those documents?'

Stefan shrugged. 'I don't know. I was told that they were legal, sir.'

Stieglitz thought for a few moments then stood up. 'Wait here,' he said unnecessarily. Stefan Gruenzweig was a broken man awaiting his fate, and his fate now lay with the inspector. Stieglitz went back to apartment 6.

'Right, Kuppers. I think we are finished here. Go back to the station and call for the morgue officials to remove these corpses. I have all the information I need. They'll start to smell before long.'

He waited until he saw Kuppers down in the courtyard talking to one of the uniformed *Orpo* men, probably updating them, or perhaps entertaining them. From the laughter, it sounded as if he was adding in quite a bit of description. Stieglitz turned away from the window and went back to apartment 5.

'You,' he said, pointing at Stefan, 'come with me. I need you to identify the bodies.'

'Please, sir—' began Stefan,

'Just do it,' said Stieglitz, raising his voice a fraction. It was enough. The two men went into apartment 6 and Stieglitz led Stefan into the bedroom. Stefan fell to his knees at seeing Klara's face and wept.

'Oh, God, Klara, what did they do to you?' He reached for her arm but recoiled when he touched it.

'Get up,' said Stieglitz, impatient now. 'Pull yourself together, man. You knew they were dead.'

In the end the inspector had to crouch down and heave the man back onto his knees so that Stefan's chin was resting on the mattress, looking straight at Klara's buttocks.

'Couldn't you at least cover her up, Inspector? Please, I beg of you.'

'Well maybe I will, but you need to first stand on your own two feet for God's sake.'

Stefan slowly got to his feet and then gasped, staring.

'What is it?' asked Stieglitz

'It's not her!' cried Stefan. 'That isn't Veronica!'

Stieglitz frowned. 'Are you sure?'

'Yes. I am absolutely sure. This is, was, another woman.'

Stieglitz went over to the pile of clothes that he had already searched earlier. He picked up the dead woman's jacket and reached into the pocket and drew out some documents.

'Then how do you explain this?' he asked, handing one of them to Stefan. Stefan took the white sheet of paper with trembling hands. He had not seen it before of course but one glance was enough. He knew that this was the document he needed to gain entry into Palestine. And there, amongst the many English words under the main headings 'Government of Palestine. Palestine Citizenship Order 1925. Certificate of Citizenship', he could see his own name typed in four different places. He held on to it.

Stieglitz smiled. 'I am going to have to ask for it back, Herr Gruenzweig. It is evidence in a murder investigation.'

He held out his hand. But, he could see Stefan Gruenzweig was quite unable to open his fingers and let it go. With two hands, the inspector gently but forcefully prised it away from him, folded it and put it into his own pocket. 'And of course,' he continued, holding up a railway ticket and some more papers, 'that's not all there is, is it? You would have wanted these too. For your journey to Palestine. Passage on a ship, though I am not at all sure that this boat is a luxury passenger steamer.'

'Please…' begged Stefan, holding out his hands.

The inspector though, stepped away. 'Let's go into the other room away from these,' he said, gesturing towards the corpses. They sat down on the chairs by the wireless set. 'You say that you were waiting for this Englishwoman to bring you your documents and she was then going to accompany you as far as Rumania, from where you would get on this ship. Is that correct?'

Stefan nodded.

'Well, if this isn't your Englishwoman, why does she have your documents just as you were expecting?'

'I don't know. I don't understand it, but I have never seen that woman before in my life.'

'And there is something missing, isn't there?' persisted Stieglitz.

'I… I don't know, sir,' replied Stefan, 'what do you mean?'

'Well, if she was coming with you, where is her train ticket?'

'I don't know. I am sorry, sir.' There followed some moments of silence as Stefan waited and the inspector was staring at the wall beyond him, thinking, Stefan knew not what. In fact Stieglitz was thinking that his original theory that the blonde was a non-Jewish foreign national, had, for a short moment, answered why they might have wanted to make it look like suicide. Make it look like a couple of Jews to hide the fact that this was a murder with very different motives. But now, he thought with frustration, he was back where he had started. This blonde might be a German Jewess after all. Finally Stefan cleared his throat.

'Sir, please may I ask something of you?'

'What?'

'I have used all my savings to get these documents. I have no job and I no longer have anywhere to live or any means to pay my rent. I don't know if you are going to kill me or arrest me. Perhaps you are going to let me go. But, without these documents, you might as well kill me now.'

To Stieglitz's surprise and disgust, Stefan Gruenzweig got down on his knees.

'I beg of you, sir.'

For a horrible moment, it looked to Stieglitz as if the man was getting ready to kiss his shoe. Stieglitz hurriedly stood up and stepped away. The documents were of course evidence, but in an investigation that all his instincts told him was not going anywhere. Nor was it one that he should be seen to take too keen an interest in. He knew that the Nazis were behind it somehow and what were these but more regime murders, most of which anyway now had the force of law. His job as a police inspector was really no more than investigating petty crimes whilst ignoring government-sponsored murder on a far larger scale. That might be fine for the Kuppers of this world but not for him. He was suddenly tired of it all. He took the documentation out of his pocket. At least he could do some good. He was about to hand them to the man, hesitated, looked closely at the railway ticket again, paused, and then handed them over.

'Take these and go,' he said. Now Stefan was too scared to do so. 'Take them,' Stieglitz repeated gently. 'It's not a trick.

We will go down the stairs together as if you came out of an apartment on a lower floor. I will then go to my colleagues in the courtyard and will tell the policeman at the street side to let you out. Come. Take your case and let's go.'

FORTY-SIX

30 SEPTEMBER 1938

BERLIN

BILLY SAT IN HIS SMALL HOTEL ROOM IN LIETZENSEE, looking out over the lake and chain smoking. He had been surprised to find that his first response to Gunther's report of Veronica's death had not been one of vengeful joy but more of relief that her threat to him had been removed. Now, he even allowed himself a moment's reflection. She had been good between the sheets. No. He admonished himself; it had been more than that. She'd been beautiful and engaging. Yet she had also played him for a fool, doubtless going back to her Jewish controllers and had had them all laughing at him. She was dangerous too. On her return to England she would have raised questions about Hilary Masterson's own untimely end. So he'd had no choice. Gunther had assured Billy that she hadn't suffered 'too much', making clear that that phrase had left Gunther some scope to enjoy himself. Billy remembered back to that night in the Tiergarten and a part of him was aroused at both the memory and at his imagining what might have happened to Veronica. The other part of him, disgusted by his perversion, prevented him from asking Gunther for any details.

He wondered how long it would take before the police realised who she was. Possibly they would never know. By the time she was reported missing in England and her family realised that she had gone to Berlin, he would have emptied her room at the Adlon of her things, making it look to all the world as if she had left on the morning train as planned.

The sunlight pouring into the hotel room woke Veronica. She rolled over and reached for a pillow and pulled it over her head to cut out the bright light. As she did so, her eyes briefly opened and she noted the strange surroundings. *Where was she?* It took her a few moments to remember that she was in Daphne's bed. She remembered now that she had caused quite a stir at the Adlon, walking through the lobby with bare, dirty feet. She had had to explain the problem to the doorman and show him her broken shoe and even then he had insisted in escorting her to the manager just in case she was a problem that the hotel needed to deal with. Only after that had she been able to retrieve her room key from reception along with the envelope containing Daphne's own key. Veronica had bathed in her own room, packed her bags ready for departure the next day, and then gone to Daphne's room to fulfil her end of the bargain she had made. She had put on her nightdress, phoned reception, asked for a call to be put through to the room for 9am, and gone to sleep.

She looked at the clock by the side of the bed. It was 8:30am. How ironic that, having finally caved in and made herself available to Daphne, it was Daphne herself who had failed to make the appointment. She stretched and relaxed for a few moments, enjoying the unexpectedly long and uninterrupted night's sleep. It was possible that she would now be able to put Daphne off indefinitely. In London, Daphne would be back with Reggie and Veronica could come up with endless excuses once they were home. She got dressed and went back to her room. She rang Klara. No answer. She tried again. Surely they couldn't have already left for the station. It would be far too early. Or perhaps they had decided to allow themselves enough time to eat at the café in the station. She rang the operator.

'Yes. How can I help you?'

'I have been trying to phone this number and am not getting a reply. Can you please check for me that there is no fault on the line?'

The operator took a note of the number and a few moments later came back to confirm that there was no fault. Veronica thanked her and turned on the wireless. Tuning to the BBC World Service took too long and the reception had been so poor that she had in the end left it tuned to the same *Reichs-Rundfunk-Gesellschaft* national broadcast that the rest of Germany listened to.

> '...Before he left Munich Premier Edouard Daladier made a statement saying, "I believe the Munich meeting may mark a historical date for Europe. The Duce, Benito Mussolini, has also returned home but Prime Minister Chamberlain stayed on after the last work of the four-power conference was completed. For an hour and a half he talked with Chancellor Adolf Hitler. This conversation brought a joint statement in which the two statesmen declared that the Munich agreement is symbolic of the decision of Germany and Britain never to go to war with each other again. They committed themselves to the processes of consultation should future questions arise.'

Veronica listened with growing confusion to the triumphant tones of the German broadcaster. Weren't France and Britain standing firm against Hitler after all, or was it Germany who had backed down? The answer came a couple of minutes later:

> '*Following their discussion, Prime Minister Chamberlain announced that he had always had in mind that a peaceful solution to the Czech question might open the way to general appeasement in Europe.*'

She looked at the wireless in disbelief. Britain seemed to have given way without so much as threatening to fight for the Czechs. It didn't seem possible given the information that Hilary had shown the Prime Minister. And despite the threat to France, it seemed the French were giving way too. Slowly her incredulity gave way to fear. With Germany getting her way without any threat from France or Britain, there would be no officers' coup. Captain X would no doubt think that she, Veronica, had betrayed them and they might be coming after her. She thought rapidly. Her tickets for the train out of Berlin had no name. It was time for Veronica Beaumont to disappear. By the time the train arrived at the border for document checks Veronica would no longer be on the train. In her place would be Miss Hilary Masterson. From her suitcase she removed the bottles of hair dye that had been her constant companions over the past weeks.

'FOURTHLY,' continued the radio announcement, '*the occupation, by stages, of the predominantly German territory by German troops will begin on October 1st. These territories marked on the map will be occupied by German troops in the following order—*'

Veronica turned off the wireless.

A native Berliner, Inspector Stieglitz never failed to be moved by the splendour and sheer scale of the Anhalter Bahnhof. The portico, with its three giant arches to the front and flanked to the east and to the west by another two arches, towered twenty metres over him as he moved into the enormous hallway, all diffused in a warm light, partly a reflection of the unusual pale mustard colour of the ornate brickwork. And that was only half the story, the inspector would think proudly, the arched roof which rose up to dwarf even the portico, reached to maybe as high as thirty-five metres.

Today, however, the inspector, without Kuppers this time, was moving swiftly towards the platform onto which the morning train from Prague was just pulling in. It would be a while before it started on its return journey but Stieglitz wanted to be there well ahead of even the earliest boarding passengers. He looked at the large clock high up across the other side of the concourse. He had at least thirty minutes before the train was scheduled to depart.

He leant against a wall, lit a cigarette and pushed his hat low over his face. To the average passer-by, had they noticed him at all, it would have looked as though he was dozing, but his eyes, hidden in shadow, were constantly scanning the approach to the train, waiting for Stefan Gruenzweig.

It wasn't hard to spot him when he did arrive, the man clearly waiting for someone and anxiously scanning the concourse before finally taking up a position on the other side, sitting on a wooden bench. There were a few women, all with hats, who may or may not have been English, or blonde, or Veronica Beaumont, but Inspector Stieglitz didn't bother sparing any of them a glance. Stefan Gruenzweig would spot her for him. There were still another twenty minutes to go.

FORTY-SEVEN

30 SEPTEMBER 1938

ADLON HOTEL, BERLIN

Hans returned one more time to the Adlon. Although they now had all they needed from Helga, he had already booked the hotel room and she had promised an hour together. Two weeks of courtship were paying off. She had finally decided to trust him, she had said, believing that he truly cared for her. So, today, he would finally get to sleep with her and then he would never come back. She would be devastated of course, but it wasn't his fault her timing was so bad.

Afterwards they lay there smoking. It was, he mused, in some ways a shame. She had been every bit as good as he had known she would be. Hans was already thinking how best to make his exit when Helga mentioned that the Englishwoman had made another call this morning.

'You mean yesterday morning surely, Helga?' replied Hans, stubbing out the rest of his cigarette.

She laughed and slapped him lightly on his tummy, making him jump a little. 'No, silly. I mean just before you got here. One hour ago. A little more.'

'That's impossible,' said Hans, 'what did she say?'

'Oh nothing really. Even less than last time. She didn't even get through. She had been trying to place a call to somewhere in Auguststrasse and asked the operator if there was a fault on the line. But there wasn't.'

Hans felt the hairs stand up on the back of his neck. He didn't believe in ghosts but he and Gunther had finished Veronica for good last night. Rapidly he got dressed, ignoring all the questions coming from Helga. As he reached for the door, she stood in front of him, still naked. She raised her hand to his cheek.

'Wait, Hans! What are you doing? You can't leave like this. Tell me what's going on!'

Hans reached for her hair with both hands and pulled her screaming into the air before throwing her into the wall with such force that she dislodged a picture frame which fell on her head as she hit the floor, knocking her unconscious. He closed the door, locking it and walked to the lift but when it didn't come immediately, he started racing up the two flights of stairs towards Veronica's room.

He reached the corridor as a woman came out of the room, closing the door, her bags already outside. Hans stopped and stared, suddenly not sure what to do. The woman turned to see him standing there in his SA uniform and for a moment neither of them spoke. Then, quite calmly the woman spoke to him.

'Sir, please would you call the lift for me?'

Hans turned and pressed for the lift before turning back to her. Her German was good, but he did detect a foreign accent. But this woman wasn't Veronica Beaumont, he was certain. This woman had chestnut brown hair. Yet she was coming out of Veronica Beaumont's room. He helped her get her bags into the lift and got in with her.

'Are you leaving us, Frau...?' he asked.

'Masterson,' she answered. 'No, I am leaving Berlin but only to visit friends in Munich.'

Hans nodded politely. He was trying to remember back to the brief glance he had caught of Veronica some months ago at the Savignyplatz station, but all he could see was the blonde woman's face from last night as she had struggled for her life.

As Veronica came out of the lift, a hotel porter came towards them to take her bags.

'That's all right,' said Hans. 'I'm helping the lady with her bags.'

The porter backed away.

'There's really no need,' said Veronica.

'It is a pleasure,' said Hans, 'will you be taking a taxi?'

Veronica nodded, thankful that she had checked out earlier. That would have been very awkward.

The next taxi rolled up and Hans started loading the bags.

'Where to?' asked the driver.

Veronica hesitated and glanced at the SA man, but he was at the back and seemingly fully occupied.

'Anhalter Bahnhof,' she said softly.

'What was that, Fräulein?' asked the taxi driver.

She repeated it, more loudly this time, glancing nervously out the corner of her eye to see if the SA man had heard it.

Letting himself into Veronica's room at the Adlon had been easy for Billy. The problem was that the room was empty. It looked as if she really had checked out. He sat down on a hard-backed chair in the corner and tried to think. Was it possible that she had checked out the night before and taken her suitcase with her across town to meet the Jew? He shouldn't be surprised. With a pang of jealousy, he concluded that she'd probably slept with him. He wondered why her betrayal with Hilary still hurt when they were both now dead. *Concentrate.* If her things weren't here then they couldn't raise police suspicions. But then where were they? He decided to go back to reception and ask them when checkout had taken place.

As he made his way down, Hans was coming back in from the taxi rank. He and Billy met just in front of reception, their surprise mutual. Without Gunther to translate between them, they both turned towards the reception desk.

With just five minutes to departure, both Stefan and Inspector Stieglitz were beginning to think that Veronica would not show. Stefan began walking slowly towards the train, looking over his shoulder every few steps. As he came closer to where the inspector was standing, Stieglitz began to move further along the wall so that Stefan would not notice him. Then there she was. Stieglitz saw her first but doubted that this could be the one he sought. She was a stand-out beauty and was walking fast. It looked like she was trying to run but couldn't because of a limp. Stefan, however, saw her, turned away, hesitated and then stopped and turned back towards her. They both put down their suitcases and embraced, cheek to cheek on first one side and then on the other. Stieglitz threw away his third, or was it his fourth, cigarette, put his hat back on and began to move towards them. Now he would find out the identity of the dead blonde.

'Veronica!' The shout came from some way behind her shoulder, cutting through the general hubbub of a busy terminal. At the sound of the English shout from across the concourse, many of the travellers glanced around to see the source of the noise. Veronica, however, spun round, as if the voice had been attached to her by some invisible string. Her suitcase dropped to the ground. As she saw Billy running towards her she put a hand to her mouth in surprise. Stieglitz could not see the expression on her face. Was it surprise, or shock? Pleasure or terror?

Gathering herself together, Veronica hurriedly whispered into Stefan's ear. From her gestures and from his subsequent movement, it was clear that Veronica had told him to get onto the train and that she would join him in a moment. Seconds later and Billy was at her side.

It was an interesting development for Stieglitz, one that opened up new lines of enquiry. Who was this Englishman and what was his connection to the Englishwoman, or perhaps to the other dead woman? He thought of going up and arresting the pair of them but he doubted that they would co-operate, and this Englishman was far too big for him to take on with any hope of winning. A foreigner probably didn't hold the Berlin *Kripo* in as much awe as Germans had always done, even before it had become affiliated to the Gestapo. It would mean he'd have to draw his gun. Of course, Stieglitz knew he should have brought backup but he hadn't wanted to explain how he had let the Jew go last night and even removed evidence from a crime scene to give him the means to leave the country. Even if the action could be justified, by ensuring that they caught bigger fish, nowadays logical police procedure came a long way behind following the ideology of the Party. By the time he'd wriggled out of all of that, whether he solved the case or not he would still have a black mark against him. The Gestapo would remember that he had interfered in their business. Eventually, the black marks would accumulate until it was more convenient that he met with an accident than continue as a troublesome, ideologically suspect police officer.

Billy managed to force a smile as he got close to her. In his desperate race to get to the train before it left, he hadn't really thought about what he would say when he met her. What did he know and what did she know he knew? He had no idea how to start. He just knew he didn't want her leaving Berlin.

Veronica, however, spoke first with a voice devoid of any emotion. 'Billy! What a pleasant surprise. I didn't know you were visiting Berlin again.'

'You've changed your hair.' Billy had heard from Hans she was no longer blonde but it was still a surprise to see how different she looked.

'Do you like it?' She asked as if she really wanted to know his view on this and Billy didn't know whether he should answer, nor which answer would be the best for him to give.

'I've met with Hilary Masterson,' Billy said, a plan quickly forming in his head.

'Hilary? Why, is anything wrong?'

'No! Of course not. Well, not with Hilary. He is fine, of course. But… he told me that you have relatives here. They are in grave danger. You must come with me.'

Veronica was looking at him, her beautiful eyes now huge with worry. 'Aunt Sonia? Manfred? What has happened?'

Billy smiled reassuringly. He had her now. 'Yes. Aunt Sonia. There is just one chance to save her before they put her in a camp. If she has a British relative to vouch for her it will be okay, but you must come immediately.' He put his hand around her shoulder.

'But, what about Stefan? I have tickets for that train!'

Billy glanced briefly, uninterestedly, towards the train. 'Stefan is a big boy,' he said. 'You can always get a later train but first you need to save your aunt.'

Stieglitz watched Stefan Gruenzweig walk away and board the train. The two English people had their heads close together now. Perhaps the Englishman had come to kiss her goodbye. In which case which one of them should he follow? But after a couple of minutes, his dilemma was solved as they moved off together. As she picked up her case she looked back towards the train, trying to see Stefan. But Stieglitz could see that at that very moment Gruenzweig was mounting the steps to the carriage and temporarily out of her sight. Veronica waved anyway in that general direction and then turned. By the time Stefan Gruenzweig had entered the carriage and stuck his head out of the window all he could see was her walking away, the big Englishman's arm around her shoulder. Stieglitz saw the young man slump back into the seat. Maybe he had been in love with her, Stieglitz pondered as he began to follow the couple.

Veronica was not sure exactly how she might help her aunt. Sonia had not yet received her documents from the British Embassy so she could not have lost them, nor could anyone have taken them from her. But with everything sorted out, Veronica would make sure that there would be no last-minute hitch for her aunt and uncle. She assumed somebody, somewhere, was demanding money and here Veronica could help. Billy hailed a taxi and she got in, paying little attention to where they were going other than that they were heading towards the centre of town. The direct route then. Her thoughts went back to Stefan, now on his way to freedom. She had possibly saved that man's life. Certainly his health and freedom. Though she had to thank Daphne too of course. She had wanted to ask Stefan about Daphne but there had been no opportunity. She was relieved nonetheless as she had begun to worry that something might have happened to her. Clearly, Daphne had done as Veronica had requested, otherwise Stefan would not have had his papers for the journey. With a sigh she thought again about the deal she had struck with

Daphne. Perhaps she could play on Daphne's conscience. The arguments played through her mind, a welcome distraction from Billy, who must know that she was aware that he had vandalised her belongings back in their London flat.

Daphne, surely you helped Stefan out of the goodness of your heart? You have done a wonderful thing. You could let that be your reward, not me. If you insist… but wouldn't that tarnish the amazing deed you have done? You would never be able to say that you did it because it was right, but only because you wanted to live a fantasy.

Veronica knew it would all be for nothing. Daphne didn't think that way and she had wanted Veronica in her bed for years now. Suddenly Veronica felt very alone. She had, she realised, been rehearsing what she would say to Daphne so as not to dwell on Daphne's non-appearance. That empty bed, which she had enjoyed so much this morning, now assumed a more ominous presence.

Her thoughts were interrupted when the taxi stopped. Billy leant forward to pay the driver. They got out. Ahead of them, just across the River Spree, was the towering Berlin Cathedral with its neo-Renaissance dome.

'Here we are,' said Billy, 'this is where they are going to meet us.' He looked at her. 'I like the new hair colour. It suits you. What made you do it?'

Veronica tightened her lips in what she hoped might pass for a smile. 'Thank you,' she said, ignoring his last words. They started along the bridge to Museum Island. Veronica could understand that, if Billy's Nazi friends had somehow got hold of her aunt and uncle, Billy might well be able to pose as the family saviour, demonstrating his power and handing them back to her as his gift. But why would he bother? Did he want her gratitude? She didn't flatter herself that he loved her as Hilary had done. Then, with a horrible sinking feeling she realised that, if Billy knew about Sonia, he must know that Veronica was Jewish and that she had lied to him. She began to shiver.

Oh God. I'm walking into a trap. It was getting dark now and, as the lights on the bridge fell away behind them, the gloom of the island suddenly seemed to have acquired a malevolent aspect. To their left there were the gardens surrounding the cathedral. There was no light there at all and nor were there any people about at this hour. She determined that she would not let Billy take her there. She would insist he go and bring Sonia and Manfred to her at the bridge.

But, instead of turning left towards the cathedral, Billy turned right – towards the perhaps even more impressive structure that was the *Alte Nationalgalerie*. To the side, running alongside the river, was a beautiful cloister that she had never seen before. There must have been a couple of dozen heavy neo-classical columns on either side of the cloisters, supporting a caisson ceiling and leading towards the gallery building. As they started to walk down the wide, covered walkway, she had a feeling of dread that there were Nazis in their black or brown uniforms hiding behind every pillar. Slowly, she unfastened her bag, searching for the clasp that would give her access to its false bottom and to the derringer that rested inside it.

There was no one there. As they neared the end of the walkway, they were at a dead end. To the front and left rose the massive edifice of the *Alte Nationalgalerie*; to the right was the River Spree. She tried to lick her lips but her tongue was dry and she couldn't speak.

'Daphne Peters is dead.' said Billy. He watched her closely, gratified to see the look of shock on her face quickly replaced by one of despair at the implication for her. He was happy to confirm it. 'Gunther thought it was you, you see. I sent him to kill you.'

'Why?' She managed to croak that single word.

'Come now, Veronica,' he said, pushing her gently but firmly back against one of the last pillars in that vast promenade of pillars, 'where do I start? First of course, you're a Jewish sow. That would be enough. If the Party heard, I would be a laughing stock. Secondly, I know you and Hilary was fucking. You and him was laughing at me from the start.' Veronica shook her head but he ignored her. 'Third, you're not as stupid as I took you for. You probably already have your suspicions about Hilary's death and then you'd try and talk to the forger and his wife and you'd start to dig, and we can't have any loose ends, can we? You need to be disposed of, here in Germany.'

Veronica, who had until now not known that anyone was dead, was crying for Hilary and for Daphne. Both murdered because of her. Her clammy hand was in her bag unwrapping the cloth from around the derringer. God, she had been so sure of herself and her abilities. She had thought that at least she had controlled Billy, but no, not even that. And now she'd come to this. Even if she killed Billy she would be arrested within minutes of the gun going off. Paradoxically, the realisation that the game was up calmed her, and it was with a steady hand that she drew the derringer from her bag and pointed it at Billy. She expected him to step back and try to reason with her. That's when she would pull the trigger. Her hand may have been steady, but he was simply too fast for her. Laughing, he knocked the pistol out of her hand.

'You have a toy gun! Blimey, you're a regular secret agent, aren't you?' He bent down, picked up the derringer and threw it past the pillars and into the Spree. As he listened for the splash, Veronica kicked off her shoes and ran back towards the bridge. She estimated there were twenty pillars' worth of distance between her and the bridge. If only the gaps between them were not so wide. She tried to ignore the pain in her ankle but it slowed her nevertheless. With two good feet she might have made it. Instead, she had barely passed the first pillar when Billy's hand seized her hair from behind and dragged her backwards. She lost her balance completely and collapsed. Holding on to her hair, Billy dragged her back towards the last pillar at the end of the walkway. The pain was terrible; it felt as if he was going to pull her hair clean out of her head. Her hat had been knocked askew and one of the hat pins was digging into her head. She raised both her hands to his, trying to prise them away, and tried to bend her knees so that she was at least scrambling back on her feet rather than being pulled along the ground. She tried to dig her heels into the stone floor of the walkway but only ripped her stockings and bloodied her feet. She gouged and scratched but to no avail. She refused to scream though. She knew he would want that and she would not give it to him.

'I have a knife here with me,' Billy said as he dragged her. 'I was going to slit your throat, slaughter you like the beautiful animal that you are. Only thing is, I couldn't find a way to do that without ending up with your blood all over me clothes. Far too messy. I could drag your corpse to the river of course and throw you in, but that wouldn't get the blood out me clothes.'

Veronica, keeping a hand on one of his wrists, managed to remove one of the hat pins and stabbed at his hands, pushing it in deeply once she knew she had hit home. Billy screamed and let her go. He lashed out with his boot but she managed to roll away. She pulled out her second hat pin, tossing away her battered hat and managed to get to her knees, a pin in each hand. Billy laughed, looked as though he was turning away from her but suddenly swung round, kicking one of the pins from her hands. He was holding his own hand tightly with the other and he looked at the blood oozing out.

'You fucking bitch, that really hurts.'

He circled round her slowly, Veronica still on her knees and trying to swivel round to keep him in view. She tried to stand but he kicked out at her feet and she fell back on to her knees.

'You'll be pleased to know that I am going to strangle you, you little cunt. I will enjoy that a lot.'

He got behind her and grabbed hold of her hair again, careful to avoid her hand swinging at him with the hat pin. Lifting her up, he threw her back against one of the columns. She cried out as her bottom landed heavily on the ground, her back hard against the stone base. Billy aimed another kick, at her head this time, but she managed to duck and stab at his shin as it sailed past her ear. Billy yelled out again and then, to her utter horror, as if in slow motion, the front of Billy's skull came apart in an explosion of red and grey matter, the slime coming at her until it soaked her face and hair. The sound of a shot seemed to Veronica to follow a split second later. The loud screaming, she realised, was coming from her own mouth and she stuck her gloved fist into it and bit down to silence herself.

POLICE PRAESIDIUM, ALEXANDERPLATZ BERLIN, 1 OCTOBER

Kuppers respected Stieglitz but only grudgingly. He suspected that the inspector had been a supporter of the Centre Party until 1933. Certainly Kuppers had never heard him volunteer a 'Heil Hitler', although Stieglitz did, but only rarely, return the salute if he had to do so in the presence of very senior police officers. Working for an anti-Nazi who would normally have either had to join the Party or resign, was something that did not sit well with the young policeman. The issue though was that with people from the left as well as all the Jews thrown out of the force, they were very short of good detectives and as long as Stieglitz didn't advertise his politics, his position was safe. Kuppers also knew that he could have no better mentor in the force. The news that Stieglitz had solved the case of the two Jewish women in Auguststrasse only confirmed the man's genius.

'But sir, wasn't it your concern that we would have no jurisdiction?'

'Yes, and that was indeed the murderer's hope – that *Kripo* would not prioritise investigating Jew killings. But the beauty of it is that one of the dead women, the blonde, is a Daphne Peters. And not only is she not Jewish but she is a British aristocrat. The hit on her was ordered by a British fascist, Billy Watson.'

They were in Stieglitz's tiny office. Stieglitz was sitting back in his chair, feet on his desk, hands behind his head and looking up, puffing smoke up to the ceiling from the cigarette held in the corner of his mouth. He still had his coat on, though his jacket over the knitted waistcoat was unbuttoned, revealing the shoulder strap of his holster. His hat was where he'd slung it – over the telephone cradle on his paper-covered desk. The office may have been not much more than cupboard size – there was no room for Kuppers to sit and he was forced to stand in the doorway – but it was on the top floor of the building they all knew as 'the Red Fort' and Stieglitz, when he could, would swivel his chair round to stare out of the window behind his desk with its view of the nearby Town Hall, almost as big and built from the same red brick from which the police fortress, or praesidium, had derived its nickname. Inevitably, this sister building was known to all as the 'Red' Town Hall though Stieglitz realised, now he thought about it, that nobody actually mentioned the word 'Red' anymore for either building. No institution wanted to be accused of having 'Red' sympathies of any kind.

'Watson has been in Berlin quite a bit recently,' Stieglitz was saying now, 'in fact he is here right now.' He smiled, stubbing out his cigarette into an old, dirty saucer that did duty as a paper weight when it wasn't, as now, set on top of his coffee mug in an effort to retain the heat. 'We don't need to look for him though.'

Kuppers was hanging on his every word. 'Why not, sir?' he breathed, his voice low with excitement. 'Why don't we need to look for him?'

'As of yesterday evening, he's been dead, that's why.'

'You mean…' Kuppers looked pointedly at the inspector's revolver which was not in its usual place, holstered under the inspector's jacket, but had been recently cleaned and was now lying on a stained rag on the corner of the desk, glistening with oil.

'Best of all,' continued Stieglitz, ignoring Kuppers' interruption, 'it wasn't even the Gestapo or the SS who committed these murders but some rogue element in the SA.' He waited for Kuppers to respond but, when nothing was forthcoming, he spelt it out anyway. 'This means that we can, and we will, make arrests without any fear that we'd be told to drop the investigation. The opposite is true in fact: there will be much pressure to find the killer before the English start to put pressure on us to do so. Our lords and masters want to show Great Britain, at this sensitive time, that we can be trusted.'

What Stieglitz didn't tell his subordinate who,

gratifyingly, was now looking at him as if he was some sort of wizard, was that he had decided to keep his source out of the investigation completely. The report that he was just completing that morning told of how he had come across a man attacking a woman, probably a prostitute, on Museum Island, and how Stieglitz had intervened and held the man at gun point. The man had tried to bargain with him, promising to tell him about a murder the inspector could solve if only he would let him go. Regrettably, as Stieglitz wrote in his report, Watson had only given him the first name of the killer before he had pulled out a knife and begun to menace him. As the Englishman had stepped towards him, it had seemed as though Watson was, with his other hand, pulling a gun out of his coat, so Stieglitz had had no choice but to shoot him. There was no mention of Veronica Beaumont, whose suitcase he had retrieved and whom he had escorted to a new hotel nearby. He realised that Kuppers was still looking at him, waiting for his orders.

'Gunther,' he said at last. 'You're looking for an SA man who lives in Berlin, called Gunther. I don't know his surname nor do I know his rank.'

'Do you know how old he is, Inspector?'

'Nope,' he smiled. 'We don't want to make it too easy for you, do we?'

Kuppers clicked his heels, and disappeared from the doorway. Stieglitz sighed, thinking that he might yet live to regret letting the beautiful Englishwoman get away. She had been in a terrible state and once in the hotel room she had been desperate to run a bath, clear the remnant of blood and brains from her skin and go to sleep. Stieglitz had not let her. He had not even let her bathe her blistered and bleeding feet until she had told him everything she knew. It had not taken her long to spill the beans about Daphne Peters, and

Billy Watson. Her description of her dealings with Jews in Berlin corroborated perfectly what he had already learnt from Stefan Gruenzweig. She was a people-trafficker, dealing in forged documents and possibly connected to a foreign power. Everything she was doing would have been illegal even before the Nazis had come to power. In 1932, he would happily have arrested her and seen it as a career success in battling crime. He knew of colleagues back then who were not beyond accepting bribes in return for turning a blind eye to crime. He had never been one of those. Now he was letting a criminal go and he wasn't even being offered anything in return. Irony upon irony but Stieglitz had no regrets. The people she was trafficking wanted to be trafficked. They were not criminals, at least not as the term was understood by any normal society which allowed people to travel across borders without robbing them first. He knew that the Gestapo would love to get its hands on her and that was enough reason for him. It was how he could live with himself, coming into work in the Red Fort every morning, his place of employment, above the entrance to which was a large sculpted eagle – a stone swastika clutched in its stone claws – serving a stone-hearted regime.

FORTY-EIGHT

15 OCTOBER 1938

LONDON

GUILT WAS A POWERFUL EMOTION, THOUGHT Francis Bendit as he scanned the committee members now taking their seats. Just a month earlier, the mood had been firmly against any moves to recommend a relaxation of immigration rules. The contrary in fact had been the case. Then, the mood had been about Britain standing firm on this question and setting a good example to others. Only a firm stand, so the argument went, would send a message to the tens of thousands wishing to get to our shores to not even attempt it.

All eyes turned to him even though the chairman's seat remained empty. Francis though was the de facto chairman now.

When he looked back over the past two to three weeks, Francis could identify two developments that had together changed possibly the mood of the country and certainly the mood of this committee.

The first of these was the terrible news coming in from the areas of Czechoslovakia newly ceded to Germany. In the two weeks since the arrival of German troops into the Sudetenland, thousands of Czech Jews had been fleeing to Prague, forced to leave behind their homes and almost all their possessions. The same newspapers which had urged the Prime Minister to avoid war at all costs were now saying that he had betrayed these wretched people and that we had to do something to help them.

Francis stood up and cleared his throat, tapping his teaspoon against his saucer to get the attention of the room. He pushed his glasses more firmly up the bridge of his nose and focused on the piece of paper in front of him.

'Gentlemen, and Lady.'

He gave a polite nod towards Gladys Williams, the only woman on the committee. She was used to this sort of treatment on male-dominated committees and didn't look up from her notes.

'This is the fifth meeting of the advisory committee on refugees. Progress has until now been steady but slow. I think the mood of this committee this time is to make real progress. But, before we do, I want to take a few moments to salute our esteemed colleague and chairman of this committee over the past few months since its inception, Hilary Masterson.'

There was a murmur of assent from the assembled group.

'Hilary was a dedicated member of this committee. A man of principle and, may I say, a personal friend. I know that many of us admired him for his outspoken opposition to our appeasement policy, even when that policy was so strongly supported by a vast majority in the House.'

He gave a slight smile to the two men, Saunders and Gerard, to his left, whom he knew were very much in favour of appeasement and, unlike some of the other members in the room, were unlikely ever to be swayed from their opinion.

'We cannot begin to imagine the emotional strains that

Hilary was under that led him to take his own life. Others may know more but we are not privy to such information should it exist...'

As he continued to speak, Francis was calculating in his head where opinions had changed and who might now support him in his proposal. For the second development of course was the death of Hilary Masterson himself. Much as he had genuinely admired him, Francis had never understood the man's truculent opposition to allowing any Jewish refugees into the country. Hilary, as chairman, had wielded influence and was the focal point around which the naysayers had coalesced. With him gone they were now leaderless and less likely to stand fast against a changing tide. They just needed direction. And he was the man to give it them.

'...I, as those of you who know me can readily attest, have never been one to continue with meeting after meeting where the existence of a committee becomes an end in itself. This committee of experts has a duty. It is a duty to advise. We have all received our copies of the recent news reports. What has gradually been visited upon the Jews of Germany has been speedily visited upon the Jews of Austria and now, since October 1st, on the Sudetenland. We bear some responsibility for this latter development. The proposal is that we go back to the government with our endorsement of a scheme, put together by the Quakers, Save the Children, and other societies, for the admission into this country of Jewish children of 19 years and younger, as a temporary haven until such time as they can be safely returned to their families.'

He looked around the room slowly, meeting the eyes of each participant.

'We will vote by a show of hands. Our secretary will register the votes, and the name of who is for and who is against will be noted at the bottom of the proposal. This is a moral issue. A test of our humanity. I expect this proposal to pass our vote this evening. I would like it to be unanimous. Now, who will speak against the proposal?'

Saunders and Gerard whispered to each other for a few moments and then stood, nodded politely to Francis and left the room. The minutes would note that the proposal was carried by twelve votes to zero with three members absent.

Gunther was arrested on the morning of November 7th 1938. Stieglitz had got his man, though he had to acknowledge that it was Kuppers who had done the leg-work, trawling back through earlier unsolved cases and finding the statement of a woman who had been raped in the Tiergarten six months earlier. Her statement had been ignored before due to the suspected morals of the victim but Kuppers noted that she had heard the rapist referred to as 'Gunther' by his companions and that one of these had been a 'giant' Englishman. Six months later she was able to provide Kuppers with a good description of Obersturmführer Gunther.

The trial of course was political, Stieglitz knew that. Gunther had simply been unlucky that his victim had not been Jewish but a foreign and titled aristocrat. Unlucky too to have been a member of the SA when it was the SS whose star was in the ascendency. His sentence of years of hard labour in a concentration camp also took into account the rape of the Aryan woman in the Tiergarten. There had been almost no mention of his third victim, a Jewish Social Democrat, but Stieglitz hoped that Klara Stein's spirit would feel that she too had received some measure of justice.

FORTY-NINE

9 NOVEMBER 1938

SCHÖNEBERG, BERLIN

Renate had accepted Sonia's offer to let the children stay the night. It was good for them to see some new surroundings for a change and there was so little else to occupy them now. They couldn't eat out, go to the cinema or stay at hotels in the countryside. There were so few people they could trust these days. That Sonia and Manfred lived nearby was a bonus and they had the space. The children had known them all their lives and referred to them as Auntie and Uncle. Nobody had mentioned the other reason: that, in four days' time, Sonia and Manfred would be leaving for England and who knew when they would all be together again. After Manfred had told Richard the news, the woman had barely mentioned it again, other than to laugh at the idea that, officially, Sonia was going to be Veronica's maid and Manfred her chauffeur.

Driving was now out of the question and they counted themselves fortunate to have found a buyer who was willing to give them something approaching half their motor vehicle's market price. The man hadn't had to give them even that but had retained some vestige of conscience. The four of them had, therefore, walked round to Sonia and Manfred that evening. On the way they had passed police closing roads but had not dared approach them to ask why.

On their arrival, Sonia told them that she had not been so reticent. She had seen barricades going up from her window and gone out, taking care to approach the police from a different direction. Playing the part of an English tourist who was lost and confused, she had found out that a riot was being planned.

'Madam,' the police officer had explained in reasonable English, 'the Jews are going to get a bit of a beating later tonight. It is best you stay in your home.' He had pointed down the street. 'There's a synagogue down there. We think it's going to light up like a bonfire so we're trying to keep people away.'

Sonia ushered Renate and Richard away from the living room, leaving Manfred dealing cards to the children.

'It was clear to me that the police are not planning to intervene to stop the rioters getting to the synagogue.' She looked from one to the other and Renate noticed that Sonia's hand was shaking. 'Manfred and I think that this may be something new, something we've not seen before.'

Renate looked at Richard. He was staring hard at the ceiling. She almost looked up to see what he was staring at so fixedly even though she knew there was nothing there.

'Renate,' he said finally, 'I think we should take the children home. It isn't fair to have Manfred and Sonia worry about them when violence is happening nearby.'

Clearly he had seen Sonia's shaking hands too. Renate nodded.

'Sonia, we'll bring the children another time.'

'Of course,' Sonia quickly replied, glad not to have had to

suggest it herself. 'Let's talk tomorrow.'

The Gutmanns had not gone even fifty metres down the road before it was clear that the pogrom had already started. The streets seemed to be full of young men, shouting, chanting. The words, when they could make them out, were always about 'the Jews' and Renate wished she could shield the children's ears. In the distance they could see smoke rising from the direction of the *Religionsverein Westen* synagogue on Passauer Strasse, the low clouds tinged with red from the unseen flames below.

From the direction of the main street to their right, they could hear, over and over again, the sound of shattering glass as Jewish shops were looted. Renate was reminded of the paintings of Hieronymus Bosch. In this surreal world where men had become mad, how could she and Richard protect the children?

As they approached the junction of Martin-Luther-Strasse, just 200 metres from their own street, Dieter Schmidt came out of the doorway of his block of flats to greet them. His plain black trousers were held up by braces over a white shirt pushed to bursting point by a protruding belly. He was bare-headed and in his slippers. Dieter had been the concierge at number 42 for the past ten years. They didn't know him well, but from time to time Renate had chatted with him when visiting friends there, and knew the names of his wife and children.

'Frau Gutmann,' Dieter said, and acknowledged Renate's husband by standing stiffly upright and nodding his head respectfully in his direction. 'Please. Come in, come in. Do not go to your street.' The hot air of his breath was visible in the still, cold air.

'Herr Schmidt, whatever do you mean?' replied Renate. 'We don't live near a synagogue and we think that our home is probably the safest place for the children right now.'

'Yes, thank you, Herr Schmidt,' added the major, 'we do appreciate your kind offer.'

The man looked around nervously. He was feeling the cold and needed to get back inside. 'I am sorry, Herr Doktor,' he said, rubbing his upper arms now with his hands. 'You don't understand. Tonight, it is not just about synagogues.' He paused as from nearby there came the sound of more breaking glass accompanied by raucous laughter. 'Nor just about breaking shop windows. Tonight they will be attacking Jews in their homes. You, sir, as a doctor and ex-army officer, are well-known in the neighbourhood. The plan is to snatch thousands of Jewish men throughout the country tonight and hold them in camps until the Jews hand over money to the Reich.'

Renate didn't hesitate nor wonder how Herr Schmidt might know all this, but put her hands on the children's shoulders and almost pushed them in through his doorway.

'Follow me,' said Schmidt, walking down a narrow corridor which led past his small office from which he administered the common areas and kept an eye on the comings and goings of residents and their visitors.

Lise gave a startled scream, quickly holding a hand to her mouth. The others followed her gaze. Hanging from a hook in Herr Schmidt's office was an SA officer's uniform, complete with truncheon, and cap. Underneath stood a pair of shiny boots.

'I'm so sorry,' said Schmidt, 'I wasn't expecting visitors. But please do not be afraid, little girl. I am not going to harm you.' He turned to the major. 'It's my wife. She's the real National Socialist, insisting I become a party member. I enjoy the camaraderie and the singing. And I hate the communists, of course. But I've always had good relations with the Jews I have known. Come, please.'

They followed him to the door of his own poky flat and he let them in to a tiny front room containing a small sofa with threadbare covering and three hardbacked, wooden chairs. On the wall was a portrait of the Führer.

'Please sit. My wife is away visiting her sister in Hanover. Otherwise I would not have been able to help. But you will be safe here tonight.'

'And then what, Herr Schmidt?' asked Richard.

'Well,' Schmidt hesitated, not sure what to make of the major's words. 'Like I said, my wife is away, but she returns tomorrow so I can't—'

'I understand you, Herr Schmidt, and we thank you for your help. So few people help nowadays. But I meant what do we do next week, next month? How do we live here in Germany? It's all right,' Richard gave a smile of resignation, 'that's our problem, not yours. We thank you with all our hearts.'

They stayed in Herr Schmidt's front room for the rest of that night and until late afternoon the next day when he told them it was now safe to go out. On the short walk back to their address they saw sights that they never would have believed possible in their city. Shops had been destroyed, their windows shattered. The glass crunched underfoot. To avoid stepping on all the mess they would have had to walk in the road but that was now once again filled with traffic. People were going about their business as if nothing unusual had happened. A Jewish-owned shop was still ablaze and a fire engine was standing by but doing nothing to put the fire out. As they walked by on the other side of the street, burning embers blew onto the roof of the next-door shop. Immediately the fire crew swung into action, pointing their hoses and dousing the smouldering object to remove the danger to a non-Jewish property. Having accomplished this, the crew settled back again to watch the flames complete their destruction. The Gutmanns walked on, silent, fearful, trying not to attract attention, but it seemed that the pogrom was over. Apart from the raucous sporadic singing of Nazi songs by small groups of drunks, the organised gangs of the night had either disbanded or moved to other neighbourhoods. In the next street they passed Frau Frank. She was wearing a heavy coat against the cold but her hat sat awkwardly on her head and her normally neatly coiffed hair was in disarray, long strands poking out at all angles. Her stockings were laddered in several places. She was sitting on a broken chair outside her ground-floor flat crying, the contents of her home littered all around her. People were walking past her, their faces averted. In some cases they were even crossing the road to avoid walking too close to her, or stepping over her belongings.

'My God!' exclaimed the major, rushing up and kneeling next to her, 'what have they done to you?'

For a while, it seemed, Frau Frank would not be able to speak. Perhaps she had forgotten how. She was wild-eyed and seemed half out of her mind. Finally she was able to say a few words.

'They just burst through the door. No knocking, just broke it down. We were on our way to bed. Reinhardt was already in his pyjamas. They just started smashing everything, throwing it all out through the window. And then...' Here she broke down completely.

'Children,' said the major. 'Please start bringing Frau Frank's belongings back in off the street.' Renate was already walking past the outside railings, gathering up items of clothing which had caught there.

Frau Frank was speaking again and the major leant in close to hear her.

'They took my Reinhardt. They arrested him and took him

away.' She clutched his arm tightly. 'But he wasn't dressed, you see? He had nothing on his feet. And in this cold! How will he manage?'

Richard took hold of her and gently guided her back into the building and into her bedroom. He stood her in a corner against the wall whilst he quickly took hold of the bedspread, rolled it up around the broken picture frames and glass and china fragments that covered it and deposited the whole thing in the corner so that the bed was clear. He then guided her onto the bed and sat there holding her hand. A few minutes later, Renate came and sat next to him.

'Richard, we must get back home. We don't know what we will find when we get there but if our belongings are on the street, I don't want them lying there waiting to be destroyed or stolen.'

But when they got home, apart from a slogan in red paint across their front door saying 'Jews Out!' no damage had been done. Later that evening they heard that some thugs had indeed come up to their home but one of them had been a former medical student of Richard's and managed to direct them to 'richer pickings' further up the street.

The full horror hit home four days later, the day of Sonia and Manfred's departure for England. On that day a letter from Sonia, posted on the 'night of broken glass', arrived at their home.

Dear Renate, my dear, dear friend.

I hope you and your family have survived tonight. We have not. I write this sitting on the floor of what remains of our home. They tried to take Manfred away tonight and you know that he would never have survived such a thing a second time. He refused to go. When they began to pull him out of the door, he grabbed the poker from the fireplace and struck one of the men across the face. I didn't know Manfred possessed such strength and in that moment the Manfred we knew was back once more. The evil man will be scarred for life, of this I have no doubt. His friend took out a gun and shot my Manfred dead. His body is still warm next to me as I write this. I sit in the pool of his blood and it comforts me.

I am calm now. It is a calm brought about I know by the loss of hope and the certainty of death. Tonight I will join Manfred and we will be together once more. They say that death comes more quickly in cold water than warm and that the pain is far less. I hope they are right. I will walk down to the Spree and post this letter on the way.

You need to know this, dear friend, so that you will not worry about me and you won't spend time looking for me.

Do not weep for me either, for I am beyond pain now. Indeed, if I had tears to weep, I would be shedding them for you. For you the nightmare continues and for you, if you have even survived tonight, there can only be one thought: survival. Do not let them defeat you as they have defeated me. Get Peter and Lise out. 'Whatever it takes', as we say in English. And tell Veronica I am so happy to have met her. She so nearly saved us. At least she gave us hope and reunited me with a sister I thought I had lost forever. I was looking forward to that reunion with Cynthia, but at the same time I never really believed I would ever see England again.

All strength to you for the journey that lies before you.

Love,
Sonia

PS Tell Veronica to let Cynthia know that I forgive her

for everything. In the end she offered us her London home and I could have asked for no more than that.

FIFTY

18 NOVEMBER 1938

DOWNING STREET, LONDON

'Six weeks ago I was a hero. How quickly the people forget.'

Neville Chamberlain was sitting in the Cabinet room. There were just two others present, Sir Samuel Hoare, the Home Secretary, and Sir John Simon, the Chancellor of the Exchequer. It had indeed been about six weeks, thought Hoare, since he had seen the PM smiling.

'Following the recent outrage in Germany, the Americans are calling for us to allow more refugees into Palestine. The Jews are citing our obligation to them under the terms of the League of Nations Mandate. Yet we must retain the goodwill of the Arabs.'

'It's a tricky one, Prime Minister,' said Hoare, 'I do sympathise.'

'Why can't that despicable little man play by the rules? He has received everything he wants. What possesses him to indulge in such barbarity – he has no class.'

Chamberlain hadn't meant anything by it but the

Chancellor smiled, noticing Sir Samuel flinch at the description 'little man'. Sir Samuel was a small man himself and quite thin, which his always well-tailored suits did their best to hide.

Sir John, who was roughly half-way in age between the Prime Minister and the Home Secretary, looked as if he might have stepped out of *The Pickwick Papers*. His white, wiry hair had receded from most of his head and below that was a slightly jutting chin with thin lips. This was countered by prominent cheekbones, which had what seemed to be a permanent rosy shine to them.

'Yet, you have an idea, Prime Minister, which you wish to discuss with us?' asked Sir John, speaking for the first time.

'Yes, that's right. Tell me, John, do you remember that advisory committee we set up under poor Hilary some months ago?'

'I am aware that it has met a few times but I've not been briefed on the detail, I'm afraid.'

The Prime Minister took off his half-moon glasses and started to clean them with the handkerchief from his breast pocket, blowing first on one lens and then the other. It made it easier to talk without looking his Chancellor in the eye.

'Hilary's brief was to make sure that the committee would find it inadvisable to allow any more refugees into this country. Sam here was informed from the start of course, given the direct impact on home affairs.' Sir John nodded his understanding. 'However, Hilary faced considerable opposition from other members of the committee and the most he could achieve – more than enough at the time – was to keep them talking and not making any recommendations. That is why you never needed to hear about it.'

Sir John remained silent, wondering where this was going.

'You know,' continued the Prime Minister, 'that the Quakers and various Christian charities have been making a lot of noise in this area. They had representatives on the committee.' He sighed, holding his glasses up to the light and squinting at them. 'Well, with Hilary no longer able to exert influence, the committee has finally made its recommendations and they've gone against us. They recommend the immediate increase in the number of refugees. This recommendation, by the way, was made even before this latest Nazi outrage.'

'I see,' said Hoare, 'that really does put the cat among the pigeons. We can't let all those numbers in. I have a lot of sympathy for them. By God, what they are being put through is enough to turn anyone's stomach. But the risk of course is increased antisemitism over here.'

'Quite, Sam,' said the Prime Minister, 'but I've been thinking that we might turn this to our advantage. I think if we are seen to follow this advice we choose the lesser of two evils. We have to make a gesture if only to deflect attention from Palestine. If we open the door a crack here, we can prevent it being opened much more widely over there. If we can make a generous gesture early enough, we can dictate the terms.'

'Terms?'

'What's that you say?'

'You said we could dictate terms. What terms did you have in mind?'

'Children. No older than seventeen years old. Nobody can then accuse them of taking people's jobs.'

Hoare nodded. 'But what about the cost?' He looked at Sir John, who gave one of his famously cold smiles that never reached his eyes.

'It won't cost the Exchequer a penny. The Jews will pay for it. We should make that very clear. I've talked with the leaders of the Jewish community. They have repeatedly said that they will fund the cost of any immigration to these shores.'

'Refugees, John. Not immigrants,' said Chamberlain. 'We must never use the word immigration. These people cannot stay here long term. We are simply allowing them a shelter from the storm. And when the storm has passed, well, then they can return home.'

'Prime Minister.' Hoare felt it only prudent to mention what was on his mind. 'Forcing parents to give up their children? This means we are splitting up families. Might this not backfire on us – show us to be heartless, not humane?'

'Well then,' replied Chamberlain, 'let the other nations of the world offer more. Let those without sin cast the first stone.'

SCHÖNEBERG, BERLIN, 3 DECEMBER 1938

Registering their children with the *Hilfsverein* had been straightforward enough. Sonia, God rest her soul, had told Renate and Richard, when she had done this for them months ago, that it was no more than the logical thing to do. It was just an insurance policy in case things ever became really bad. In the meantime they planned to go to Palestine and forgot all about it. When that plan had come to nothing, they had started exploring alternative ways out. Sonia, after all, had told them that other families were managing to leave together. But that had all been before the November pogrom. Now things had become worse than bad. Actual separation had become a reality though, to be considered seriously, only when the British had announced their plan to have parents give away their own children. That this was seen as an act of generosity was, for Renate, proof that the world had taken leave of its senses.

Without Veronica being there in London, Renate knew she could never have agreed. Every part of her raged against this separation. What if Britain never let them join their children later? What if Veronica could only get them papers to Palestine, leaving her and Richard stranded in a desert thousands of miles away and with no means of getting to England? By the time she saw them again, they might not remember her. She might not recognise them. And Lise needed her mother. She was only ten!

'You *will* come later,' Veronica had reassured her on the phone. But Veronica herself was no longer able to come to Germany and Renate had received the impression that Veronica was less confident than in the past about her ability to get documents for them. One step at a time, she had urged. Patience. So now here they were. Tomorrow, she and Richard would face the world without Peter and Lise by their side.

They had waited until the children were both asleep and had then gone silently to their bedroom and closed the door to begin what would be their last night in a family home. In silence they moved to the bed but they did not undress. They held hands and without realising that they were doing so, they sank to their knees, the big doctor and his tall, refined wife.

They kissed, their cold lips touching briefly and then they hugged, their heads on each other's shoulders. Still no words were spoken. The tears came then, welling up from their depths until their bodies were wracked with sobs and they bit into each other's shoulders, worried that otherwise the children might hear their anguish.

Eventually, when their knees could no longer take the pressure, they crawled onto their bed and lay there exhausted, holding hands and staring at the ceiling. Sleep would not rescue them this night.

Richard tried to think of only the good things. Unlike for so many others, Peter and Lise were at least on the 'guaranteed' list: Veronica was their guarantor. She would take in Peter and Lise, give them a home and ensure they were not separated. So few of the other children knew where they would be staying and with whom. But Peter and Lise had seen some photographs of the flat in Park Lane. They knew that it was next to a world-famous hotel. They had an address, and Richard and Renate had already begun writing the first letters, ready to post them the very same day of their departure so that not too many days would pass in that strange country before they got letters from their mother and father.

Renate was remembering how, earlier that evening, she had packed their little suitcases, the muscles on her face strained with the effort of not breaking down. God help her, she had even scolded them. She had insisted on folding towels for them and adding little bars of soap.

'In England,' she'd said, 'they will insist on children being clean and washed at all times, just like here. You must wash your hands before every meal. They will need to see that you are well behaved so that they make you welcome there.'

'But Mother!' Lise had cried out. 'We're going to stay with Veronica, aren't we? She's not like that. She knows who we are!'

And then Renate had snapped at her. At her little girl.

Peter had joined in at that point as she had known he would, telling her to stop fussing and that they were too old now to be told such silly things.

'Don't be so sure of how things are there!' she had replied, her voice rising until by the end she was shouting. 'You must always set the example for Lise, do you understand? Veronica may be different in her own home. And what of her parents? They are important people there. You have to make a good impression. Promise me that you will always wash your hands, Lise. Before every meal! And Peter, make sure that Lise's hands are clean and you trim your nails. Promise me!!'

Peter had raised his voice back to her. He had never done that before. She realised now, that he too, of course, had been feeling the strain. In the end, simply to calm her down, he had promised. She wished they could have that evening back. She'd do it differently.

They lay there, Richard and Renate, eyes open, until the light came in through the windows of a clear cold day.

Nothing was said in the taxi to the railway station. For all they knew the driver could be a Jew-hater and they wouldn't let him hear their desperation. Then at the station, suddenly, it was too late. The platform was crowded with other children waving their goodbyes to their parents. Dozens and dozens of children, in many cases younger than theirs, pushing onto the train.

It was happening too quickly; they were not ready.

Some parents were already standing at carriage windows waving at their children.

Already separated.

Then a young mother, next to Renate, was shouting, 'No! I cannot do it. I will not!' Rushing up the carriage steps she reappeared a minute later with her little girl, perhaps no more than four years old, on her shoulder. The child was bewildered, unsure of what was happening but clutching her mother tightly. Her mother was beaming through her tears. 'I will never leave you, never!' Renate overheard the woman's words as she pushed past them, taking her daughter back home, back into the Reich.

Renate felt her husband's steadying hand on her shoulder.

Peter was at her side, stroking her cheek like he had used to do years ago as a little boy. When had he grown so tall?

She'd not noticed until today but she realised that he was looking down at her. She would need to adjust her memory of him. He kissed her gently on the nose.

'I'm so sorry for my behaviour last night, Mother. You were right of course. You are always right. I will look after Lise, never you mind.'

He went over to his father and shook his hand. 'Goodbye, Father. Until we meet next in London!' Richard Gutmann gripped his son's hand but then reached forward and hugged him tightly. Peter tried to fight back tears, he really did. Until he realised that he was proud of his wet cheeks. He kissed the side of his father's face, just at the point where the sideburn stopped in front of the right ear. He kept his lips there for what felt like a minute but maybe it was only seconds. Then he turned away to let Father have time with little Lise. But Renate could not let her go, so all three of them hugged each other as Peter looked at them, smiling through his tears.

Station-masters, in their red hats and blue coats, were walking up and down the platform shouting that it was time to board. Peter took Lise's case as well as his own and now they too were waving to their parents through the glass barrier of the carriage window.

A whistle was heard, shrill, horrible, in its finality. Doors slammed one after the other. Smoke from the engine funnel rose up, hitting the underside of the high glass and iron station roof. Trapped there, it began racing along towards them. As the wheels began to turn, a collective sigh rose up from the watching parents. Richard was reminded of a story Sonia had used to tell the children, of another town in Germany, Hamelin, further to the west. There another evil man, the Pied Piper, had taken children from their parents. At this moment, Richard wasn't sure whether the Pied Piper was Adolf Hitler or Neville Chamberlain.

Lise was standing on her seat so that she could wave her little handkerchief through the top window which had been pulled open for ventilation. Richard waved back and then Renate was running past him, running alongside the train.

Richard started running too. If his wife had gone mad with grief she might fall under the wheels. But then he noticed that she had a small package in her hand and was trying to reach Lise to press it up into her hands. 'Your sandwiches!' she was yelling. 'I forgot your sandwiches!' Richard grabbed them from her and, running hard, reached up to the small open window – getting the sandwiches to their daughter the most important thing he had ever done in his life. He shoved the sandwiches into Lise's hand and the train was gone.

Years later, Lise would tell Peter that she could still feel their father's fingers where they had grazed the palm of her hand.

EPILOGUE

4 DECEMBER 1938

PARK LANE, LONDON

'MAYFAIR 6123, WHO IS SPEAKING PLEASE?'

'Veronica, it's me,' said her mother, getting straight to the point. 'You cannot have two German refugee children staying in our flat. We don't know what you were thinking. That is our home.'

'It isn't your main home, Mother, though, is it? It's your London home. You don't come to London that often and when you do, whilst they are here, you could go to a hotel. After hearing your news, I would have thought that you would be only too glad to make a stand.'

Her mother sighed down the telephone line. 'We knew you'd mention that. Not everyone who is shocked at Germany's recent behaviour gives up their property to German children.'

'They're Jewish children, Mother. Do you still find it hard to acknowledge who you are? When you told Lady Susannah that you were leaving the Anglo-German Friendship Club over the pogrom, what did she say to you?'

Cynthia said nothing. 'Come now, Mother, you wrote to me about it. She said she had always known you were a rotten apple. That blood will out in the end. And she was one of your closest friends.'

'That's just English snobbery. It doesn't mean anything.'

'It means everything, Mother! Surely it is at times like this that you find out who your real friends are. You deluded yourself. In fact you were always "The Jewess". Never truly accepted. Is it so different for these children? It's just a question of degree.'

Her mother laughed. 'We can debate this all you like, Veronica, but we refuse to give up our home and it is not your decision to make.'

'I have a letter to read to you, Mother. It is from the mother of these two children. It might make you reconsider.'

'No, Veronica! It is of no interest to me what she has to say to us about this. We decide when we allow people into our home. She can write all she—'

'This isn't a begging letter. This is a proud woman who anyway had no reason to beg. I have already told her that you have welcomed her children.'

'You must be stark staring mad, Veronica. You'll have to write back—'

'She wrote to me about Sonia and Manfred.'

'She knows my sister?'

'She knew your sister. Sonia is dead. And Manfred. Thanks to you.'

There was a long pause on the line as Cynthia struggled to process this new information.

'How they died is contained in this letter. You really need to hear what she says. She mentions you.'

Taking her mother's continued silence as acquiescence, Veronica read out Renate's covering note and Sonia's last letter too, which Renate had copied out into her own letter to Veronica.

'So you see, Mother, your sister was going to be living in Park Lane. I told her that you were welcoming them both. She wrote to you of course. Lovely letters in fact. I told her to send them to Park Lane. I've still got them.'

'Veronica, what have you become?'

'What have *I* become?' For a moment she felt she would lose control, but then Sarah was at her side, rubbing her shoulders, putting a hand to her forehead, smoothing her frown away. 'At least,' she continued, calmer now, 'Aunt Sonia died thinking that you had become the good sister she had always hoped you would be.'

It was hard to tell amid the noises on the line whether her mother was crying or not. Veronica felt that she was.

'The Gutmanns were good friends of Aunt Sonia. These children knew her and they are now in our charge. You can make other arrangements if you are in London but, until their parents can join them and become established again, I want them living in Park Lane with me. You owe it to your sister.' Still her mother said nothing though she was clearly still there. 'Opinion is changing in this country, as you have yourself noted. Wooing Germany is a bit behind the times. Looking after refugees, on the other hand, might actually be good for Father's career, don't you think?'

HARWICH, ENGLAND, 7 DECEMBER 1938

Both Lise and Peter had been sea-sick on the crossing from the Hook of Holland, but as the ship finally hit the calm waters of the estuary, they revived enough to join the other children in queuing to brush their teeth and dress in their smartest clothes. There was a sense of nervousness but also excitement, the older children looking after the younger ones even though few really knew each other beyond the past week.

Lise came back to her bunk to find Peter still sitting there, staring at his open suitcase.

'Peter!' cried Lise. 'We're nearly there. I'm going up on deck to see the port! Maybe we'll be able to spot Veronica. I do hope so!' She stopped when she noticed that her brother had been crying. 'Peter, what's happened, what's wrong?'

'Can I borrow your towel, Lise?' he replied, looking up at her.

She pointed at the open suitcase. 'But you have your own towel. I can see it. Here.' She moved to take it out of the case but Peter quickly grabbed her hand and squeezed it tightly.

'Hey! That hurts!' she cried, trying to shake herself free.

'You see my towel?' She nodded, still struggling. 'Mother folded it. Look at it, Lise. She was the last person to fold it and I have decided that she will also be the next person to unfold it. I will have it with me always but will never unfold it until she is standing next to me. Do you understand?'

Lise nodded, her eyes large as she looked at the towel in his case. Peter let go of her hands.

'Promise, Lise, that you will never touch this towel.'

Lise nodded, red-faced. 'I wish I hadn't unfolded mine now,' she said a little tearfully.

'It doesn't matter, Lise, because this is for both of us. You too will be here when Mother next touches it.' He smiled. 'So, can I borrow your towel or not?"

'Of course you can, Peter, and whilst you're gone I could guard the towel?'

He smiled at her, took her towel and went across the passageway to the toilets.

As they came down the steep gangway to the quayside, Peter began to feel afraid. There were a lot of policemen there in their tall hard police helmets, quite different from the German police. It was raining a little and some of the policemen were wearing dark blue capes. Nervously he eyed a couple whose truncheons were visible and it was as if he could feel his bones being broken all over again. He stumbled slightly, holding tightly on to the rail.

He could see a throng of people being held back between barriers and he looked for Veronica's blonde hair, but too many people were holding up umbrellas for him to see clearly. He suddenly felt very foreign and insignificant. He didn't know how to look after Lise; he didn't even know how to look after himself.

They were on the quayside now and suddenly, in a horrible replay of his worst nightmares, a policeman had got hold of Lise. Before Peter could react, the man had swung her up into the air and sat her on his shoulders, supporting her by holding each of her hands in one of his.

Peter stood in front of the policeman, uncertain what to do. He pointed at Lise, his English quite forgotten.

'Sie ist meine Schwester.'

Lise, rather daringly, knocked once on the policeman's helmet till he glanced up at her.

'Und das ist mein Bruder.'

'Ah, so brother and sister, are we?' He looked down at Peter and smiled.

Peter stared at him, surprised. Then he smiled back.

'Lise!' came a shout from behind him. He turned to look. The barrier had been opened and there was Veronica.

ACKNOWLEDGEMENTS

WRITING IS IN MANY WAYS A SOLITARY PURSUIT and writers stumble, blinking, into the light, as I suppose do other writers, never being sure of the reception awaiting their creation. The encouragement of good friends and family is, therefore, paramount. Through a three-month creative writing course, led by the wonderful Charlotte Mendelson, I met other aspiring writers who, meeting as the 'Write Club' in the months following the formal course, provided me with a forensic analysis of my sample chapters along with pertinent suggestions, many of which eventually made their way into this story. If there are passages you don't like, they're to blame. Thank you then, my fellow club members and newly acquired and dear friends: Emily Ballantyne; Clive Collins; Natasha Cutler; Max Dunne; Richard Gough; Jenni Hagan; Jenny Parks; Zoe Miller; Clare Pooley and Maggie Sandilands. The first people to read my full manuscript were Andy and Miriam Marsden, whose feedback was invaluable, and the last were Adrian Daniels and Shani Rabinowitz, both of whom provided me with such insightful suggestions (and last-minute headaches) that I find it hard to believe that they both chose legal over literary careers. In between and throughout this writing journey, was my wife, Sally, who would unhesitatingly read through passages whenever I requested. My daughter, Hudi, read the entire manuscript so that she could discuss my characters with me in depth, bringing to bear her usual intelligence and common sense. Of all the characters, Sarah Levtov in particular owes Hudi a special debt for her very existence. Thank you to my parents, John and Melna, who read my manuscript most critically and with an especially sharp eye for anachronisms. Thanks too are due to Miriam Selby and Charles Daniels, whose suggestions and praise for my work came at just the right time for me. To Sidney Myers, thanks for his diligent, thorough reading and honest feedback. Also to my sister, Anna-Deborah, for her encouragement and joy in my progress.

Some years ago, my son, Gideon, moved from reading fiction to fact and my efforts to recommend great novels to him were in vain. To encourage me in my writing, however, he promised that my published book would be the next book of fiction that he would read. Thank you, Gideon, for helping to give me the incentive to get to this point. The ball is in your court now.

I am grateful to Adam LeBor, who reviewed my work through the eyes of a professional and without whose belief in this project, his support and advice, this book would not have seen the light of day. Thanks go to my PhD tutor, Professor Matthias Strohn, for critiquing those chapters relating to the German army, for directing me to those Berlin suburbs where I could most profitably spend my time, and for the twenty-minute crash course he gave me one afternoon in the lobby of the Hotel Bristol in Berlin on the design and layout of Berlin apartment buildings of the 1930s. I am indebted to Elliot Jager and also to Lisa Clayton, of the Hebrew University of Jerusalem, for drawing my attention to the immigration certificates scheme that saved so many lives. My thanks also to the Clandestine Immigration and Naval Museum in Haifa, where I was able to view their amazing collection of real and forged British-Palestine passports and various document stamps used to forge life-saving entry visas. Thanks too to my eyewitnesses: to the late Rachel Deutsch who on one memorable afternoon shared with me and with her own family, for the first time, her childhood memories of the *Kristallnacht* pogrom in Berlin in 1938; and to the late Miriam Eris (née Keller) who shared with me her heart-rending experiences of being chosen by her parents to go to England on one of the last *Kindertransports*, leaving them and her younger siblings behind in Germany to be consumed by the Holocaust. She arrived at Harwich the day war broke out.